JOE HANNIBAL,

and

THE BRUTAL BALLET

"Hannibal is the type of private investigator—tough and hard-edged, but also sexy and sensitive—that many mystery buffs will take to heart."

—Flint *Journal* (Mich.)

"Readable . . . engaging . . . an old-fashioned private eye who smokes cigarettes, drinks bourbon, beds beautiful dames and hews to an old-fashioned code of ethics."

—*Publishers Weekly*

"In-depth porn facts, raunchy back talk, and steamy interludes." —*Kirkus Reviews*

"Blessed with a voice as clear and pure as a Midwestern breeze, Joe Hannibal, Wayne Dundee's tough but human detective, brings a blue-collar sensibility to the genre that is as refreshing as it is real."

—Max Allan Collins, author of *Neon Mirage*

"[Wayne Dundee gives us] the sexy, sensitive Joe Hannibal . . . interesting characters . . . good prose, sexuality minus violence and brutality, and strongly independent men and women." —*Houston Chronicle*

Wayne D. Dundee

THE BRUTAL BALLET

(A JOE HANNIBAL NOVEL)

A DELL BOOK

Published by
Dell Publishing
a division of
Bantam Doubleday Dell Publishing Group, Inc.
666 Fifth Avenue
New York, New York 10103

ISBN: 0-440-20719-3

Printed in the United States of America

Published simultaneously in Canada

January 1992

10 9 8 7 6 5 4 3 2 1

OPM

This is for my brothers and sisters—tag-teammates for life.

And in memory of my grandfather, Eddie Smith, who, according to family legend, as a young man growing up around Nekoosa, Wisconsin, regularly tossed on his can during bouts of adolescent horseplay another Nekoosa youth who went on to become the legendary grappler Ed "Strangler" Lewis. To his dying day, Grandpa was ready, willing, and very likely able to lick any man who claimed pro wrestling was fixed.

"Ave, Caesar, nos morituri te salutamus!"
(Hail, Caesar, we who are about to die salute you.)

—the chant of Roman gladiators
upon entering the arena for
combat

1

Three seats to my left, a stocky woman was on her feet shouting and shaking her fist so vigorously it caused loose tendrils of iron gray hair to snap about her face like pennants on a blustery day. The woman looked to be in her middle to late fifties and was built along the lines of a Chicago Bears defensive tackle. She wore a bulky, shapeless, pink sweatshirt above bulky, shapeless, faded jeans. Black lettering across the broad expanse of her back proclaimed: BULLSHIRT. Even amid the surrounding din, her shouts carried loud and clear.

"Attagirl! Attagirl! Tear that bitch's blond hair out by its black roots!"

The focus of my noisy neighbor's attention—as well as that of the rest of the crowd packing the acoustically bankrupt old high school gymnasium—was the activity taking place on the elevated wrestling mat that had been erected at midpoint of the gym's basketball court. Ringed by red, white, and blue ropes and skirted by a colorful apron bearing the logo of Big River Wrestling Promotions, this squared circle was center stage for tonight's card of professional wrestling. The participants in the match currently underway happened to be a pair of young women, one of them a statuesque blonde encased in shiny black spandex, the other a shorter, somewhat chunky brunette clad in pale orange. By their curves and colors ye shall know them.

Up until a few minutes ago, the blonde, introduced as Paula the Platinum Powerhouse and minus any visibly dark roots in spite of the hefty pink woman's allegations (although the perfection of her pale locks did encourage suspicions that Mother Nature might have had some help in that department), had been getting all the best of things, largely due to a hearty lack of respect for the rules as well as for the physical comfort of her opponent.

The latter, presented as Bouncing Betty, had lived up to her billing nicely by allowing herself to be tossed and flung and dribbled about the ring mercilessly at the hands of Paula, these actions usually precipitated by underhanded deeds involving hair-pulling or eye-gouging or the like. The crowd, although vocally protesting, was loving every minute of it. What they liked even better was the recent turn of events that had seen Betty, after being pounded and pummeled nearly to the point of unconsciousness, display miraculous recuperative powers and come surging back on offense, using many of Paula's own unsportspersonlike tactics against her.

The only person in the gym—aside from the suddenly beleaguered Paula—who demonstrated dismay over this shifted tide of battle was the dark-suited, mustachioed, cane-wielding man who was prowling back and forth at ringside like a lame tiger on a chain. He, too, had been introduced by the ring announcer prior to the start of the match—as Paula's personal manager, "Terrible" Tommy McGurk. In point of fact, he was the main reason I was there.

I had first met McGurk a few years back, back when he had been just plain Tommy McGurk, an up-and-coming young wrestler, a hometowner from my adopted city of Rockford, Illinois; a nice enough fellow with a swell wife and a fine young son and a growing reputation as a dedicated athlete striving to inject as much dignity as possible into his chosen "sport."

The "Terrible" tag and the cane and the mustache and the shenanigans outside the ring on behalf of his rule-bending charge—all in sharp contrast to his former approach to the game—I knew had been recent acquisitions. I knew, also, that in the interim McGurk had been dealt a couple of pretty devastating dropkicks by that big, roughhousing, totally unpredictable opponent we all try to go the distance with . . . Life.

Life's a bitch, the popular saying goes, and then you die. I felt reasonably sure McGurk would brook no argument with at least part of that statement; only in his case it had been something far more dear to him than his own mortal existence which had been taken away.

I thought about that as I watched him limp back and forth at the edge of the mat, shouting abuse at the referee and at Bouncing Betty, slapping his cane distractingly against the frayed canvas, working the crowd, pumping their baser emotions. I thought about it as I listened to the names they called him, wondering if they knew. Knew what had been taken from him, understood what it was he was seeking to regain there before them.

"Wrap that cane around his neck!"

"Shove it up his nose!"

"No, shove it up his ass—and break it off!"

This last variation of popular sentiment was roared loudly by the pink mountain off to my left and met with an encouraging volley of applause and shrill whistles. Down at ringside, the terrible one turned with a sneer and brandished the offensive cane menacingly in response. The woman in the sweatshirt shook her fist right back at him, her hair snapping so sharply I half expected to hear it crack like a whip.

In the ring, Bouncing Betty, with the Platinum Powerhouse hanging in her grasp as limply as a boiled blanket, couldn't help but take note of the heightening crowd noise and then the cause for it. McGurk happened to be standing with his back to her now, so busy trading insults with the paying customers and threatening those in the nearer seats with his slashing cane that he'd apparently all but forgotten the match in progress. Unceremoniously dropping her disdained opponent, Betty stalked across the ring, reached through the ropes and—cheered on by a thunderous roar of approval—snatched the shiny cane out of the unprepared McGurk's grasp. That is, she *almost* snatched the cane away. Reacting with slapstick desperation, McGurk whirled about and somehow managed to hang on, clinging, it appeared, barely by his fingertips. The crowd hooted and continued to cheer as Betty, still leaning through the ropes, began to whip the cane back and forth in long swings, causing McGurk on his bum leg to stutter-gallop awkwardly first one way and then the other in an exhaustive effort to maintain his precarious grip. If that sounds somewhat tasteless as a basis for entertainment, then you don't know your average wrestling crowd.

The referee—a leathery-skinned, balding little guy wearing a zebra shirt and baggy trousers belted high around a waist not quite as thick as Betty's thigh—inserted himself through the ropes and tried to get Betty to release her hold on the gasping manager and his prized possession. The crowd roundly booed this attempt to restore order. The ref and Betty argued animatedly and all the while McGurk was kept dangling, his hold slipping a fingernail's length with each jerk of the cane.

And then, rising up off the canvas like a battered, sweaty, devilishly curved wraith, unnoticed by the struggling trio although immediately jeered and cursed by hundreds of onlookers whose faces began to assume uniformly glazed expressions of anticipated carnage, Paula the Platinum Powerhouse stood and smiled a wicked smile before dropping into an attack crouch and leaping full onto the unprotected back of the distracted Betty. In the same instant, McGurk, sighting what was coming, released his hold on the cane and—in a cruel variation of the old unexpectedly dropped end in a tug-of-war contest —provided backward momentum on Betty's part directly into Paula's first blow. The point of a raised knee thudded meatily into the tender kidney area beneath taut back-flesh. The impact was audible where I sat five rows up in the bleachers, even with the crowd noise. I winced in spite of myself. To whatever degree you believed pro wrestling was fake or not, that particular shot had been as real as the icy beauty of the grappler who delivered it. Far too real, I was certain, for the set of kidneys on the receiving end. But the show must go on, and Betty—with damn near all the bounce knocked out of her—showed she was a trouper right to the end. She managed to stay on her feet for the arm whip across the ring and the slingshot off the ropes, then took a ripping clothesline to the jaw that flattened her hard onto the already brutalized kidney region before being rolled into a tight cradle and counted one-two-three for the pin that ended the match.

The crowd remained in a frenzy for several minutes. In my immediate vicinity I was the only one who stayed seated. Everyone else around me was on their feet, hurling insults and obscenities and anatomically impossible suggestions down at the strutting pair of victors in the ring. Wadded-up candy wrappers and empty popcorn boxes and not-so-empty beer cups were also being hurled.

Paula and McGurk withstood this barrage, baring their teeth in sneers and tauntingly displaying the ladies' championship belt Paula had retained as the ring announcer crawled through the ropes and gave the official time and decision on the match over the P.A. system. His voice, even amplified, was nearly drowned out by a rumble of boos. In the meantime, the referee and a couple of ring attendants were assisting Bouncing Betty down off the mat and back toward the dressing rooms. Almost no one in the audience paid any attention to her pained withdrawal. The fans were too busy letting the Platinum Powerhouse and Terrible Tommy know how much they hated them.

2

It was a terrific spring night. A zillion stars in the sky, a warm, almost balmy, breeze stirring. The smell of budding leaves and growing grass in the air. The kind of spring night that causes poets to write love sonnets and old farmers to gaze out off their back porches with a lump in their throats and an itch in their calloused palms and remember what it was that made them farmers to begin with.

I was soaking it in from the vantage point of a leaning position against the grill of my rust-pocked Honda. I had a cigarette going, its smoke rolling up to make dark patterns in the wash of silvery starlight. Behind me, beyond the brief length of the stubby little car and across the parking lot, the shadow-cut rear side of the high school loomed in the same silver wash. With many of the building's doors and windows cracked in deference to the warm night air, the sounds of the crowd and the occasional thudding smack of a wrestler hitting the mat leaked out to reach my ears.

A twenty surreptitiously tucked into the dress uniform pocket of the chief of the local volunteer fire squad, whose men were serving tonight as ushers and backup security for the big show, had gotten the section of the parking lot reserved for the wrestlers pointed out to me. As a bonus, he threw in a nod toward the long, sleek, late model Pontiac in which the platinum-haired ladies' champ and her manager had arrived.

Luck had arranged for me to already be parked in a spot from where both the Pontiac and its likely exit route from the premises were well within view. Following Paula's win over Bouncing Betty, I'd roamed on out to be ready for the sleek car's departure. With three matches remaining on the card, I was in hopes of that being some time in advance of the show's-over rush.

I blew some more smoke at the stars and reflected on my reasons for needing to keep tabs on the Pontiac and its passengers. It was the kind of job that has long smudged my profession with a semi-sleazy tarnish; the kind of job you try to avoid taking on, but nevertheless do under certain circumstances.

In the past when I'd hired out for divorce work, it had been because my wallet was too flat to allow any choice. This time it was for somewhat different reasons and, strictly speaking, divorce wasn't necessarily the desired end. But the moves I found myself going through were the same, and so was the way they made me feel.

"So many things have changed since the accident," Lori McGurk had put it to me the previous day as she worked her way into telling me why she'd sent for me, what it was she felt she needed the services of a private detective for. "That horrible instant that took Tommy Jr. from us was just the start. What came next was like a series of delayed shockwaves. The trauma of losing a loved one is something that smacks you head-on, something you either come to grips with or allow to devastate you. The rest of it, though—the denial, the depression, the guilt, the blame—those are slower, sneakier processes. But they can be just as devastating."

Lori McGurk was "Terrible" Tommy's wife. Petite and delicately pretty on the outside, but as tough at the core as a space-age hardball. I'd learned that much the first time I got involved with her and her husband. That had

been almost five years ago, when a bottom-rung bookie
with high-rise dollar signs in his eyes had tried to guarantee Tommy's ring performance in a no-bullshit "shooting" match the book had hyped to a level that was way
over his head if the dice—in this case, human dice tossed
on a wrestling mat—didn't roll strictly to plan. Never
mind every detail, but before it was all over there were a
number of nasty threats and some physical abuse and
Lori was taken hostage in an attempt to ensure Tommy's
cooperation, only to be snatched away in a violent last-
second rescue by yours truly so that the match could go
down as the best-man-wins event it was meant to be. She
came through the whole thing, like I said, displaying an
inner toughness that belied her outer delicacy.

Yesterday I could see more of the toughness showing
through. Her prettiness had matured into genuine
beauty and there was an assuredness in her manner and a
degree of carefully controlled assertiveness that hadn't
been there before. The cupid's bow mouth had been
enhanced somehow, made fuller, more sensual, and the
straw blond hair had been highlighted with streaks of
richer color and styled into a shorter, bouncier, more
with-it bob than the simple bangs and shoulder-length
cut I remembered. I'd wondered about those changes as I
sat and listened to her. The transformation was easy
enough on the eyes, but it still made me wonder.

The series of traumas she mentioned were the same
ones I alluded to earlier when I said Life had delivered
some awfully rough wallops to Tommy McGurk's chin.
The roughest was the auto accident that claimed the life
of their only child, a son, Tommy Jr. I'd never met the boy
because he was sent away to stay with grandparents during the shooting-match business, but I'd seen dozens of
pictures of him on the walls of the McGurk home when I
was there. Bright eyes, a smile bracketed by impish dim-
ples, energy that vibrated even out of a photograph—
everything a healthy kid ought to be. And loved crazy by
his parents. But then suddenly gone. A wet snow driven
by hard winds, a treacherously slick patch of ice, a bridge
abutment . . . then nothing. A black hole where life had
been. A wrenching ache in a place that had been filled

with love. I knew the feelings well; both of my parents had been killed in a car accident when I was nine. But when you're young it's easier to adapt.

"The same crash that killed Tommy Jr.," I'd said to Lori, trying to move her along, "was also the one that injured Tommy Sr., right?"

She'd nodded. "Yes. His leg was so badly broken and crushed in so many places, there was no chance to set it, to ever make it fully functional again. They gave him a titanium hip socket, fused the knee and ankle. Bad as that was, it seemed relatively minor at the time. At least he was alive. It was only later—one of those delayed shockwaves I told you about—that we both came to realize what a big part of him had died, too."

A life ended. A career over. Two casualties, any way you cut it. It was just a matter of degrees. And for somebody like Tommy McGurk—never taking anything away from his deep and abiding love for his son—the difference wouldn't be that great.

Lori had continued, in her roundabout way, getting to what it was she wanted from me. "Money," she said, "became a problem almost immediately. Once our son had been put to rest and Tommy came home from the hospital, we quickly realized how financially vulnerable we were. We'd carried a small life insurance policy on Tommy Jr. that took care of the funeral and all. But there's no insurance company in existence that will underwrite the medical expenses of a professional wrestler —at least not with realistic premiums. So there we were, income that had been quite substantial cut suddenly to zero, no future in any field Tommy was prepared for, no insurance, and skyrocketing medical bills. Not to mention everyday living expenses in the range we'd become accustomed to, which were several notches above poverty level. Oh the wrestling community took up some collections for us and had various benefit cards, all very touching gestures, don't get me wrong, but futile when actually compared to our need. What savings we had were wiped out in a matter of weeks, days practically. And our beautiful house on Springcreek—you remember—had to be put up for sale. All of that on top of our loss, our emptiness, and Tommy's physical pain . . . it was a hell of a time."

You never know what to say to something like that—at least I never do—and I hadn't then. I'd attended the funeral service for Tommy Jr. and afterwards heard bits and pieces concerning the McGurks' ensuing troubles as they unfolded, mostly from our shared friend Bomber Brannigan. But I'd never felt close enough to the couple personally to figure it was any of my business. Listening to Lori McGurk relive it all these years later, I still wasn't sure it should be.

"But eventually you were able to get a good job," I'd said, gently prodding her on with it regardless. "That's what took you away from Rockford, brought you down here."

"Down here" was the Rock Island segment of the Quad Cities, four closely grouped towns whose boundaries have meshed over the years into one interbred urban sprawl that straddles the Mississippi and covers a good chunk of two states—Rock Island (which really isn't an island at all) and Moline in Illinois, Davenport and Bettendorf over in Iowa. It was there that her phone call had summoned me and there—in a moderately posh restaurant overlooking the fabled Mississippi from a cantilevered riverbank perch—that I was trying to find out why.

"I reapplied for my realtor's license," she had explained, "something I'd been fairly successful at before I got pregnant with Tommy Jr. and gave it up. It was no piece of cake getting back into it, but I was determined and it finally started to come together again. One of my best friends from high school had a solid business here in the Quad Cities area. When I heard she had an opening on her staff and was willing to take me on, it was too good an opportunity to pass up. Tommy was going through a very bleak, listless stage, indifferent to most of the things that were happening in our lives. And we'd long since given up our house and were just renting a one-bedroom apartment. So there certainly was nothing tying us to Rockford."

I'd made a gesture, indicating the nice restaurant and

her polished appearance. "Looks like the move worked out pretty well, money-wise anyway."

"Yes. Money-wise. The area has been struggling economically since the pullout of the farm-implement industry, but there's still a good living to be made here, especially since the start-up of the riverboat gambling. Only money's not the be-all and end-all, is it? You realize that quickly enough, even when you've recently done without. You realize it when . . . other things are still lacking."

She'd lighted a cigarette at that point, one of those extra-long jobs with a flower pattern around the filtered tip. I couldn't remember that she'd smoked before. I lit up, too, one of my Pall Malls, and through the dueling clouds of smoke I'd said, "What's this all about, Lori? What do you want from me?"

She'd taken several beats to answer, but when she did she finally got into the meat of it. "You've heard, I suppose, that Tommy is back in the wrestling game. Not in the ring, of course, but as a manager. One of the smaller organizations—Big River Wrestling Promotions, based just across the river in Davenport—made him an offer about eight months ago. You remember how Tommy used to feel about the hype and the carnival aspects of wrestling, how he avoided them as much as he could. Well, that's pretty much all this consists of. They've got him wearing a gunslinger's mustache and dark suits and carrying a silver-tipped cane, really playing up his bad leg, interfering with the refs and the opponents, pumping the crowd, pulling all sorts of underhanded tricks to help his wrestler win. All the kinds of things Tommy used to hate. But he loved the game so much and he wanted to . . . to *contribute* so badly, that he accepted their offer. And—money-wise, once again—it's working out pretty well. For Tommy *and* for BRW. He's still capable of drawing crowds, getting people to the arenas, getting them to shell out the price of admission, even if now they're there to boo him and call him names instead of cheer the way they used to."

"But . . . ?" I'd said.

She'd stabbed out her half-smoked cigarette angrily. "The wrestler Tommy is managing is the BRW ladies'

champion. She's billed as Paula the Platinum Powerhouse, real name Paula de Ruth. If you've never seen or
heard of her, she's quite a stunning creature. Nearly six
feet tall, breathtakingly proportioned, with Monroe platinum blond hair, only cropped punkishly short. The day of
lady wrestlers built like fireplugs with breasts seems to be
over. Anyway, to make a long story short, I think she and
Tommy may be having an affair."

Of all the things I'd expected to hear—or *wanted* to
hear—that was way the hell down on the list. "Jesus,
Lori," I'd said, "I hope you aren't asking me to—"

"It's not that, not what you think. I'm not after a divorce. Unless Tommy wants one, that is. Unless it's gone
further than I suspect. I just need to know for sure. Know
the truth so I know what I'm up against. I can't very well
ask him, accuse him—a man like Tommy, that would just
drive him away whether I was right or wrong. God knows
there are some rocky spots in our marriage. But after
everything we've been through you think I'm going to
just throw in the towel and let that bitch take him?"

So there it was. The why of it. Why she'd sent for me
and why I ended up lurking halfheartedly in a shadow-
shot high school parking lot on one of spring's finest
nights. I hadn't been able to say no to the earnest pleading in Lori McGurk's eyes nor to her determination to
find out for sure what it was she was "up against." But at
the same time, my acquaintance with her husband—I'd
always liked Tommy, even though no lasting bond ever
developed between us—made duty that was generally
distasteful even more so.

I tossed my butt to the ground, mashed it out under a
boot heel, and told myself to knock it off. You took the
lady's money, pal, you owe her a job. Simple as that. So
just do it and quit mentally pissing and moaning over it.

Shortly after dishing out—and digesting—that morsel
of stern advice, I noted some activity at one of the exit
doors. A handful of people emerged from the building.
One of the taller ones had hair that caught the starlight
like a wet pearl. This gleaming-haired individual and a
second person, equally as tall but bulkier and moving
laboriously, started across the parking lot. The others re-

mained milling just outside the door, watching. Members
of the town's volunteer fire squad keeping an eye out for
the safe departure of Paula the Platinum Powerhouse and
her manager, Terrible Tommy McGurk. Something
they'd be bragging about to friends and relatives for
months to come.

I waited until the pair had crossed to the sleek Pontiac
and were inside, Paula in the driver's seat. Then I crawled
behind the wheel of my Honda and keyed the ignition.
When the big car rolled out onto the street, I was half a
block behind.

The town—I forget its name—was a community of only
a few thousand and we quickly put it behind us. In a
matter of minutes we were cutting through broad, flat
Iowa farmland, traveling east on a smooth stretch of two-
lane highway. It was soon apparent that, in addition to
her ring style, the platinum one also displayed plenty of
aggression at the controls of a car. She punched it up past
seventy and held it there, causing my little Honda to
strain and shiver and wheeze desperately in order to
keep pace.

After thirty or so minutes, the Honda groaning for
mercy, we rolled into Clinton, a sizable factory town with
rows of tall smokestacks belching noxious gray clouds that
flattened out over the waters of the Mississippi and dis-
persed there into scraggly wisps that hung from the sky
like dirty whiskers. By my reckoning, this still left us close
to fifty miles north of the Quad Cities. If the Pontiac
turned south and started down along the river, I'd be in
for another merry chase. On the other hand, if the big car
headed that way it seemed an odds-on bet that would
indicate the subject was going straight home like a good
little boy. One of the inconsistencies that had aroused
Lori McGurk's suspicions had been her husband's erratic
habits following matches that took place within reasonable driving distances. Sometimes he came home
straightaway, other times he would check into a hotel or
motel—allegedly alone—and complete the trip in the
morning. His excuse in such instances invariably was that
his leg was bothering him and he hadn't felt up to the
drive. A plausible enough line on the surface, but one my

client thought she was being asked to swallow too damn often.

If the pair in the Pontiac were going to check into a hostelry tonight for the purpose of practicing the kinds of wrestling holds applied between the sheets instead of between the ropes, then I had a hunch it would be right here in Clinton. It was a safe distance from their home turf, there was a varied selection of inns—why keep those hormones in check any longer? It would make my task simple if that was their plan, get the case over in one shot out of the gun, so to speak. Sure couldn't complain about that. But a part of me—not because I wanted to milk the job for more than it was worth, and in spite of the fact I was supposed to be a dispassionate, strictly objective observer—was pulling for Tommy to show a little more class.

Ahead, the Pontiac began to reduce its speed. Its left-turn signal flashed and then it swung smoothly into the parking lot of a Denny's restaurant. I rolled on by.

We'd been the only two cars on the road a good share of the time. With traffic so sparse and Clinton a logical destination (as opposed to the handful of nameless, wide-spot-in-the-road burgs we passed uneventfully through), there should have been nothing alarming in this. To pull into the very same eatery, though, would have been begging to be noticed. It was only ten thirty, there were plenty of other places open. I drove down four blocks, then turned off and looped around and reapproached the Denny's. Before reaching it, I pulled into a neighboring Taco Bell. I parked in the shadow of a large garbage dumpster, obscuring my presence somewhat but leaving myself an unobstructed view of the Denny's lot. The Pontiac stood out nicely from the small pack of other vehicles and Tommy and Paula were even obliging enough to have taken booth seats inside before a wide front window.

This side of the street seemed to be a long string of small shopping centers and fast food joints with an occasional corner service station. Across the way was a polyglot of hulking, smudge-windowed factory buildings rising up behind rusted chain link fences. Every few blocks a tavern with a grime-dimmed neon beer sign had been squeezed in. The smells of industrial waste and cooking grease intermingled in the night air.

I cut the Honda's engine. The little car heaved a sigh of relief then went quiet.

I lit a cigarette and dragged the smoke deep to keep company with whatever other pollutants might be piling up in my lungs.

Over in the Denny's window, McGurk and Paula were giving their meal orders to a round-shouldered waitress in a pale green uniform. When the waitress left, the two leaned their heads somewhat closer together over the little tabletop and continued to talk. After a minute or two, Paula threw back her head and laughed. Lots of dazzling, perfect white teeth put on display and I was willing to bet the laugh was throaty and rich, well practiced. Even from a distance, her smile and her flashing eyes and the spectacular profile of her face and body were all pretty breathtaking. Up close, could this combination be enough to cause a man to forget his marriage vows? That remained to be seen. But it would damn sure be enough to make most men at least a little absentminded, I was already sure of that much.

Even tainted by factory stink, it didn't take long before the various cooking odors that were drifting up and down the street started getting to me. I'm a sucker for greasy fast foods in the first place, and in the second place, except for a bag of popcorn at the wrestling matches, I hadn't eaten since around noon. No way I was going to be able to sit patiently by and watch somebody else fill their face without slipping in few bites for myself.

When the waitress returned bearing a tray of food for the pair in the window, I bailed out of the Honda and ducked into Taco Bell. I ordered a Mexican pizza and a beef burrito and a large Coke. While they were putting my order together, I used the facilities. Relieved and refreshed and armed with sustenance, I went back out to the car and resumed my vigil.

The unhurried pace at which the subject and his companion completed their meal and the way they went on to linger over coffee had me fairly convinced that a tryst at some hotsheet motel was hardly in the offing for tonight. Nobody works up to it *that* goddamned leisurely, not when they're doing it on the sly. Of course that didn't mean they'd never done the dirty deed together, or that they wouldn't again. All it meant for sure was that it looked like the case was going to be dragged out a while longer as far as I was concerned.

I toyed with the idea of calling it quits for tonight and heading home. Rockford lay across the river and the state line, about two hours' drive east and a little north. I could be in the sack by two. If I followed McGurk all the way back to the Quad Cities to make absolutely certain nothing went on, I'd tack a good two and a half, three hours onto that. The alternative was to stick with him until he'd lighted at home or wherever and then find a motel room for myself. The prospect of spending the night in a strange bed in a strange town—alone—was about as appealing as punching a time clock for a living in one of those factories across the street.

As I fired up a fresh cigarette, still undecided as to which way I should play it, McGurk and Paula stood from their booth and made ready to leave. I guess the fact that I remained sitting there, waiting for them to come out and get in the Pontiac, indicates I was probably going to do it right and tail them all the way. But the events of the next few seconds took care of my having to make that particular decision at all.

The Dodge Diplomat wheeled off the street and into the parking lot and screeched to a halt crossways directly behind the Pontiac. Tommy and Paula were just emerging from the restaurant. My first thought was that the recklessly arriving car held some overly enthusiastic wrestling fans who had recognized the pair from the street as they were driving by. But the guy who clambered out the passenger side of the Dodge didn't look enthusiastic—he looked pissed. He was of average height and build, middle thirties or thereabouts, sharply dressed in a light-colored blazer, dark slacks and shirt, no tie. His longish, carefully arranged hair remained sprayed to rigid perfection even with all his excited movement. In fact, the only thing about his appearance that wasn't perfect were the blotches of anger that clouded his face.

Since I was parked with my windows rolled down to accommodate the warmth of the night, I had no trouble overhearing most of the conversation that ensued.

"So," the newcomer snarled, jabbing an accusing finger at the startled couple, "I've caught you and your lover redhanded!"

"Oh, for God's sake, Alex," the tall blond woman responded wearily. "Don't be ridiculous."

"Ridiculous? Here the two of you are—what more do I have to see?"

"We're sharing a ride and a late dinner, you fool. Where's the crime in that?"

Alex's body language indicated how loosely in check his anger was. He was a coiled whip ready to unfurl, to lash out. "Yeah," he sneered, "and don't think I don't know what you've got planned for dessert."

"That's a lie," Tommy McGurk said.

"Fuck you, gimp. You expect me to believe you've been spending all the time together that you two have and there's nothing going on? Yeah, you're managing her all right. You're managing to slip it to her every damn chance—"

"Stop it," Paula insisted. "Just stop it, Alex. You're causing a scene."

"*I'm* causing a scene? I'm not the one sleeping around like the cheapest slut on the boulevard."

"No, you wouldn't dream of doing anything like that, would you?"

"Hey. You knew all about my past when you hooked up with me, baby."

"I think somebody needs to remind you that I'm not your 'baby' anymore and you no longer have any claim on me. If I *did* choose to sleep around, it would be none of your damn business."

"As long as you're carrying my name—"

"That won't be my misfortune any longer than absolutely necessary."

A second man, the driver, got somewhat warily out of the Dodge. His appearance seemed to be purposefully in contrast to the first guy's. Wearing a rumpled dark suit and tie, this one was short and stout, balding, fiftyish, had virtually no neck and an enormous stomach. I could hear him puffing hard just from the exertion of climbing out of the car.

Addressing the stout man now, Paula said, "I'm surprised to see you're a part of this, Abe."

He spread his hands in a helpless gesture. "We were driving by. He saw the car."

"I told you back at the school that I wanted to talk to you after the matches," Alex said to Paula.

"And I told you there was nothing more to say."

"Goddamnit, there's plenty more to say." His protest was shrill on the night air.

The round-shouldered waitress and a young black guy wearing a dishwasher's apron had come over to the front window and stood there looking out. Another car had pulled into the parking lot, emitting an elderly couple who stood nervously eyeing the exchange taking place between them and the entrance to Denny's.

"Look," Abe said, "this is no good. We're drawing a freaking crowd here. You guys should be settling your differences in private somewhere."

"That's what I'm *trying* to do," Alex said.

Tommy McGurk said, "I think the lady has made it clear she feels their differences are beyond settling."

Alex's eyes flashed. "Hey, gimp, nobody gives much of a shit *what* you think."

McGurk took a step toward him. "You call me that again, mister, I'll make you eat—"

Paula got between them. "Come on. Come on. Jesus!"

Abe stepped into it, too, and the four of them struggling looked for a minute like they were doing some sort of slapstick folk dance. When things had settled down a little, the stout man panted, "Now that's freaking enough, you hear? Enough."

Almost plaintively, Alex said, "I just want to *talk* to her, for Chrissakes. Is that too much to ask?"

"She seems to think so," McGurk answered.

This brought about another round of shoving and shuffling.

Finally Paula threw up her hands. "All right, we can talk. We'll go somewhere and we'll talk. It won't do any stinking good, but we can get it over with and maybe you'll get it through your thick head once and for all that it's no good between us."

"No," McGurk said.

"Let 'em," Abe told him. "We can't stay here waltzing around in this parking lot all freaking night."

"It's okay," Paula said. "Maybe it's not even a bad idea."

"It's a *good* idea," Alex insisted. "There's things that need to be said between us."

McGurk continued to glower at him.

"Please, Tommy," Paula said. "Take my car and go on. I'll pick it up tomorrow. We'll ride from here with Abe. It will be okay, really."

"Are you sure?" McGurk asked her.

She nodded, said nothing more.

McGurk hesitated. He studied her face for a long moment, then gave Alex another hard look. After several beats, he allowed a resigned nod. Swinging around the group, he started toward the Pontiac. The others watched him.

Suddenly, without warning, Alex's foot shot out, kicking away Tommy's cane. The lame man stumbled and fell heavily to the pavement of the parking lot. His attacker was on him in a flash, swinging more kicks to his back and shoulders, leaning awkwardly to throw punches down at the side of his face and neck. I heard the dull thuds of the kicks landing and one or two sharp cracks of a fist striking meat and bone.

"Sonofabitch!" Alex was shouting. "I'll teach you to mess with my wife, you sonofabitch."

It was one of the most cowardly attacks I'd ever witnessed and responsive anger flared hot and bright inside me. I had the car door open and was halfway out before I checked myself. Tommy McGurk knew me—how would I explain my presence there? It was a bitter pill to swallow, being forced to hold off under such circumstances, but for the sake of the case and Lori's confidentiality a pill I made myself choke down. Besides, it was only a matter of seconds before Paula and Abe were pulling Alex off anyway.

The stout man displayed a strong dose of his own anger and some surprising aggression to go with it. After throwing a bear hug around Alex and slinging him away from the downed McGurk, Abe shook a clublike fist in his face. "That was chickenshit, man. Pure chickenshit. You think I'm going to stand by for something like that?"

The old couple across the parking lot were hurrying back into their car. The waitress in the window was pushing the dishwasher away, pointing in the direction of the lobby. Probably sending him to phone the cops.

Paula knelt beside Tommy. He seemed dazed. His cane lay several feet from him. I wanted in the worst way to go over and get it for him, give it back, and help him to his feet. My knuckles were stark white where I gripped the steering wheel as I continued to watch without moving.

Abe retrieved the cane and helped Tommy stand up. Then, still angry, he addressed both Paula and Alex. "You two had better get your freaking act together," he said, "and quit spreading your mess around where other people can step in it. The both of you get out of my sight. Go on, get. You deserve each other. I won't have you in my car, Alex, stinking it up with your chickenshit ways. I'll see that Tommy gets home okay, and the devil take the pair of you for all I care."

"What did I do?" Paula wanted to know.

"Come on, honey. This is Abe. Remember? Don't try that Miss Innocent act on me."

"Fat lot you'd know about innocence, you toad," Alex prodded.

Abe pointed a sausagelike finger at him. "I'm anxious to be on my way before somebody calls the cops on this little party we're having here. But I could be persuaded to stick around long enough to belt you right in your smart mouth, sonny, you give me much more reason."

Mention of the possibility of cops seemed to dissipate any steam there might have been left to continue the fracas. A couple more rounds of sullen looks were exchanged, then Abe assisted Tommy over to the Dodge. McGurk balked momentarily at that point, his anger apparently trying to surface through his stunned condition, but the stout man got him settled down and in before he got too agitated. They drove away.

Alex and Paula followed in a matter of moments. He stepped close to her and said something low that I didn't catch, tried to touch her. She jerked away from his hand, not having any. But they rolled off together nonetheless, with her behind the wheel of the Pontiac, him sulking beside her.

I stayed and finished smoking my cigarette, giving no thought to following either of the departed vehicles but instead reflecting on all that I had just seen and heard and wondering how it fit with my reasons for being there in the first place. Too much of it had been innuendo and unclear motivation. But one thing had come across loud and strong. Lori McGurk certainly wasn't the only one who suspected there might be more than a business relationship taking place between Tommy and Paula.

3

The phone call came at ten the next morning.

I was sitting at the kitchen table in my undershorts, smoking my first cigarette of the day while waiting for a pot of coffee to brew. A cloud cover had rolled in sometime during the wee hours after I'd gotten home, causing the new day to dawn gray and dreary, perfect for sleeping in and recharging the batteries too many hours and too many miles had drained low.

When I hooked the phone, Lori McGurk's voice said in my ear, "Mr. Hannibal? Joe?"

"You got him, kid. I was going to call you in a little while. What's up?"

"Oh, Jesus, it's awful. It's Tommy . . . he's . . . they've . . ." Her breathing was rapid and her voice broke with sobs she was fighting to keep under control.

"Take it easy," I soothed, at the same time feeling a trickle of ice slide down between my shoulder blades. "What about Tommy? What happened?"

It seemed like a long time before she got the answer out. "He's been arrested . . . for murder."

The phone in my hand suddenly weighed a hundred

pounds. "Holy balls," I responded brilliantly. "Who? Who's murder?"

"A man named Alex de Ruth. He's—"

"Never mind. I know who he is."

Alex—the snappy dresser from the parking lot last night. Estranged husband of Paula, the woman more than one person suspected Tommy of having an extramarital affair with. The guy who'd sucker-punched McGurk and left him lying in the dirt in front of witnesses. Christ, it had all the earmarks of a custom-wrapped package the cops would be creaming their pants over. A crime of passion, everybody's favorite. A love triangle. Humiliation . . . retribution . . . motivation plus.

"Tell me exactly what happened," I said into the mouthpiece, keeping my voice much calmer than I actually felt.

"They came earlier this morning. The police. They asked Tommy a bunch of questions, then said they needed him to accompany them downtown so they could ask him some more. He called from there later. To tell me they . . . he'd been placed under arrest."

"Do you know any of the details of the murder?"

"It's been on the TV and radio some. Nothing about Tommy yet. They're saying Alex was shot to death in his driveway just before daybreak."

"Daybreak? Wasn't Tommy home before then?"

"Not . . . not really. It was already starting to get light when I heard him come in. The police got me to admit that before I realized what was going on."

"What's Tommy saying?"

"What do you mean?"

"The murder—is he denying it?"

"Of course he's denying it. What kind of question is that?"

"Just checking. Have you arranged for a lawyer, or do you have one in mind that you can get?"

"I know a number of business attorneys through my realty dealings. I'm sure I can get a recommendation from one of them. But this . . . this is all some kind of dreadful mistake. Surely they'll come to their senses before Tommy has to stand trial."

"Let's hope so. But you can't count on that. You need to make every preparation, the sooner the better."

"All . . . all right."

"They'll be setting bail. Possibly yet today, more likely tomorrow. You'll need to get some money together to cover that."

"I understand."

"I can be there in a few hours. How about The Bomber? You want me to fill him in, see if he can come along?"

"Yes. I haven't seen Tommy, I'm not sure what kind of state he's in. But I think it would be good for him to have Bomber here."

"Okay then."

"Joe . . . ?"

"Yeah, kid."

"You were with Tommy last night. Watching him, I mean. Watching *them*. Did you see anything . . . well, that I should know about?"

"I'll give you a full report when I get there. You've got enough on your mind for right now. But as far as what went on between Tommy and Paula last night, I saw nothing you need to add to your worries."

"Thank you. Thank God for at least that much."

We broke the connection. I put the phone down, wishing she would have held off with the thanks. The part directed toward me anyway. Like maybe until I'd done something to deserve it. The way it stood right then, I wondered if I needed to be ready to shoulder some share of the blame for the predicament Tommy McGurk was in. Inasmuch as the cops had gone ahead and booked him, it seemed logical to conclude that not only hadn't he been home at the time of the killing but neither had he been anywhere else he could substantiate. In the wake of the incident at Denny's last night, with Tommy and Paula clearly parted for a while, the job of monitoring any potential romantic interlude between them had seemed for the time being to be stalled. I had to consider now, though, that if I'd stuck to him in order to be positive—

rather than opt for the self-serving action of turning home—I might have been on hand to provide an alibi.

Or, I thought sourly, maybe to have prevented a murder . . .

4

Bomber and I made the drive down to the Quad Cities later that afternoon. The overcast sky stayed with us the whole way, tossing down occasional spurts of hard, cold rain that streaked the windshield and drummed on the hood and roof of Bomber's big Buick. We'd decided to travel in his vehicle—despite its appetite for premium gas in quantities that would bring a smile to the lips of the coldest-hearted Arab—because it better accommodated the pair of us. At six-one and two hundred thirty-odd pounds, I'm hardly a runt; and Bomber's got five full inches on me in height and more than a hundred pounds in weight. He's forever razzing me about my "cute little" Honda, sometimes threatening to buy one just like it and carry it around in his hip pocket as a spare.

For over two decades, Bomber Brannigan—so dubbed after one of his early opponents claimed getting hit by him was "like having a bomb dropped on you"—had been one of the squared circle's fiercest competitors, first as a pro boxer then as a wrestler. At the close of his wrestling career, he'd settled in Rockford to open The Bomb Shelter and turn it into one of the city's most popular watering holes. He and I met at that point and have been solid buddies ever since. As Bomber was phasing out of wrestling, I knew, Tommy McGurk had been just starting and it was at the side of the battle-scarred old veteran that the rookie learned the basic ins and outs of how to survive the rough game. That's how far back their friendship went. And, even though time and circumstances had diluted their relationship somewhat in recent years, getting hold of Bomber was still one of the first things Lori McGurk and I had thought of in light of Tommy's current fix.

When I hit Bomber with it (if there's a subtle way of working up to telling someone that a close friend has been arrested for murder, I'd like to know what it is) his initial reaction had been more or less what you'd expect. "Is everybody nuts? There's no way in hell Tommy would have shot a guy to death!" After he got past that, he went into a kind of a pout over my involvement in the whole thing. "Christ, if they were having troubles why didn't somebody tell me? Why didn't Lori come to me if she thought Tommy might be messing around—I'd have kicked him in the ass and got his act straightened up in a damn quick hurry." I had to point out that the likelihood of such a tactful response on his part was probably the exact reason Lori *hadn't* gone to him. "The thing is," I'd summed up, "Tommy needs you now—they both do." That did it; he was okay with it after that. Ready to accompany me down and do everything he could to try and help a pal. It remained only for us to each throw some things in a suitcase and make arrangements to be away for an indefinite amount of time before we were ready to head out.

We rolled into Rock Island a little past six, with an early dusk descending around us and our headlight beams dancing like sparks on the rainslick pavement.

The McGurk home was a simple but attractive one-story cottage on a tree-lined street in a quiet-looking neighborhood of neatly manicured lawns and hedges wrapped around other modestly attractive houses. Ozzie and Harriet-ville. A spot where not even the shadow of something as ugly as murder was supposed to touch.

The yard light was on. Bomber parked at the curb and we walked up a narrow sidewalk under the watchful eyes of ornamental deer and ducks stationed on the wet grass.

Bomber's knock was answered promptly and somewhat surprisingly by the stout man I had heard called Abe, the fourth party from the fracas in the Denny's parking lot last night. He thrust out his right hand almost before he had the door open, saying, "Bomber. Good to see you again, good you could make it down. Lori said you were on the way."

"Been awhile, Abe," Bomber replied, the two of them exchanging an aggressive handshake.

"Too long. Too damn long. And now it has to be under shit circumstances like these."

His eyes swept to me. "And you must be . . . Harrigan, is it?"

"Hannibal," I corrected. "Joe Hannibal."

"Abe Lugretti," he said, pumping my arm. "Now I only know you about ten seconds, son, but I'll take it on myself to warn you right up front you got to watch yourself keeping company with this character"—a jerk of his head to indicate Bomber—"because he can get you in more trouble in five freaking minutes than most guys can in five lifetimes."

Bomber grinned easily. "And I suppose you didn't get a kick out of every minute of it? Besides, the way I remember, I didn't exactly have a patent on getting us in dutch. You held your own in that department, and then some."

"That must be why," Lugretti said, "Duke Dukenos always claimed what one of us couldn't dream up, the other one could."

Both men laughed heartily. I smiled along with them, but couldn't help feeling a little awkward and out of place, alienated by their reminiscences.

"Abe and I used to wrestle on a lot of the same cards for old Duke," Bomber explained, sensing my discomfort. "Trouble was, we had a bad habit of sometimes doing more damage in the local saloons after the matches than we did in the ring."

"Hey," Lugretti said, suddenly smacking the heel of a hand to his forehead. "Look at me—I got you standing here in the freaking rain like a couple unwelcome in-laws. Holy cow, come in. Come on in."

The McGurk house was tidy and bright, sensibly fur-nished. Plush (but not overly so) carpeting, comfortable-looking chairs and couches. Everything thoughtfully arranged, colors and styles well matched. I vaguely re-membered a few things from my visits to their Rockford home.

The focal point of the living room—where Lugretti led us—was a large oil painting hung over the fireplace. The painting was of Tommy and Lori and their now-deceased son. The tracking gazes of the faces in the painting seemed to have a sobering effect on the banter between Bomber and Lugretti.

"How's Lori holding up?" Bomber wanted to know.

Lugretti shrugged. "Not too bad. Well as can be ex-pected, I guess."

"Where is she—in lying down or something?"

"No, as a matter of fact she ain't here. Her and the lawyer she hired went to the police station, where Tom-my's being held. That's why she called me to come over—so somebody'd be on hand when you showed up."

"She get herself a good lawyer?" I asked.

"Supposed to be. Name's Hatfield. Supposed to be a real crackerjack, about the best there is."

"A criminal lawyer, right? Not some deed-shuffler who drew up the papers on the last house she sold?"

"Guess so. What's the difference? Ain't a lawyer a law-yer?"

"Relax, Joe," Bomber said. "Lori's no fool. She'll do whatever's best for Tommy, you can count on that."

Lugretti frowned in my direction. "Lori said you're a private eye. That right?"

"Right enough."

"No offense, but I'm not sure I understand what brings you in on this. You been hired, too?"

"Joe's a friend of mine, Abe," Bomber said. "A good friend. What's more, he's also a friend of Lori's and Tommy's. He's here to lend a hand if needed, just like you and me."

Lugretti nodded. "That's good enough for me then."

"So what's the deal?" Bomber said. "We supposed to go and meet up with Lori at the police station?"

"Wouldn't be much sense in that. The lawyer wasn't even sure he could get Lori in to see Tommy. She was hoping for a few minutes, though. What she said for us to do until she got back was to just make ourselves at home and wait."

"Shit, I didn't drive all the way down here to sit on my hands and wait," Bomber grumbled.

Nevertheless, it looked like our best option for the time being. I pointed this out to Bomber, echoing Lugretti's observation that we weren't likely to be able to accomplish anything at the cop shop even if we went to the trouble of going there. Plus there was the chance we might miss Lori en route.

"That's the ticket," Lugretti agreed. "So why don't you just sit tight and make yourselves at home like she said? She shouldn't be much longer anyway, she really shouldn't. You guys been on the road awhile, you must be hungry or thirsty or something, ain't you? How about I build us a plate of sandwiches and pop us some beers? By the time we finish those, Lori'll probably be here. Whatya say?"

Bomber scowled a minute more, then made a resigned gesture with his hand. "Hell, I guess. Yeah, Abe, a sandwich and a cold beer'd go pretty good about now if it's not too much trouble."

"Hey, no trouble at all," said the stout man, moving toward the kitchen. "Be back in a flash."

Once he was gone from the room, I said to The Bomber, "It was pretty obvious from your old pal's questions that Lori hasn't told him the full story on me. Now that I think about it, she probably hasn't told anybody about her suspicions concerning Tommy's fidelity or about hiring me prior to the murder. And on top of everything else that's suddenly hit the fan, I doubt she'd be anxious to have those facts aired right now."

"So we need to be careful what we say. I get the picture. I'm not too crazy about holding out on old friends, though."

"It's her play to call. Just remember that."

While we waited for Lugretti, Bomber and I each took a turn in the bathroom, where we relieved and refreshed ourselves accordingly. By the time we were finished, the food was ready. We regrouped at the dining room table.

In between mouthfuls of salami and cheese and swallows of ice cold Bud, Lugretti filled us in on everything he knew about the circumstances surrounding Alex de Ruth's murder and Tommy's subsequent arrest.

"I got to tell you," he started out, "as far as I can see it looks kinda bad for the kid."

"What the hell," Bomber responded. "You saying you figure Tommy actually killed that guy?"

"No, that's not what I'm saying. But it don't matter much what I figure, see. The thing is they got a whole pile of, whatycall, your circumstantial evidence mounting up against Tommy."

"I'll tell you what they got a whole pile of," Bomber grumbled.

Lugretti went on. "I guess you both know about Tommy getting back in the wrestling game, right? Strictly as a manager, of course, on account of his bum leg and all. Well, that's where it starts—with who he ended up managing. She calls herself Paula the Platinum Powerhouse and she's the BRW ladies' champ. Her real name is Paula de Ruth; she is—or was—Alex de Ruth's wife. If you've never seen this gal, wow, she generates enough steam to run a locomotive. Lady wrestlers these days are a whole different breed than the two-legged Clydesdales they had back when we were climbing in the ring, Bomber. A lot of these chicks could be *Playboy* centerfolds, and Paula is one of the hottest of the bunch."

Bomber said, "So Tommy and this Paula got to fooling around with each other, is that what you're getting at?"

"That's sure the way it looked to a lot of people. Naturally, they had to put in quite a bit of time together due to their manager-client setup, but it wasn't long before talk was going around that all the time they were spending together wasn't strictly business. Hell, it wasn't hard to picture—I mean, Tommy's still an attractive enough guy and, for his part, a man'd have to be made of freaking wood not to feel some kind of tug around Paula."

"I take it Alex de Ruth got wind of this at some point?"

"He sure did. And he was fit to be tied, let me tell you. Never mind that he was a randy sonofabitch who was ready to jump anything female in a hundred-mile radius. There was no way he was going to let some one-legged wonder—that's a quote—beat his time with his own wife."

"How about Lori?" I said, playing along. "Did anything leak back to her?"

Lugretti frowned thoughtfully. "I'm not sure. Not that I ever heard of, no. If it did, she never made any kind of scene over it. 'Course that wouldn't be Lori's style anyhow."

"But de Ruth *did* make a scene?"

"Oh, yeah. More than one. Paula and Tommy denied anything was going on between them, but that didn't stop people from talking and it sure didn't stop Alex from showing his freaking ass. When Paula moved out on him a few weeks ago, it only made matters worse. And then last night, that was the worst of all."

"De Ruth getting murdered, you mean?"

"No, I mean before that. That's the part that makes it look so bad for Tommy."

Still playing dumb, I said, "I'm not following you, Abe. What else happened last night besides the killing?"

He took a long pull of beer, swallowed and expelled a heavy sigh. Then, mouth twisted wryly, he related the events at the Denny's parking lot the previous night. He told things pretty much the way I'd seen them, but with the added perspective of having been alone with de Ruth prior to the incident and then alone with McGurk afterwards.

"I never saw Tommy so damn mad," he said. "Sucker-punched and hurt and humiliated the way he was in front of everybody, you couldn't hardly blame him. At first it left him sort of stunned, I guess that's how I was able to get him out of there without more trouble. But the longer we drove the more chance it had to work on him and the

madder he got. Lord knows he threatened to do plenty to
Alex, but hell, you know how that kind of stuff rolls out
when you're so pissed you can't see straight. By the time
we got back to Davenport and I dropped him off at the
BRW building where he'd left his car to ride to the
matches with Paula, I thought he'd cooled down okay. I
made him promise not to do something dumb."

"What were you and de Ruth doing riding together?"
Bomber asked.

Lugretti shrugged. "Since him and Paula split up we
been swapping rides to some of the away matches. You
know, to break up the monotony of the drive, cut down
on expenses."

"What time was it when you left Tommy?" I said.

"About one thirty, quarter to two."

"How much of this do the cops know?"

Lugretti's expression sagged like melting plastic.
"Thanks partly to me, they know all of it. First Paula must
have told them about the trouble between Alex and
Tommy—they naturally contacted her right away after
the shooting. Then, because it came out I was a witness to
the fight in the parking lot, they came to see me. When
they started asking all their blasted questions, I had no
idea yet what had happened. What I figured was that
Tommy had caught up with Alex somewhere and poked
him in the nose, maybe roughed him a little. So I didn't
hold nothing back on the blues, I laid it all out trying to
make it sound like Alex had asked for whatever he got.
Which he did . . . short of murder, that is."

"There you go again," Bomber said. "Still sounding like
you believe Tommy *did* kill that jerk."

Lugretti's eyes remained heavy with regret, but his
gaze didn't waver under Bomber's scowl. "I guess what I
believe is that he *could* have. He was mad, he'd been
pushed too far, he maybe got a little crazy. I don't mean
just from what happened in that freaking parking lot, but
. . . well, a lot of things. You haven't been around
Tommy much in the last couple years. He's changed. The
accident, the string of bad luck—they all took their toll.
And God knows Alex de Ruth had—and Paula has, too, for

that matter—a special knack for bringing out the worst in just about anybody."

Bomber said, "But *murder*, Abe? Tommy?"

"Hey, you think that's what I *want* to think? Jeez, I'd never say it to another living soul. But it's there in my head, I can't help it."

Both men's voices had been raised and now the silence was sudden and strained.

I gave it a minute or so, then said to Lugretti, "How about the alleged romance between Tommy and Paula? What's your reading on that—has there actually been anything going on?"

The stout man made a gesture with both hands. "You two are grilling me worse than the cops! What's the idea anyway?"

"The idea," Bomber said, almost gently, "is to try and help Tommy. That's all we're here for. This is what Joe does for a living—asks questions to get different angles on a thing so he can start to sort out the truth. In this case we're lucky to have somebody like you, an old and trusted friend, to help lay the groundwork. We need to take advantage of that."

Lugretti continued to look glum. "I feel like I'm being asked to tell tales out of school."

"This is a pretty extreme situation, Abe," I pointed out. "It has to be dealt with in ways we can't necessarily be happy or comfortable with."

"All right," he said, sighing again, "if it'll help you get to the bottom of things, I'll admit that, yeah, I figure Tommy and Paula have been messing around some. Don't ask me why exactly, I never heard or saw anything specific. But when you know somebody pretty good and you're around them enough, well, you sort of pick up on things, you understand?"

"Shit," Bomber said. "I thought the kid had better sense than that."

Lugretti made another gesture. "Like I said, I got no proof or nothing. You asked for my gut feeling, that's what it is."

And my gut feeling was that the stout man wasn't telling us everything, that he was more certain of what had gone on between Tommy and Paula than he was saying. Keeping mum out of some sense of loyalty, I supposed. None of which had anything to do with the question of McGurk's criminal guilt except it removed him at least one step from the person everybody who believed in him thought—hoped—that he was. Whether or not that put him a step closer to being a killer remained to be seen.

5

Lori McGurk returned home about half past seven. She seemed somewhat wrung out by tension and up close, when she embraced Bomber and me and told us how grateful she was that we were there, you could see redness around her eyes and nose from crying. All things considered, though, she appeared to be coping okay.

She reported that she had been allowed a few minutes with Tommy, that he was holding up well, was insistent about his innocence and determinedly confident of beating the charges against him. She assured us that Nicholas Hatfield, the lawyer she had retained, was one of the best around and that he, too, exuded confidence. Tommy's arraignment was scheduled for ten the next morning, during which his bail would be set. After that it would be time to start channeling all that confidence into building a case for his defense.

Abe Lugretti stuck around long enough to hear this and to finish off the beer he had open, then excused himself to leave. He said his good nights to Bomber and me. Lori saw him to the door, thanking him for coming over and covering our arrival. He downplayed the effort and made her promise not to hesitate calling on him again if there was anything else he could do.

With Lugretti departed and all the latest developments recapped, Lori allowed the strain she was operating under and the point of near-exhaustion she had reached to show through. It was there on her face suddenly, as if she had whisked off a mask. Bomber and I both spotted it and old Doc Brannigan wasted no time in prescribing a long, hot bath and a good stiff drink. Despite Lori's halfhearted protestations and much as I wanted a chance to go over certain things at greater length with her, I had to concur.

While Lori was in the bathroom, soaking in a sudsy, steamy tub with a tumbler of Cutty on the rocks for company, I carried our bags in from the car and Bomber and I made ready to settle for the night. Lori had effectively deep-sixed any notion of us staying at a motel by pointing out she not only had plenty of room but genuinely *wanted* the company. Sleeping accommodations amounted to a choice between the bed in the guest room or the huge overstuffed couch in the living room. Bomber won a coin flip for the bed, but the couch promised not to be much of a hardship.

Lori emerged from the bathroom wrapped in a fuzzy robe, rosy cheeked and sleepy eyed. We sat at the dining room table with her and made small talk while she sipped partway through another drink and picked at the sandwich Bomber had made for her. At each lull in the conversation her eyes would drift shut a little quicker and her head would tip a little lower. It wasn't long before Bomber was shooing her off to bed.

He and I cleared the table, put away the sandwich makings, did the dishes. Since I'm not much for turning in early, I let Bomber have next shot at the shower and getting ready for bed while I fiddled with the TV until I found an old John Wayne Western playing that I hadn't seen in a long time.

Bomber came out during a commercial and announced he was going to hit the sack. He had on a pair of the loudest pajamas—patterns of tropical fish and exotic sea flora—I have ever seen.

"Hope you can keep the noise from those things down low enough for the rest of us to sleep," I told him.

He waved good night with one finger, the middle one.

6

Nicholas Hatfield was a tall, lanky, loose-jointed type, all knobby elbows and wristbones and an Adam's apple that stuck out almost farther than his nose. It was surprising to hear the booming, Shakespearean-stage-actor voice that emanated from his stickman frame.

"The burden of proof is on the prosecution," he was saying. "They've got motive, opportunity—the whole nine yards short of an eyewitness or a smoking gun. But they've still got to *prove* beyond a reasonable doubt to a jury that Tommy McGurk was the one who pumped those slugs into Alex de Ruth. Now we can sit back on our smug duffs and wait for them to fall on their faces because we know Tommy is pure and innocent, or we can break some sweat and build a case of our own we're damn sure is going to substantiate that innocence."

I said, "I sort of figured that's where I might come in."

Hatfield nodded thoughtfully. "I could retain you as my case investigator, thus shielding you from cop hassle for sticking your nose into an ongoing murder inquiry. That the way you figured it?"

I nodded back. "You got it."

We were seated, the bony lawyer and I, at a postage-stamp-sized table in a cramped diner around the corner from the court building where Tommy McGurk's arraignment had taken place. Earlier that morning, over breakfast, I had reviewed things with Lori McGurk to the point of establishing that she had wisely told Hatfield everything concerning her suspicions of infidelity and my initial hiring, but, as I'd suspected, her adamant desire under present circumstances was to keep those facts from everyone else—especially Tommy. The arraignment and the accused's release on bail had gone as expected. Following that, while Bomber and Lori scooted Tommy out through a gaggle of reporters and headed home with him, I'd hung back and requested some additional time with Hatfield. He'd led the way to the diner.

"Naturally," he said now as he buttered a crisp English muffin half, the knife making a soft scraping sound, "I have from time to time employed the services of a private investigator when building a complex case. And for the most part with satisfactory results, I'll admit. The thing is —and with all due respect to your generous offer—I'm not sure I see the need for it at this juncture."

"You just got done saying—or inferring, at least—you saw the need to 'break some sweat' in building a stronger case on Tommy McGurk's behalf."

"I do have an experienced staff, Mr. Hannibal, not to mention one or two adequately functioning facilities of my own. We manage every now and again to struggle successfully through a job without outside assistance."

"The point is, counselor, I'm already here, already involved. I got what you'd call a personal interest. Why not make use of me? If you think I'm trying to take advantage of the situation and gouge some extra money out of it, then up yours. But that still don't get rid of me."

Hatfield smiled calmly around a bite of muffin. "I was told you could be a bit . . . er, short fused, shall we say?"

"A hell of a lot worse has been said about me. Who laid that particular adjective on you? And why?"

"The who was a Lieutenant Ed Terry, Rockford PD. The why was because I called him up and asked. When Lori McGurk first told me about you and that you likely would want to remain involved—indeed that she would welcome that—then I took the liberty of doing some checking. Even though a client may show great wisdom in hiring me, there's no guarantee that wisdom extends to other areas."

"So you were scouting me as a potential teammate?"

"Something like that."

I tapped out a cigarette and lit it. "No offense, but for a lawyer you seem mighty particular about who you toss in with."

"One of the little quirks that hopefully sets me apart from the pack."

"Judge Hugh Farrow says you've got a number of little quirks that set you apart."

He furled his brows over that one. "Judge Farrow? I don't believe I've ever . . ."

"He pounds a gavel up in my neck of the woods. You may never have counseled before him but he knows about you all the same. Matter of fact, there isn't much on the legal scene that goes on in this part of the country he doesn't know about. That's why I called him from the McGurk house this morning and asked about you." I gave it a beat and showed him some teeth in the interim. "You see, counselor, you're not the only one particular about who plays on your team."

When Hatfield broke the silence, it was with a loud, glass-rattling, muffin-crumb-spraying laugh. It was the kind of full, genuine, infectious laugh you can't help at least smiling along with. Even the other customers around us, at first startled by the outburst, ended up turning back to their own business with a grin.

"Whoo," Hatfield said after catching most of his breath, "are we a couple of trusting souls or what? Lieutenant Terry said you were stubborn and hot-headed and liable to go off half-cocked at any minute, but you were also tough and lucky and basically honest and once you had your nose stuck in a thing it was usually better to have you inside the tent pissing out than outside pissing in. I think I just got a firsthand sample of what he meant. And what kind of scouting report did your omniscient judge pass along on me?"

"Said you were quirky, like I told you. Abe Lincoln on the surface, Attila the Hun down deep. Said you work a jury—and I'm quoting here—with the schizoid energy of Robin Williams in concert. Said your tactics usually keep judges on their toes and knock the opposition on their asses. I think he's sort of a fan, but at the same time I got the impression he's glad you're not practicing in his jurisdiction."

Hatfield spread his hands. "Guess that settles it then. Sounds like a couple rascals like us were meant for each other. To not throw in together now would look chicken-shit, right?"

"At least."

"I'll have the necessary papers drawn up to establish you're working for me. You come to terms on payment with Lori and Tommy, let me know; I'll adjust my bill accordingly and show transfer to you. You turn up something above and beyond the call of duty that helps me lock the case, you and I will discuss a bonus."

"I told you I'm not in this one for the money."

"But if some just happens to land in your pocket, you could stand it, couldn't you? Don't get too frigging noble on me, Hannibal."

"Okay. I could stand it, yeah."

A waitress was headed our way with a pot of coffee to refill our cups but Hatfield waved her off. He stood up, digging a loose wad of bills from his pocket which he tossed on the table to cover our fare. "Let's walk and talk," he said. "Too many ears here."

Outside, spring had coughed up just about the finest day anybody could ask for. Gallons of warm sunshine poured out of a cobalt sky broken only by scattered wisps of pure white. Everything smelled clean and new in the wake of yesterday's rain. Even the river smelled fresh. And everywhere streaks and splashes of brightening green.

Hatfield walked with both hands shoved deep in his pockets, feet kicking out ahead in jaunty strides. The posture caused his pantleg cuffs to ride high, each step flashing rows of orange unicorns scampering back and forth across the navy blue of his socks.

"From what we know so far," he said, "it sounds like our murder victim—de Ruth—was just a tad less popular than hoof-and-mouth disease. He was a fan favorite as BRW's lead announcer for its televised matches and promotional interviews, but to his coworkers behind the scenes he was a conniving, manipulating snake. Now a lot of that comes from Tommy and Lori McGurk so maybe we need to take it with a grain of salt, but I've heard rumblings of it elsewhere, too, so I think it's definitely worth checking out."

"Checking out," I said, "as in seeing if his alleged charming ways might have given cause for someone else to have wanted to murder him."

"Exactly. He came to BRW a little under two years ago from one of the bigger promotions in the southwest. He left there 'under a cloud,' as they say. Might even need to take it back that far, find out just what the nature of that cloud was. But that can wait, I'd think, until we've had a closer look at his more immediate past. Your association with that big ex-wrestler pal of yours, the Banger—"

"Bomber," I corrected. "Bomber Brannigan."

"Yeah. Him. Anyway, having him at your side should give you a certain advantage in digging into the BRW scene. The pro wrestling community isn't exactly known for its openness to outsiders, you know. No matter how much dirt there might be on Alex de Ruth, he was one of their own, and I don't think they'll be eager to blab to just anybody about him."

"Tommy McGurk is one of their own, too," I pointed out.

"True. That may be a balancing factor. But McGurk now has a murder charge hanging over his head, don't forget. People are funny. The law of the land might be 'Innocent Until Proven Guilty,' but that isn't necessarily how it works in people's minds. Even though they probably won't admit it, when the average person reads in the paper or sees on TV that so-and-so has been charged with a serious crime they tend to think whoever it was *must* have done something to deserve it. And even if a court of law goes on to find the charged individual innocent, then the doubt over all those 'legal loopholes' that lowlife shy-

sters like me know how to hop through sets in and the
must-have-done-something taint still sticks to some degree."

"Real cheery picture you paint."

"The way it is, pal. Just telling you the way it is. All the
more incentive for us to ferret out Alex de Ruth's real
killer. I don't have much doubt I can beat this crapola
case they've got against our client, if they're even able to
get an indictment. But the taint has already been stuck to
him, see. He's had enough shit dumped on his life, he
doesn't need any more. So the only way to *really* clear
him is to hand over the bastard guilty of what he's being
blamed for."

"I like the way you think, counselor."

"Yeah, well, thinking it and getting it done are two
different things. That's where you've dealt yourself in."

"You know, something that no one seems to be considering yet strikes me as a big point in Tommy's favor: the
way de Ruth was killed. If he'd been beaten or even
stabbed—something more physical—I'd say that would
be more to Tommy's disadvantage. He is, after all, a physical guy, that's his history. Operating on the emotions and
motives he allegedly has, actions along those lines would
be easier to swallow. But to take a gun and cold-bloodedly
shoot the man, that seems too ill fitted to be anywhere
near believable."

Hatfield twisted his mouth thoughtfully. "I see what
you're saying. I considered the same thing. But then I
found out Tommy's a long-standing hunting advocate—
that much has been documented, among other places, in
the pages of a number of wrestling magazines. He pos-
sesses a current small game license, owns a rack of guns,
and is a card-carrying NRA member. I'm afraid that's
plenty for the state to paint a very convincing picture of
him as someone quite capable of resorting to firearm use.
De Ruth was killed by a hunting rifle, remember—although a 7mm, luckily not a caliber compatible with anything registered to Tommy."

"Nuts," I said, only partly under my breath.

"Eloquently put."

We walked a ways before I said, "Strictly you to me, one

renegade to another—you as all-fired confident about beating this thing as you're letting on, or is that part of your act?"

He didn't hesitate. "No, I feel good about beating the state's case as it looks to be shaping up. They jumped too hard too fast and in the process shut the door on too many options they can't go back and open now without helping me make them look like asses."

"Legal angles aside, how solid is your personal belief in Tommy's innocence?"

"If I thought he killed de Ruth, we wouldn't be having this conversation."

"A man is capable of doing some pretty screwy things where a beautiful woman is concerned."

Hatfield stopped walking. "Maybe I should be asking you how strong *your* belief in his innocence is?"

"Strong enough so that I'm not afraid to hold it up to the light and look at it, even question it a little."

He considered this for several beats. Then: "Maybe that isn't such a bad answer."

"Maybe it's even a good one," I said, grinning. "Maybe it's just one more thing that makes me the best man for the job that needs done here."

7

Headquarters for Big River Wrestling Promotions were housed in a chunky, single-storied white brick building that looked as if it had been initially designed for an automobile or major appliance dealership. Located as it was on the fringe of Davenport's formerly depressed west side riverfront area, it wasn't surprising to find the original business folded. The spot was still too far out to have been resuscitated by any of the riverboat gambling overflow that had pumped new life onto much of the scene. The glass-walled front of the structure, the former showroom, had been sectioned off into a reception area and a handful of offices. Beyond this (I would soon learn), what had once been the service and storage bays had been transformed into a training gym complete with a full-sized ring.

Bomber and I stood in the reception area a few minutes before three in the afternoon. The receptionist, a rail-thin, middle-aged woman with limp hair and tired eyes, had picked up her desk phone to announce our arrival and then relayed that Mel Dukenos would be with us shortly.

After Hatfield and I had finished our talk and stroll, he'd given me a lift back to the McGurk house. There, I'd gone over the gist of our conversation with Lori, Tommy, and the Bomber, dwelling on the point of de Ruth's alleged unpopularity and the plan for me to try and uncover anyone else who might have honed their dislike for the man to the point of wanting to see him dead. This approach had met with immediate approval, and Lori and Tommy were fairly brimming over with suggestions on who, why, and what should warrant my attention. Even Bomber, who had previously heard a thing or two about de Ruth's antics through the various contacts he maintained with the wrestling world, provided some input. I tried to assimilate as much as possible of what got tossed around, scribbling names and observations into my pocket notebook as well as a few downright accusations.

Once the exercise had run its course, it had been Bomber, in his typical charge-ahead style, who'd suggested he and I pay a visit to the BRW building. There was no disputing Hatfield's assessment that the pro wrestling community is very much a "closed" segment of society, and gaining the sanction of Big River's Powers That Be could be one more important step toward circumnavigating that barrier and making our investigation as thorough as possible. Plus (something that occurred to me, whether it was part of Bomber's reasoning or not), getting away from Lori and Tommy for a while would provide them with their first opportunity to be alone together since this latest bit of misfortune had clobbered their lives. The flip side to such a provision, of course, was the chance that maybe that was the last thing in the world either of them wanted.

"Bomber Brannigan, I do declare!"

Mel Dukenos strode into the reception area, her smile brilliant, her words coated by a faint southern accent. She was a compact, attractive woman of forty-something, wearing the years as comfortably as the simple skirt and sweater that complimented her trim curves. The whole package came as a bit of a surprise. I'd been informed that "Mel" was short for Melanie, so it wasn't the fact she was a woman that caught me off guard; but inasmuch as I'd also

been informed she was the widow of old-time promoter
Duke Dukenos and had at one time spent a couple years
among the ranks of female wrestlers, I guess I was expecting someone a little older and built more after the fashion
of one of those "female Clydesdales" Abe Lugretti had
alluded to before.

She proceeded directly to Bomber with both arms extended, reaching out and up to grip his beefy shoulders.
"It's great to see you again, you old rascal. You're looking
as fit as the day of your farewell match."

Bomber smiled. "It's good to see you again, too, Mel.
But we both know I'm fifty pounds and a couple dozen
years past my fighting prime, so you're as full of beans as
you are beautiful."

"Well, you still look fine to me and I can darn well say so
if I want to."

They traded smiles a while longer before Bomber directed her attention toward me with a nod of his head.
"Mel, I'd like you to meet Joe Hannibal, a good friend of
mine."

"Mrs. Dukenos," I said. "My pleasure."

"Make it Mel, Joe, and it'll be my pleasure right back."
We shook hands.

She rocked her head back and peered up at Bomber
again. "Abe Lugretti mentioned you were in town. But I
had a hunch you'd be showing up, even before he said
anything. You're never very far away when Tommy Mc-
Gurk gets his butt in a jam."

Bomber frowned. "There a note of disapproval in there
somewhere?"

"Not at all. I'm pulling for Tommy, too. But this time
I'm afraid he may be in a jam too sticky for you or anybody else to get him out of."

"That's what brings us here all the same," Bomber said.
"Spare us a few minutes to talk?"

Big River's petite exec motioned us back to her office. It
was a big, square room with a big, square desk and green
metal filing cabinets. The walls were covered with posters advertising various wrestling cards. A handful of well-
tended plants had been placed about here and there,
providing a hint of femininity. Otherwise, I got the feel-

ing the room was largely unchanged from the time when Duke Dukenos had been its main occupant.

His widow seated herself on a corner of the desk, gesturing Bomber and me into visitors' chairs, then said, "I hope everybody understands my position in all of this and bears me no kind of grudge. Regardless of my personal feelings—and I truly am pulling for Tommy, as I said—as the head of BRW I have to consider above all else what is best for the organization. We are very much dependent on public acceptance, up to and including our weekly television spot which sells the tickets to our live shows and is made possible through a potload of advertising dollars paid to the stations. The complexities of the whole ball of wax absolutely prohibit me—BRW—from using or in any official way sanctioning Tommy as long as he has anything like a murder charge hanging over his head."

Bomber's mouth pulled into a tight line. "I take it your advertisers must never have heard of a catchy little phrase that goes 'Innocent until proven guilty,' huh?"

"Noble words on a piece of paper," Mel Dukenos said. "I've got some other words on a different piece of paper that spell out a morals clause in Tommy McGurk's contract, you want to talk about that? I'm already out my lead announcer and one of my top draw performers—maybe two, if Paula decides to go on some kind of grieving-widow kick. Can't you see that I can't afford to risk anything more right now?"

"The lady has a point, Bomber," I said. "And you busting her chops over what ought to be instead of what is isn't going to help anything or anybody." I felt like I was chiming in on a good cop/bad cop routine and swiping lines from Nicholas Hatfield to boot.

Bomber gave me a look. I weathered it. After a little bit his eyes swung away and he clamped his hands on his thighs, digging the clublike fingers deep. "Yeah, yeah," he sighed. "I guess sometimes my mouth has a mind of its own."

Mel Dukenos managed a smile. "Don't worry about it. Most of the time it's one of your more endearing traits. This mess has everybody wired tight as hell."

I turned my attention to her. "When you say you're pulling for Tommy—exactly what do you mean?"

She blinked. "Why, I . . . I mean I hope he comes through this okay."

"Do you believe he's innocent?"

She took time to gnaw her lower lip some before putting an answer past it. "I *want* to believe he is, yes. But there's no denying Tommy has quite a temper. Let's face it, you have to have a certain amount of innate aggression in order to cut it in the wrestling profession. And there's also no denying Alex de Ruth had a masterful capacity for being able to bring just about anybody to the boiling point. Put the two together . . ."

"You seem to be dodging the question, ma'am."

"All right. Let's say I'd be somewhat surprised if it turned out Tommy allowed himself to be driven to murder—but not really blown away by it."

It still wasn't a clear answer but it looked to be as close as I was going to get to one. I moved on to the next question. "Was Tommy having an affair with Paula de Ruth?"

Her reply tumbled out above a firmly set jaw. "I don't think I care to answer that."

"Come on, Mel," Bomber said. "I thought we could count on you to help."

"What's the point of a question like that? How can it help, except maybe to provide a cheap thrill if you get off on dishing dirt?"

"It can help," I said, "by arming me with as many facts as I can get. If Tommy and Paula *were* having a fling and the prosecution can prove it, then that strengthens their case—especially if our side is caught flat-footed because everybody was being too damn polite to level with us."

"I thought Abe said you were just a private eye? You're coming on like you think you're some kind of hotshot lawyer or something."

I wondered how many rungs of the ladder separated the two in her mind. It was obvious my profession was the one farther down.

"That's right," I said. "I'm just a P.I. But I'm working in

close conjunction with McGurk's attorney on this, therefore whatever I know he knows and vice versa."

"This is Joe's kind of thing," Bomber said, "and he's
damn good at it. He came through for Tommy and Lori
once before, when they were living up north, back when
Tommy was still wrestling."

She chewed her lip some more. "Yeah," she said
thoughtfully, "I remember hearing something about
that . . ."

"I'm not out to shovel any unnecessary dirt," I told her.
"And by the same token I don't mean to whitewash anything. I want to get to the bottom line on this and because
I'm on Tommy's side I'm counting on that to add up to
proof of his innocence as far as murder."

I got a resigned wave of one hand. "All right. I don't
have a juicy eye-witness report or an incriminatingly
stained bedsheet I can hand over for evidence, but, for
what it's worth, I'd long since formed the opinion there
definitely *was* something going on between Tommy and
Paula. I can't exactly put my finger on what it was made
me reach that conclusion, except it was a feeling I had
even before Alex started making all his noise. Something
about the way the two of them would look at each other,
their body language when they were in the same room
together, that sort of thing. Then, too, it was no secret
Paula and Alex had a pretty wide-open relationship. The
only surprise was that Tommy might be foolish enough to
get caught in it and that Alex would end up getting so
bent out of shape."

"You're saying Paula and Alex had both fooled around
outside their marriage before?"

"That's a polite way of saying it. At least Paula had the
decency to show a little discretion. Alex, on the other
hand, short of actually doing it right in front of her, was a
blowhard and a braggart who loved nothing better than
to regale anyone who'd listen with every lurid detail of
exactly how much—as he so quaintly put it—pipe he was
able to lay."

"Sounds like a real charmer," Bomber grunted.

"He could be . . . in an oily, obvious kind of way."

"So why in hell did you keep a jerk like that around?"

"One very simple and very mercenary reason—he was good for business. Within six months after I hired him as our lead announcer, the ratings on our TV spots had nearly doubled. And a bigger TV audience relates directly to bigger crowds at the live matches. Oh we'd made a number of other changes, too, of course, but there's still no denying Alex was a big part of BRW's increased success. He got more mail than many of our wrestlers. And when he attended the live matches to do TV tapings, he always had a flock around him, a flock from which he wasn't above plucking an impressionable young female for a little off-camera squeeze and please, I might add. Let's face it, he had plenty to offer as far as fan appeal. He was handsome, knew the sport well, did colorful analysis and play by play, put just the right mix of irreverence and intimidation into the interviews he did. Hell, I knew it was just a matter of time before I was going to have him lured away by one of the bigger federations. I just didn't expect to lose him quite so soon or so permanently, that's all."

I said, "It's rumored that, before coming to BRW, de Ruth had worked for a wrestling promotion down south and that he left there under some sort of cloud. Know anything about that?"

"He did announcing for a handful of different outfits, I know that one or two of them were in the south. But I don't know any of the details of his departures from them."

"Did de Ruth have any close friends?"

Her smile was sardonic. "Hardly. I suppose you'd have to say Paula, before they split up. And then of course himself. Alex always liked Alex best. Anybody will tell you that."

"How about the other end of the spectrum—enemies?"

"Well, almost anyone who got to know him eventually grew to dislike him, as we've been discussing. But I don't know how many of them would rate as full-fledged enemies, not in the way I think you mean."

"The thing is," I said, "if Tommy *didn't* kill de Ruth then that obviously leaves somebody who did. The logical place to start looking for that somebody is among those who were closest around de Ruth, relatives, coworkers, and the like. Especially since there's indication plenty of ill will toward him existed in that group."

"In other words we need to dig into your organization, talk to your people, Mel," Bomber said. "The surest way to clear Tommy is turn up de Ruth's *real* killer."

"Either way, it doesn't do me a hell of a lot of good, does it? Not if I end up trading one of my people for another."

"Except it will be the right one, the one who deserves it," I pointed out.

"I hope you'll back our play, not try to stand in our way," Bomber said.

Mel Dukenos looked from one of us to the other. Hung a long, probing gaze on each. After a minute, she said, "No, I wouldn't do anything like that. I want the truth found out, too. I certainly don't want to see Tommy railroaded. I'll hold out hope that the real murderer turns out to be nobody connected with BRW, but I won't try to stop you from digging to make sure."

Bomber nodded. "I knew I could count on you, kid."

Having stated her decision, Mel Dukenos almost immediately looked less than comfortable with it. "I suppose you'd like to go out into the gym now and start your questioning?"

I nodded. "Anyone in particular you'd recommend we pay attention to?"

"Oh no you don't," she said with a hard shake of her head. "You're not going to get me to bite on that, no way. I'll take you around and introduce you, help break the ice a little for you, then you're on your own. I'm not about to be a finger-pointer for you."

"So what do you think?" Bomber wanted to know.

"About her proposition, you mean?"

"No, about the shortage of sheep dip in Saskatchewan. Jeez."

"Okay, okay, no need to get testy. But it's your decision to make, not mine or anybody else's. Sounds like it should be interesting, maybe even fun. And probably profitable to boot."

"Hang the profit angle. What about the investigation, helping Tommy? I wouldn't want anybody to think I was abandoning a sinking ship."

"Anybody who knows you knows a damn sight better than that. Besides, you'd still be helping Tommy by protecting his job for him. If and when this thing blows over, the stage will be set and the scenario all written for his return. And you'd still be plenty useful to the investigation, too. Hell, it might be for the good if we're split up. You'd be even more integrated into the wrestling scene, on the inside where you could keep your eyes and ears open while I was on the outside making noise, shaking the walls, trying to jar something loose. You'd be in a good position to spot if I started getting results."

We were rolling across the Mississippi on the Centennial Bridge, passing from Iowa back into Illinois. The sinking sun sprayed streaks of silver on the muddy blue water. As Bomber slowed to drop a quarter into the exact-change toll basket, I swung my gaze upriver where, through the steel girders, I could see the sandy, wooded tip of Arsenal Island. The island serves, geographically, as the hub of the whole Quad Cities layout. Even before the coming of the white man, the Indian tribes of the region had recognized its strategic location, sitting at the juncture of the Rock and Mississippi rivers with surrounding high lookout bluffs. In the hands of those who claimed it since, Arsenal Island has been home to old Fort Armstrong during the Black Hawk Indian War, the site of a prison for captured Confederate troops in the waning months of the Civil War, and for the past century plus has garrisoned the U.S. Army arsenal which gave it its name. In more peaceful times it shouldered the load of the first bridge to span the mighty Mississip.

I thought of all those things fleetingly as I squinted across the flashing water, but the thing that leaped most prominently to mind concerning the historic island was perhaps the darkest event to take place upon it and one tied by a certain irony to present circumstances. Between the Black Hawk War and the Civil War, Colonel George Davenport, pioneer settler of the area after whom the Iowa city was named, established a residence on the island. On a fourth of July morning while his family was in town doing holiday shopping, Davenport was attacked in his house and tortured and finally killed by a gang of seven river rats who falsely believed he had a fortune in gold buried on the grounds. All they got for their trouble was $300 in cash from a dresser drawer and eventually a hanging in Rock Island after they were caught and tried. Legend had it that the Indians, hearing of the death of their good friend "Saganosh," gathered from throughout Illinois and Iowa and as far away as Wisconsin and performed ceremonies for days before helping to lay the good colonel to his final rest.

I pondered the "big" death of a prominent, well-respected man like Davenport and the "small" death of a cad like Alex de Ruth. Both messily murdered at their own homes. Only it was a safe bet de Ruth wasn't going to go down in the history books, and it seemed equally evident that no one was going to dance a ceremony of mourning for his passing. But none of that did Tommy McGurk a lick of good. If Hatfield or the rest of us couldn't prove otherwise, in the eyes of the law he'd be just as guilty for killing an unpopular man as Davenport's attackers had been for killing a popular one.

The bong of the Thank You/Go Ahead signal and the motion of Bomber accelerating away from the toll stop swung my gaze back around and broke my reverie. Brought me back to the matter currently under discussion between him and me, an intriguing little sidebar to the murder case per se that had cropped up near the close of our visit to the BRW building.

We'd spent roughly an hour in the gym, getting set up nicely by Mel Dukenos and then left to mingle at will with any and all present. Not surprisingly, our purpose and our questions had been met with a certain amount of suspicion and reluctance to get involved. Although BRW employed a handful of veterans, in addition to Tommy McGurk and Abe Lugretti, who had been part of the game when Bomber was still wrestling, it was our bad luck that none of them were there that afternoon, leaving us unable to trade effectively off his "in" status or even his reputation. It was poignantly amusing to watch the expression on the big guy's face when only a couple of the sweating hulks we talked to seemed to recognize his name, and then only vaguely. As far as the case went, at least we established our intent and the fact we had the sanction of the head office. Word would spread. We'd be back and, one way or another, we'd have to be dealt with.

It was when we were ready to go that Mel Dukenos had asked us back into her office and dropped her out-of-left-field proposal in our laps. More specifically, in Bomber's lap. The thing was, she explained, she had this dilemma and seeing Bomber had triggered an idea how he could help her out of it. It seemed BRW had one of its biggest-ever shows upcoming soon in St. Louis. The problem was that Tommy McGurk, as the colorful manager of the ladies' champ, and Alex de Ruth, as lead announcer for the pay-per-view cable TV hookup that had been arranged, were important ingredients to the success of the card and now were suddenly out of the picture without sufficient time to seek out polished replacements. Mel's inspiration was to trade off Bomber's former popularity and his well-known association with Tommy and to insert him not only as the Platinum Powerhouse's new manager but, during the other matches, as color commentator to beef up the play-by-play duties inherited by Abe Lugretti. She was quick to assure him she would provide adequate compensation for however long the arrangement lasted.

"So you think I should do it, huh?" Bomber pressed me.

"Did I say that?"

"You just rattled off about forty reasons why it wouldn't be a bad idea."

"That's a far cry from saying 'go ahead and do it.' "

"Well, dammit, should I or shouldn't I?"

I gave him a sour look. "You *want* to do it, don't you? But you want me to give you the go-ahead so if it turns to shit then you can bitch and grumble and blame it at least partly on me."

"All I'm after is a little bit of friendly advice. Sounds like you got some kind of complex, pal."

I studied his craggy profile as he steered the Buick through the Rock Island traffic. "It got to you back there, didn't it? The gym. The sweat, the smells, the smack of the wrestlers hitting the mat. And I saw the look in your eyes when you were scanning the posters on the walls."

"I was on a lot of those cards, you know."

"Yeah, I saw that."

"It was my life for a lot of years, Joe. A hard life, a crazy one, but not a bad one by any means. At least I always figured it did good by me."

"I never realized you missed it so much."

"I didn't. Never let myself. I got too old, too fat, too many aches from too many broken bones and ripped muscles. There was no going back, so why mope over it."

"But now you've got a way to go back."

"Maybe."

"Wouldn't be the same up home without your ugly mug shoving me a beer across the bar of The Bomb Shelter."

"Oh, hell, I wouldn't give up The Bomb Shelter. Liz and Old Charley can handle things fine there, like they always do when I'm off on something else. I don't see this as a very long-term thing, no matter how it turns out with Tommy. It's just . . . an opportunity I'd hate to pass up, you know? A lark, a working vacation sort of. And as long as you honestly don't think it would queer anything as far as Tommy's situation . . ."

"I told you how I saw that. Having you deeper on the inside could even work out better."

Bomber glanced over, flashing a somewhat sheepish grin. "There's one more reason I want to try Mel's deal on for size."

"What's that?"

"Those punks back there at the gym who had no idea who the hell I was? . . . I aim to show 'em."

Lori had supper ready when we got back to the Mc-Gurk house. We sat down to a fine meal of lamb chops, scalloped potatoes, and steamed vegetables. Bomber and I gave a rundown of how things had gone at BRW, in the process passing on Mel Dukenos's best wishes to Tommy along with the fact that she and a lot of others in the organization were pulling for him. For the time being, we held off mentioning the offer that had been made to Bomber. I left him to bring it up in his own way and in his own time; he'd pretty much decided to accept as long as the McGurks had no problem with it, and I couldn't see why they would.

For their part, Tommy and Lori appeared to be holding up as well as could be expected. They seemed very much at ease with each other, indicating their time alone together had been welcome or at least hadn't been a strain.

When supper was finished and the table cleared and I sensed Bomber was getting ready to tell them about Mel Dukenos's dilemma and proposed solution involving him, I topped off my cup of coffee and moseyed out into the backyard with it. I figured they could get through the talk okay without me. Besides, I needed some solitude, a chance to sip the coffee and enjoy a leisurely cigarette by myself. The way my life has worked out, I guess a sizable portion of me has reached confirmed loner status; my contact with people—even ones I consider friends, like the Bomber—is strictly bump and run. When I go too long without a stretch of being alone—like I hadn't been for a couple of days now—I start to feel cramped, edgy. I suppose it was that same part of me that had been sensitive earlier to the McGurks possible need to be by themselves for a while.

In the middle of the backyard, I found a picnic table. I sat down with my coffee in front of me, tapped out a Pall Mall and got it going. It was dark by then. Tommy had snapped on the yard light for me, but the light from a skyful of moon and stars overhead made its yellowish glow seem feeble and unnecessary.

The yard had a chest-high wooden fence around it and in one corner was a formidable dog house. From this, a glossy Irish setter had emerged to the end of its chain when I came out and sat now on its haunches, watching me hopefully. I decided the mutt either wanted to play or wanted to bum a cigarette off me. Whichever he had in mind, I was ignoring him.

One of the things I do best when I'm alone is think. Sometimes I think too much and get to feeling sorry for myself, but that's another story. This night I had plenty else to mull over. Once I'd taken Lori McGurk's money and agreed to look into things for her, the case had taken off like a runaway roller coaster, long since jumping its track and sucking me along for a white-knuckled ride in directions I'd no way in hell anticipated. I needed a chance to reflect on it all. I'd started out after a man I hoped wasn't guilty of one thing, and now suddenly I was digging like crazy trying to prove that same man wasn't guilty of something a lot worse. And the trouble was, everything was moving so fast I didn't have a *feel* for any of it. No feeling, that is, except a growing conviction my man hadn't measured up as far as the first count I'd pinned my hopes on and a sinking, letdown realization he was only human and therefore probably a damn sight more capable of the greater guilt than any of us in his corner wanted to admit.

I don't know how long I sat there. The coffee was nothing but a residual taste at the back of my mouth and that first cigarette had turned into another and another, their burnt-out butts in a neat row at my elbow along the edge of the tabletop. The dog continued to watch me with patient hopefulness and I continued to ignore it.

I heard the house door open and close behind me. The dog perked up, came to all fours. Its long tail began whipping back and forth and it started whimpering and woofing eagerly. I turned to see Tommy McGurk coming across the yard. He was carrying a couple of cans of beer.

"Mind some company?" he asked.

I shook my head and said, not altogether truthfully, "Nope. Not at all." Hell, it was his place.

"Ready to chase that coffee with a cold brew?"

"Now you're talking."

The dog was galloping back and forth by then, short arcs on the end of its chain, its barks getting louder, more insistent.

Tommy put the cans of beer on the table next to me. "Pop yourself one. I've got to go let that rascal loose, let him work off a little of that energy or he'll drive us crazy."

I punched the tab on a can, blew away the first surge of foam, tipped it high. It tasted cold and crisp and golden and great.

Tommy returned to the table and sat across from me. He reached for the other can of beer, thumbed it open. He looked good in the soft focus of the night lighting. Calm. Gone was that haunted, trapped look that hollows a man's eyes and draws on his face after only a few hours behind bars; the look that had been on him when I'd first seen him at the arraignment that morning. Behind him, the dog, loosened from its own restraint, was tearing repeatedly back and forth across the width of the yard. The way its ears stood straight out behind its head made me think of the flowing cape on a comic book superhero.

Tommy said, "To have that much vitality again, huh?"

"Again? Don't recall that I ever had that much."

"Maybe not," Tommy said, almost wistfully. "Maybe not."

We nipped at our beer. The dog continued to run.

"Ever do any hunting with him?" I wondered.

"You bet. You might not guess it—around the house here he mostly acts like he ain't got a brain in his head—but out in the field he's a damn fine animal. I used to take him out a lot, before I got back into wrestling." He stared down at his can of beer, rolling it slowly between his palms. "Looks like I'll be having some time on my hands for a while, give me the chance to get him out again."

I let that one drift away, then said, "How did it go inside? Bomber talk to you?"

"About Mel's offer to him?"

"Uh-huh."

"I told him to go for it. I got no problem with it, sounds solid to me. It'd help out Mel, and Bomber said you didn't figure it would hurt the investigation any, right?"

"Not that I can foresee."

"He's on the phone with her now, giving her the go-ahead to set it up, suggesting some polishing touches."

"I guess the obvious next step is to make sure Paula de Ruth is willing to go along with it."

"I think she will. Paula's got a pretty good head on her shoulders, she knows enough to trust Mel's instincts." He rolled his can of beer some more. "Speaking of Paula, have you, uh, had a chance to talk to her yet?"

"No, I haven't. I need to obviously, but with the funeral tomorrow and everything, the timing hasn't been right."

"Uhmm. I was just wondering how she's making it through all this."

"You haven't talked to her either, uh?"

His eyes swung up with an "are you nuts?" look in them, then fell away again and he said simply, "No. Uh-uh."

I drank some of my beer. "While we're on the subject, Tommy, I guess this is as good a time as any to ask—were you having a thing with Paula?"

His mouth twisted into a bitter smile. "Everybody figures I was, don't they?"

"About everybody, yeah."

"Does Lori?"

He caught me a little off guard with that. "That one I can't answer," I said. "You'll have to ask her yourself."

"Yeah. Right. That's the kind of thing a guy is in a real hurry to ask his wife."

"You still haven't given me an answer."

The dog came trotting up with a chew toy in his mouth, a badly mangled rubber chicken he'd scrounged from some corner of the yard. He dropped it at Tommy's feet and rocked back on his haunches with an expectant look on his face. He was panting hard from all his activity, his wet pink tongue painted orange by the glow of the yard light. Tommy picked the rubber chicken up and threw it and the beast went bounding happily after it.

Tommy remained turned partly away, gazing absently after the running dog. "Some guys cheat on their wives as a matter of course," he said. "They're always on the prowl, always looking, always ready to sample something different. I never was one of those. And don't think I didn't have plenty of chances. Pro wrestling has its groupies, just like other professional sports or rock and roll or what have you." I caught the corner of a rueful smile. "The only difference is that our groupies tend to be more of legal age."

The dog returned, only to go racing away when Tommy threw the chicken again.

"But things change in a man's life," he went on. "Pieces of him get rubbed off, chipped away, sort of like the outer layer of paint or plaster on a building. And sometimes what gets exposed is pretty different than what used to be there. That's how it got to be with me. One day I looked around and there were a lot of pieces of me missing. What was left didn't feel right, didn't feel the same anymore. And then Paula came along and made me feel better . . . made me feel whole again. Do you understand what I'm saying?"

Yeah, I thought to myself, you're saying you boffed her, you dumb shit. Outwardly, all I did was nod.

"But I never went looking for it," Tommy said, "I never prowled or planned and I haven't changed into the kind of guy who figures to in the future. I want you to know that."

"It all comes under the same heading," I said.

He sighed. "Yeah. No getting around that."

"And there's no getting around the fact it doesn't help your case one damn bit either. Do you love her?"

"Paula?"

"That's who we're talking about, isn't it?" I was suddenly short tempered, irritable. He'd disappointed me and even though I was more or less expecting it, it still made me sore.

Tommy tried to find the right words. "I have a . . . deep feeling toward Paula. I *care* about her, especially with what's happened. I'm grateful for the time we had together. But I don't think I love her . . . not in the way I love Lori." He let his wife's name hang in the air for a long time. Then: "She'll have to be told all this, won't she?"

"It's going to come out one way or another. I think it would be best if she heard it from you."

The dog, finally tiring a little, had come to lie beside Tommy's feet and gnaw noisily on the rubber chicken. Tommy's hand drifted down to pet him.

"Another thing I want you to know, Hannibal," he said.

"What's that?"

"I may have done a dumb thing with Paula and I may have gone through some miserable periods of depression and feeling sorry for myself—but I never meant to hurt Lori and I never stopped loving her."

"You don't have to convince me. It's Lori who needs to hear that."

"And I never killed that prick de Ruth, either. I'm not saying I never thought about it or that I wouldn't have if I could have gotten my hands on him. But it never worked out that way. That's the part that's important for *you* to believe."

"Why don't you tell me about that night?"

"What's to tell? I never caught up with him so nothing happened—at least not as far as I was concerned. Yeah, I was hot after what the sucker-punching bastard did to me in that parking lot. Boiling hot. Crazy mad. Luckily Abe was able to get me out of there. And he even got me calmed down some during the drive back. But after I picked up my own car from the BRW lot and was by myself, it all came back and I was boiling all over again. I tried to figure out where they would have gone—Paula had agreed to go somewhere with him and hear him out, let him talk his talk one more time. I drove by her place, drove by his place, couldn't find any sign of them. All I could think about was getting my hands on the sonofabitch, smashing his face, paying him back for all the shit he'd been spreading and for knocking me in the dirt. I'd held everything back for too long, let too much build up inside me."

"His neighbors described your car, said it drove up and down the street several times that night. Claimed at one point there was quite a commotion, some hollering and swearing."

"Yeah, that was me. Being even more of a horse's ass. After I drove around and drove around and couldn't find them anywhere, I got it in my head maybe he was at his place all along, laying low, hiding from me because he somehow knew I was on the prod. So I went back again and banged on his door and threw rocks at his upstairs windows and hollered for him to come out. Called him a chickenshit and every name I could lay my tongue to. Real mature behavior, right? When I saw lights popping on in some of the other houses I at least had enough sense to get out of there before somebody called the cops."

"What time was that?"

"Hell, I don't know. I wasn't paying any attention to the time."

"Abe Lugretti says he dropped you off at the BRW lot about one thirty. You go along with that?"

"Sounds about right, yeah."

"So altogether you drove around—what?—a couple hours maybe?"

"Couldn't have been much more or much less than that."

"So you caused the commotion at de Ruth's about three thirty and took off when you saw you were disturbing the neighbors. Then what?"

"Well. I guess I drove around some more."

"You 'guess'? Come on, man, this isn't a trivia quiz we're doing here, this is fucking important—important to *you.*"

"All right. I drove around. That's what I did."

"Where'd you go?"

"No specific place. Just around."

"You didn't go back to de Ruth's any more or try to find Paula at her place?"

"No. I didn't go anywhere in particular. I just goddamn *drove around* I told you."

"Did you stop for gas, coffee—do anything where somebody might have seen you at a certain time?"

"Nothing that I can think of, no."

"That's pretty lame, Tommy. Somewhere between the time you raised enough hell to get yourself noticed at de Ruth's house and then finally returned home, after daylight, the man you admittedly were enraged at and had been chasing after into the wee hours of the morning managed to get himself blown away. Can you see why the cops are wetting their pants over you as their prime suspect?"

"Of course I can see it. You think I'm dumb? But that doesn't change anything. I can only tell you what I can tell you."

He continued to pet the dog, as he'd been doing, his eyes gazing off and away, not meeting mine. I didn't think he'd actually lied to me, but at the same time, as with Abe Lugretti the previous night, I got a clear impression he was holding something back. *I can only tell you what I can tell you.* Maybe it didn't mean shit, just an awkward choice of words, and I was trying too hard to flex my intuitive muscles.

At any rate, the exchange had accomplished one important thing: It had brought me to believe more completely that Tommy McGurk wasn't a murderer. What I could do to help Hatfield prove that and exactly what it was—if anything—Tommy was hiding were extenuations that remained to be seen.

Eventually, Tommy got around to looking at me again. He said, "What I came out here for, Hannibal, was . . .

well, to say thanks. Seems you always show up to try and help when I put my ass in a sling. I realize that probably has more to do with the friendship between you and Bomber than any overwhelming concern on your part for my well being, but I'm grateful all the same. The last time, that business with El Bandido and Eddie the Sleeve and his bunch, I'm afraid I didn't express my gratitude too good. In fact, I probably seemed a little resentful. What I resented, what I was really mad at, was the fact I couldn't handle the problem myself. But I'm a little older and a lot smarter now and I've learned all too well there are plenty of things in a man's life he can't handle all by himself. This is another one of those. So I want you to know I appreciate everything you're doing on my behalf."

"There are a lot more people supporting you in this than just me and the Bomber," I reminded him.

He nodded. "I know. I hope I don't let any of them down."

I looked at him for a long time, then gave a nod of my own. "So do I."

9

They buried Alex de Ruth the next morning. Naturally, neither Tommy nor Lori attended the funeral services. But Bomber and I were there, in the company of Mel Dukenos. For Bomber it was a first step toward establishing himself on the BRW scene; I saw it as an opportunity to connect some faces to the various names I'd been listing in my notebook.

Given all the ill will reputedly felt toward the deceased, the turnout was stronger than I would have bet on. I saw this as a comment on human hypocrisy. Mel Dukenos offered an even more cynical opinion, suggesting that many of those on hand were there not to mourn but rather to make *damn sure* the man was planted and gone.

In any event, the minister, a painfully sincere young man with a receding hairline and a double chin, must have been clued in about the mixed feelings for the earthly remains he was reading over because he kept his sermon brief and considerably less saccharine than usual.

Paula de Ruth sat next to a frail-looking, freckled blond woman purported to be Alex's sister, his only other surviving relative, flown up from San Antonio, Texas. The sister snuffled repeatedly into a crumpled hanky throughout the service, the widow remained rigid and silent, a column of wondrously curved ice beneath a veil and a clinging sheath of black.

Afterwards, I was introduced to a number of BRW personnel, notable among them: Sam War Cloud, a beefy, aging veteran of American Indian descent long past his prime physically but apparently not in spirit; Leticia Cloud, his lovely and much younger wife, a popular wrestler in her own right under the ring banner of Princess Silver Dove; a pair of massive, mustachioed, shaven-headed brothers named Kolchonsky out of Chicago who tag-teamed as the Savage Sheiks, mat terrorists allegedly from the volatile sands of the Middle East; and, last but not least, there was BRW's current men's heavyweight champ, Brick Towers, a square-shouldered young giant with the kind of soft-spoken manner and cleft-chinned, blue-eyed good looks that added up to quintessential Clean Cut All American Hero (at least in Mel Dukenos's opinion, and that, I was told, accounted for the gold around Towers's waist far more than his actual wrestling abilities). Abe Lugretti was there, too, and I spotted Bouncing Betty and the wiry referee from the matches I'd seen a few nights before. A more colorfully bereaved bunch you would be hard-pressed to find anywhere.

And there had been another presence to consider. A pair of them. They remained on the background fringe, silent, somber suits, somber expressions, eyes that never stopped moving. When the procession made its way from the funeral parlor to the cemetery, they were there, too. Eyes behind mirrored sunglasses now, but you could still feel the ceaseless movement. To the uninitiated they might have been anything, business associates paying their last respects perhaps. For me, they might as well have been carrying neon signs and wearing vaudeville-sized badges. They were cops. Certainly not unheard of for a cop to visit the funeral of a murder victim; but in this case, if they were so solidly locked on Tommy McGurk as their man, why bother? I didn't know the reason, but I got the uncomfortable feeling they were there doing the same thing I was—matching faces to names.

Paula de Ruth and the snuffling sister left straightaway at the conclusion of the ceremony, with only cursory nods to those they came unavoidably in contact with.

Once things had broken up and we'd quit the cemetery and dropped Mel Dukenos at her place, it was time for Bomber and me to turn north and make the drive home to Rockford. With the case expanding and splintering off in unexpected ways, we both needed to make arrangements for more extended absences than we'd initially planned.

Back on home turf, we split up. I spent the afternoon at my office making phone calls and putting the finishing touches on a handful of reports, tying off as many loose ends as I could. A couple ongoing cases I transferred to other agencies. Later in the evening I lured Liz Grimaldi —Bomber's Gal Friday and a special kind of friend to me (all in addition to mother henning the both of us every chance she gets)—away from her Bomb Shelter duties long enough to keep me company through a leisurely supper at my favorite steak house. It seemed important to gorge myself on the familiar and the good in my life before heading out once again into the badlands. I capped off the evening drinking deeply from Liz's smiling eyes and sneaked a couple extra peeks down her cleavage.

That night I slept hard in my own bed, dreaming scattered dreams populated by chubby Indian chiefs and marauding Arabs with thick Polish accents and suggestively beautiful women masked by mysterious veils and sugar plum fairies dancing on stardust and tall, silent men with mirrors for eyes.

I rolled back into the Quad Cities behind the wheel of my Honda shortly past noon on the following day. I found the motel where I'd made a reservation via phone and decided to try their coffee shop for lunch. By the time I had a serving of the day's special (meat loaf) under my belt, my room was ready. I signed in and lugged my single grip up to the second floor slot they'd assigned me.

I'd known I wouldn't feel comfortable bunking at the McGurks's over a drawn-out stretch, especially without the Bomber around. So when Mel Dukenos had requested that Bomber (for appearance' sake, given the new capacity he was assuming) find a different place to stay, I'd taken that as a cue to do likewise. When BRW's top exec additionally found an apartment for her new hiree to sublet, he and I had discussed sharing it but in the end agreed to remain split up. I guess Bomber has a loner streak as well.

I used the motel room phone to call the McGurks, report in, let them know I was back in town and back on the job. Lori picked up and we talked briefly. She seemed in decent spirits, said Tommy was doing okay, too. No, they hadn't heard from the Bomber so far today, didn't know if he'd returned from Rockford yet or not. Hatfield had been in touch, to go over some details with Tommy and to offer his continuing encouragement. Lori said she planned to go to her real estate office later and put in a few hours, see how things went. I told her I'd be on the move, starting to question people, starting to stir things up. We wished each other luck and rang off.

Outside, the day was another beaut. Blue sky, sunshine, a soft, warm breeze. Mother Nature strutting her finest. Spring is about the best it gets in the Midwest, a transition without extremes. Fall runs a close second, offering a brilliantly colored respite between the blistering heat of summer and the marrow-freezing breath of winter, but there is a gloomy downside you can never get all the way past. It is, after all, a dying season, an ending, a passage *from*. Spring comes on clean and vital and exciting, a beginning, a passage *into*.

I drove from Rock Island across the river to Davenport with the Honda windows down, letting the warmth and freshness of the day pour over me.

I had in mind the first person I intended to call on. It was the obvious choice, even if the timing was lousy. I couldn't see where there'd be a *good* time, not in the near future.

First I tried the apartment she'd taken after leaving her husband. Paula de Ruth wasn't there. I drove next to the house where they had lived together, the address at which Alex de Ruth was shot to death.

The house was your basic split level, pale blue trimmed by darker blue, but extraordinarily maintained. Not a smudge on the window glass, not a hint of cracked or chipped paint, not a single blade of ragged grass on the lawn. From what I knew of the man I somehow couldn't picture Alex de Ruth having sweated away his spare time keeping things up to this degree. Nevertheless, I parked my decidedly shabby set of wheels at the curb a respectful distance away.

From the police reports I'd scanned over Hatfield's shoulder at the arraignment, I knew de Ruth had been gunned down in the driveway right out front of his house. As I walked up the sidewalk, I automatically looked over that way. I don't know what I expected to see, but there were no ominous patches of bloodstained asphalt, no remnants of a chalk outline marking where the body had fallen. Parked in the driveway was the sleek Pontiac I had seen Paula de Ruth driving the night I tailed her and Tommy McGurk, the night that had culminated in her husband's death. Parked beside it was a gleaming black Chevy IROC Z.

I thumbed the bell button and listened to its chimes go rolling into the house.

Paula de Ruth answered the door so promptly it was almost startling. The way she looked finished the job. She had on skin-tight designer jeans and a matching denim jacket with silver studding and sleeves rolled precisely to three-quarter length. The jeans were tucked into knee-high black patent leather boots with stiletto heels that lifted her already formidable height to eye level with my six-one. Beneath the unbuttoned jacket she wore a low-cut, lacey black silk something that shimmered and rippled from the movement of her unrestrained breasts like there were kittens scampering back and forth under the fabric. Crowning it all an abbreviated sweep of milk-blond hair, eyes as blue and sharp as chips of cobalt, full mouth painted wet blood red.

Her gaze slid over me with measured deliberateness, down one side and up the other, the way a binge-primed bulimic might eye a buffet spread before either digging in or throwing up beside it.

Before I could say anything, she announced, "I'm on my way out."

I dug a business card from my pocket and handed it over. "I only need a few minutes of your time, Mrs. de Ruth. It's important that I talk to you."

She examined the card. "Oh. You're the detective they hired to try and help Tommy."

"That's right."

Her eyes returned to me. "What makes you think I have anything to say of importance to your investigation?"

I retrieved my card. "Come on, Mrs. de Ruth. If you don't want to talk to me, that's your prerogative. Just say so. But I'd appreciate it if you didn't jerk my chain."

I thought I saw her red lips twitch with the hint of a smile. "Did you know my late husband, Mr. Hannibal?"

"No. Never met him."

"Good. You shouldn't feel obligated to act saddened by his death then. Let's go."

She hooked a purse from somewhere inside, pulled the door shut as she stepped out. Brushed by me in long, heel-cracking strides and headed for the two parked cars.

I became aware that my feet were carrying me after her.

"Where are we going?" I said.

"Anywhere away from here. This place is smothering me. I've spent the past three days cooped up with a blubbering sister-in-law in between being bombarded by police questions and phone calls dripping with syrupy condolences. I need to get somewhere where the phony bullshit level is low enough to allow me to breathe."

She chose the IROC Z, commenting, "Hell, it's black. What could be more appropriate for a widow in mourning?"

As she keyed the ignition and gunned the powerful engine to life, I leaned in the window and said, "Mrs. de Ruth, maybe right now isn't a good time—"

"Mr. Hannibal," she said above the snarl of the engine, "I assure you I am perfectly capable of carrying on a conversation while operating an automobile. Aren't you able to ask your questions while riding along?"

It turned out that, no, I wasn't.

I wasn't for the simple reason she proved to be a fucking maniac behind the wheel. If I thought she'd displayed aggressive driving tendencies the night I followed her and Tommy in her Pontiac, that had been nothing. Today, at the controls of the sportier, more powerful Z, she acted almost suicidal. With a heavy metal tape punched in and the stereo player cranked to ear-splitting volume, we laid a block-long patch of rubber tearing away from the house, then proceeded to shoot through a gridwork of side streets and lesser-traveled routes like a runaway Indy 500 racer. As best I could tell we were traveling in an easterly direction, following the line of the river. I rode it out in white-knuckled, clenched-teeth silence. If she'd been a man, I probably would have yanked the keys out of the ignition and cuffed her alongside the head. But some dumb, primitive Male thing dictated I couldn't allow myself to be intimidated by a mere woman when it came to anything involving that supreme icon of masculinity—the car.

When we finally came to a halt, amidst a cloud of dust and a spray of gravel pellets, it was in the heart of a small but lush riverside park crowding the far border of Bettendorf. Paula skidded up to within an inch of a reflective guard rail and cut the engine. Directly ahead of us, down a rolling slope and through the budding trees, you could see the river, the grand old man, the Mississippi. The smell of it and sound of it—a kind of ghostly perpetual whisper, perhaps more a sound of the imagination than of the senses—reached up to us.

Paula got out of the car, extending her arms in either direction, and arched her back in a long, luxurious stretch. I took my time getting out on my side, gingerly unkinking my legs, making sure they still had circulation going through them and were ready to hold me up after being locked in a brace-for-your-life posture during the past quarter hour.

Over the Z's gleaming top, Paula said, "Mr. Hannibal, you haven't asked me a single question yet."

"All right," I said, forcing a tight smile, "how about telling me where I can find the nearest pay phone?"

"What in the world do you want a pay phone for?"

"So I can call a cab. If you think I'm crawling back into this kamikaze coupe again with you in the driver's seat, you're nuttier than that row of walnut trees over there."

She laughed. "Was I going a little fast for you?"

"I get the feeling you go a little fast for a lot of people, lady," I told her, "and not necessarily only behind the wheel of a car."

She looked thoughtful. "I guess maybe that's been the trouble my whole life. You always so good at reading people?"

"Sometimes I get lucky."

"What else can you tell about me?"

In for a penny, I decided. I said, "I think it's safe to say you don't find widowhood terribly devastating."

"People show their grief in different ways and for different reasons, Mr. Hannibal. Great outward displays of teeth-gnashing and sorrow often have more to do with self-pity than anything else. Alex and I had been through for a long time, even if he was too stubborn to admit it. I'd already made the adjustment. I'm sorry he's dead, sorry if he suffered, but the prospect of his being absent from my future is nothing new for me to deal with."

We'd moved around the front end of the car and meandered onto the grass beyond the guard rail by then. Off to our right, a hiking trail paved with wood chips wound along the edge of the trees and down toward the river. Paula was pressing us casually but steadily toward it, her impractical footwear causing her no apparent concern or hindrance. Her long, relaxed, coltish strides seemed suited enough to the setting while her attitudes and sense of style seemed in sharper contrast.

As if somehow tuning in on my contemplation over this contrast, she said, "I like coming here. It makes me feel good to be near the river. I'm from west Texas originally, grew up in the middle of heat and dust and emptiness. What rivers we had around were nothing but muddy cracks in the ground. You Midwesterners take all this greenery and beauty for granted, don't realize how truly special it is."

"Texas," I said. "That where you first met Alex?"

"Uh-huh. I'd made it as far as Galveston, was dancing in a topless joint on the bay. It didn't take much for him to convince me there was no future in what I was doing, that dancers and strippers are a dime a dozen. He said he could make me a star."

"In reference to wrestling, I take it?"

"That's right. I was always a big girl, strong from the work I had to do when I was growing up, in good shape from the dancing. Alex had been announcing for a couple years at that point, mostly on independent cards for one or two of the smaller federations through the Southwest. He saw an upsurge in women's wrestling coming, and was convinced I could play a major role in it. It took a few tries to hit on the right gimmick, the right image for me, but when we did it started to pay off and it hopefully hasn't stopped yet. I think that's what made it so hard for him to accept our breakup, not that he was losing me but that I was still climbing and if I continued to do so he might miss out on a share of the glory. Usually when Alex was through with someone they were on the downslide, not the other way around."

"According to Mel Dukenos, Alex was pretty successful in his own right, extremely popular as an announcer."

"Yes, that's true. But it's also true that Alex got a far greater rush from manipulating others than from his own accomplishments."

We'd reached the hiking path and started down it. The sunlight filtering through the trees struck silvery highlights off Paula's hair and her perfume mixed intriguingly with the green, growing scents coming from all around us. It would be impossible to be near her under any circumstances and not be keenly aware of her potent womanhood.

She inhaled deeply with her head tossed back, her face upturned. "I get my own rush from the crowds and the excitement and the competition, no doubt about it. But I need to come here, places like this, for quieter moments, too, to keep it all in balance."

"Did you and Alex ever come here together?"

She laughed shortly. *"That* would have been the day. You know what you said before, about me going too fast for most people? Well Alex wasn't one of them, I promise you. He was hardly a 'stop and smell the roses' type. Not ever, not even for the briefest second."

"How about Tommy McGurk?" I ventured. "Ever come here with him?"

She gave me a look. "That's a strange thing to ask."

"Not really."

"Oh, I see. You've heard about Alex's accusations that Tommy and I were having an affair."

"More people than just your late husband seem to think that might have been the case."

"People have dirty minds."

"The point is, did those dirty minds reach the right conclusion or the wrong one?"

"That's a pretty bold question, don't you think?"

"Yeah, but I worked up to it kinda smooth, didn't I?"

"Did you work up to asking it of Tommy?"

"Matter of fact I did, yeah."

The answer and whatever implication it carried hung between us. Neither of us said anything more for a time. This was partly due to the fact that we'd reached the river's edge. The Mississippi of legend and song spread before us, the impact of it a humbling thing, making two little piss-ant human beings and their puny exchanges seem, for a few minutes anyway, as inconsequential as a pair of buzzing bugs.

Arsenal Island and the brunt of the Quad Cities sprawl lay downriver, out of sight around a gradual bend of the rolling water. It gave the spot a remote, tranquil feel. I could see why someone would find it soothing to come here.

Because I needed something to do with my hands, I dug out a cigarette and lit it. I blew smoke in the face of the big river. Defiant.

"Got another one of those?" Paula asked softly.

I shook out another and snapped a flame to it for her. She pulled the smoke deep then tipped her head back the way she had done on the trail and exhaled.

Grinning with half my mouth, trying to ease the tension a little, I said, "Is that a good idea for the ladies' champ? I'd hate to think I was contributing to a title loss or anything."

She shrugged. "I still enjoy a cigarette now and then. That's the difference when you only have one once in a while—you actually enjoy them. But don't worry, I start extensive training tomorrow for the big St. Louis card coming up. I guarantee I'll be working off this cigarette and more. And tomorrow I'll also be meeting the new manager Mel has arranged for me—a friend of yours, I understand?"

I nodded. "Bomber Brannigan. You'll find him quite a guy."

"Mel says he's a real pro, a natural to the game. She assures me he'll make the transition a smooth one and I'll enjoy working with him. She has this scenario all worked out. We'll be playing off the well-known fact that Bomber was Tommy's mentor back when they were both still wrestling. Considering all the sensationalistic press the murder and the so-called 'love triangle' has received, we'd be foolish to try and deny or ignore it so we'll use it as the springboard for Bomber's arrival on the scene, his purpose to clean up the mess his former pupil has made of things. I'll remain a heel, more of a vamp now, a seducer and destroyer of men's souls, and Bomber will spur me on to new nastiness. Mel's long range plan then—if everyone remains agreeable and things work out right—is to bring Tommy back if and when he's cleared; only he will be reformed, having 'seen the light' while incarcerated, and that will set up this huge struggle in which he tries to regain managerial control of me in order to save me from my rotten ways and rescue me from the evil influence of Bomber."

I shook my head in wonderment. "Shakespeare with turnbuckles."

"Don't laugh. The fans will eat it up. If it really catches on, it's the kind of thing that could propel the whole organization several notches up the ladder."

Out in the deep middle of the channel, a grain barge, sunk low in the water from the weight of its cargo, was sliding along slowly. A couple of speedboats—water revelers rushing the season—went skimming by it like it was literally standing still.

"Actually," Paula said, shifting gears to a more reflective mood, "I did come here a few times with Tommy. To talk, much as you and I are doing right now."

"Everybody needs a time and a place to say their piece," I allowed. "And somebody to listen."

"That's the important part. Somebody to listen. Tommy was a good listener, that's what first attracted me to him. And when it turned out he also had some things to unload, I tried to be a good listener for him. I guess you already know where that eventually led."

"How serious was—or is—it?"

"Tommy loves Lori. Any blind person can see that. What happened between us was never a threat to either of our marriages. Mine was already in the dumpster. Tommy had some . . . personal insecurities, I guess you could call them, he needed to work out. I'd like to think I helped him. The sex thing was a sidebar that just sort of happened. If I hadn't foolishly let something slip to Alex in a moment of anger and he hadn't gone on to make a huge production out of it, no one else would have ever known or had to speculate about it."

"You sure Tommy feels the same way about how things stand between you and him?"

"I'm sure."

"Then you don't believe he gunned down Alex in some sort of jealous rage?"

"No, of course not. I've told the police that."

"You also told them about the fight between Tommy and Alex in the restaurant parking lot."

"That's not fair! Yes, I told them about the fight. Jesus, they woke me from a sound sleep with the news Alex had been shot to death. They started hammering me with questions; I was stunned and confused and a little frightened. The fight had taken place only a few hours before, naturally it came to mind for me to mention. That doesn't mean I *sicced* them on Tommy, for God's sake."

"Tommy admits he went looking for Alex that night, after his sucker attack in the parking lot. If not out of jealousy, mightn't he have caught up with and killed Alex for plain old revenge?"

She made a throwaway gesture with her hand. "Anything's possible, I suppose. Alex could certainly be infuriating, and Tommy certainly has a temper. But I don't believe it could have happened that way either, not with a gun, not so cold-bloodedly."

"The next obvious question then—if not Tommy, who? Did your husband have any enemies?"

She gave another of her short laughs. "Do you want a list? Do you have a lot of pages in that little notebook?"

"Let's keep the list manageable. How about just enemies capable of murder?"

Her jaw muscles tightened and she took a hard final drag on her cigarette before flipping it out into the water. She scowled after it for several beats, then turned to face me full on. "This private eye bit—it really all it's cracked up to be like on TV and in the movies? I mean, are you really willing to sit on things, keep your mouth shut about them for the good of your client?"

"I've been known to sit on a thing until it sprouted feathers and started chirping 'Mommy' at me."

"This is serious."

"All right. It goes without saying there are certain lines I won't cross. But if I need to I'm willing to walk to the far edge of them and lean way the hell out. That's all I can promise."

"Tommy told me about you once. How you helped him before. I guess you've already proven yourself, haven't you?"

"I'd like to think so. What are you trying to get at here? What's this all about?"

"We have to go back to the house," she said, stepping around me and starting back up the hiking trail. "I have something there to show you."

10

I gambled another ride with Paula after eliciting from her a promise to take it easy on both my nerves and my eardrums.

Back at the house, before piling out of the car, she said, "There. I kept my part of the bargain. Now yours is to handle what I'm about to disclose to you with the utmost discretion."

"Fair enough," I agreed.

Inside, the house wasn't quite the showplace it was on the exterior. However, this was primarily due to superficial clutter—clothing, papers, and sympathy cards scattered about, empty pop bottles and dirty coffee cups left here and there—so I figured it was a temporary state rather than the norm. Either from Alex de Ruth's bachelor period just prior to his death or the hectic days since the shooting, or a combination of both.

Paula led me directly back to the master bedroom.

The first thing you noticed was the wine-colored shag carpeting that swallowed your feet up past the ankles. Then the mirrors. Walls of them, all reflectively magnifying the light spewed by the ornate French chandelier, all with a pinkish marble-veined pattern running through them. All, that is, except the eight-foot square slab suspended over the black satin-sheeted bed. No silly designs there to distort or alter, nothing but sparkling crystal clarity. Toss around some frail-looking boudoir furniture continuing the quasi French motif, display a sliver of black-tiled bathroom with sunken tub through an ajar mirrored door, wrap it all in a heady mix of musky male and female perfumes clinging to the air, and it wasn't hard to conclude that here was a spot not intended exclusively for sleeping.

I let out a low whistle. "Welcome to Adventureland, boys and girls."

"Spare me the wisecracks please," Paula said somewhat wearily. "I obviously can't deny that Alex and I enjoyed certain stimuli in our sexual practices. At this point I suppose I could lay the reasons for that all on him, but I won't. When things were still good between us, I appreciated a bit of novelty as much as he did. It was only within the last twenty-four hours, though, that I discovered his tastes ran a lot kinkier than I'd ever imagined."

She had proceeded to the far wall of the room. Rather than a full wall, the center section of this proved to be a row of sliding panels opening onto a long walk-in closet. Paula shot a pair of the panels back and I followed her between them.

"After Alex's death," she explained, "I knew I'd be moving back into the house and figured to keep it for the foreseeable future. After all, I put as much in it as he did. Or at least I thought I had. When his sister came up from Texas for the funeral, the need to move back in became more immediate. I didn't have room to put her up at my apartment and she was in no shape to stay by herself at a motel or anywhere. So the two of us stayed here until this morning when I got her on her plane back to San Antonio."

She pushed aside some hanging garments. "It was last night, while I was in here putting away some of my things, that I spotted that."

She pointed to a corner of the closet. The inside of the space was done in cheap woodgrain paneling. At the juncture of the back wall and the end that was to our right as we stood facing in, down near the bottom, a chunk of the paneling had been pried at and partly broken away. Splintered shards of it lay on the carpet where a row of shoes had been shoved back.

"It's one of those things you can't be a hundred percent positive of," Paula said, "but I'm as sure as I can be that wasn't like that before. I rummaged through this same closet thoroughly only a couple of days ago, picking out the suit they dressed Alex in for the funeral. I don't see how I could have missed it if it was like that then."

I knelt down to examine the damage more closely.

"Follow that seam up. To the fourth woodscrew there, or what looks like a screw, and press it."

I did as instructed. A cleverly concealed, albeit flimsy, door popped open at me.

"I discovered that by accident while I was looking around," she said over my shoulder. "There's a string hanging down from a lightbulb in back. You go ahead on in first. There isn't a lot of room back there."

I ducked through the cramped doorway, reaching for the light cord. The single bulb illuminated a narrow, tunnellike area running between two unfinished inner walls. A handful of 1x6s had been nailed between some of the upright studs, creating a chest level line of shelves which were about half filled with videocassettes in cardboard sleeves. In the middle of the tunnel floor stood an unfolded three-step, kitchen-helper type stepstool. Directly above the stool, on a pivot stand attached to a metal track reaching across the top of the closet shell I had entered through to another exactly like it on the opposite side, was fastened a video camera.

My brain clicked ahead, starting to fit the pieces together in the only ways that seemed to make sense.

"Get up on the stool," Paula urged. "You'll see what's in range of the camera."

I stepped up, the metal tubing and hinges creaking under my weight. Cranking my head to the left I looked across the top of the closet housing and through what was evidently a special two-way pane of mirror. There was the master bedroom, everything as plainly visible from this vantage point as it had been when I'd walked through it only minutes ago. Turning my head the other way, I looked over the top of the opposite closet housing and into another bedroom, this one somewhat smaller and more standardly appointed.

"That's the guest bedroom you're looking at now," Paula said.

I hopped down, slapping dust from my hands. "Real interesting setup."

She cocked an eyebrow. "Interesting indeed."

"And last night was the first you knew about any of this?"

"Absolutely. Oh, Alex and I had fooled around with a camcorder some, taped our own lovemaking on occasion and even a swing session once with another couple. Like I said before, we both enjoyed novelty and I was as much for it as he was. But those were times when everybody knew what was what. I sure as hell never knew about *this* and it's obvious nobody else was supposed to either, for sure nobody who might have got caught in the act."

I made a gesture, indicating the array of videos. I said, "If all these were made here, then your guy Alex was an awful busy fella—not to mention a pretty fair amount of other people, by the look of it."

Paula twisted her mouth wryly. "If I know Alex, you can bet he's in a good share of them himself. Him and some of the air-brained bimbettes he was so fond of picking up. Can you believe the bastard? He not only brought them into our home—our very bed—and fucked them, but he had to capture it on film. God only knows what he got out of the other room."

"You haven't checked any of the tapes?"

"I had Alex's sister here until this morning, remember? I doubt very much these are the kind of home movies it would have been proper for us to reminisce over. And I don't know that I want to see them, regardless."

"Aside from what you've already mentioned, did you and Alex do much entertaining? You know, parties, guests spending the night or maybe the weekend, that kind of thing?"

"More than probably the average couple, yeah. At

least, we did prior to the past six months when we really
started going for each other's throats. We never spent a
lot of time alone together, not even when things were
better between us. Alex liked a crowd around, and I guess
I did, too. Plus, Alex was a wheeler dealer, always had
something going. He'd have guys in from all over the
country to discuss this or that, and often these guys would
be accompanied by a 'mate' who may or may not have
been their real wives. They'd spend the night with us, or,
like you said, sometimes a weekend."

I made another gesture. "Considering all this, you see
the next logical possibility, don't you?"

"Blackmail. Right?"

"You think Alex was above something like that?"

"Hell no. More and more I'm realizing there may not
have been anything he was above. Even at the nice, simple parties we had, there were times when couples who
didn't really belong together would slip off . . . if they
were foolish enough to choose one of these bedrooms,
under the watchful eye of Alex's little peeping video
setup here, then there's no telling who or what he might
have captured."

I said, "Judging by the way that trick door was pried at
and broken, especially if it was done just recently, as you
believe—*after* Alex's murder, in other words—then I'd
say somebody who knew they were on one of these tapes
came looking for the evidence. Is there any way to tell if
they got it?"

Paula shook her head. "There are still tapes here. I have
no way of knowing how many might be missing because I
have no idea how many there were to begin with."

I picked up a couple of the videocassettes. Each had a
strip of masking tape on the end with identifying markings done in black ink. One said 18-13x20-6, the other
1-4x12-3. A quick scan of the others on the shelves indicated they were similarly marked.

"What do those numbers mean?" Paula asked.

My turn to shake my head. "I don't know. Yet. It's a
code of some kind. I could figure it out, I think, with a
little time."

"A code? Jesus Christ, Peeping Tom with overtones of

James Bond. That late husband of mine was a dilly, wasn't he?"

"If it is a code, then he may have had a decoder book, or just a sheet of paper perhaps. Have you seen anything like that around? Any kind of list with numbers like these?"

"No, I haven't. But I've been too busy with the funeral and Sister Stephanie and so on to have had time to go through anything, really. I'll keep my eyes open."

"Yeah, do that." I gave the tunnel another good visual sweep, thoughtfully tugging at the end of my nose. "Something more about this I've got to wonder," I said. "If you and Alex picked out this house together and lived here together until just a few weeks ago, how did he manage to rig up something like this without you knowing about it?"

"I wondered about that, too, at first. But it really wouldn't have been so hard. In the first place, we made the deal on the house before ever moving to the area and then decided on some work we wanted done before we took occupancy. Alex made all those arrangements, he could have included this then. And even if he got the idea to do it later, he had a number of opportunities. I've done a couple tours of Japan for BRW that he didn't accompany me on, I had two or three extended hospital stays from ring injuries. He could have had this done any of those times. And I'm hardly such a dedicated housekeeper I would have noticed the shrinkage in closet space or anything like that. Never."

She made it a convincing pitch. But that still left one more biggie.

"We've got to consider another thing," I said. "All the possibilities here add up to a dandy motive for murder. A lot better one, for my money, than the stack of circumstantial crap they've got against Tommy McGurk."

"I agree."

"There's even the chance the break-in took place sooner than you figure. Like on the night of the murder maybe. What I'm getting at is, the cops ought to be made aware of this."

Her eyes flashed. "No way! You're a detective—the private kind—that's why I'm showing it to you. I'm willing to let you dig and ask your questions and do whatever you need to do. But I'm not ready to go public. Not for my sake or the sake of the people who might be on those tapes or for a lot of other reasons."

"What about for Tommy McGurk's sake? He's the one with his ass on the line."

"Naturally I'd be willing to do whatever it takes if that was the only way to save Tommy. But surely we have some time before it gets down to that. And aren't you showing a distinct lack of confidence in yourself? Aren't a lot of people already counting on you to be the one who clears Tommy by uncovering the real killer and shouldn't this improve your chances of doing just that?"

"So what if I do? It will damn sure have to be handed over to the cops then."

"But that would be an entirely different set of circumstances. Merely a buttoning-up process. It wouldn't result in anything like the media circus a prolonged police investigation into something like this would cause."

I sighed. She seemed to have an answer for everything. I wanted a cigarette, but was reluctant to light up in our tight and already musty surroundings.

Paula said, "Will you at least look at the tapes? Make sure they are what we think they are, and see if you can narrow anything down from what's on them? Then we can discuss further what we should do next."

"All right," I said. "Yeah, I can do that much. Where do you have a video player?"

She glanced at her wristwatch and frowned. "It's getting awfully late to start now, isn't it? It will take hours to go through those and I don't think I want to be around when you do. Besides, I was on my way out to blow off some of these mourning widow blues when you showed up, remember? Tell you what, I'll give you access to the house tomorrow while I'm at the gym and you can view the videos then. In the meantime, you can get me out of here and take me somewhere where we can not have to think about death or dirty pictures or dirty little people with dirty little secrets. How does that sound?"

It sounded intriguing as hell. After all, she was a striking woman and I've got as many hormones as the next guy. In spite of everything, I'd been very much aware of our close proximity and the female heat emanating off her ever since entering that cramped space. Nevertheless, there was also a part of me that wondered at her unexpected frankness and what her long range motivations might be.

But none of it stopped me from asking, "You got a particular place in mind?"

11

It was called Rocky's Rib Shack and in the gloom of settling twilight the word 'shack' appeared to be the operative and very appropriate choice. It lay a half hour's drive south of the cities, a pile of unpainted lumber, mossy shingles, and smeared windows perched on the rim of a swampy pool of Mississippi backwater blurrily reflecting the neon beer signs.

I parked Alex de Ruth's IROC Z in a gravel lot already crowded with pickup trucks, motorcycles, and every variety of car, some nothing but rolling collections of rust and dents (in whose company my Honda would have felt right at home) but a surprising number of others as sharp and snazzy as the Z.

Paula and I went inside, she with an eager swagger in her stride, me dragging my feet a little. She homed in on an unoccupied booth, cutting through the smoke-laden air as confidently as a sonar-equipped luxury liner gliding through ocean fog. I was aware of several dozen pairs of male eyes picking up her progress with their own kind of sonar.

The layout of the place was simple but effective, a long,

low-ceilinged rectangular room with a dance floor and a live band playing at the far end and the bar and wall booths up near the entrance. In between were a handful of small tables and chairs. The kitchen appeared to be through a pair of batwing doors past the curve of the bar, on the opposite side of the room.

Once we'd landed in the booth, a frizzy-haired barmaid with pendulous breasts barely contained by a knit tube top showed up to take our order for a pitcher of beer and a double rack of ribs with all the trimmings.

The beer arrived first and we wasted no time partaking of it, making small talk about this and that between drinks and when we could be heard above the music. While not exactly my idea of appropriate mealtime entertainment (I prefer *McHale's Navy* reruns on the tube), the band was pretty good, sticking to mostly country rock oldies done with hard drum licks and growlingly intense vocals as delivered by a portly, bearded lead singer trying for the Charlie Daniels look with a rakishly curved stetson dipped low over his eyes.

When the food came, it was excellent. Tender, fall-off-the-bone-at-a-touch chunks of meat steaming under a juicy, generous layer of barbecue sauce, all complemented by bowls of tangy slaw and mounds of golden French fries. Heart attack on a plate according to some, but who gave a shit. We ordered a second pitcher of beer to wash it down and plenty of wet-naps to wipe it off, then dug in.

During the meal, I reached two very crucial decisions. One, there is absolutely no neat way to eat barbecued ribs. Two, sharing a meal of same with Paula de Ruth definitely ranked as sexual foreplay. We've all heard of erotic eating, we've all seen the old Albert Finney movie, *Tom Jones;* but until you've sat across the table from a drop-dead blonde and watched her very deliberately, very precisely suck every morsel of meat and sauce from a platter of spare rib bones, you have no real idea what it's all about. I fully suspect that if I'd happened to spill any beer in my lap at that point, it would have steamed like water hitting a hot griddle.

At meal's end, Paula took a long pull of beer, licked

foam from her saucy red lips, and said, "A rowdy bar, plenty of cold beer, greasy hot food, and pounding honky tonk music—do I know how to show a fella a good time or what?"

"Yeah," I agreed somewhat huskily. "You're full of surprises."

If her eating display had left a dry male lap anywhere in the vicinity, Paula took care of that a few minutes later when she dragged me out on the dance floor. While I huffed and shuffled and flapped my arms in what is my standard imitation of contemporary dancing, she put on a show most guys there would have paid money to see: shimmying and shaking and gyrating, lots of suggestive bumps up against me that probably would have got me to sweating even if my own exertions weren't already doing so. And that was just warming up. When the band cranked into the Jerry Lee Lewis classic "Whole Lotta Shakin'" for their next number, Paula really got into it. By song's end it was almost like a scene from one of those corny old musicals, with the rest of the dancers fallen back in a wide circle, clapping their hands to the beat while only Paula and I remained in the middle of the floor. My part of it was mostly grinning idiotically and clapping along, too, leaving Paula to indeed shake it, baby, shake it. The whole thing ended to the loudest applause of the evening. Paula and I headed back to our booth, out of breath and laughing, getting sporadic slaps on the backs from some of the other dancers, mostly men. A few of the women were shooting very unappreciative glares in Paula's direction.

As we sat down, Paula said, "Are you all right? You look kinda wasted."

"A little winded is all. Been awhile since I've boogied."

"You should do something to keep in better shape."

"Okay. I'll go to the gym tomorrow, you stay home and watch Alex's dirty movies."

She made a face. "We aren't supposed to talk about the case, remember?"

"Right. I forgot."

She picked up the pitcher and emptied it, bringing our glasses to even levels. "Come on," she said. "Let's go get some fresh air. I could use some and you definitely look like you could, too."

Outdoors, it was full dark by now. A calm night, muting the voices and music from inside. A railed porch belted the Rib Shack, becoming a sort of cantilevered deck on the back side, jutting out over the pool of backwater. Heavily shadowed, a pattern of the night's moon and stars bouncing off its surface, the pool didn't look so bad right then. For the time being you could forget about the weeds and cans and old tires cluttering its perimeter, not look for the patches of scum floating among the stars.

We carried our glasses of beer around there and leaned against the rail, looking up at the sky and listening for sounds coming off the river not so far away. When I lit up a cigarette, Paula asked for one also.

"Did you say you quit smoking or just quit buying your own?" I said, trotting out the tired old joke.

It got a smile out of Paula even as she replied, "Just shut up and give me one."

We smoked in quiet for a while.

"This place reminds me a lot of the places we had in Texas when I first started going out," Paula said. "I guess that's why it makes me feel good to come here."

"You come here often?"

"I go in spurts. I doubt if they consider me a regular or anything."

"They'll remember you after tonight, you can bet on that."

"Did I embarrass you?"

"Embarrass *me?* Nah. No way."

"I did, didn't I?"

"Look, it's every guy's fantasy to be seen in public with a woman who's such a knockout she stops traffic and turns every other guy's head. Why would it embarrass me to have that come true?"

She eyed me in the moonlight, not fully convinced. "Well," she said, "I'm not usually such an exhibitionist. Really. Tonight it just felt good to let loose like that. But if I embarrassed you, I apologize."

"Apology not accepted because there's none needed. Let's just drop it, okay?"

Whether she would have or not became a moot point when company arrived and interrupted any further possible discussion.

"Company" consisted of a half dozen scruffy biker types, four men and two women. We heard the porch boards clump under their heavy boots and then the railing creaked as the pack milled around us and fanned out to lean against the weathered slats on either side. Their presence and particularly the surrounding maneuver sent a trickle of tension through the night air.

Their leader proved to be a tall, heavy-shouldered galoot with a bush of orangish hair and a thin, dark beard. An animal fang on the end of a glittery chain dangled from one of his ears. He wore greasy jeans and a denim vest, no shirt. His tattooed arms were corded with muscles but his bare, pale stomach sagged like a sack of wet sand. When he smiled, his teeth were bad and he smelled like something that had lain in the muck of the pond for a couple of weeks. Probably the responsibilities of leadership didn't leave him a lot of time for personal hygiene.

"Hey there, folks," he said easily. "Don't mean to bother you, but we just wanted to stop out and say how much we appreciate your showing up to pump some life into this tired old scene. Little lady's a right fine dancer."

Paula managed a cautious smile. "Thank you."

Past Fang's shoulder, one of the women, a massive creature with dark blue tattoos on her doughy biceps and huge, loose breasts that sagged under a faded tank top to just above a roll of stomach flab bunched by the waistband of her too-tight jeans, opened a permanently petulant mouth and said something. I didn't catch all of it, but the words "prick-teasin' bitch" came out clearly enough.

Fang grinned, showing us even more of his gray-green teeth. "Don't give no never mind to Fat Fran. She gets a little jealous is all when I pay any double attention to another woman. 'Course she's got sorta double reason to be jealous of you, ma'am, 'cause I was payin' attention to you even before I saw you dance tonight. I'm a big rasslin' fan, you see, and I watch you on the TV every chance I get. You *are* Paula the Platinum Powerhouse, right?"

"That's right," Paula acknowledged.

Fat Fran got it all out real clear this time. "Yeah," she sneered. "Phony hair, phony tits, phony profession."

The bullying taunt from the female hulk was almost funny in a twisted kind of way, but as Paula's escort I felt it my onus to do something more than just stand there like an impotent dummy. "I think you'd better tell your girlfriend to watch her mouth," I suggested to Fang.

He aimed his grin my way this time, but there was no humor in the slitted eyes he aimed along with it. "And who might you be, bub, and why should I give a flyin' fuck what you think?"

I tossed his grin right back to him. "I just might be the 'bub' who's ready, willing, and able to teach you and your tricycle terrorists here a few manners, if that's what it takes."

Fang's mouth pulled straight and he went stone rigid, all six-and-a-quarter feet of him. Behind him, Fat Fran's eyes became as narrow and dangerous as his. All around us, I could feel the rest of the pack tightening up.

"Hey, take it easy, Hannibal," Paula said, clutching my arm. "The lady has a right to her opinion. After all, this is America, isn't it?"

Everybody kept glaring at everybody else, clenched postures maintained. For a minute or so the only sound was the muffled music from within and the ratcheting of some bullfrogs over by the pond.

Slowly, Fang's grin returned to split the bearded lower half of his face. "Well now," he said. "On top of everything else, sounds like the lady's got a right reasonable head on her shoulders."

"Yeah," Fat Fran chimed in. "Right reasonably chickenshit, if you ask me."

Paula looked at me. "See? Another example of the great American right of free expression." Her gaze swung to Fran. "Of course I have a few rights also . . . like the right to knock you flat on your lard ass if you don't can it, cunt."

The petulant mouth dropped open wide and everything went into freeze frame for a long second before Fat Fran let out a bellow and lunged past Fang, clawed hands reaching for Paula's throat. The tall blonde swept the outstretched arms to one side with a perfectly timed block and in the same motion swung her left fist hard into the flab roll directly under Fran's right breast. The charging woman stopped short with a loud "haawff!" Paula brought her blocking arm around in a close arc and slammed the elbow across the ridge of Fran's eyebrows, snapping her head back sharply. Fran fell heavily, her broad bottom smacking the deck. I felt the boards shiver through my feet.

While the dust was still shaking loose from Fran's one-point landing, before anybody else could decide to move, I went into a quick crouch and came up with the derringer snatched from the spring rig in my right boot. It's a two-shot .22 Magnum carried basically for emergencies, and that seemed to be exactly what we had on our hands. Never breaking my flow of motion, I reached for a handful of Fang's bushy hair, jerked his head around and pulled him back against me, jamming the derringer's stubby barrel into the soft pocket of flesh under the ridge of his jaw.

"Everybody stay as still as you are," I ordered. "Take it real easy or your fearless leader gets some extra ventilation in his head."

"Had to go for a gun, didn't you, wimp?" Fang snarled in my grasp.

"Six against two ain't exactly *mano a mano*, asswipe," I pointed out to him.

Paula's eyes flashed angrily in my direction. "Hannibal! I'm handling this, goddamnit."

"How do you figure?"

"It's between the cow and me, and she's on her ass. I'm in control, that's how I figure."

"You heard her," Fang said. "It's between the two of them. Your mama against mine. The rest of us are strictly observers. You and me can maybe lock stud horns another day."

The rest of the pack was watching us with slackened mouths and shiny, expectant eyes. Watching me.

"This is nuts," I said.

"That's the way I want it," Paula said. "I aim to teach this pig a lesson." Her eyes were shining, too, with a strange and wild light. I suddenly remembered the way she had pounded Bouncing Betty unnecessarily at the matches the other night, the expression on her face then which I had thought was part of the act.

Fang strained in my grasp, rolling his eyes away. "Fat Fran!" he called. "You hearin' this, mama? This chick's callin' you names, sayin' she's in control, gonna teach you a lesson. You figurin' to let her get away with that?"

From where she still sat sprawled on her can, Fran reached up with one hand and wiped a smear of blood from the end of her nose. "No fucking way," she mumbled. "She got in a lucky punch is all."

Paula laughed derisively. "And I can get in two or three dozen more any time I want to."

Fang rolled his eyes back to me. "Let 'em get it on, man. Leave me the hell go and let's cut to the action. No tricks. Shit, it'll be a blast."

"Do it, Hannibal," Paula urged, her eyes bright with an even wilder glint now. "You'll still have the gun if they try anything afterwards. This won't take me long, I promise."

The next few minutes are a kind of blur in my memory. I recall lowering the derringer and letting go of Fang—reluctantly. Exactly what was said and done right after that I'm not sure. Everything flowed into a jumble of motion and excited voices. Next thing I knew all of us were gathered on a grassy patch at the edge of the parking lot. Paula and Fran, in fighters' crouches, were circling each other on the grass. Fang and his pack were all around me, shouting and whistling and clapping. Other patrons were pouring out of the Rib Shack and were quick to pick up the whistles and cheers.

Paula had stripped off her denim jacket. I held it clutched in my left hand. In my right, shoved in the pocket of my own jacket, I still gripped the derringer.

In the silver-blue moonlight, augmented in this remote corner of the grounds only slightly by the high parking lot floodlights, with the fighters and the crowd casting long, dancing shadows, the whole scene took on an eerie, almost surrealistic aspect. Or maybe it was just the way I felt. Call it sexist or chauvinistic or old-fashioned or whatever you want, but in the handbook I carry it says that men sometimes fight over women, not the other way around. And not that Paula and Fat Fran were fighting *over* Fang or me exactly; but it seemed close to it. It was his "mama" against mine. He and I were the principal watchers, the cheerers . . . the comforts most likely to be sought at the end of the combat. It all felt alien and wrong somehow, twisted around. But at the same time I couldn't deny the surge of excitement welling inside me at the sight of the muscles playing up and down Paula's bare arms, the wolf's smile she wore, the feral fire flickering in her eyes.

When the two women threw themselves together, meat and muscle thudding audibly, grunts of effort sounding, my voice was as loud as any in the roar of approval that went up from the crowd.

As Paula predicted, it didn't take long. But while it lasted it was as down and dirty as any fight I've ever witnessed. With her superior knowledge of leverage and countermoves, Paula repeatedly dumped her opponent to the ground, each time slipping in a vicious punch or kick or chop. Fran, her greater weight and strength her advantage if she could work in close enough to use them, kept getting back up and charging again. When the big woman was able to force a clinch, the infighting got nastily brutal. Fran rained blows with her clublike fists and ripping knees, Paula countered with slashing chops and elbow smashes and finally a head butt to break out.

As Fran staggered back, one of her giant breasts spilled free from the torn tank top. Blood was already pouring from her nose and mouth and moments later, as she picked herself up from being tossed yet another time, the exposed mam showed scraped and bleeding.

Paula's lacey-silky top lasted only a little longer. When she slashed free once more from Fran's clambering, bearlike grasp, the top remained dangling from one of the big woman's fists. A ripple of response went through the crowd at the sight of a barebacked Paula. Glistening with sweat, her hair reflecting like ice in the moonlight, splendid breasts rising and falling with deep breaths, she was indeed an amazon of legend, a warrior woman of magnificent proportions.

It came to an end shortly after that. When Fat Fran, sucking air and desperate, was able to hang on for another clinch she saw fit to add biting to her repertoire. Her gnashing teeth drew blood from Paula's stomach and shoulder. Cursing, enraged, Paula pounded her back with a flurry of blows, then crouched in close, hooking the big woman's head and one arm, and swung her up and over in a move known as the standing suplex. The recipient of such a maneuver lands directly on the small of their back with greatly increased velocity, the shock to the spinal nervous system like a hammer blow. In her anger, Paula fell on her victim and threw a couple of extra punches, but they were strictly icing on the cake. Fat Fran was finished.

The crowd went abruptly quiet.

I walked forward with the denim jacket and gently wrapped it around the blood- and dust-streaked torso of my amazon. Out of the corner of my eye I saw the other biker mama and a couple more members of the pack going to aid the still supine Fran.

The crowd became animated and audible again. Buzzing with a hundred conversations at once, all containing lines like "did you see the time the fat one did such-and-such?" or "how about when the blonde did so-and-so?".

It seemed like a good place to be gone from. I steered Paula in a turn and we started for the car.

Fang was directly in our path, blocking our way. His expression was solemn, no green-toothed grin. I slipped my hand into my pocket and wrapped it around the derringer.

"That's a helluva woman you got there," Fang said to me. "I seen my Frannie go to it with badass chicks from all over and she never been the one left layin' before. She got what she wanted, to go up against the best. No hard feelings now, eh?"

Paula rubbed her chewed shoulder under the jacket. "I'll let you know that after I'm sure your friend tests negative for rabies," she said.

We walked around him.

After we'd gone a dozen or so steps he called my name. When I looked back, he was grinning. Not the taunting grin from before, but one that actually looked genuine, almost friendly. "Hey, Hannibal," he said. "You-all come around again, you hear? Maybe next time you'n me can try each other out for size, give the folks another good show, what do you say?"

I didn't say anything. He was still grinning when I turned my back on him and Paula and I resumed walking.

I drove back to the city. Paula and I barely spoke during the ride. She sat in the seat next to me with her head tipped back against the cushion rest and her eyes closed, but I don't think she ever really slept.

When we reached her place she went immediately to fill the sunken tub with water as hot as she could stand. I fixed us drinks; bourbon-water for the lady, bourbon on the rocks for me. While she soaked in her bath and drank her drink, I carried mine out into the living room and waited there restlessly. I flipped through the channels on TV, flipped through the pages of a magazine, couldn't seem to get interested in anything. Mostly I thought about the baser instincts that are in all of us and our pathetically inadequate abilities to deal with them.

Upon emerging from the bath, Paula lay nude on her stomach across the bed. Instructing me where to find the necessary items in the medicine cabinet, she asked that I administer to her wounds.

I guess her blasé attitude and the fact I'd already seen her topless during the fight, plus the somberness of my assigned task should have all combined to prevent the moment from arousing me. But I'm only human, and merely a male of the species at that. Her shape and muscle tone were flawless, her skin warm to the touch, soft yet firm, velvet stretched taut over pliant steel. I swabbed on peroxide and iodine and bandages where needed, trying to concentrate strictly on the wounds and on the process, to block any notice of the whole that each bit of damage was a part of.

As I finished her back side and she rolled over so I could do her front, Paula said, "I guess I behaved pretty outrageously tonight, didn't I?"

"Did you?" I replied. "I couldn't say; I don't know how you behave on a typical night out."

"Well this was hardly typical, I assure you."

"Like I said before, they're going to remember you from now on at Rocky's."

I'd taken care of the bites to her stomach and shoulder, the ones that had broken the skin, and now I spotted a third, a more superficial one, a purplish oval of dotted teethmarks on the underside of her left breast. As I dabbed iodine to it, Paula said, "Maybe it's you. Maybe you bring out the beast in me."

"Maybe," I allowed.

Apparently I brought out something in her. Much as I tried not to, I couldn't help noticing that, as I doctored the area, her nipple began to swell and rise up, hardening. Her breathing had grown more rapid.

I let my gaze slide from the wound, over the blossoming nipple, to Paula's face. She was watching me, her eyes steady, mouth pouting provocatively.

"You know," she said, a sandpapery whisper, "not all bites are undesirable, not even in the tenderest places. It all depends on the circumstances under which they are received."

Suddenly the iodine bottle was gone from my grasp, dropped, forgotten, and my hands and arms were full of Paula. She curved her body to meet mine, hers as supple as a serpent's, her own hands reaching, tugging, demanding. She tore at my shirt. With her hands. With her teeth. In a matter of seconds I was as naked as she, our bodies flushed with passion, stained by streaks of spilled iodine.

I glided my hands over her with a very different purpose than before, kneading the flesh of her stomach and hips. She groaned. I lowered my face. The silk of her thigh caressed my ear. The rush of blood inside my head pounded like a Krupa solo.

"Don't be gentle," I heard her say. "Don't be."

12

After three hours of watching people who were mostly strangers to me engaged in a variety of sexual antics (some of which were pretty strange, too), I was reduced to feeling cramped and bleary eyed and more than a little disgusted with my job and myself and the whole situation in general.

Hell, it was hardly the first time I'd dug through the festering crud hidden in a corner of some poor bastard's life. And it almost certainly wouldn't be the last. But that morning for some reason it got to me more than usual.

Maybe because I felt closer to it than I normally did. Remorsefully so. Because, only hours earlier, I had romped in the same bed as shown in many of the videos, performed a number of the same acts I watched performed over again, enjoyed the very same body I had now seen others enjoy. This time there could be no kidding myself; I wasn't so far removed—and certainly not above—that which I was digging through.

Damn.

Dumb.

It was a little past one in the afternoon when I snapped

off the VCR and the television monitor and tossed the remote down on the coffee table next to the stack of still-unviewed cassettes. I got up off the couch and stood for a minute rolling the kinks out of my shoulders and back. Then I carried my empty coffee cup from the living room into the kitchen.

I had the de Ruth house to myself. Paula had left at ten for the BRW gym, to begin her intensive training for the upcoming big match. Before leaving, she'd set me up with the VCR, TV, remote, the stack of videos from the hideaway tunnel, and a pot of coffee. Told me to go to it, do my stuff.

The remote and its various features proved to be good allies. The Fast Forward had allowed me to zip through twenty-odd tapes in the three hours, condense them down to sequences that mattered; the Pause had frozen faces and profiles for me to study at length.

Trouble was, there had been so few faces that meant anything to me, no matter how long or hard I studied them.

Paula's was there, of course. And Alex's. The two of them making love to each other. The two of them swinging with another couple (the taping she had spoken of). And then there had been Paula in two additional sessions, each with a different man, neither of whom I recognized. Incidents she hadn't bothered to mention, perhaps because she hadn't suspected they would be on tape or because they had been of too little significance for her to remember. Made me wonder how long last night with me might be carried in her memory, without so much as a snapshot to jog the recollective process. Maybe part of the remorse I was feeling had to do with jealousy, which was even dumber yet.

As for Alex, exactly as Paula had predicted, he turned up in practically fifty percent of the cassettes I hit the Play on. His partners ranged the gamut from young to old, thin to heavy, black to white, blond to brunette to redhead and back again. From a standpoint of sheer numbers, the odds were that I should spot someone I knew among his conquests. As a matter of fact, I knew two of them. The first was Bouncing Betty, the much put-upon

opponent I had seen Paula pound to the mat on that night
less than a week past that seemed so long ago. The second
was a dusky-skinned, raven-haired beauty I recognized as
Leticia Cloud, the young wife of the beefy old Indian
grappler, Sam War Cloud. I didn't know anything about
Bouncing Betty—not even her real name—but every instinct I had for judging character and relationships told
me that Sam War Cloud was hardly the type to take
lightly to being cuckolded, especially by the likes of Alex
de Ruth. I chalked up the potential in that situation as
being very volatile, which translated to real promising as
far as what I was looking for.

The next familiar face to show up had been quite a
surprise. You might even say a shock. Balding and bul-
bous-bodied, Abe Lugretti had flickered onto the screen
naked and ready. His coupling with a frail, unsmiling girl
had been desperately frantic, almost to the point of being
comedic. But there was nothing funny about it when you
knew that wasn't the intent. And there was nothing
funny about the expression on the face of the girl. And
damn sure none of it was funny when you were acquainted with the fat man, when he was an old friend of a
good buddy, when you had only recently decided you
liked him okay yourself. There were unspoken volumes
behind what was on that piece of tape. I didn't know if
any of it had anything to do with de Ruth's murder, but
what I did know—just as sure as I knew it was something I
was going to have to see to—was that the story once put
into words wasn't going to be a pretty one.

It was somewhere around that point in my video view-
ing marathon that the distaste for what I was doing
started getting real hard to keep swallowed down.

But it didn't reach choke level until three or four cassettes later, when the next face I recognized came into
focus. It was the face of BRW's popular heavyweight
champ, Brick Towers. Handsomely chiseled, framed by a
flowing shock of wheat-colored hair, riding proudly atop a
bronzed, superbly muscled body. In the taped sequence I
was watching, another face figured prominently in what
was going on—that face busily buried in Towers's lap. The
hair and the thick neck and shoulders had me braced

somewhat for it. But I found out I wasn't braced nearly enough for when the second face lifted . . . and Alex de Ruth smiled lewdly up at his lover.

Expand the range of Alex's conquests one more notch. Jesus Christ.

In the kitchen, I rinsed my cup at the sink then filled it with cold tap water and drank deeply from it. The water tasted clean and fresh. I needed that.

Outside it was another bright day, but a blustery one. Through the window over the sink I watched the lawn grass ripple, saw the sunlight pouring down on it broken by the flickering shadows of wind-pushed clouds scudding across the sky. I decided what else I needed was to get out there and breathe some of that gusty air. A chaser to the water.

Before quitting the house, I gathered up the videos from the living room and carried them into the bedroom but not all the way back to the hidey-hole. In the event Paula received any unexpected visitors, the cassettes scattered in plain view could lead to some embarrassing questions. I piled them on the floor in front of the closet, grouping them as to the ones I'd already seen and the ones I had yet to look at. The latter was my task to complete, but one I'd had my fill of for the time being.

I drove to my motel, the Honda buffeted by the whipping afternoon wind.

I'd showered at Paula's that morning but I showered again now, a quick one, then brushed my teeth, pulled on all clean clothes, and wiped down my boots with a damp towel.

At the motel diner I ordered a late lunch; a hamburger, a bowl of bean soup, and a glass of milk. I sat at the counter, enjoying the sizzle and smells coming off the old-fashioned grill in back and, more covertly, enjoying the sway of the pretty waitress's hips as she eeled in and out with her duties up front. Waiting for the food, I lit a cigarette and fanned through my pocket notebook while I smoked. I lined out one or two of the earlier entries, added a few random thought scribbles here and there.

At least the case was taking on some new shape, offering different avenues for me to explore. What's more,

most of those avenues appeared to lead handily away
from Tommy McGurk.

They waited until I was through eating. I'll give them
that.

I was blowing the steam off a post lunch cup of coffee,
pondering whether or not to team a piece of pie with it,
when they came in. Moved up on either side of me,
dropped onto the empty stools there. We had the counter
to ourselves. The one on my left, the younger and beefier
of the two, tugged a napkin out of the holder and began
wiping his mirrored sunglasses with it. The older, thinner
one on my right looked bored, but I had the feeling it was
a carefully calculated expression. They smelled of stale
cigarette smoke and faded aftershave. And they smelled
of something more: The Law.

They were the pair of plainclothes cops I'd spotted at
Alex de Ruth's funeral.

I tipped back a sip of the coffee and waited for them to
make their next move. But they seemed in no particular
hurry. I guess it was supposed to be a psychological thing,
make me feel boxed in, trapped, work on my nerves.

The waitress started over but then read something in
the situation that caused her to turn away and leave us be.

My notebook still lay on the countertop in front of me. I
turned it to a blank page, dated the top margin, and
below that wrote: TWO POLICEMEN CAME CALLING
TODAY. THEY WERE THE STRONG, SILENT TYPE. I
put it in big block letters and printed it slow and neat,
holding my hands back so their inquisitive eyes couldn't
miss it.

After about thirty seconds, the one on my left grunted.
"Real cute."

The other one, the one who up until now had looked
strictly bored and disinterested, said, "Good penmanship,
good spelling, a certain amount of originality. But lacking
in genuine sincerity, I feel. I give it a B+."

"Darn," I said. "I knew I should have gone with 'strong,
silent, and handsome.' "

Lefty pointed a finger. "Don't get too goddamned
cute."

"If you're going to start pointing things at me, how about pointing some ID?"

"You know A-fucking well who we are."

"I know *what* you are, not who. Let's see it."

With grudging sighs they dug out their wallets and opened them to their shields and photo tags. I learned I was in the company of Detective Anthony Brell (formerly Lefty) and Detective Sergeant Henry Janky (holding up the right flank), two stalwart examples of Davenport's finest.

When their wallets were put away again, I smiled politely and said, "Good afternoon, officers. What can I do for you?"

Janky's grin hung lopsided and sardonic on his narrow face. "Oh, you *could* tell us all about why you're poking in the de Ruth murder case and what you've found so far, if anything. And where you're headed next with your investigation. How'd that be?"

"Kind of tough, that's how it would be. Pretty much goes against the grain of what I'm all about, you know?"

Brell said, "I'd like to go against your grain sometime, smart guy. Show you what *I'm* all about."

"Put a sock in it, Brellsy," Janky told him, wearily but firmly. "This ain't one of your raw meat days. Besides, remember what the captain said."

Brell looked sullen, like a little kid who'd been scolded in front of company.

I said, "I'm going to be real disappointed if you two are trying the old Good Cop/Bad Cop routine on me."

Janky shook his head. "No routine here, mister. Brellsy there is just about the most miserable cuss ever got a badge pinned on him, and I've been blessed to have him for a partner. But he has his uses. And if you keep egging him, I won't stand in front of you every time."

"Fair enough," I allowed. "So what do you really want from me?"

Janky shrugged. "About what you'd expect. You're on our turf, sticking your nose in something we figure is not only our business and none of yours but something we've already taken care of. Sort of goes against the grain, as you put it, to have somebody come in and start redoing your

job for you. On the other hand, we're willing to be fair. If
you know something we don't—or think you do—we'd
like to hear it. But if you're just stirring shit, trying to
make us look bad, that we definitely would take exception
to."

"It's not a matter of trying to make anybody look bad,"
I told him. "It's a matter of trying to save a guy's bacon—
Tommy McGurk's."

"What for?" Brell sneered. "The asshole's as dirty as the
bottom of my shoe. He got a hard-on for de Ruth—a
different kind of hard than he'd been getting for the
dumb bastard's wife—and popped him right there in the
driveway. End of story."

"Where's the murder weapon?"

"It'll turn up. They always do."

"Maybe. And maybe it all went down the way you
figure," I said. "But it nevertheless *could* have gone down
some other ways. Somebody needs to check those other
possibilities out before shutting the door on them and
that's what McGurk's lawyer has brought me in to do. De
Ruth wasn't exactly Mr. Congeniality, you know."

"Big step from being unpopular to being made dead."

"Happens all the time for a hell of a lot less cause."

"Yeah, but not as often as it happens over pussy."

Janky winced a little at his partner's crudity. "Look,
Hannibal," he said to me, "you got a job to do. We can
appreciate that. We're working stiffs ourselves. We got a
job to do, too. So you go ahead and do your snooping, we'll
go ahead and keep an eye on you. That's the way it works.
Hell, you're the legal representative of a prominent attorney, we all know our hands are tied from doing anything
to stop you anyway. But if it turns out you're keeping
pertinent facts from us or you start riling up our citizens
or try to pull some kind of shady shit to muck up the
works, then we'll find a way to land on you all the same.
Understand what I'm saying? I'm not Brellsy talking just
to make noise, I'm telling you something worth listening
to."

I looked in his eyes—eyes set in a face no longer pulled
slack by an expression of boredom, far from it—and I said,
"I believe you."

* * *

Nicholas Hatfield said, "And the names again were . . . ?"

I gave them to him.

His voice came back through the phone receiver. "And Janky's the senior man, Brell's the twerp."

"That's the picture."

"What else did you read off them? You think maybe they tried leaning on you because they have something to cover up?"

"No, I didn't pick up on anything like that. I think Janky laid it out pretty straight. Natural enough for them to resent somebody like me scuffing up a floor they've already swept. I do think, though, they maybe aren't as comfortable with all their chips riding on McGurk as they're trying to put across. Like I told you, I spotted them the first time casing de Ruth's funeral. Maybe the order to button the case came from higher up and they got no choice in the way they're playing it."

"I'll pour it all through a sieve and see if any chunks get stuck. I've got a pretty good pipe into the Davenport PD. What else?"

"Going back to Alex de Ruth's little video enterprise," I said, having already given Hatfield the bare bones of it after reaching him at his uptown office, "what are the chances of backtracking any bank transactions he might have made over the past six months to a year?"

"Should be doable. What are you thinking? Blackmail? See if he shows a pattern of deposits that might be linked to payoffs?"

"You guessed it. He and his wife—widow, now—maintained separate checking and savings accounts. She has access to whatever records he kept at home, I can have her start chasing the question from her end, too. But the way he liked to play his little secrets, he could've had a whole other gig going somewhere and in some way that won't turn up so easy."

"I can get a sweep of the entire area. See what shows. Computer interfacing is a marvelous toy."

"Uhmm. How about taking it another step then? I don't have a list ready right now, but what if I culled some names from the faces on the videos—could you run a similar screen from that direction? See if any of them showed odd patterns in their withdrawals or check cashing habits?"

It was quiet on his end for a minute. "You're sliding over on some pretty shaky legal ground there. Backtracking de Ruth is one thing, he's a definite principal in the case. But a random selection like the one you're proposing . . ."

"Let me put it another way. If some unscrupulous lowlifes—not anybody at all like you or I—wanted to do such a thing, would it be feasible?"

"It wouldn't yield anything admissible in court, of course, but I expect it could be done." Translation: Hell yes, just don't ask me to go on record for it, and especially not over the phone, you dope.

I sighed exaggeratedly. "Ah, the burden of wearing this damn white hat and playing by the rules all the time."

"Yeah, it's a bitch, ain't it? Tell me, though, you wear yours *all* the time? Like, say, even when you were putting the moves on Paula de Ruth?"

"What do you mean 'putting the moves' on her? She's merely a subject it was necessary for me to interview in the course of my investigation."

"Yeah, 'merely' my ass. Come on, man, don't forget I've seen this chick. The Pope would end up hitting on her. Besides, you expect me to believe you got all the cooperation you got out of her with only your snazzy interrogation technique?"

"Just me and my silver tongue."

"Aha. But where did you *put* said silver tongue, that's what I'm getting at."

"Counselor, you have a dirty mind."

"Secret of my success. But, hey, all kidding aside, pal, sounds like you're off to a helluva start. I'm optimistic enough to believe there's a good chance this video bit you discovered could really lead to something. You're going to end up making me look good and earn that bonus for yourself in the bargain."

"Let's not count our chickens, counselor. Do everything you can on your end, especially to keep Janky and

Brell off my back. If they decide to Band-Aid themselves to me, my effectiveness will be knocked to hell."

"Done. And done I guess is what this conversation is, too, since you obviously aren't going to give me any of the juicy details on you and the Platinum Powerhouse."

"Good-bye, counselor."

13

I spotted the familiar outlines of Bomber's height and bulk from all the way across the gym. At least I thought I did. The closer I got, the less sure I was. The size and shape were right, and the booming voice as it came into earshot, but there had been some new touches since I'd seen him last, some refinements that couldn't help but pull a smirk, albeit a cautious one, out of me as I walked over to him.

He was talking to a couple guys I remembered from the introductions that had been handed around at Alex de Ruth's funeral. They were the Kolchonsky brothers, their shaved heads and flamboyant mustaches—trademarks of their ring personae as the Savage Sheiks—making them pretty hard to forget. They stood before Bomber with thick arms folded benignly, eyes attentive. The expression "hanging on every word" would be suitable. Bomber was regaling them with some colorful bit of lore from his own days in the squared circle.

He broke off in mid-story when he caught sight of me out of the corner of his eye. "Jesus Christ, Joe," he said, turning, "there you are. I was starting to think you must have dropped off the edge of the world."

"Maybe I did," I said, still wearing my smirk, letting my gaze sweep pointedly over the changes in him. "Maybe I landed in the Twilight Zone."

I guess it was the hair I mostly couldn't get over. The three-piece suit, the gleaming wingtips, the dinner plate-sized Rolex, the aluminized briefcase dangling like a toy from his curled paw—none of these were affectations of the Bomber I had ever known before, but they were merely *things*, adornments to the surface. What had been done to his hair, though—that bristly, unruly, gray-white thatch worn perpetually in a kind of half grown-out crew-cut—the change there seemed too personal, like a scar carved onto him. The fiercely independent, shooting-off-at-odd-angles growth had been captured, crimped, and curled into a tight, neat cap of puffed rice ringlets hugging his head with lacquered obedience. Rows of defeated soldiers.

Reddening slightly under my examination, Bomber said, "So what the hell are you looking at?"

"I'm not at all sure," I told him.

"Well, I'll *tell* you what you're looking at," he came back. "You're looking at Bombastic Bomber Brannigan, the new manager of Big River Wrestling's undisputed lady champion, Paula the Platinum Powerhouse."

"I dare you to try and say that five times fast."

At that, Bomber's devoted two-man audience decided they didn't care much for my attitude. Crowding forward, they said in simultaneous growls, "What's this jerk's problem?" and "Is this guy bugging you, Mr. Brannigan?"

"Take it easy, fellas," Bomber said, but only after showing me a smug, maybe-I-oughta-let-'em-kick-your-ass grin. "Believe it or not, this rude individual is a friend of mine."

I never felt truly threatened by the two bruisers, not with Bomber standing right there, but the fleeting incident did serve to drive home one glaring fact: For the remainder of the case, I was going to spend a big share of my time going up against people who were physically superior to me. Now maybe that doesn't sound like such of a much, but to a guy my size in the knock-around racket that's been putting beans on the table for a good many years, it was a sobering realization.

I've never considered myself a bully: I have in fact done my share and more of pulling for the little guy, the underdog. Ironically, though, my beef and raw muscle have often been the tools I've used in those pursuits, tools I've learned to depend on the way you would any machine or implement that gets the job done for you. I know when to count on other things as well—my guns, my friends, my contacts—but at the core of it has always been my own inner and outer strength. At the risk of sounding chest-thumpingly macho (or what has become mistakenly perceived as same in the general mindset), I have to say there is a certain serenity that comes with being able to walk onto nearly any scene and feel confident you can physically handle most persons there. This particular scene, however, wasn't going to allow me that slice of serenity.

"Joe," Bomber said, "you remember Mike and Bob, right? They're a couple of real comers for BRW. I watched them working out in the ring a little while ago, and you're going to be hearing plenty more about them, believe me. Fellas, Joe here never played the game but I'll tell you he's the only guy ever knocked me down in a fair fight."

My standard line when Bomber uses that worn-out introduction is to point out how he climbed promptly back up and threw me through a wall for my troubles. But I held my tongue this time, not wanting to get into any long-winded explanations about how a solid friendship had formed from that rocky beginning or a retelling of any of the war stories that followed. The introduction had served to put the two bruising brothers at ease, that was good enough.

One of them, Mike, I think it was, said, "So you're the P.I., huh? The detective looking into the de Ruth murder thing, trying to make sure Tommy McGurk isn't getting railroaded?"

I nodded. "That's me."

"Then you're okay in our book," the other brother

rumbled. "Tommy's a good guy, no way he gunned down that creep de Ruth. Besides, whoever did off the asshole should be given a medal, not tossed in the clink over it."

"Interesting sentiment," I said. "Happens to be exactly the angle I'm playing. Since de Ruth was from all reports so thoroughly disliked, doesn't seem too much of a stretch to figure there could be any number of other people who might've wanted him dead."

"So what you're after is a better candidate, or suspect, I guess you'd say, than Tommy. Sort of a variation on the old 'best defense is a good offense' line of reasoning, right?"

"That's one way of putting it."

"Damn good way of putting it, you ask me," Bob said.

"Yeah," Mike agreed. "That's our kind of thinking, mister."

"Even if I turn up a new suspect who happens also to be a friend?"

They exchanged glances over the question, then heaved a matching set of fatalistic shrugs.

Any further discussion at that point was interrupted by the approach of a young woman who said from several feet away: "Hey, guys, we're next up for an interview. We'd better get our stuff on and get ready."

The newcomer, a black girl in about her middle twenties, was somewhat small in stature, especially by contrast to most everyone else inhabiting the gym this busy afternoon. What she lacked in formidable height or muscularity, however, was offset by certain other features that made her impressive all the same. Hers was a lithe dancer's body in tight, faded jeans and a T-shirt bearing likenesses of the Savage Sheiks in full wrestling regalia. A thick, lustrous mane of black hair spilled past her shoulders, framing a face dominated by sultry, heavy-lidded dark eyes and a mouth sensual enough to melt chrome.

"Oh, good," Mike Kolchonsky said in response to her announcement. "Is today the day we get to change together?"

"In your dreams, sucker."

"I know about that part. What I want is to bring those dreams to life."

"Come on," Bob Kolchonsky protested, "look where you've got our mouths at this very instant." He pointed at the girl's chest, where the unmistakable bumps of her nipples were poking against the facial images of him and his brother silkscreened onto her shirt. "How can you be willing to be so intimate with a couple stupid pictures and pass up on the real thing?"

The black girl smiled only slightly self-consciously. "You guys. You never give up, do you?"

"Now pretend you really want us to."

"Yeah, it would break your heart if we ever stopped."

She checked her wristwatch. "If we're not ready and we end up costing Mel extra bucks because we kept the video crew waiting, she'll break more than our hearts."

The brothers turned back to Bomber and me.

"Guess we got to close this off, Mr. Brannigan, Hannibal. Been nice talking to you."

"Yeah. Good hunting there, Hannibal. See you around."

The three of them receded across the gym, the Kolchonskys moving in that compressed-power kind of rolling gait that is the signature of so many heavy-duty jocks, their massive frames bracketing the girl protectively in spite of all the teasing.

"So who was that?" I asked of Bomber.

"Name's Ava something-or-other," he answered off-handedly. "She plays a harem girl to the boys' sheik bit. You know, decks out in a sexy little costume with beads and gold chains and a veil, dances around the ring during the introductions, holds the sheiks' robes and paraphernalia during the matches, all like that. I guess she wrestles sometimes, too, under a separate identity. The veil hides her face, see, so she can show up at a different spot on the card and not be recognized. It's an old trick a lot of masked wrestlers use. The double duty gives them a chance to earn extra bread and the promoters like it because it gives them one less body to sign up and keep track of."

"I guess that's one of the many reasons I wouldn't cut it as a wrestling promoter. To my way of thinking she's too cute to have her face hidden, even part of the time."

"I noticed you noticing."

"Let's just say I found her a refreshing change from most of the citizens you've got here in Steroid City."

As I said this, I made a gesture indicating the array of sweating, bulging, straining meat and muscle at work throughout the gym. Except for the sheer bulk on display, the place was no different than a hundred other gyms I'd been in. The sounds were all there, the clank of iron plates, the creak of pulleys and cables and joints, the grunts of effort and the exuberant "yahs!" of accomplishment. And the smells; sweat and disinfectant and liniment and determination and pain and fleeting physical glory.

It was a high-ceilinged oblong room with a row of fluorescent lights running down the middle and a haphazard arrangement of shaded bulbs hanging off to the sides. This created contrasting patches of glaring brightness and sharp-edged slices of shadow that the trainees slid in and out of as they did their routines, all with the same unnoticing, grimly determined expressions.

"Yeah, I hate to admit it," Bomber said, scanning the scene with me, "but I'm afraid you're right. That steroid shit was just getting a foothold when I left the game, but it sure as hell looks to have a firm grip nowadays. Dumb asses, don't they know what it can do to them in the long run? Look at me, sure I got fat and out of shape, but I can still get my peter up and my arteries aren't filling with blood clots the size of doorknobs or my bones turning to cracker crumbs."

"That's right. Although you do seem to have developed that recent kinking problem with your hair . . ."

"Will you for Chrissakes lay off my hair? Mel decided it was necessary to soften my appearance to fit my new image. Said with my hair the way it was before I only looked like an ex con who'd stolen the rest—the suit and the watch and all."

"And you went along with it?"

"She's sharp, Joe. Got damn good instincts, knows the game as well as anybody I've ever seen. In the three years since Duke died, she's brought BRW steadily forward through the ranks of all the different federations. Duke was stubborn, tried to stick to the old ways too long after the glitz and the cable TV deals and the pay-per-view events and all the rest of it arrived to change the face of wrestling forever: hype it to a level of popularity it'd never seen before. A lot of people were against Mel taking over after he was gone, but she's shut up every one of her detractors damned tight I'll tell you."

"Sounds like you're really getting caught up in this," I observed.

He grinned. "I gotta admit I'm having fun. It'll wear off I suppose, I really don't think I'm ready to get back into it full time. And even without your ribbing, I'm not all that crazy about my new 'do either. But so far the good has way outbalanced the bad. And there's enough ham left in me to look forward to working in front of a live crowd again, too. This'll be the first time I've ever been the heel. Everybody tells me it's a whole new kick."

"Your wrestler ought to know about that. You had a chance to spend any time with her yet?"

"Paula, you mean? Oh, sure. We hung for a long time this morning. She's a knockout in the looks department just like everybody said, and what's more she is one hell of an athlete. I watched her go through a workout routine that would've left me gasping like a grounded fish even back when I was boxing, which was when I figure I was in my best shape ever."

"Yeah, I've seen her in action, too," I said drily.

He nodded. "She mentioned you were by to talk to her yesterday, that you took her out to supper last night. Apparently she was cooperative with your investigation."

More than you know, pal, I said inside my head, then felt myself flush slightly at my own dirty thoughts. Out loud, all I said was, "Uh-huh, she was."

"That's the way it's been around here. Cooperative as hell. No sign of the animosity we were afraid we might run into, at least not so far. What I'm getting mostly is pretty much what you heard from Mike and Bob just a minute ago, that everybody liked Tommy too well to buy him as a murderer and that nobody's real sorry about what happened to de Ruth, no matter who did it. I guess the biggest surprise is that even Paula seems to fit in that category."

"Doesn't quite make it as a grieving widow, does she?"

"From all reports, she has pretty good reason for that," Bomber said.

The degree of defensiveness in his tone caught me a little off guard. But then, considering he'd spent a big chunk of the day with her, I guess it shouldn't have come as so much of a surprise. Whatever else she was or wasn't, the platinum one surely demonstrated the mythical sirenlike ability of being able to muddle men's senses.

"So where is Paula now?" I wondered.

"She's in getting a rubdown. She should be out before long, we're scheduled to tape a series of interviews as soon as the others are through."

"What's this videotaping and interviewing business all about anyway?"

Bomber rolled his eyes. "What is it? Man, it's the backbone of the whole wrestling foundation. It's what sells the tickets to the live matches, it's what establishes the ring personalities of the wrestlers, it's chest-pounding, drum-beating, eye-to-eye Medicine Show snake oil advertising done through a TV tube."

"And you're pumping up for it, practicing on me right now, aren't you?"

He laughed. "I guess I am. Let's face it, I was never exactly shy to begin with and now I've been tagged to be 'bombastic.' Hell, I always *loved* hamming it up for the camera. I never had any big hangups about the so-called 'serious' aspects of the sport like, say, Tommy used to. It should be obvious to any idiot that there's a theatrical side to what we do and it should be equally obvious that there's a damn tough physical side to it. I always figured the fans and viewers could sort that shit out for themselves; all I ever wanted to do was put on a good show and have some fun between the bumps and bruises."

In all the years we'd been buddies, it was surprising how little the Bomber and I had actually talked about his wrestling career. It had stayed pretty much a closed chapter of his life, one I wasn't particularly interested in hearing about and one he'd never seemed particularly

interested in talking about (other than a handful of especially wild tales I'd sat through over and over again). As I
listened to him now, however, watching the excitement
dance in his eyes, I found myself wondering if there'd
been times he *had* wanted to talk more about it and I'd
been a shitheel friend for not showing greater interest. I
made up my mind that whenever and however this case
ended, once we were back home in Rockford and settled
into more normal routines, I'd make it a point to bring it
up again, give him the opportunity to go with it as much
as he wanted.

I reached this monumentally humanitarian decision
only moments before spotting Mel Dukenos and Paula de
Ruth winding their way through the gym crowd toward
us. Mel wore an expensively cut blazer with matching
skirt. Paula's costume—black spandex tights, gold boots, a
flowing full-length black cloak with gold trim and tie cord
—was equally businesslike as long as you took into consideration what her business was.

"Don't look now, but here come both of your boss ladies," I said to Bomber.

"Yeah, but to hell with not looking. Everybody else is."

He was right about that. Even the two beefcakes swapping holds up in the ring took time out for quick, appreciative gazes after the women.

"Hello again, Mr. Hannibal," Mel Dukenos greeted me.
"I see you've met the 'new' Bomber Brannigan. What do
you think?"

Dutifully, I said, "Oh, I think he looks absolutely bombastic."

That got a good laugh from everybody.

"I understand," Mel went on, "you've already met
Paula here as well. You certainly seem to get around."

"Yes indeed," Paula said, with a twinkle in her eye
aimed strictly at me, "Mr. Hannibal showed me quite a
nice time last night. Not only helped me get my mind off
my troubles, but managed to sneak in some pretty thorough investigating techniques at the same time."

"No hard feelings I hope," I said, trying not to let her
coy double entrendres rattle me in front of the others,

even though I could feel patches of heat crawling up my neck.

"Not in the least. I'm very willing to help your cause. I won't mind anytime you think of more questions to ask me."

There it was again. The voice, the challenging ice blue stare, the fantastic assemblage of curves—the whole damn mind-blowing package. I'd gotten out of her bed that morning feeling not very proud of either of us. My grainy-eyed session with the videotapes had left me feeling even lower, resolved to cool it with her. Don't fuck with the merchandise, son. That's a cardinal rule in any business, no matter what. Yet here I was, my resolve melting like August ice after only a handful of minutes back in her presence, my mind spinning ahead with schemes to take her up on that "anytime you think of more questions to ask me" remark. It was like she had an invisible chain tugging at my crotch, and part of the problem was that I knew she had too many of those invisible chains leading to too many other crotches.

"Speaking of questions to be asked and answered," Mel Dukenos said, "they should be ready for Bomber and Paula in the interview area practically any second. Why don't we head that way? I pay a small fortune to bring that video crew in here every week, I like to keep things on schedule."

14

The interview area was set up at the far end of the building in a boxy corridor whose ends led off to the men's and women's locker rooms. The back wall of the corridor had been covered by a huge poster displaying the BRW logo. The interviews taking place in front of it were being conducted by Abe Lugretti, looking surprisingly dapper and unrumpled (if somewhat incongruous) in a black dinner jacket and red tie. Everything that transpired was being captured by a two-man camera, sound, and lighting crew.

We came in at the tail end of the sheiks promising into Lugretti's hand-held mike to do all sorts of bodily harm to another tag team they had an upcoming match with. As they verbally destroyed these future opponents, the black girl, Ava, in her exotic harem girl costume, danced alluringly in and out of the shot while muted sitar music played in the background.

And they say pro wrestling lacks culture.

Bomber and Paula were on next. While they were getting situated, Mel Dukenos stood next to me and said, "I'm really looking forward to this. Bomber used to give some of the best interviews ever. He's such a natural, so spontaneous. One of the classics was the time he had a cage match scheduled with Cyclone Kramer and Bomber showed up for an interview taping carrying this huge, overripe tomato with a face drawn on it that was supposed to be Kramer. The interview was shot behind a sheet of chicken wire, simulating the cage, and as he ranted and raved and carried on about how badly he was going to beat the Cyclone, all the things he was going to do to him, Bomber pushed the tomato face *through* the wire, shredding it, causing all the pulp and juice to run down for the camera. It was so outlandish the switchboards virtually ignited when the spot ran on TV. After that, every promoter in the country wanted a Brannigan-Kramer match. The fans couldn't get enough. I think Bomber and Cyclone spent most of that spring and summer fighting practically no one else but each other, on cards from coast to coast and border to border.

"That Bomber," I said, "a real master of subtlety and understatement."

Ignoring my sarcasm, Mel went on. "My only regret, aside from the basic one over the whole tragic murder, naturally, is that we don't have enough time ahead of the big pay-per-view card to properly promote the fact Bomber is back. The stuff we're taping today will only run twice before then. And there's no chance at all of making any of the newsletters or magazines that cover our sport." She sighed. "But it'll work out. It could be worse, I could be stuck in the same situation with no Bomber to fall back on."

If her sentiments seemed somewhat lacking in compassion for the predicaments of others such as Tommy (to say nothing of his alleged victim), at least she wasn't being hypocritical about where her priorities lay. We each have our own fish to fry on this hot skillet of a planet.

A series of shushings and palms-down hand motions signaled that the camera and related equipment were ready to roll again.

The interview that followed went something like this:

ANNOUNCER: (voice and expression very somber) Ladies and gentlemen, it can be no secret that the tragic events of the past few days you have all undoubtedly heard and read about has shaken the Big River Wrestling organization to its very core. Each one of us here at BRW is troubled and deeply saddened by what has taken place, by the losses we have suffered. But in the tradition of great athletic competition, a tradition cemented in our common memory by instances such as the Munich Olympics continuing after the man-made horror of a terrorist attack or the more recent World Series contest completed after the natural horror of a devastating earthquake, we are determined to carry on in the face of adversity. For the sake of you, our loyal fans, and for the sake of our tremendous sport of wrestling we can do no less.

And there can be no braver example of this determination and dedication than the young woman I am about to bring on. Ladies and gentlemen, it is with great pride that I present the undisputed ladies' champion of Big River Wrestling, Paula the Platinum Powerhouse.

PAULA: (moving onto camera, expression thoughtful, equally somber) Thank you for that introduction, Abe. I have to say it was more respectful than usual.

ANNOUNCER: Well, you and I haven't always seen eye to eye in the past, Champ. I, like many of the fans, have never cared for some of your ring tactics or your frequent disregard for the rules. Nevertheless I applaud the spirit and fortitude you have shown to me and to the world in your handling of these shocking events and all that has been written and implied by the media.

PAULA: Ordinarily I could care less what you or the fans or the media think, say, or do. I have to admit, though, that the support I've received through all of this has been both helpful and welcome. But by far my greatest strength came from my love for the sport of wrestling and my resolve to remain at the top.

ANNOUNCER: That leads up to a question I have to ask then, Champ, *the* question that I'm sure has been weighing on the minds of so many—are you going to go ahead and defend your title, as planned, against Queen Cobra during BRW's spectacular pay-per-view card in St. Louis on the 24th?

PAULA: (hanging head in contemplation for a dramatic length of time, then suddenly lifting her face and staring straight into camera) You can damn well bet I am, Abe!

ANNOUNCER: That's the answer I anticipated and I certainly admire you for it. But surely you must realize that, under the circumstances, everyone would understand if you chose to postpone defending your coveted belt.

PAULA: That may be. But a true champion has to be ready to protect that championship at all times. The greater the champion, the greater the challenges he or she should be able to overcome. I've been telling you and all the people out there I'm the greatest champion you have ever seen, I look at this as an opportunity to prove it. And if that over-the-hill bimbo Queen Cobra thinks she had a chance of sneaking a cheap victory from me because maybe my mind is a little messed up, my concentration off a beat or two, well, let her go ahead and try and we'll see who's messed up when the bell rings at the end of the match.

ANNOUNCER: Allow me to play devil's advocate and say that a lot of people might agree with the reasoning you could hardly be at your sharpest under the circumstances. Good heavens, in the course of less than a week you have been widowed, your manager of long and successful standing is facing serious allegations that render his services unavailable, and the press has laid bare every secret and every outrageous accusation imaginable concerning you. Given all that, how can you possibly maintain a mental peak for what will undoubtedly be one of the toughest tests of your career?

PAULA: The heart of a competitor—make that a *champion* competitor—beats inside me, Abe. I've demonstrated many times that I'm willing to do whatever it takes to win. This will be no different.

ANNOUNCER: Let me go back a minute to the subject of your manager, or I guess I should say the sudden lack of one. You've got to be having pretty mixed feelings about Terrible Tommy McGurk right now. But more important, you've had great success with him in your corner, shouting instructions and encouragement and sometimes doing considerably more. Isn't that going to be a major adjustment for you, suddenly being completely on your own, and coming at such a crucial time?

PAULA: If I didn't know better, Abe, I'd say you're starting to sound like you expect, or maybe *want*, me to lose in St. Louie.

ANNOUNCER: Nothing could be further from the truth, Champ. I'm merely trying to examine for the fans all the possible ramifications of what has taken place.

PAULA: (smiling shrewdly) Well here's another ramification you can examine. You see, in addition to having the heart of a champion I also have the *brain* of a champion. That means always being prepared, always thinking ahead, planning five or ten or twenty moves in advance of anyone else.

ANNOUNCER: So what are you saying?

PAULA: I'm saying, you round little man, that I've already hired myself a new manager. He will not only be a *replacement* for Tommy McGurk, he will be an *improvement* over him. He's one of the true living legends of wrestling and he's going to be in *my* corner from now on.

ANNOUNCER: Who? Who are you talking about?

BOMBER: (voice from off camera) She's talking about me, that's who. The man who walks where he wants to walk, says what he wants to say, and leaves a trail of broken hearts and broken noses wherever I go.

ANNOUNCER: (eyes bugging) Holy cow, I don't believe this! It's . . . it's . . .

PAULA: (smiling triumphantly) It's my new manager, Bomber Brannigan!

BOMBER: (moving on camera, wearing a big smile as he grasps Paula's right hand in his and pumps enthusiastically) *Bombastic* Bomber Brannigan, doll. That's what all the wheeler-dealers and so-called movers and shakers have taken to calling me. I talk a big story, and then I'm damn well able to back it up.

ANNOUNCER: Ladies and gentlemen, I can hardly get over this. Bomber Brannigan, gone from the wrestling scene for more than a decade—back now, and back as the new manager of Paula the Platinum Powerhouse!

BOMBER: You bet I'm back, Abe Lugretti. I've been away conquering new frontiers, swimming with the sharks, running with the wolves. But all the while I kept my eye on the wrestling scene. And do you know what I saw? I saw the sport I love being turned into a big, fat joke. I saw people laughing. I saw guys trying to act tough with painted faces and funny haircuts, bringing birds and snakes and dogs and cats and chickens and who knows what else to the ring with them. I saw little kids playing with wrestler *dolls,* for crying out loud! But one of the few bright spots I saw was this gal right here. It doesn't matter that she's a woman, just like it wouldn't matter if she was black or yellow or polka dot. All I care is that she's a tough, savvy competitor—a champion who deserves to stay a champion, and I aim to help see she does. When I heard what happened with Tommy McGurk, that she would be going into one of the toughest battles of her life without a manager, that's when I knew it was time for me to get back into the wrestling game. I called her up and offered my services.

PAULA: And naturally I accepted. Who in their right mind would pass up the chance to have Bombastic Bomber Brannigan—one of the greats of all time—in their corner?

ANNOUNCER: Ladies and gentlemen, this is phenomenal. You are truly witnessing history in the making. For those of you who might have forgotten or are too young to remember, let me remind you that Bomber Brannigan was Tommy McGurk's mentor when Tommy first broke into the ranks of pro wrestling. And now, irony of ironies, the teacher has returned to replace the pupil in guiding this lady who wears the gold around her waist.

BOMBER: That's right, and don't you ever forget it.

I'm the teacher—the *master*—Tommy McGurk is the pupil. That's the way it will always be, whether a decade passes, or a hundred decades. I taught that punk everything he knows. But I sure never taught him to be stupid enough to get caught. And the other key thing to remember is that even though I taught him everything *he* knows, I would never teach him everything *I* know. That's the difference that will make Paula the Platinum Powerhouse an even greater champion under my guidance.

ANNOUNCER: (looking shocked) I can't believe your lack of compassion for an old friend.

BOMBER: I don't care what you believe, Abe Lugretti. You know what they say, a friend in need is a pain in the gazeekus. Besides, is it my problem if some chump can't keep his nose clean? Tommy McGurk had the world by a string on a downhill pull, and he blew it big time.

ANNOUNCER: According to the law of the land that remains to be seen. What about "innocent until proven guilty?"

BOMBER: What about it?

PAULA: (sneeringly) Yeah, what about it? If you want to play that game, how about "do unto others" ? You didn't see me going out and screwing everything up right on the brink of a super important match, did you? I don't owe Terrible Tommy a thing, and Bomber sure as hell doesn't either.

ANNOUNCER: But he was a tried and proven commodity. I'll be the first to salute Bomber's past glory, only he's been away from things for a long time. And having been a great wrestler doesn't necessarily translate into being a successful manager. What if he's, well, lousy at it? Or, at the very least, what if he's a little rusty? Can you afford to have that as another concern going into this match with Queen Cobra?

PAULA: You let me worry about that. And I assure you it is a worry I do *not* have.

BOMBER: (scowling) What kind of questions are those, anyway? You talk like I've had my rear end planted on a rocking chair in some nursing home while I was away.

I've been chewing raw meat out there in the dog-eat-dog real world, mister, and I don't mind telling you I gnawed my way to the position of lead husky everywhere I went. I'm Bombastic Bomber Brannigan. The Bomber. The Bombastic One. I can out-fight, out-think, out-cuss, out-drink, out-eat, out-walk, out-run, out-swim, out-ride, out-shoot, out-love, out-hate, out-manage, out . . . out . . .

ANNOUNCER: Out-talk?

BOMBER: Yeah! And out-*talk* any pot-bellied, gimpy-legged has-been like Tommy McGurk on the best day he ever had. You might do well to remember that, Abe Lugretti, you over-inflated beach ball, and to start showing a little more respect.

15

That evening, Bomber and I took Lori and Tommy McGurk out for an early supper. We went to the same restaurant Lori and I had lunched at the day she first hired me.

Bomber was in lofty spirits, still running high on the rush he was getting off being back in the wrestling lime-light. His booming laugh filled the place and his toothy smile was infectious enough that I could feel myself wear-ing a grin of my own through much of the meal, pleased at seeing my buddy so upbeat, so happy.

Lori did some smiling and even a little laughing, too, sharing Bomber's mood. She also related she was able to close a house sale just that afternoon that she'd been sweating over for some time, the double good news there being not only the commission check that would be forth-coming but the implication her business, at least so far, wasn't being negatively affected by any fallout from the murder case.

It was Tommy who struck the only discordant note in our quartet. From the minute we started out he acted pensive, morose. Not that he didn't have every right, I guess, with all that hung so ominous over his head. And I suppose from a certain standpoint it might appear the display of lightheartedness by the rest of us was somewhat cold and unfeeling for what he was going through. But you can only console a man's grief so far before your caring becomes part of the fuel and then it's time to go another direction.

Except Tommy wasn't ready to make the turn. When I tossed a couple shots at Bomber's new hairdo and left him plenty of opportunity to join in on the ribbing as he normally would have, he merely continued picking halfheartedly at the salad he'd been served. When Bomber recited a handful of the more outlandish exchanges from the interview he'd done, all he got for his trouble was a wan smile. And when Lori excitedly listed some of the things they could pay off or purchase now that her deal had gone through, he looked downright bored.

By the time we were through eating and our plates had been cleared for a round of after-dinner coffee (and a bowl of mint ice cream for the Bomber), Tommy's glumness had managed to drag everybody else down instead of the other way around. Even the smile on the face of our waitress seemed to have faded somewhat from what it was earlier.

A trip to the rest room by Tommy finally offered we remaining three a chance to dip our heads together conspiratorially and discuss what we'd been able to relay only with our eyes up until that point.

"I don't know what got into him," Lori said. "He's been like this all day. And he had a pretty rough night. Lots of tossing and turning, some bad dreams I'd guess, but he wouldn't talk about it. I woke up once and he wasn't in bed, instead he was over by the window just staring out at the night. When I asked him what was wrong, all he'd say was that he couldn't sleep because his leg was bothering him. That's his old catchall excuse. I heard it plenty during the bleak times after the accident, and then again more recently when . . . well, you know."

"Has anything changed?" I asked. "Have the police been bugging him, or has Hatfield hit some kind of snag I didn't hear about?"

Lori shook her head. "Nothing like that. I think maybe everything has come together all at once in his mind and its weighing pretty heavy. Plus, he's probably starting to feel cooped up. First jail, then he hasn't left the house since he got home. Until tonight."

"That's what tonight was supposed to be all about," Bomber pointed out.

"I know. And I still think it was a good idea."

"Maybe it's me," Bomber said. "Even though he gave the idea the green light, maybe inside it bothers him that I'm filling in for him at BRW. Could it be he's worried I'll be some kind of big hit or like it too much or something and there won't be room for him when he's ready to come back?"

"Don't be silly," Lori said with another shake of her head. "He knows you'd never be a part of anything like that. It could be something less personal along those lines, though. It could be he's just feeling left out in general. We're all going on about our business and he's stuck in a kind of limbo."

"No matter what it is," I said, "the answer isn't to keep feeling sorry for him. Besides, most of the business we're going on with is related somehow to getting him *un*-stuck from his limbo."

"Maybe it's her," Lori said.

" 'Her' who?" Bomber said.

"Paula. Maybe he's acting the way he is because he hasn't seen her, been with her."

Bomber made a face. "Aw, Jeez, don't think that. That wouldn't be it at all."

"I don't buy it either," I chimed in. "Strictly from a practical angle, with you returning to your real estate work and Bomber and I gone from the house he's had all kinds of time to get together with her if that was what he wanted."

Lori's expression eased somewhat but she still didn't look fully convinced.

The scream that cut through the restaurant changed all our expressions. It came from the direction of the front lobby, a child's screech of terror rising to an alarming note before being swallowed by the crash and clatter of something—several items—falling and scattering in disarray.

I was on my feet, moving, vaguely aware of the conversational buzz of the other diners halting for a moment then restarting at a heightened level of intensity. With Bomber at my heels, I weaved through the arrangement of tables and trotted around the end of a dark wood divider draped by foamy green plants.

The kid was due ahead, in the mouth of a short hallway that led off from one side of the hostess's station. He was a boy of seven or eight struggling to climb back to his feet and escape out of the tumbled pile of hard plastic serving trays he had apparently run into and capsized. He was still making scared noises, sobbing, and I got the impression it was more than the accident with the trays that had him so shook up.

Tommy McGurk stood in the middle of the short hall beyond the youngster, seemingly frozen in place, his face pained, his hands outstretched as if pleading with the boy. The frightened glances the kid was throwing over his shoulder as he struggled were aimed directly at Tommy.

I dragged my feet, trying to figure out what the hell was taking place. Bomber bumped against me, grunting a curse.

And then a man shot past us from behind in a hard, determined run. He was a skinny, middle-aged guy wearing a sweater and a tie. The tie was flapping and the strands of hair he'd had carefully arranged to cover the bald spot on top of his head were flying in all directions.

"Daddy!" the kid wailed, spotting the skinny guy. "The killer is after me. The killer!"

The pain and confusion on Tommy's face twisted tighter and he took a jerky step forward.

The skinny guy kicked aside several of the spilled trays and reached to pick up his son. A woman scurried past Bomber and me, a pale-skinned birdlike edition wearing a flowered dress with a matching hat perched on tightly permed hair. She hurried to where the man was straightening up, holding the boy now.

"Watch out, Mommy," the boy called to her. "It's him. It's the man you said was a killer."

Tommy advanced, his feet shuffling noisily into the scattered trays on the floor, his hands still outstretched in an imploring way. "I was coming out of the rest room," he said. "He bumped into me on his way in . . . then he screamed and ran . . . but I didn't . . . I never meant . . ."

"You killer!" the boy shouted at him, secure and suddenly brave now in his parents' embrace.

It became wretchedly clear at that point what had happened. A bit of hushed, holier-than-thou sniping on the mother's part over a family meal out on the town. "Look over there. It's him. Tommy McGurk, the killer, the one they arrested for murder. Shot his girlfriend's husband to death. It's disgusting they let him make bail. He shouldn't be allowed out in public among decent people." Whatever the words had been exactly, that would have been the gist of them. And to the ears of a boy of eight they would have been gospel. Some time later the kid has to pee and because he's a little man now there's no reason he can't find his way there and back alone, even in the crowded restaurant. Nobody counted on him running into the bogeyman that had been planted so recently and so vividly in his mind.

"I'm sorry," Tommy said weakly.

It knifed my guts to see the anguish etched around his eyes.

"It's okay," the father said, hugging his son, not looking at anyone, obviously embarrassed by the whole matter. "It's okay."

But his wife was too emotional to share his good sense. "No, it's not okay," she hissed at Tommy. "You should be ashamed of yourself, parading around in public like you have every right, frightening poor innocents. You belong behind bars!"

The distraught hostess and a dark-suited man who evidently was the restaurant manager or owner closed in, flanked by two wide-eyed busboys poised to clean up the mess that had been made.

"Please," the dark-suited man said. "Enough."

"You're damned right that's enough." Lori McGurk pushed between Bomber and me and strode intently over to Tommy. She nestled into the crook of a thick arm that lifted out of habit to embrace her, half turning so that her jaw jutted in the direction of the distraught mother. "I regret if your child got upset, lady, but I'll remind you that my husband *does* have every right to be here. If you don't like it you can either go somewhere else to eat or go to hell. And that holds for anybody else who might think they're so pure and innocent."

"Please," the dark-suited man said again.

The hostess made an urgent gesture, signaling the bus-boys to start restacking the trays. Maybe she hoped the noise they made would partially drown out any further unpleasantries that might be exchanged.

The dark-suited man lifted both arms for attention. "Please ladies and gentlemen," he said unctuously. "Return to your tables. Continue dining. The disturbance is over, there will be no more problems."

The crowd that had gathered began to disperse obligingly.

The woman in the flowered dress and hat sniffed indignantly. Lori glared icicles at her. Tommy stood with eyes downcast, as did the man holding the boy.

"You must understand," the dark-suited man said to the four of them, "that I have to ask you to leave. I don't know what started this, I don't choose to know. Your bills will be taken care of, you will be welcome here another time. But not tonight."

The flowered woman tried to protest but her husband cut her short. "He's right, Ellen. It's time to go."

Lori looked as if she, too, was ready to start an argument. Bomber and I moved on her before she got anything out. Tommy said nothing, seeming either not to comprehend or not to care what was going on.

Outside, as we piled into Bomber's Buick, I saw Tommy pause for just an instant to follow with his eyes the departure from the parking lot of the car carrying the man and woman and little boy. In that instant and in those haunted eyes I caught the silvery glint of tears.

The knife in my gut dug deeper as I tried to imagine what might be going on behind those tears. Was he comparing back, seeing the hundreds of young boys with hero worship glowing on their faces who used to attend his matches and cheer for him when he'd been a wrestling hero, a good guy? Did he wonder at the disappointment those same faces might hold for him now? Was he in some context conjuring the image of his own son when he'd been alive? Or was he merely replaying what had happened in the restaurant and wallowing in the agony of it?

I longed, as I'm sure Bomber and Lori did, for something to say to him to make him feel better. But there was nothing there.

When we dropped the McGurks back at their house, Tommy found voice to thank Bomber and me for the night out, even with the way it had gone awry, and to assure us hollowly that he was fine, that he'd get over it all right. Behind him, Lori couldn't help looking grim and unconvinced.

Back in the car, Bomber said to me, "You know, during the past couple days I guess I got caught up a little too much in the fun and excitement of being part of the whole wrestling show again. I sort of lost track of what this is really all about. Tonight, I got put back on track."

"I hear you," I said.

The dashboard lights cast his features in stark shadows. "We got to nail the bastard that killed de Ruth, Joe. We got to do it for Tommy. Fast. Nobody should have to go through what him and that kid went through back there."

I knew what he meant. I've spent most of my adult life in professions—first as a public cop, then as a private one —that have crowded me against the harder edges of society. I've seen and done and walked away (sometimes with my hide barely intact) from things no "proper" citizen should ever be exposed to. All this has leathered the hide I've managed to keep, made a pretty tough cookie out of me. You could say I've seen it all twice, been there and back, supply any appropriate cliche of your choosing.

But I never again want to see the look that had been on Tommy McGurk's face in that dim hallway when the little boy was crying out and fleeing from him in blind terror. That I don't think I'm up to.

16

It was nearly nine when I thumbed Paula de Ruth's bell button. She answered the door wearing a pair of stylishly baggy black gym shorts and a man's ribbed sleeveless undershirt that was anything but baggy.

"I'd almost given up on you," she said by way of greeting.

"Slow but steady wins the race," I responded. And then, thinking of Fat Fran's handiwork, I asked, "How are the wounds?"

"Maybe you missed your calling. Maybe you should have been a doctor instead of a detective." She smiled. "I found your bedside manner most effective."

At that point she totally surprised me by slipping an arm around my shoulder and pulling herself against me for a long, hard kiss. Her tongue slid between my teeth and busied itself inside my mouth. In spite of my better judgment, that triggered my own tongue to get busy and then my hands, gliding all up and down the splendidly firm contours of her back and bottom.

When the kiss ended, she stepped back. "Mmm. That was nice. Wasn't it?"

"I've had worse. But I'm not sure if it was a good idea, right here in the doorway and all."

"Because of the neighbors? To hell with them. They never had anything to say when Alex was running what must have been a goddamn *parade* of his video playmates in and out of here."

We'd only had a brief chance to talk privately at the gym that afternoon. Following the interview taping, she'd had a publicity photo sitting scheduled and then a live phone hookup with a local radio talk show and then something else after that, all woven around the constant comings and going of Bomber and Mel Dukenos and assorted other BRW personnel, making it virtually impossible to get her alone for more than a minute at a time. When I explained I had some of the secret videos yet to view and that I needed her help to put names with more of the faces, we'd set up this get-together for later. She hadn't been crazy about the idea of having to watch the videos after all, but I'd made her see the necessity of it if we were going to get the full benefit out of them.

She ushered me into the living room now, asking if I cared for something to drink. I told her bourbon rocks. She left and returned with a tumbler of the smoky liquor for me and a glass of beer for herself. I remembered that her kiss had tasted tangily of beer. Watching her make the trip to the kitchen and back—the flash of her long, shapely legs, the suggestive quiver of her unencumbered breasts under the thin shirt fabric, nipple points prominent—I struggled to regain my resolve to keep this on a strictly business basis.

We took seats on the couch. I saw that she had brought the cassettes back out of the bedroom and placed them on the same coffee table I'd used that morning.

"I was careful to keep them arranged the way you had them," she pointed out. "I hope to heck the smaller stack has the ones you haven't seen at all yet."

"Uh-huh. It does."

"I'm no prude by any stretch of the imagination, but I can't tell you how much I'm *not* looking forward to this."

"I tried to leave the ones I went through set at a point where you'll get a good look at the faces right away, without having to put up with much of the accompanying activity."

"Thank God for at least that much. Have you told anyone else about these?"

"I almost told Bomber a little while ago, but I decided to hold off until I had a more complete idea of everything they contained. I did discuss them earlier today with Tommy McGurk's defense attorney. He'll be able to help us go after bank records and so forth in case there's a blackmail angle."

"While I was waiting for you, I went through a lot of Alex's bank statements and other records he kept here at home but I saw nothing that looked wrong or suspicious. I also had an eye open for any sign of a code book or sheet like you suggested, to help decipher those markings on the cassette boxes, but I struck out there too."

"It'll start coming together. These things take time."

We sipped from our drinks.

I tapped out a cigarette and got it going.

Paula sighed. "Well, I guess there's no sense putting off the unpleasantries any longer, is there? The controls are there by your arm and you're the one who knows what it is you want me to look at. Let's get this over with."

It took about an hour to go through the tapes I'd already screened, and then another hour to check out the remaining ones. Paula's reactions to what we watched ran the gamut from groans of dismay to coughs of edgy laughter, a muttered epithet here and there. Mostly she sat in stony silence.

When all was said and done, she was able to provide sixteen additional names over the handful I'd managed on my initial run at it. These represented about half of the thirty-seven videos we'd found in the hidey-hole. Most of the faces she couldn't identify were on the assortment of females seen coupling with Alex ("bimbette sluts" she called them, along with even less flattering terms for her late husband). There were also a number of participants she remembered as being in attendance at their parties—attendees who'd evidently paired off to do some extracurricular partying of their own, only to be captured in the act by Alex's camera—but who she couldn't put names to other than vague recollections of them being called "Kippy-something" or "Mickey-something" or some such meaningless tag.

Part of what we put together I wasted no time in mentally relegating to back burner status. The swing couple segment, for example, featuring Sid and Nancy, no last names please, from Lubbock, Texas. Inasmuch as all involved had been aware of the camera's presence well in advance and had proceeded willingly, it didn't seem a likely basis for any kind of backlash that might have led to de Ruth's killing. Also, the incident had taken place some two years in the past, the only tape in the collection not shot in this house. As an aside, the pop psycholologist in me couldn't help wondering if that session had been the triggering mechanism behind this whole more elaborate setup by Alex de Ruth.

Other episodes I downgraded to low priority included three separate sets of married couples, also party attendees, who evidently had been moved to covertly "try out" the de Ruth's exotically appointed bedroom, unaware of its lack of privacy. It was curious how the sex act took on a whole different context when you recognized it was being done by two people genuinely in love and devoted and attuned to one another, in no conscious way performing for anyone else's pleasure except each other's. It wasn't any less erotic to watch, but it was a gentler, more subtle stimulant—intoxication brought on by the sipping of fine wine as opposed to jolts of raw whiskey. Regardless of any of that, though, I calculated these entries as having little more potential than the source of possible teasing and/or embarrassment—hardly grounds for murder.

And while the two tapes showing Paula with other men carried somewhat more potential, I bottom-slotted them in the same manner. It hadn't been necessary to actually play those tapes over again. When I got to them and told Paula what was on them, she had remembered well enough the circumstances under which they would have been shot. It had been about eighteen months ago, she explained, and the two men were business associates of Alex's, a pair of wheeler-dealers from Florida he was try-

ing to get to take him in on one of their big money-
making ventures. That had been just when the de Ruths
were beginning to get a foothold in the BRW organization, before she was the ladies' champion, before they felt
their future was secure. So when Alex asked her to be
"nice" to the two guys—each on a separate occasion—he
made her believe it was important enough to go along
with. Whatever deal Alex was trying to cook up with
them eventually fell through, Paula couldn't remember
exactly why. But she was sure there had been no serious
hard feelings over it. And she could only recall that one of
the men was named John-Something and the other was
Earl Collingford . . . or was it Collingwood?

But even with those ten culled for the time being from
the lineup, I still had plenty to work with. One dozen
names, faces, and bodies as starting points on the road to a
killer.

And two of those starting points I was keeping to myself. I hadn't shown Paula either the tape containing
Brick Towers or the one with Abe Lugretti. Lugretti I
held back out of a sense of loyalty to the Bomber. Towers I
held back for reasons of my own. In the first place I never
like to lay down all my cards any sooner than I have to,
just on general principles. In the second place the Towers
tape seemed to pack the most potent punch for an ace in
the hole. Among the many possibilities it contained was
the additional motive it gave Paula herself. One thing to
be cheated on by a no-good louse of a husband for the
sake of tumbling with other women; something quite
different when the objective was to play backdoor buddies with another man. I didn't think it was stretching
plausibility too far to conjecture a woman of Paula's
beauty and temperament just might find such a revelation unbearable. Not to totally disregard her openness
and cooperation up to now, but still . . .

By the time all of this had been physically and mentally
sorted through and the cassettes were shelved back in
their hidey-hole, it was well past midnight. We spent another quarter hour employing the phone book and Paula's memory and a haphazardly maintained address log
out of Alex's desk to determine residences and/or contact

points for the names I'd given priority. This information I added to my notebook.

When we were finally through, I followed Paula into the kitchen, carrying my full ashtray and empty glass. I dumped the accumulation of squashed butts while she rinsed my glass along with hers and tipped them upside down on the drainboard.

When she turned away from the sink, drying her hands, I said, "It's awful late."

"I noticed," she said.

"I realize how tough this must have been for you. Took guts to put yourself through it. I appreciate it."

She looked as exhausted as I felt. But she still had things on her mind. She came across the kitchen and pushed herself against me. "I don't want to *hear* how goddamn appreciative you are. I want you to show me."

We kissed. More dueling tongues. Her hand slid up my thigh, then over. She cupped my balls through my pants. Her breasts were hot, alive things where they mashed against me. Her hand was hotter, even more alive.

"It's late as hell," I said when her mouth let mine breathe.

"So let's not waste any more time."

I held her at arms' length. "I don't think this is a good idea right now."

Her eyes darted down to the bulge her busy hand had produced. "Part of you seems to think it's a very good idea."

"That part of me isn't real strong on showing good sense."

She pulled away. "I see. The damn videos. You some kind of bluenose, now that you've seen me riding a couple other cocks you're too good to touch me?"

"Oh, for Chrissakes."

"For Chrissakes is right! Did you think I was a virgin last night? Did you think I learned those little games we played—games you enjoyed a great deal as I recall—in a fucking convent or something? None of that seemed to bother you then, you hypocrite."

"The tapes have nothing to do with it," I said, not altogether truthfully. "I'm in the middle of a case. An important case, goddamn it. I can't afford to get distracted, get too involved in anything else."

"Involved!? I'm not asking you to run away to the Fiji Islands with me, you egotistical jerk. All I wanted was a couple hours of your time—our time."

"All right, why was that so important? Look at you and look at me. I ain't exactly Paul Newman, baby, and I know it. But you, you could rub that bod against just about anybody you wanted and have them panting after you like a hound in heat. So why me? Could it be you're just a little too anxious to keep tabs on where my investigation takes me?"

"You bastard. After all I've done to help you."

"That's exactly my point."

"I don't believe this. What's next? Are you going to ask me if I have an alibi for the time Alex was shot?"

"Good idea. Do you?"

"Fuck you. Get out of here."

"You're developing some serious mood swings."

"Get out, I said."

"Jesus. Does it have to be one way or the other? I'm grateful for your help. Sincerely. My investigation wouldn't be off the ground without you and if I really thought you were a viable suspect I would have never gotten this close, no matter how beautiful you are. Can't we walk away from this with some kind of truce?"

She sighed wearily. "Just take your gratitude and go, okay? That's what you wanted, so do it."

For just an instant I saw a glimmer of vulnerability showing through. But it didn't last long and I wasn't sure there was enough there to risk trying to coax out again. At least not right then.

I got out of there.

All during the drive back to my motel I was more aware than I wanted to be of the empty-feeling places where her body had pressed so hard against me.

17

"Damn it to hell, Joe. That's a lousy thing to ask a guy to do."

Bomber wasn't happy. He stabbed at his scrambled eggs so hard I thought he might crack the plate.

"It'll be a helluva lot easier on him coming from you than somebody else," I pointed out. "Besides, you were saying last night how you wanted to get back in the thick of this again, do everything we could as fast as we could to clear Tommy. I've got some good leads here, Bomber. Abe is one of them. He's got to be checked out like all the others, until we find the one that breaks the thing open."

"What if none of them has anything to do with it? You just throw shit like this in people's faces and see what runs off?"

"That's the way it's done, pal."

"It stinks."

"If you're not up to it, go ahead on down to the gym and do your mugging and fight your pretend fights there. Leave the real battle to me, only don't practice on me with phony bullshit about how bad you want to 'nail' the killer then. One way or another, though, Lugretti gets talked to."

He stabbed at his eggs some more, jaw muscles working furiously as he chewed.

I tipped up my cup, drained the last of the coffee from it.

My phone call had gotten him out of bed that morning. We'd met at this diner—his choice, my treat—for breakfast. I'd told him about the videotapes while we were waiting for our orders to arrive. He hadn't been ready for it and he sure as hell hadn't been ready to be handed the task of confronting his old friend about having a role in them.

"Look," I said after a waitress had come by to refill our cups, "I sort of walloped you over the head with everything. I don't blame you for not wanting to be the one to talk to Abe."

He shook his head. "No, you were right the first time. It *should* be me. I guess I forgot for a minute what the bottom line is on all this." He scowled through the steam rising off the coffee he had poised to his mouth. "But you *do* tend to wallop a fella with stuff, you know."

I grinned ruefully. "Maybe you could give me a lesson or two sometime on being more tactful."

After wincing through a sip of the coffee, Bomber said, "I keep seeing Tommy's face, the way it looked last night after . . . well, you know. I can't get it out of my mind. That how it is with you?"

It was my turn to shake my head. "Not any more. I keep seeing a killer's face out there somewhere, laughing because he thinks he's getting away with something. That's what I'm staying focused on. I aim to change the fucker's expression."

While Bomber trudged off to deal with Abe Lugretti, I decided I'd warm up with what looked to be one of the less promising entries on the list.

The Hubners lived a block and a half down from the de Ruth house. Roger Hubner, I'd been told, was a slick-talking, slick-all-around successful new car dealer with a stereotypically dumb blond-type wife, Missy, who he con-

stantly and booringly called attention to as having "the
best set of headlights and chassis I ever handled." I'd
never had occasion to hear his spiel, but I had a pretty
good idea what he was talking about because Missy had
been one of Alex de Ruth's video playthings and I'd seen
her put to an impressive road test.

The morning was warm, the air hazy with humidity.
There was rain in the forecast. It was a little past nine
when I pulled up at the address Paula had provided for
her neighbors. I figured my timing was just about perfect;
a successful businessman ought to be out of the house by
now, and his "homemaker" wife likely wouldn't be gone
on any errands or shopping trips this early.

The house was what might be called a modernistic
ranch style: low-slung, plenty of brickwork and dark
wood, slabs of glass at odd angles. There was a brass
knocker on the front door in the shape of a surrey-topped
antique car. I guessed it was more for show than function,
especially since there was a bell button only a foot or so to
the side. I jabbed the button and heard chimes to the
refrain of "Fun, fun, fun, 'til her daddy takes her T-Bird
away" go rolling off inside.

I had no trouble recognizing Missy Hubner, even with
her clothes on. She had the kind of face that would always
be called "cute," never pretty or beautiful. Factor in a
puff of cotton candy blond hair and twin rows of daz-
zingly perfect teeth and it added up to your basic Perpetual High School Cheerleader model. She *had* to be
named Missy, or Muffy or Buffy or some such. It was in the
stars.

She stood in the opened doorway and hit me with a
couple hundred watts of smile. "Hi. What can I do for
you?" She had on a sleeveless, V-neck sweater and a pair
of stone-washed jeans. She wasn't in the statuesque
league of Paula de Ruth (too short and too close to being
plump), but the headlights and chassis looked to be in
very good working order all the same.

I used one of the oldest tricks in the book. Flashed my
P.I. ticket with the flair and bored confidence of a cop
showing his shield. "My name is Hannibal," I said, putting
the same slightly bored air in my voice. "I'm a detective

working the de Ruth homicide of a few nights ago. If you're Mrs. Hubner, I'd like to ask you some questions."

I could have flashed her a lottery ticket stub for all the attention she paid. It was the words that made the impression. "Homicide? My goodness. Uh, yes, I'm Mrs. Hubner. It was awful about Alex. Come in, won't you?"

The interior of the house was airy and well appointed. Lots of outside light pouring in through all that glass. On a cloudless day you'd need to wear sunglasses to keep from walking into things.

"Can I get you anything? Coffee? Orange juice?"

"All I need are a few minutes of your time."

We took seats in the living room, in overstuffed chairs facing one another over a low, gleaming coffee table.

"I'm not sure I understand this, Mister—er, Detective Hannibal. I mean, Roger and I aren't, like, suspects or anything are we?"

"We're just making sure all the bases get touched, Mrs. Hubner."

"But hasn't the killer already been arrested?"

"It's true an arrest has been made. But in a case as serious as this there are always ongoing lines of investigation."

"Oh."

"You *were* friends with the victim, the deceased—is that correct?"

"Yes. We were never real, real *close* friends, but being neighbors and all, the four of us got together from time to time. Alex bought his last car from my husband."

"Were you aware that Alex de Ruth had a reputation as being something of a ladies' man?"

She actually blushed. "Well, I have to admit I heard things. I mean, Alex *was* awfully good-looking and certainly flirtatious. But you never knew how serious he was, at least I never did. And, not to tell tales out of school, but I think it was sort of a two-way street with him and Paula, if you know what I mean."

I cleared my throat. "I want to be as delicate as I can be, Mrs. Hubner. It turns out Alex de Ruth took his flirting very serious. That fact has been pretty well documented. You see, we discovered a collection of videotapes—files, I

guess you could call them—of many of his conquests.
Were you aware of such a collection?"

She flushed with color again, a much deeper shade.
"What on earth kind of question is that? Why would I
know about a disgusting thing like a collection of dirty
movies?"

"Because you're on one of them, Mrs. Hubner," I said.

All of a sudden the color was completely gone from her
face. Her mouth hung open stupidly and her stare hung
on me for an uncomfortable length of time.

And then she shut her eyes tight and leaned forward
and threw up on the carpet between her feet. Needless to
say, it wasn't one of the reactions I'd been hoping for.

While she was being sick, I found my way to the kitchen
where I rummaged through the cabinets around the sink
until I found a bowl and a squeeze bottle of dish soap. I
filled the bowl with warm, soapy water and unsnapped a
roll of paper towels from the dispenser on the wall. Carried the whole works back into the living room.

I handed her a fistful of dry towels so she could blow her
nose and wipe her face, then held the bowl so she could
wet more towels and clean herself better. The moment
wasn't exactly a glamour highlight from a career pretty
short on glamour to begin with.

"Oh my God," Missy Hubner groaned. "Oh God, I'm so
ashamed."

I wasn't sure if she meant she was ashamed for tossing
her breakfast or for being in de Ruth's video collection.

When we'd finished cleaning the worst of her mess, I
took the bowl and the used towels back into the kitchen. I
washed my hands there. Returned with a glass of cold
water for Missy.

By the time she got that down, she'd regained enough
of her composure to continue. The first thing she asked
was, "Does my husband know?"

I shook my head. "Not from me."

"Will he have to be told?"

"Not necessarily. It depends on what else you're able to
tell me."

"What do you want to know?"

"Alex's videos: were you aware of them before this?"

She considered lying. I saw the thought play across her face. But she decided not to try it.

"I didn't know about any other tapes," she said. "But I knew about the one with me. Oh, yes, Alex made sure of that."

"How?"

"What do you mean?"

"How did Alex make sure you knew about your tape? Did he try to use it against you in some way, threaten to show it around?"

"The creep showed it to *me*, that's who he showed it to. He came by the house a couple days after . . . well, after what happened on the tape. It was in the afternoon, Roger was away at work, the kids still in school. Alex said he had something he thought I'd find amusing. He had a videocassette with him. He punched it into the machine over there, turned on the TV, hit the Play. When I saw what came on the screen, I almost got sick. You'd think I would have handled it better this time, wouldn't you, instead of worse?"

"So what happened after he played the video for you?"

"Well, I wanted to know how he got it naturally, demanded he give it to me so I could destroy it. He just laughed and said there were plenty more where that came from. He said I should be proud I came across so hot on the screen. He called me Miss Photogenic-Energetic, made a joke out of it. He said I'd better be sensible if I didn't want a lot of other people seeing what a great whore I'd make. Then he sat in that chair right there where you're sitting and told me . . . made me go down on him while he finished watching us on the tape."

Her voice had taken on a kind of hollow, wooden tone as she related the incident. Her eyes wouldn't look at me, were focused in a kind of glazed, faraway stare.

"So that was how he used the tape against you?" I asked. "For repeated sexual favors?"

She blinked at the questions, then shook her head. "No, only the once. I hardly saw him after that. I made up excuses for Roger and me not to attend the next couple of parties the de Ruths threw because it was at one of those damn things where he got to me in the first place. Roger was making ga-ga over Paula like he always did and Alex took advantage of me feeling sorry for myself, convinced me I should show my jerk hubby that two could play at that game. Got a couple extra drinks in me, then got me in the bedroom. You know the rest. Anyway, we didn't go to any more of their parties and pretty soon they quit having them. Rumors said they weren't getting along so hot. We bumped into them a time or two when we went out for dinner or to catch a show. Alex was always very proper, but he'd have a wink or a smarmy, I've-got-a-secret smile when no one else was looking. Once we were positioned in a crowded restaurant foyer in such a way that he was able to rub my bottom without anyone seeing the whole while the four of us stood there talking. I couldn't let anything show on my face. I think that's what the tape meant to him: It gave him a kind of power, a control over me that he could use any time he wanted. But *having* the power was actually more important to him than *using* it, you understand?"

"He never asked for a payment in money or anything like that?"

"Never. Roger and I live well but we're always right at the financial edge. I think Alex knew that, knew I couldn't have managed anything along those lines."

"When you heard Alex had been killed, did you think of the videotape?"

"You bet I did. Talk about waiting for the other shoe to drop. I even went over to the house to offer my condolences to Paula. I guess I was thinking . . . hell, I don't know what. Like the cassette would be right there on a bookshelf with my name on it and I could reclaim it as my property or something, right?" She winced at a connected thought. "Does Paula know about my tape?"

"She was the one who discovered the cache of videos, but I don't think she's viewed each of them," I said, glossing it as best I could to save her added concern.

The room around us got quiet. A kind of awkward emptiness settled in the air between Missy and me. I could feel it was time for me to leave.

I stood to do so. "Thank you for your time and your

candor, Mrs. Hubner. I'm sorry to have had to put you through it."

"And I'm sorry for my initial lack of control." She looked drawn, like someone who'd just broken a hard fever, but she managed an embarrassed little smile. "I assure you I don't usually greet guests in that manner."

At the door she touched my arm. "Detective Hannibal? What will become of the video with me on it?"

"I'll do everything I can," I said, "to see that all of the tapes not pertinent to the case are gotten rid of. That's the best I can promise."

She gave a tight nod. "That's fair. That's better than I had a little while ago."

I reached for the jangling instrument, pulled it to the side of my head and said, "Yeah."

It was a pay phone, one of those bubble-on-a-pole jobs that aren't worth shit for blocking out background noise but have made the old-fashioned booths all but extinct, ever since some artsy engineer some damn where group-sucked a bunch of brain dead board members into believing he had a "better" idea. Fifty years from now a new idea boy will probably sell a different boardful of suits on a visionary concept: *closed in* public phones to maximize privacy and minimize outside interference, and won't everyone just gush?

The voice shouting through the receiver right now, though, was strong enough to make conflicting noise a moot point. "Who the fuck is this!?"

"I yam what I yam and that's all what I yam," I said, then added "harf, harf, harf" in my best imitation of Popeye's throaty chuckle.

"You'll be laughing out your asshole if I ever find out who this is, wiseguy. What's this shit you told my secretary about wanting to market some kind of 'sports special' video I made for Alex de Ruth?"

"Ah, Mr. Ives," I said in my normal voice, "I think you know exactly what video—not to mention what special sport—I'm talking about or you wouldn't have taken time out of your busy day to return my call."

The fish I had on the line was one Brian Ives, general

manager at WMRQ, a Moline independent TV station. I'd gotten a call through to his personal secretary and had left my message, suggesting she get it to him ASAP along with the pay phone number where I could be reached for the next five minutes only. I'd smoked a cigarette while I waited. Because he, in the company of a marginally pretty young woman who happened to be married to his most popular sportscaster, was featured very prominently in one of Alex's videos, the fish rang back with thirty seconds to spare.

Ives's breath snorted angrily in my ear. In a barely controlled voice, he said, "All right what's the pitch? How much are you asking?"

"How much you got?"

He sputtered. "You expect *me* to set the price?"

I sighed. The guy sounded like a jerk, but that was no excuse for twisting it in, or for getting a kick out of it the way I was starting to do. "Ives," I said, "I'm no shakedown artist or blackmailer. My price is reasonable, probably more reasonable than you deserve. All I want from you is some time and information."

"What are you talking about?"

"I'm talking about talking. A dialogue, a discussion. You, me, and Mrs. Morrissey. I need to know more about the circumstances surrounding the videotape, what transpired concerning it between the point it was recorded and the point Alex de Ruth got killed."

"What kind of shit is that? You trying to rope me in on a murder?"

"Should I be? How bad did you want the tape?"

"Not bad enough to kill for it. If I had, we wouldn't be having this conversation, would we? Because I'd have the damn thing and you wouldn't."

I didn't like him sounding so smug. I said, "Maybe you fucked up. Maybe you killed de Ruth and then the tape wasn't where you could get at it. Maybe there was more than one copy. Those are the kinds of things we need to discuss."

"If I agreed to meet with you—and that's a big if— where might it be? And when?"

"As soon as possible. A public place: a bar or a restaurant. Your town, you name one."

He thought it over. "There's a place not far from here . . . the Green Galley. An out-of-the-way spot. A public place where you can have some privacy, if you get the picture."

"Sounds about right. The Green Galley in an hour, then."

"Now wait a minute!"

"You picked the place, I pick the time. You're a businessman, we'll 'do' an early lunch."

"I already have a luncheon appointment."

"Break it. I want Penny Morrissey there, too."

"How can I speak for Penny? I can't guarantee that on an hour's notice—"

"Ives," I cut in, "in addition to being her husband's employer, I've seen you and the lady do your imitation of a jigsaw puzzle with each other's body parts. I'd say those are pretty good indications you have some influence over her. Get her there."

I watched from the bar and let them sweat it out an extra ten minutes or so. This wasn't just a streak of meanness on my part, but rather a calculated softening-up tactic. I wanted their anxiety to override any degree of preparedness they might have built up, any two-on-one confidence they might be harboring. I wanted them edgy and uncertain, not cocky.

The Green Galley was set up like an old-fashioned country tavern. Living quarters upstairs, the business down. Bar and booths in one room, tables with real cloth tablecloths and softly glowing lamps in the other. Plenty of moody, shadowy corners where you could get lost for a little while even in the middle of the day.

Brian Ives and Penny Morrissey had chosen one of these. When I decided the time was right to make my move, I left the bar and walked over carrying my bourbon.

"I've got the yo-yo, who's got the string?" I said.

They both looked up, frowning. "Huh?" Ives said.

"Code words," I said, pulling out a chair and sitting

down. "We blew a great chance to set up some code phrases. You know, I say something like, 'The geese seem to be returning much slower this spring,' and then the right thing for you to reply is, 'That's because they're being extra careful so they don't quack up.' Like that."

"What the hell is he talking about?" Penny Morrissey wanted to know.

"Sometimes he thinks he's a funny guy," Ives said.

"Is he the one we've been waiting for?"

"I'm afraid so."

"I should have known. He *looks* like a thug."

I smiled at her. "You can never judge a book by its cover, Mrs. Morrissey. Take you, for instance—who'd ever guess just by looking at you how much you enjoy it doggie-style?"

She reached across the table and slapped me. She wasn't very good at it.

I smiled at her some more with the sting of the slap prickling the side of my face. "If I was the kind of person you think I am, that could have been a very expensive move on your part." I swung my gaze to Ives. "Since you're the bankroll end of the team, I'd caution your partner to be a little more polite."

"For God's sake, Penny," Ives said to her, "people are watching. Get hold of yourself."

She was a slender woman with thin lips and a narrow face made even more pinched-looking by thick blond hair hanging down straight on either side. Only her eyes, wide and expressive, saved her from seeming just skinny and rather plain. What those eyes were expressing in my direction right now wasn't meant to give me a warm feeling. But I could live with dirty looks as long as she kept a civil tongue in her head and her hands to herself.

"Look," Ives said, "can we try to do this like business people, like at least half-assed professionals?" He was imposing in a well fed, corpulent kind of way. He puffed up his bulk to make the request, in a manner he probably relied on to bully his way at board meetings and such.

But the Morrissey woman wasn't so easily cowed. "Can I help it if he looks like a thug?"

"Goddammit, Penny."

She held up a hand. "All right, all right. Businesslike. Professional."

A waitress showed up to see if we were ready to order yet. Ives kept it to another round of cocktails. He was a martini drinker and so, somewhat surprisingly, was Penny Morrissey; I signaled for another bourbon on the rocks.

After the fresh drinks had been delivered, Ives said, "Now. Let's start over. For openers, do you have a name, something we can call you?"

"Besides 'Mr. Thug,' you mean?"

"Please."

There was no reason for them not to know who I was. I handed over one of my cards.

"Joe Hannibal," Ives read. "Private investigations."

"We've all heard of his kind," Penny Morrissey said. "The sleazy, double-dealing private dick."

"Never mind that," Ives said quickly. "What matters is that he has an item, a commodity, if you will, of interest to us. Mr. Hannibal, what do you have in mind that can be to our mutual benefit?"

"I need to know more about the history of the 'commodity' in order to better determine how it might fit into a bigger picture."

"That bigger picture being the murder of Alex de Ruth?"

"That's right."

"That's a closed case," Penny Morrissey said.

"Not to everyone it isn't."

Ives said, "Am I to understand that this commodity—"

"Oh, for crying out loud, Brian," the woman cut in, "call it what the hell it is. It's a videotape, a dirty little record of a dirty little deed that's been hanging over our heads like a sword on a string."

Ives flushed, looking undecided as whether to be angry or embarrassed. He cleared his throat. "All right, the videotape then. Are there others?"

I nodded. "Matter of fact there are."

"I figured there would be. So you're trying to find out if and how de Ruth was using these tapes, is that it?"

"On the button. If it turns out he was keeping them to

himself, using them for nothing more than some sort of private gratification, then I don't have much. But if I find out he was pressuring people with them, using them for gain of any kind, then I have some alternative motives for his murder."

"Sounds like you're asking us to incriminate ourselves," Penny Morrissey observed. "Under those circumstances, we'd be damn fools to tell you if he *was* using the tapes against us."

"Not really. The tapes exist, and I have them. There's no getting around that. If you have nothing else to hide except that you were unlucky enough to get caught doing what you got caught doing, then you'd be damn fools not to take advantage of this chance to level with me. Besides, Mr. Ives' initial reaction and the fact you're both sitting here now indicate this isn't the first you're hearing about the tape, that you obviously were made aware of it prior to this. The only question is, how and why did de Ruth let you know?"

They cast sidelong glances at one another. Their eyes told each other to be careful.

Ives cleared his throat. "The how is simple enough. It was at another one of his and Paula's parties, not that different from any of the others, not that different from the one where—well, when he caught us. Always making references to that fancy bedroom of theirs, practically extending an invitation. Anyway, this next time Alex got me aside at some point in the middle of things and steered me into his study, told me he had some unique footage that I, as the head of a TV station, would surely appreciate. I get that kind of shit all the time, but Alex insisted. I guess I don't have to tell you what he played for me."

"And what was his point? What did he want?"

Ives tipped up his martini, then lowered it with a rattle of ice and glared into it as if it had betrayed him by being empty. "That was the weird part," he said, his eyes finding me again. "He didn't seem to *want* anything. Just for me to know he had the tape. He clapped me on the back after showing it to me and do you know what he said? He said, 'Every man's equal when their ass is hanging out,

Brian. Then it comes down to who's the biggest prick.'
That's all. As we went back out to join the party—I was in
sort of a daze—he said something about how it would be
nice if the sports segments of our newscasts would sometimes carry the results of the pro wrestling cards. But that
was almost like an afterthought, not an ultimatum or a
condition for me to meet."

"Were you at that party, Mrs. Morrissey?"

She nodded. "I was there."

"Did de Ruth approach you in a similar way?"

"Not at all. It was chivalrous Brian who couldn't wait to
pull me aside and whimper the bad news."

"Did de Ruth *ever* confront you about the existence of
the tape?"

"Never."

"And he never brought it up to me again either," Ives
said. "If he'd been making demands, asking for money,
that would have been, well, understandable. Something I
would've had some idea how to deal with. But this way
there was nothing. Just the knowing what he had, and the
waiting and wondering how he was going to try to put it
to use."

I understood the feeling. I was waiting and wondering
if this tail chase I was on was ever going to turn up anything I could sink my teeth into. I didn't find the pair
before me particularly likable, but nevertheless watching
them squirm on the hook of their past indiscretions
hardly ranked as preferred entertainment. "You just
throw shit in people's faces and see what runs off?"
Bomber had asked. Yeah, that's about the size of it. Sometimes I don't feel much better than what I'm shoveling,
but the motions come automatic after all these years so I
don't have to think about it as much.

"Waiting isn't exactly my strong suit," Penny Morrissey
said into the silence. She used the brightly colored, impractical little straw to poke at the ice cubes in her own
empty drink. "I haven't told anyone this, not even Brian,
but not so long ago, when the waiting was getting to me
pretty bad, I paid a visit to Alex. I asked him about the
tape, asked him flat out what his intentions were. I offered
him . . . things. Money. Myself . . ."

Ives looked pained. "My God, Penny."

She put one of her hands on one of his, patted it. "Don't look so crushed, darling. Mr. de Ruth wasn't having any. At least not that day. He was nice enough to inform me, though, that if he was ever in the mood, and I quote, for 'a ball-breaking ice bitch' he would be sure to let me know."

Her eyes bored into me. "The point is, Hannibal, Alex de Ruth was an evil man. Evil simply for the sake of being evil. That's what you should be concentrating on. I think he sought out wickedness in others not to exploit, but to embrace and to fuel himself, to add to his sense of power. In my own warped way I love my husband, as I believe Brian does his wife. If I'd thought Alex was a threat to my marriage or my happiness I might have considered killing him. But I didn't sense that. You won't have any trouble finding people who wanted Alex dead because they felt threatened by him, by what he knew . . . but don't limit the focus of your investigation only to his victims. Alex's evil was immense, which means he must have made immensely evil enemies. Don't ignore that possibility."

18

I found Bomber waiting for me at the BRW gym.
He was sitting backwards on a metal folding chair, thick forearms crossed in front of him, watching two female wrestlers trading slams and tosses up in the ring, working out a routine. One of the fighters I recognized as Ava, the black girl I had met yesterday in the company of the Kolchonsky brothers.

"You're late," Bomber grumbled over his shoulder as I walked up.

"Had myself what you'd call a full morning," I explained. "Ran on a little long."

"Get anywhere?"

I shrugged. "Learned some things. Not as much as I would've liked, but you take what you can get. You?"

"Oh, I had more fun than a barrel of fucking monkeys. Nothing starts my day off better than to dig up some dirt on an old friend and then go rub his nose in it."

"So what did you find out?"

He stood up. "We'll talk about it, but not here. You had lunch yet?"

"Matter of fact, no." We'd somehow never gotten around to that at the Green Galley.

"They tell me there's a place around the corner. Has the thickest burgers and greasiest onion rings in town."

"Cold beer to wash 'em down?"

"Plenty."

"Sounds like my kind of place. Lead on."

"Let me just touch base with Mel before I go," he said. "She decided at the last minute to add me and Paula to a card she's got put together for tonight, some burg down south. Wants to generate as much word-of-mouth hype as she can, I guess. I need to make sure I got the time and directions straight."

He headed off toward the offices.

The gym was far less crowded today than it had been yesterday. Aside from the gals in the ring, there was a clump of dedicated lifters over in the free weights area and a sprinkling of others on the various machines. That was it, twenty people tops.

Made it easy to decide where to focus my attention while killing a few minutes waiting for Bomber, at least. Never pass up an opportunity to do a little girl-watching, even stomping, kicking girls.

Trouble was, my timing was off. I'd no sooner settled onto the chair Bomber had vacated than the pair in the squared circle decided to call it quits. After exchanging "attagirl" pats on the back and some muttered final bits of shop talk, they climbed wearily out through the ropes. The one I hadn't seen before—a hefty dishwater blonde with legs like you'd hope for in your next order of drumsticks from the Colonel—angled away from me, trudging to where a robe and towel were draped over the end of a utility table. Ava, the sensual dark beauty, moved to a chair hung with similar garments nearer to where I sat. She aimed a brief smile my way as she shook out her mane of hair and toweled the sheen of sweat from her shoulders and throat.

"Hi there," she said.

" 'Lo," I responded.

"You're the private eye everybody's talking about, right?"

I grinned somewhat self-consciously. "I'm a private detective. Don't know how popular I am as a topic of conversation."

"Oh, you're hot. In the pro wrestling biz we're used to Nazis and mad Russians and various foreign terrorists, not to mention masked marvels and painted warriors and a whole assortment of bullies and crazies and gym rats. All of that is old hat. But a real live P.I. is a novelty."

"Well then," I said, "I'm glad I could add a spot of color to your otherwise drab landscape."

She laughed and thrust out her right hand. "I'm Ava Coltrane."

"I know," I said. "We sort of met yesterday."

"We did? Oh yeah, when I came to get Mike and Bob for their interview."

"That's right. And I'm Joe Hannibal, by the way."

"Technically speaking, Joe, when we met yesterday I wasn't me."

"You weren't?"

"No. I was Arabesque, harem girl for the Savage Sheiks."

"I see."

"And up in the ring just now I was The Pagan, or at least I was practicing for when I *am* her, like on the card tonight down in New Boston. Of course I'll be Arabesque part of the time down there, too."

If Bomber hadn't explained to me yesterday about the different roles she undertook for Big River, I might have thought she was a nut case. As it was, I found her immediately likable for her willingness to make light of this grunt and groan show she was a part of.

I said, "Sounds like you lead a complicated life—or should I say lives?"

She shrugged. "Most of the time I'm just plain little Ava."

Her present scant attire, displaying the tight roundness of her rump and the thrust of her high, small, perfectly coned breasts, in addition to the exotic beauty of her face, made it clear she was anything but plain. But I got the feeling she was fishing for a comment along those lines, so I passed.

"How long have you been this triple threat?" I asked instead.

"How long have I worked for Mel and Big River, you mean? Let's see. Little over a year. About fourteen months, I guess."

"So you must have gotten acquainted with Alex de Ruth and Tommy McGurk in that time?"

"Sure. But I didn't get as well acquainted with Alex as he would have liked—not as well as plenty of others did."

It was like she was reading my mind. I said, "So there's something to all these stories I'm hearing about Alex's prowess with the ladies?"

"Quite a lot to it."

"I don't get it. On the one hand everybody tells me what a unlikable jerk he was, on the other it's what a heavy scorer he was with babes. Back and forth."

She arched a brow. "One doesn't necessarily exclude the other, you know. Stop and think how many times you've seen somebody who's a genuine asshole at practically every other level be a hit with the opposite sex. It works both ways. Men are called cads or scoundrels or cocksmen, women are called man-eaters or just bitches. But no matter what they're called, they keep right on mowing down their targets, don't they?"

I wondered if she was speaking as a mower or mowee.

"The point is," she went on, "for anybody who gets that kind of reputation it almost becomes an asset. Say you're a girl and an Alex de Ruth makes a move on you. You've been warned, you've heard all the stories, you've made up your mind to be polite but cold. Firm. And then he turns out to be actually *nice*—gentle, witty, even makes jokes about this crazy 'rep' he has, how misunderstood he is. You start to sway. How could everybody be so wrong? Poor guy can't help it he's got drop-dead good looks that intimidate other men and turn on their women. He's a victim, see. A victim of other people's jealousies and dirty minds. And right about then, when he's got you at your weakest and most gullible, he senses it and—whammo!— the sonofabitch nails you."

"Came that close, uh?" I asked when she was through.

She made a face. "Closer than I like to think about. For damn sure closer than I ever admitted before."

"When was this?"

"Only a month or so after I started. Alex didn't waste any time."

"How did he treat you afterward, after your, er, near miss?"

"Distant. Chilly. About what you'd expect. I thought he might try to make trouble for me, but he didn't. At least not that I ever heard about."

"Was that something he'd do to girls who turned him down?"

A rueful smile. "From what I can tell, not a hell of a lot of them did. I figure that's maybe why I got away with it. Caught him off guard, caught him without a game plan for that contingency."

"What became of all of those conquests? Any ongoing romances develop?"

"No way. Alex was strictly interested in putting notches on the bedpost. A tumble or two and he was gone, off looking for fresh meat."

"Must have made for some devastation, some hard feelings."

"Not necessarily. All the participants went into it with their eyes open. Like I said, there were always plenty of warnings. And one tiny sliver of credit you had to give the bastard was that he was honest about being married, made no false promises, told no lies about planning to divorce his wife, no whining hard luck stories about how bad she treated him. He was right up front: All he was after was a little side action."

"That 'side action' must have put some strain on the marriage, regardless."

"Paula and Alex were split up at the time of the shooting, if that's what you mean. I don't know how much that was a result of his shenanigans or how much it had to do with . . . well, other things."

"Other things like Tommy McGurk?"

"Look, I'm willing to answer your questions but don't treat me as dumb as you're trying to act, okay? Everybody knows Paula is cooperating with your investigation, how much time the two of you've spent together over the past couple days. If you haven't got the straight of what went down with her and Tommy and Alex by now, then you're not much of a detective."

Her words shoved my eyebrows up. "Maybe compared to you I'm not," I allowed. "But then I'm also not three people rolled into one."

"I like to be aware of what's going on around me, that's all," she said somewhat defensively. "I was raised in a field hand's shack not a hundred miles from here. Spent the first ten or twelve years of my life with my head hung in shame, the curious guilt of being born poor. Finally decided to lift my head up, look for a way out. Found one. Been making sure to always look up and pay close attention ever since. It's my way."

"And not a bad one by any means."

"Doesn't leave room for a lot of surprises."

"Did it surprise you when Alex de Ruth got killed?"

"Yeah. Wow. That one caught me. Beaten up by a jealous boyfriend or husband, punched by somebody he'd insulted one too many times, any of those were overdue. But getting killed, getting shot to death . . ."

"Do you believe Tommy McGurk could have done it?"

"*Could* have done it? Anything's possible. But do I believe he did? —no way."

"Any better candidates?"

"That's one hell of a heavy-duty question."

"From you I expect a heavy-duty answer."

"There's the boyfriends, husbands, and fathers of girls who became notches on his bedpost. It'd be a long list."

"You also said something about people he insulted. He do a lot of that?"

"Only all the time. Cameramen, ring attendants, wrestlers who were out of shape or on a losing streak, rookies just getting started. And a lot of this would be right on the air during broadcasts or interviews. Hey, make no mistake, unless you were the chick he happened to be hitting on at the moment or someone in a position of power he figured might be of some use to him, Alex de Ruth was pretty much a twenty-four-hour-a-day prick."

Out of the corner of my eye, I saw Bomber returning.

Ava followed my glance.

"Your partner," she said. "He's a character."

"That he is. But don't underestimate him."

"Guess you and him have things to do. Guess that means our talk here is finished."

"Doesn't mean we can't pick it up again some other time."

"You coming to the matches tonight?"

"Hadn't really thought about it. I just heard about them a few minutes ago."

"You should. Be a good show. New Boston, that's down near where I grew up. You'd get to see me—well, The Pagan—win in front of a hometown crowd."

"You sound awful confident."

She grinned. "I read the script. Maybe you didn't know it, but you were watching part of the dress rehearsal a few minutes ago."

As Bomber drew close, she touched my arm, the grin suddenly gone. "Candidates, Mr. Hannibal?" she said. "Don't overlook the obvious just because of what it is. Nobody had more reason to want Alex dead than Paula."

19

Outside, the gray day had finally started leaking rain. A steady, cool drizzle that rinsed the rundown buildings and littered streets, giving them a fresher, cleaner look at least for a little while.

Bomber and I flipped up our collars and walked through the drizzle. Double-timed it down the block and around the corner to the bar with the burgers and onion rings.

Even in my hurry I didn't miss the Chevy parked at the curb across the street. It was new enough and sporty enough to stand out in this neighborhood like fresh paint in a junkyard. Dumb. I'd seen the car before, on and off in my rearview mirror during my drive from the Green Galley. That could have been coincidence. This wasn't.

The bar—no name, just a chipped Pabst Blue Ribbon sign hanging over the entrance—was warm and dry, filled with the tangy smells of alcohol and disinfectant riding under the heavier odors of cooking grease and cigarette smoke. There were a half dozen customers in the place, all seated at the bar. One of them was a faded redhead with equally faded green eyes that followed

Bomber and me through the door. She could have been a hooker, could have been just looking; bored, on the watch for some excitement to walk into her life. Her face didn't say whether or not she thought we might be it. Nobody else paid us any particular attention.

We took a booth near the far end of the room. I sat facing the door. Bomber plopped in across from me.

The bartender, a tall, pear-shaped guy with a scraggly goatee and forearms like beer kegs, called over to us. "What can I get you gents to drink?"

Bomber called back, "A couple beers. Bud." When the barkeep asked "draft or bottles?" I answered quickly "bottles." Bomber frowned at that departure from habit, but didn't pursue it. He had other things on his mind, things he wanted to get to.

After the pear-shaped guy had brought over our beers and left again to fill our food orders, Bomber said, "Want me to go first?"

I swallowed some Bud. "You want to get it over with, don't you?"

He grunted. "I wanted it over with before I ever started."

Past his shoulder, two new customers came in. A couple of huskies, one slightly taller and trimmer than the other. The bulkier one had on a checkered sport coat that looked immediately out of place here. It hadn't stood out quite so bad in the new Chevy, visible through the rain-pebbled glass. Dumber and dumber. Too much so to be greatly alarmed about, but not enough to ignore. At least they'd had the sense to follow us in, make sure we didn't double-door them.

"Okay, so I went to see Abe," Bomber said as the newcomers took seats at the bar. The redhead gave them the same looks she'd given Bomber and me, got the same nothing in return. They were too busy pretending not to be taking notice of me to notice her. Bomber was saying, "I didn't take a lot of time with it, couldn't see any way to sort of ease up to it gentle. So I took a page out of your book and just clobbered him with it."

"Sometimes it comes to that no matter how much time you take," I told him.

"Uh-huh. When I told him we came across this video-tape, part of a collection, had him and a young girl in it, his first reaction was to take a swing at me. Try to clobber me back. After we'd danced around that, he went to the opposite extreme. Sat down and started blubbering like a baby."

Bomber paused to heave a big sigh. Took a long drink of his beer, sighed again. What he'd had to put his old friend through was mirrored on his own face.

Without looking at me, watching instead the bubbles feed into foam through the dark glass of his bottle, he continued. "To understand what comes next, you have to know a little more about Abe. He was married once, see. Married late, to a stout little woman named Maisie. Homely as a footprint in the mud, she was, but so sweet and nice it made you clean forget about that round little mutt face of hers, and so devoted to Abe it made you ache for wanting somebody to love you that much. The two of them together were something special, something you just wanted to be *around*, you know?"

"Anyway," Bomber went on, "just shy of their fifth anniversary, Maisie came down with bone cancer. No treatment, no hope, the doctors said. In six months she went from two hundred pounds to eighty-seven. Pain all the time, suffered awful. I shouldn't have to say how hard it was on Abe. Ripped the guts out of all of us. When she went, it was a blessing. Right up to the end, though, her main concern was Abe, never herself. 'Take care of him,' she'd tell everybody who came to see her. 'Look out for him when I'm gone.' Like she knew something. What it was, Abe took to drinking heavy after she died. For awhile we tried to control him by using her name—you know, 'What would Maisie say if she saw you like this?' But that never worked for very long because that was the whole thing, what he was trying to drown was the pain that Maisie wasn't there to see him at all. He finally just went deeper with it. Started doing his drinking in private. Alone. That's when the pain got him, that's when he dealt with it. Been like that for a number of years now. He functions okay as long as you don't get him too early in the morning. He isn't hurting anybody but himself and it looks like the only way he can keep going, so the rest of us decided to leave it be, pretend not even to know."

He paused to tip up his bottle. I had some with him, my eyes making a busy sweep under my raised forearm. The guys from the Chevy were nursing mixed drinks and watching a car race on the TV playing behind the bar, when they weren't sliding glances in my direction.

"What we *really* didn't know," Bomber continued, "was this thing Abe developed for younger women. Girls. I don't mean underage, not babies, but young *looking*. That's the way he described them. Said whenever he tried to meet women his own age he couldn't help thinking of Maisie, like he was cheating on her, on her memory. Couldn't make things work. So he started concentrating on young stuff. Strictly for release, not relationships. He was willing to pay."

I could see what was coming. I helped Bomber along with it. "And Alex de Ruth found out."

Bomber rolled the half-empty bottle of Bud in his big hands, wrenching it like he wished it was de Ruth's neck. "Yeah, the sonofabitch found out," he said. "Pounced on it like a cat on a bug. Seeking out another person's weakness and turning it into his own strength, that was his thing according to Abe."

I nodded. "Fits with a lot of what I've heard."

"He set up the bit with the girl in the video. Brought her to one of his parties, sicced her on Abe. Afterwards, after he had it on tape, de Ruth trotted out papers proving the girl was underage."

"Did he put the package to any use or did he just wave it under Abe's nose to watch him grovel?"

"No, he put it to use. After he'd sweated Abe, humiliated him, made him beg, de Ruth suggested ever so casually that Abe ought to think about cutting back on his work load at BRW. All of this was a while ago, see, shortly after Alex and Paula arrived on the scene here. De Ruth hired out as a backup announcer to Abe, who'd been top dog at the mike for years. He was no spring chicken any more, not in the best of health with his weight and his drinking, but I remember how it caught everybody by surprise when he went to Mel and told her he wanted to start taking it a little easier, drop down to color commentary, maybe a special interview here and there, not much else."

"Mel went along with it that easy?"

"She thought it was what Abe wanted. Besides, the new guy—de Ruth—was already coming on strong, getting positive fan reaction, looking sharp whenever he was on the air. Everything was in place, no hassle, all she had to do was switch them around, let Abe start drawing a little slack, bump de Ruth up to lead spot."

"De Ruth use the tape on him any more?"

"Wasn't that enough?"

Yeah, I thought grimly. Enough to give Lugretti a festering, boil-hot motive for murder.

Bomber pulled his Bud down closer to empty. "But there's more."

The pear-shaped bartender showed up with our food. Steaming heaps on two thick platters which he deposited in front of us along with a handful of paper napkins and shakers of salt and pepper. Bomber and I took turns with the shakers, doctoring the fare to our individual tastes.

"Turns out," Bomber said around a mouthful of juicy burger, "it was Abe who tried that break-in at the de Ruths, cracked away the closet panel that caught Paula's eye and ended up leading her to the cache of videos."

"*Tried* the break-in?" I said.

"He chickened the rest of the way out," Bomber explained. "He picked an afternoon he knew Paula would be busy with her sister-in-law, the one up from Texas for the funeral, and got into the house and into the bedroom and found the hollow-sounding area behind the closet. Wasn't hard to figure that much out after seeing the angle the video was shot from. He got as far as prying on the closet wall, trying to find the opening. When that piece of paneling broke away, that's what finally spooked him off. He said it sounded loud as a cannon shot. That, on top of the way his heart had been hammering the whole time already, convinced him half the neighborhood must have heard him by then, must know he was in there. He couldn't finish it. Panicked and ran the hell out."

I shoved a couple curves of onion ring into my mouth

after the bite of hamburger I was working on. You had to believe it, I decided. Number one, Lugretti wouldn't have had to admit to that part at all. Number two, the tape involving him had been left behind. If you've ever been in a break-in situation, you understand how every tiny sound seems magnified, every floor creak, every drawer rasp, how your nerves can pump them up until you're ready to believe they are loud enough to be heard a dozen blocks away.

"The existence of that tape must have been working on him pretty hard," I said, remembering how I had sensed that first night at Lori's that he was holding something back.

Bomber nodded. "For a long time. Once de Ruth was dead, all Abe could think about was getting his hands on it, stopping anyone else from finding out."

There was the kicker. *Once de Ruth was dead.*

"How did you leave him?" I asked Bomber.

He rolled his big shoulders in a shrug. "Fair, I guess. In a way I think it must have been a relief for him to have it come out. At least it's in the hands of somebody who isn't going to gouge him some more, isn't threatening to go public. It's done. And he's got the wrestling to occupy him, the matches tonight and the big ones coming up. He's too much of a professional to fold right now, to let BRW down. He'll make it okay."

We chewed for a while in silence.

Over on the end of the bar, the two guys from the Chevy were starting to look fidgety.

Bomber killed the rest of his beer, frowned at the empty. "Shit. Should've had that barkeep bring us another round when we had him over here."

I slid out of the booth, stood up. "Let me chase us a couple of fresh ones," I said.

I carried our empty bottles over to the bar, plunked them down, signaled for reinforcements. Down the way, the guy in the checkered sport coat and his buddy were concentrating mightily on an underarm deodorant commercial that had interrupted the race on TV.

The bartender handed me a new pair of Buds, foaming slightly from the action of being uncapped. I took these

back to our booth, informing Bomber loudly from a couple steps away, "While I'm up, I think I'd better go see a
man about a horse."

He rolled his eyes above the mouthful of onion rings he
was chewing as if to say why the hell tell him about it?

I leaned over to set his beer in front of him and, in a
much lower voice, said, "Do you remember when Eddie
the Sleeve's thugs had Lori hostage in that sleazey motel
room that time, how you took out the front door when we
went in after her?"

"Huh?" he said.

"In about three minutes," I said in tight, "follow me
into the bathroom that same exact way."

I straightened up and left him with that "huh?" look
still on his face. He'd figure it out. I went down the narrow hall indicated by an arrow on a hand-lettered sign
that said Rest Rooms. Behind me, I could hear the growl
of race cars revving on the TV again. If I was right,
Checkered Coat and his pal wouldn't be pretending to
pay attention to that anymore.

At the end of the hall I pushed through a door marked
Stallions, the letters burned fancily onto a chunk of
varnished wood shaped like a horse's head. On the other
side an identical piece of wood was lettered Mares. I
wondered how many thousand drunks had come down
that hall over the years and whinied and pawed the floor
at sight of those plaques, trying to be funny. Opposite
ends of the horse.

The bathroom was a big square room, surprisingly
clean smelling and looking. It had recently been redone, I
decided. Apple green walls, white tile on the floor. There
were two urinals, a booth, a sink with a stainless steel
mirror. Also a row of condom vending machines and one
of those stupid hot air blowers for drying your hands.

I walked over to the far urinal, hitched up close, got
situated. Got a satisfactory stream going, burbling nicely
into the bright plastic Sani-Gard. On the newly painted
wall in front of me some wiseguy had already scrawled:
Why are you looking up here for a joke when you've got
one in your hand?

If he only knew.

I heard the door open behind me. The scrape of shoes on the tile.

I didn't have to look around. I knew who it would be. I braced myself.

Making your move on a guy standing at a urinal is one of the oldest tricks in the book. In New York City I hear they've developed it into practically a whole separate art form of mugging. Something instinctive with us guys, when we've got our peter in hand, for whatever reason, the last thing we're able to think about is letting go. Not to fight, not to run. Our priorities take on a completely different order. Just one more way the damn thing can get us in trouble.

I turned my head to one side, hoping to avoid a broken nose. Did it just in time.

A thick forearm crashed heavily onto the back of my neck, angled so that it also landed across my right ear. The left side of my face slammed hard against the wall and was held there. In the same instant a hipshot with some big bastard's full body weight behind it thudded into the small of my back, bowing me sharply inward, driving me into the hard, cold wrap of the urinal, pinning my arms there.

It was neatly done, you had to give them that. Maybe the two jerks couldn't hang a tail worth shit, but they knew how to throw their beef around. It occurred to me that I might have underestimated them, that the plan I had rolling might not be such a hot one.

The one who'd slammed into me held me expertly. A pair of hands—the other one's—started patting me down, rummaging the pockets he could get to, tugging at my shirt.

"I told you he wouldn't have it on him." The voice of the one holding me, his mouth close to my ear.

"Had to make sure." His partner.

A pause. Feet scraping on the floor, positioning. Then a fist cracked into my ribs. It wasn't a hard punch, too awkward the way it had to be thrown around the guy pinning me. But it bit in painfully and knocked some air out nevertheless. An attention getter.

"Where is it?" A demand from the puncher.

"Where's what?" I grunted. "What's this all about?"

Another shot to the ribs. "Wrong answer," Puncher warned.

"Jesus, I don't know what you're talking about," I insisted.

"Don't waste time," Holder growled in my ear. "You know damn well what we're after—the tape."

"What tape?"

Fist to the ribs again. "Think you're as tough as you are stupid, don't you, asshole? We'll get it out of you one way or another—hard or easy."

"Okay," I said, trying to catch my breath. "The tape. Now I remember. Yeah. I must have left it up your mother's dress after I got done—"

They doubled up on me for that. Puncher swung another one into my side, Holder lifted his arm and re-slammed it across my neck and ear. My cheekbone skidded on the wall.

Fuck, how long had it been? Could Bomber tell time? Maybe I should have told him to wait only two minutes. Or one.

Speak of the devil. I heard the latch snap like a rifle shot and then the back side of the swinging door whap wallboard a micro-second later. Beautiful noise.

An instant of diverted attention. I felt the one pinning me go rigid, his body twist slightly, his pressure against me release momentarily.

That's what I'd been waiting for. All I needed.

I butt-bumped him a half step off, pivoted, swung my right hand around and up. In the hand I clutched a beer bottle—empty now, but full when I'd sneaked it in to hold in front of me and start pouring measuredly down the urinal drain to create the proper sound effects for the arrival of my visitors. A handy club now, one I uppercutted into the throat of the slob who'd had me pinned. I thumped it solidly under the ridge of his jaw, not a larynx crusher but a devastating blow all the same. He wouldn't be able to turn his head for weeks. It knocked him to one side, off his feet and down.

Still holding my bottle club, dropped into a fighter's crouch, I swung my eyes and body for Puncher, the guy in the checkered sport coat. But there was nothing for me there anymore. Bomber had read the situation quickly, known to do more than just kick open the door and wait for applause. He had Puncher in a headlock—a *real* headlock—twisting him down to his knees, grinding. I could hear neck vertebrae crackling.

A glance back told me Holder was out of contention. I moved quickly to where Bomber was at work.

"Not a lot of time," I said. "I need him under control but able to talk."

He jerked Puncher upright by the hair of his head, slipped around behind him, pulled one arm back and up in a hammerlock, hooked the other one in a half nelson. Puncher's face was nearly as white as the tile on the floor, all the blood squeezed out of it. He hung in Bomber's grasp like a scarecrow on a rack.

I reached out, smashed my bottle on the edge of the sink. Stepped in close then, hooked one of Puncher's legs under my left arm, cranking it high while I stood on his opposite foot. I pressed the jagged maw of the broken bottle into his wide open crotch.

"Now it's your turn, asswipe," I said through my teeth. "Only I won't be near as patient or gentle as you two fuck-ups were."

He worked his mouth, his tongue flicking out dry and pink against the stark white of his face. His bulged eyes were locked on my hand between his legs. "G-God," he sobbed.

"Who sent you after me!?" I wanted to know, letting him have a twist of the bottle for emphasis.

He gave it up in a rush. "Ives. Brian Ives. W-We work security for him at the station. He said you were a blackmailing b-bastard, causing him a lot of grief. Said you had a videotape. Paid us extra to f-follow you after you had lunch with him. Said bring the tape back whatever we had to do."

Just like that.

All of a sudden the big bartender was in the doorway. "What the fuck!" he roared. "What are you sonsabitches doing in here?" He was waving a baseball bat. Not one of those miniature jobs either. This one looked the size of a small tree.

I let go of Puncher's leg and stepped back. Dropped what was left of my bottle into the sink, held out my empty hands. Bomber released his holds, too. Puncher slid to a puddle.

"Couple of goddamn faggots," I said to the barkeep, improvising fast, indicating the two guys on the floor. "Tried to corner me there in the stall and hobbyhorse me. Lucky my buddy came to check. What the hell kind of place you running here anyway, mister?"

The bartender's brows furrowed, two wooly horns butting together above his eyes. "Now wait a minute. I never saw those two before today. Just like I never saw you two."

"It wasn't us two you should have been worrying about," I said indignantly.

Some of the other customers were crowded into the hall behind him. I heard one of them say, "It was the one in the checkered coat I bet. I thought I saw him eyeballing me funny when he was at the bar."

Somebody snickered. "Yeah, but it was a different kind of balling he was after."

"Fucking queers," somebody else grumbled.

The bartender held up a hand and said to everybody, "Look, I don't hold no truck with their kind either. Damn sure not in my place. But don't think I'm going to stand by and let any of you bust them up. We'll get them out— run 'em the hell out—and that'll be the end of it, you hear? I don't want no goddamn NAACLU or some shit coming down on me."

A general rumbling from those in the hall.

"Ought to run them out on the end of that ball bat."

"No, they might like that—might try to bend over and stop quick, get it?" Nasty laugh.

"Goddamn fucking queers."

Bomber and I stood back to make room for the group of regulars, let them proceed with kind words and understanding to escort Puncher and Holder from the premises. Pretty soon it was just us and the bartender standing there in the john.

He gave us the fisheye for several beats. Then he said to me, "I've been gay—the closet variety, because of ass-holes like you and the bunch that just marched out of here—for thirty years. There's two things I'd like to know. Number one, what makes you think anybody would *ever* want to rape your ugly ass? Number two, how the fuck do you 'hobbyhorse' somebody?"

20

I cradled the phone hard, hanging up on Brian Ives in mid-sputter. He was trying to tell me how sorry he was, how he'd arranged for his security goons to follow me before we'd met in person, before he understood what I was really about, but by then it had been too late to call them off. He sounded sincere, nerves jumping in his voice. My message to him had definitely been sincere: I told him I thought he was too fucking dumb to be a killer so I didn't intend to waste any more time on him, but if I caught a whiff of his goons again or if I heard he was even wondering out loud about my business, I would come around and put him in the hospital before sending copies of his tape to every piss-ant news team in the country. He'd be dealing with the repercussions while in traction.

I made the call from my motel room. After hanging up, I lit a cigarette and lay back across the bed. I had no lights on in the room. I blew smoke at the dim backdrop of the ceiling and listened to the rain fall outside.

Inside my head parts of the case were rolling around, spinning like the smoke patterns on the ceiling. Pieces of a puzzle I was mentally shuffling, trying to arrange into a pattern that would tell me something I didn't already know.

I thought about what I had, what I did know. It mostly boiled down to a handful of conclusions based on instinct, gut feelings. I hadn't really ruled anybody out or in beyond some question of doubt. The single absolute was the collection of videotapes. If we turned them over to the cops they'd be forced to reopen their case, forced to deal with a number of other suspects packing motives at least as strong as Tommy McGurk's. But that would be a whole other can of worms, a can that would scoop up people like Abe Lugretti and Missy Hubner and roll them in dirt for the public before the sifting was done. And the heightened activity level would alert the killer, make him/her more careful, cause them to burrow deeper. The way it stood now the bastard could afford to be a little smug; everybody seemed fooled except this hardheaded private eye who was going around bumping into dead ends.

I lay on my back feeling restless but undecided what move to make next.

I considered calling Nicholas Hatfield, seeing if he had anything for me. Decided it was too soon.

Bomber would be back at the BRW gym by now, with Paula, working out a routine for tonight's spur-of-the-moment match. Nothing for me there.

There were more video stars on my list left to contact, but I felt like I'd burned a day's worth of that string already. Couldn't get fired up for another run at it yet this afternoon.

I thought about Penny Morrissey's ominous statement: *Alex's evil was immense, which means he must have made immensely evil enemies.*

I rolled off the bed after awhile, squashed out the last half inch of my smoke in the ashtray. I snapped on the bathroom light, washed my face and combed my hair. Traded my damp shirt for a fresh one, pulled a jacket on over it. Outside, in the rain, even the rust spots on my Honda looked slick and shiny.

I drove to the McGurks.

* * *

Tommy was home alone.

He must have seen me drive up, was standing with the front door held open for me when I came puddle-hopping from car to house.

He was unshaven, looking somewhat haggard but not too bad.

The clock on the living room wall said three thirty. *Wheel Of Fortune* was playing on television.

"Am I interrupting anything between you and Vanna?" I asked.

Got a wisp of a smile out of him. "She'll get over it," he said.

He motioned me toward a chair but I didn't feel like sitting down. I still felt restless, needed to prowl. I wasn't sure why I'd come here.

"Bomber called a little while ago," Tommy said. "For the second or third time today. Checking up on me, I guess, after last night. I think he thinks I might try to blow my brains out."

"He got reason?"

He shrugged. "Everybody thinks about it sometime or other, don't they?"

"Maybe everybody thinks about it. Only chickenshits do it."

He walked over by the window. "Don't be so sure. I used to think that way, too. But I'm not convinced anymore it's a matter of courage, maybe just a matter of smartening up. You reach a point where you realize dying isn't so bad. It's living that kills you."

I watched the water trickling down the other side of the window glass make squirming shadows on his face. "That's a crock, and you know it," I said.

He sighed. "This damn rain don't help, I know that much."

He stood watching the rain. I stood watching him. The eyes on the faces in the big oil painting that dominated the living room—Tommy, Lori, and Tommy Jr. from that happier time—tracked both of us.

Eventually he turned away from the window.

I said, "So where's Lori?"

He made a catchall gesture with one hand. "She's at

some board of realtors meeting somewhere. They get together every few weeks, chew the fat, pretend it helps business. No telling how long she'll be gone."

It crossed my mind that she must not have picked up on the depth of his mood or she wouldn't have left him alone. I said, "Did Bomber tell you I had some luck digging, came up with a handful of leads that look pretty promising?"

"Yeah, he said something about it."

"You want a rundown?" I'd decided I could tell him and Lori about the videos as long as I didn't attach any names for the time being. They were, after all, my clients.

Tommy pondered the question for what seemed like too long. When he responded, it was with a question of his own. "You know what I really want, Hannibal?" He went ahead without waiting for me to say anything. "I've got a couple fifths of Jack Daniels Black Label in a cupboard in there and I've got one hell of an urge to take them for a ride, play rock and roll music till the windows rattle, and get smashed out of my gourd. What I need from you is to either talk me out of it or go along and help keep my sorry ass out of more trouble. Whatya say?"

My turn to ponder. "Daniels Black, uh?" I said at length.

He nodded, starting to grin.

"If I talked you out of it," I mused, "then it would just keep setting in there going to waste. Seems a terrible shame. I don't see how I could let myself be a party to anything as irresponsible as that."

I drove. Tommy drank. We found an all-oldies station on the car radio, cranked up the volume, and played the shit out of rock and roll.

We sang along with some of the songs. Tommy more than me because he was the one drinking. Mostly. I had a nip now and then. The Jack Daniels went down wickedly smooth, the songs came out rough and raucous.

It was primitive, I guess, maybe even childish. The kind of thing you're supposed to outgrow, especially in this new climate of temperance that has gripped the country. Everything in moderation, everything—booze, sex, food

—that used to be so much fun, that we used to couldn't get enough of. And who's to say they're wrong, these extollers of restraint? Not me. Christ knows I've woken with enough hangovers, tried to focus bleary eyes on enough morning-sorry one-night stands, done enough puke pushups off enough toilet bowls to question the wisdom of it all without any outside influence. But neither was *this* wrong. Not tonight. It felt too right, looked too right seeing Tommy laugh and sing, seeing the trouble slide off his face. Even if only for a little while. Some prices are worth paying.

Darkness descended on us, making me glad I'd left the hurriedly scribbled note for Lori on the kitchen table.

The Honda's headlight beams bit into the rainy night like yellow fangs.

At some point the radio volume got knocked back and the snatches of singalong turned into talk. Not talk about anything in particular, not at first. Just rambling observations and opinions, reminiscences. Cars we'd driven and/or owned (segueing from yet another crack at my Honda), women we'd loved and lost or never attained at all, places we'd been, jobs we'd held, chances we'd blown. Old jokes. A smattering of politics (more jokes).

Tommy talked for a while about wrestling. His basic love of the sport, dating back to his high school days. The raw attraction of the one-on-one competition, the simple grace to be found in its leverage and balance, the explosive excitement of the power moves. He spoke of his own distaste for the show biz aspects at the pro level, then lamented over the perceived raw deal dished out by the sports media and others willing to applaud the equally choreographed routines of gymnasts and skaters yet deny even the slightest nod toward any athletic prowess on the tights-and-turnbuckles scene. We both marvelled at the game's phenomenal rise in popularity during the past decade, even though, in Tommy's estimation, it came at the cost of using some of the most strident sideshow antics ever.

Sometimes you're only as drunk as you want to be. When we eventually worked our way around to his current state of affairs, Tommy downshifted from the liquored-up overdrive he'd been running at. His voice turned low and steady, his eyes became intense glints.

He started out with his reentry into wrestling, how it simultaneously excited and revolted him—the feeling of turning whore, of selling out to the side of the game he'd always detested, serving as an interfering, rule-breaking manager to the ladies' champion. But overriding everything was the feeling of being able to contribute that it returned to him. Contribute again not only to the sport he loved, but to his marriage and his life. Contribute again after the bleak years following the accident that had robbed him of his son and the use of his leg. Bleak years during which he had done little but feel—and cause—misery.

"You know, Hannibal," he said, "you can deal with almost anything when the boundaries are clear. When you know who to hate, who to love, who to trust. But who was I supposed to blame for that accident? Who was I supposed to hate, aim my anger at? Myself? God? I wasn't driving recklessly, I wasn't not paying attention to conditions, the car wasn't poorly maintained. But no matter. Boom. My son is gone forever, my leg is fucked up. My life is turned upside down and spilled out and I don't know how to put it back again. And if *I* didn't know who to blame, what about Lori? What was she feeling? She wasn't there, it was me behind the wheel. How could she *not* blame me? There was never anything said, never anything in her actions, but once I got the notion in my head it didn't matter; I couldn't shake it. Add to that my physical problems . . . you ever try making love to a woman on only one pin, with one of your goddamned legs flapping around useless, like somebody'd nailed a sack of bones to your hip?"

There was, of course, no answer to that.

He went on. "Going back to work for BRW restored my sense of worth as a person. Getting involved with Paula restored my sense of worth as a man. Sounds lame, I know, especially saying it out loud. But there it is. Hell, I never loved Paula. I don't think either of us ever spoke the word when we were together. All we did was . . . well, use one another to each get through something else."

"Now what you need to do," I said, "is get through the rest of it. Only this time use the person you *do* love to help you through, the one who's been there for you all along, except in your own misconceptions. Talk to Lori, tell her the truth. Everything. Exactly the way you've just told it to me."

We'd long since driven out of the city. The rain had let up and overhead I could see broken patches of starlight showing through the dispersing, rapidly shifting cloud cover. For a while we'd rolled south and west along the river, crossing to the Iowa side at Muscatine, where we turned and aimed north. Overshot the Quad Cities to the west, following no particular course, gradually angling back toward the river on narrow blacktop roads that twisted and curved through the sodden countryside. Recrossed the Mississippi, swollen and angry looking far below, a hungry black tongue lapping up the storm. The more serious talk unfolded as we cut east into Illinois and it was on this stretch that Tommy also began suggesting some specific turns, an unspoken destination obviously in mind.

The cemetery covered a high, tree-fringed knob on the northwest edge of Dixon, a community of about fifteen thousand straddling the Rock River, its main claim to fame as the boyhood home of one Ronald Reagan. At last report, the former president's suspiciously selective memory still included this quiet burg on the shrinking list of things he seemed to think it was safe to recollect.

Tommy directed me up the looping gravel drive, to a spot near the crown of the knob, on the back side. I stopped when he told me to, cut the Honda's engine. In the wake of the storm, the night was so still and quiet you could hear the soft spattering of residual droplets of rain working their way down through the leaves on the trees. On all sides, the still-wet tombstones shone dully in the emerging starlight. Away in the distance to the north I

could see the strobelike pulse of the lights on the cooling
towers of the Byron nuclear plant. About thirty miles
beyond lay Rockford, my home base. So near and yet so
far.

Tommy got out of the car. I did likewise.

He leaned back against his closed door and was still,
eyeing a row of tombstones as if part of him wanted to go
over to them but another part was uncertain. I walked
around the car and stood beside him.

"Over there," he said, pointing to a smaller marker
near the end of the row, "is where our son is buried. Back
down the hill a ways is where Lori's parents are, that's
how we came to chose this place. Our plots—Lori's and
mine—will be there beside Tommy junior."

His words sent a strange sensation running through me,
a kind of mild panic, a sudden feeling of vast loneliness—
the realization that *I* had no eternal resting place picked
out. To say nothing of anyone to share it with.

"When we put our baby in the ground there," Tommy
continued, "it was like we buried a lot of the good parts of
my life with him . . . my luck, my good fortune. Whatever you want to call it. Seems like everything has been
mostly one shit brick after another ever since." He
paused, rolled his head to look at me. "That's why I came
here on the night de Ruth was shot. After I couldn't find
him, after I made an ass of myself at his place . . . I came
here. I sat back and had a hard think on it and I finally
decided that here was where my life had taken a wrong
turn—at least the symbol of that—so here was where I
had to come to try to get it back on track. You see, Hannibal, I'd never returned here since the funeral. Lori came
all the time. She'd ask me, beg me, and I wanted to, I
really wanted to . . . but I never could. Eventually, of
course, she quit asking. And that became one more problem between us."

I thought of that evening we'd talked in his backyard,
when I hadn't been able to pin him down about where
he'd driven to on the night de Ruth was killed and how I'd
felt he was hiding something. This explained it.

As if reading my thoughts, he said, "I held off saying

anything because . . . well, because I felt sort of silly about it. I mean, coming here with the crazy notion of swapping my bad luck for good. Then, too, I thought it might hurt Lori that after all this time I came here without her. Besides, there still wasn't anything about it that could establish me an alibi—nobody I ran into, nobody who'd remember seeing me."

All I could do was shake my head.

"Let me show you," he said, finally moving toward the marker. I followed him over and we stood looking down at the modest stone slab. On the grass in front of it lay a handful of wilted, wind-scattered dandelion stems, petals long since turned to milkweed puffs and blown away.

"I picked those and put them there when I came," Tommy said, his voice discernibly huskier than it had been. "Like most kids, I suppose, dandelions were the first flowers Tommy junior paid any attention to. When they started showing up on the lawn, he'd pick a handful every day and bring them in to his mom. When he was real little, I remember, he couldn't pronounce the word flower, got the 'l' screwed up, said it like 'fowler.' So he called dandelions 'fowler-lions.' 'Look at all the pretty fowler-lions I picked for Mom today, Dad,' he'd say to me when I got home."

Tommy squatted down, awkwardly with his bad leg, reached out and began picking up the dead stems, brushing the grass clean over his son's grave. I saw the broad span of his shoulders shudder once, then heard the first sob as he started to cry.

Jesus. I wanted to crawl behind one of the tombstones.

I walked back to the car. His sobs followed me, ragged and mournful on the still air. The poor bastard. I could feel his ache.

I dug out a cigarette and got it going. My hands were shaking. Went to take a long drag of smoke but couldn't. My breathing was too choked, I had to keep swallowing for some reason. Jesus Christ. Sonofabitch. Pretty soon I tossed down the cigarette and let the tears come. Who knew exactly why? I leaned on the Honda, fists pressed impotently against its cold steel. The sounds I made were soft echoes to the wails of anguish coming from behind me.

A breeze stirred out of nowhere. The trees trembled and wept with us.

Or maybe for us.

21

The following day I was back on the job early, the unexpected solemn turn the outing with Tommy McGurk had taken once again spurring my resolve to make some kind of headway with his case. Not even the "couple of juvenile horse's asses" remark Lori had tossed at us when we finally got back to the house was enough to discourage me.

Harriet Spoonerman was a gaunt, fiftyish woman with somewhat weary, dark-circled eyes above the kind of cheekbones and wide mouth many fashion models would make a pact with the devil to possess. The inheritor of a small but quite successful chain of department stores ("Spoonerman's—hard-wearing products for hard-working people"), Ms. Spoonerman was from all reports, however, in no position to require any such desperate bartering. Nevertheless she'd managed for some reason to cross paths with at least one incarnation of the devil in the form of Alex de Ruth: I'd seen the video proof.

I found her in her spaciously renovated office on the top floor of the Moline building that housed the store her father had started the chain with some seventy-five years ago. My early-bird tactics (geared specifically to appeal to her reputation for same) had worked well enough to gain an audience without prior arrangement.

"Mr. Hannibal," she said, reading from the card I'd relayed to her through her secretary. "It says here you are a private investigator, and you told Karen you wished to see me about a matter I would find important on both a business and a personal front."

I nodded. "That's right."

She smiled. "How could I fail to be intrigued by such an introduction? The possibilities it conjures are endless. I suppose you counted on that."

"You're right," I admitted, "I *was* counting on that kind of reaction."

Her smile stayed in place, but became different somehow. "Then I'm glad I didn't disappoint you. Because from here on out I suspect you may be in for a great deal of disappointment."

"You do?" I said, bewildered.

"Oh, I can almost guarantee it. You're not from around here, are you, Mr. Hannibal?"

"No, like it says on my card there—"

"Rockford, yes. If you were from around here, of course, you would know better than to even attempt this. Believe me, it has been tried before and tried by some of the best."

I sat there with her smile pouring all over me for another long minute and I didn't have the faintest idea in hell what she was talking about.

Carefully, I said, "Look, Ms. Spoonerman, I'm not sure—"

"Which one is it?" she asked.

"Which one what?"

"Oh, come on, for God's sake. Surely you didn't expect to get anywhere without at least telling me which one of the ungrateful little sluts is behind this. Or is it another shocked and outraged mother? God, I get so sick of them."

I tried again. "Ms. Spoonerman, I don't think you—"

She cut me off again. "It's Giselle, isn't it? It's Giselle and that fat little phony French mother of hers, the one with that mole on her upper lip that looks like a fly has landed there permanently. Ugh, how revolting. If she thinks what I do is disgusting, the pig ought to look in a mirror sometime."

"I don't know any Giselle," I told her.

"It must have been Patricia then! Shit, I was hoping it wouldn't be my sweet little Patty." Her smile had sort of slid around, gotten lopsided and nasty, and her words were coming faster and more stridently. "What is she trying to use? Those letters I wrote her? Well you can tell that little missy for me—"

"Lady," I interrupted firmly and loudly, "will you please shut the fuck up before I belt you one?"

The smile went away. Her mouth clapped shut like a small animal trap. She shrank back in her big wraparound chair and glared at me and for just an instant I saw the way she had looked as a little girl, pouting.

"That's better," I said.

"What now?" she asked in a smaller but far from subdued voice. "Strongarm tactics?"

I shook my head. "What comes now is that I tell you why I am here. It has nothing to do with whatever you started babbling about. At least I don't *think* it does, since I haven't figured out for sure yet what set you off."

She frowned. "You mean you aren't here about one of my . . . girls?"

"I'm here about Alex de Ruth."

"Alex? Good heavens, he's dead."

"I know. Murdered, to be exact."

"Couldn't happen to a nicer fellow." She suddenly sat forward again, eyes brightening, a new kind of smile flashing below them. "My God, am I some sort of suspect? Is that what this is about? How delicious!"

"Why do you think you might be a suspect, Ms. Spoonerman? Did you have reason to want Alex de Ruth dead?"

"Everyone who spent more than five minutes with that phony jerk—certainly every woman—had reason to entertain thoughts of his demise."

"It's been my understanding de Ruth was pretty popular with the ladies."

"Only until he got what he wanted. Only until the poor fools figured out how blatantly they had been used."

"What brings me here specifically," I said, "is the fact that de Ruth kept a sort of, er, record of his conquests. A video record, if you will. Were you aware that you'd been included in this manner, Ms. Spoonerman?"

"Hell yes, I'm aware of it. That's old news. The only thing that surprises me is that he actually kept the tape."

"Matter of fact, you have the distinction of being the only individual, aside from Alex and his wife, to be featured more than once in his collection."

Her eyes turned shrewd. "And you came here anticipating he might have tried to use that against me for blackmailing purposes. Thus giving me a two- or threefold reason to want him dead so he couldn't leach me dry."

"It scans as a logical possibility."

"Not very original."

"So tell me a different version."

She stood up and paced thoughtfully in small circle patterns behind her desk. Through the partially opened vertical blinds on the broad window in back of her, I could see a slice of the Mississippi beyond rooftops and trees and tall industrial stacks, dimpled and gleaming in the bright sun of the new day. In less cluttered times, say seventy-five years ago when old man Spoonerman first built here, it would have been a spectacular view. As I watched, one of the old-fashioned paddle wheelers specially reconstructed to travel the water corridor legislated to allow riverboat gambling slid into view, the sight of it hinting at grandness even further past.

"How many videos are there of me, Mr. Hannibal?"

"Two."

"Who has them now?"

"I can't say."

"You mean you *won't* say."

"Same difference."

"But you've viewed both tapes?"

"Enough."

"Without going into great detail, please describe what is on them."

A simple test to evaluate if I might be bluffing. I said, "On one you're having sex with Alex de Ruth, on the other you're having sex with a dark-haired young woman whose name I wasn't able to determine."

Hearing myself say that last part out loud suddenly jarred into place a clearer realization what was behind some of her earlier remarks.

She brought it the rest of the way into focus a moment later when she said, "In case it wasn't obvious, my personal preference in those proceedings was *not* for Alex de Ruth. I am, you see, a lesbian. I suppose I could try to split hairs and claim to be bisexual inasmuch as I've been intimate with a number of men—Alex and others—but the plain truth of the matter is that I enjoy the sexual favors of women far more. The dark-haired girl, by the way, was the Giselle I mentioned before. She was my frequent companion during that period, although we have since split up."

I smiled wryly. "And you initially thought I was here as her representative in an attempt to shake you down for past indiscretions?"

"Precisely. It has been tried before. More times than I care to think about. The price of possessing wealth. I'm looking for a relationship, unfortunately many of the lovers I have the poor taste to choose are only looking for a meal ticket. When I eventually wise up and dump them out on their ungrateful little asses, they sometimes make one more desperate attempt to gouge out a final handful of easy money."

"Have they ever been successful?"

"Never. Let them blab their lurid claims if they think it will do them any good. I don't flaunt my sexual tastes, I don't march in parades, I don't hit indiscriminately on every female Spoonerman employee: I don't do these things out of respect for the values of most people, their belief that mine is not a natural lifestyle. But by the same token, I make no apologies for what I am and I will not tolerate any ill treatment because of it. If a customer decides not to buy from Spoonerman's due to the fact they've heard I am gay, then to hell with them. I see it as their loss, they're turning their back on top quality at a fair price. Luckily most people are smart enough to realize this and the occasional 'scandal' that has leaked out about me has never been harmful to business."

"But Alex de Ruth took a shot all the same, didn't he?"

"A shot at blackmailing me, you mean? Oh, yes, in his own peculiar way he did. And in my own peculiar way I went along with it. The tape with Giselle and me was shot first, quite without our knowledge. And when Alex came around with his smarmy smile and made me aware of its existence I thought he might be trying to wangle some sort of extra consideration for Big River Wrestling. Spoonerman's is chief sponsor of their television spot, you understand. But no, it seemed all Alex wanted was a turn at getting in my knickers. I think the poor deluded ass had some kind of ultra-macho vision of redefining my sexual persuasion with his stud prowess or something."

"And you say you went along with him?"

"I said I went along in my own peculiar way." She aimed a sharply arched eyebrow at me. "You haven't watched the tapes at any great length, have you?"

"Just enough to ascertain who was on them and what was taking place."

"Mmm. That explains it. Had you watched the tape of Alex and I all the way through, then you would have seen that things worked out . . . well, not entirely to his satisfaction. I consider myself a student of fleshly delights, a scholar if you will. There are ways—and not at all unpleasant ones—to absolutely devastate a sexual partner, to leave them so totally drained and sated that they are simultaneously begging for more yet whimpering to be left alone. Suffice it to say I employed some of these techniques on Alex and left him . . . confused, I guess, would be a good word. That is why I'm surprised he kept that tape. I would have thought he'd find it an embarrassment."

"That's it?" I said. "That's all that ever came of it?"

"Sorry to disappoint you, but yes. You see, Mr. Hannibal, I may have despised Alex de Ruth but I really had no reason to want him dead. Hell, when you actually stop to think about it, men like Alex provide women like me with tremendous opportunities."

I found a pay phone in the lobby of the Spoonerman Building and put through a call to Nicholas Hatfield. Got lucky and caught him at his office.

"Nothing but strikeouts trying to turn up any unusual bank transactions by de Ruth," he reported when he came on the line. "I ran him seven ways from Sunday. So far—zip."

"Doesn't surprise me," I said. "I'm beginning to think the whole idea might have been a bum steer. The more I hear about this character the more I'm finding out what a sick puppy he was. He was using the videos alright. But not for money, not in any of the more standard ways you might think of." I proceeded into a brief rundown of who I'd talked to and what I'd come away with.

When I was through, Hatfield said, "It's true it doesn't sound to be panning out as well as we'd hoped, but how often does anything so soon out of the gate? Don't get too discouraged. Your list is still the best thing we've got going. On the other side of the whole magilla, every indication is that the state's attorney is figuring to go to the grand jury for an indictment. They're still convinced Tommy is their man."

"Poor unlucky schmuck," I muttered. I related the incident in the restaurant, then told him about Tommy's and my excursion last night and the way it had culminated in that soggy cemetery.

Incongruously, this seemed to brighten the lawyer. "Hey, that's not too bad," he said. "Not too bad at all. First, it makes Tommy sound stronger, more definite, now he's saying he cut the crap chasing around looking for the blonde and her husband. Drove away from it, went to a specific place. Second, look at the sentiment in where he went, what he did. Jesus, puts a lump even in my cynical old throat. If push comes to shove and we do go to trial, you think I can't milk something out of that? Give me just two or three middle-aged dames in the jury box and I'll *win* the fucking thing right there."

"Swell," I said, feeling perhaps a pang of guilt for baring Tommy's deep personal wounds and then hearing them so coldly and bluntly incorporated into a battle plan (yet at the same time realizing that was exactly the right attitude for Hatfield to have). "If you've got it so sewn up then, I can pack my bags and shake this burg."

Hatfield chuckled. "Who you shitting, pal? Certainly

not me. You can grumble all you want, but I know your kind too well. Once you get your spurs dug in, you'll stay on until the horse is done bucking. No matter how distasteful you find that list, you're going to keep working it. Besides, it hasn't actually been a complete wash. I'd say it's yielded better than you seem to want to admit. The Lugretti guy, for instance. As much motive there as McGurk, and no better alibi."

I sighed. "Yeah. And you could say the same for Paula. Trouble is, after Tommy, those are the two I least want it to be."

Hatfield was quiet on his end for a minute. Then: "That ain't something we get to choose, pal."

He was right, of course.

It never is.

And that was the hell of it.

The address I'd established for Bouncing Betty (real name Betty Ryerson) turned out to be a bait shop in Milan, a small community hinged to the southern edge of Rock Island. Upon discovering this, my first thought was that I'd either gotten some bad information or had fouled up the numbers somehow when entering them into my notebook. Spotting what appeared to be living quarters above the shop, however, I reconsidered and nosed the Honda to the curb out front, deciding to give it a try anyway.

Like the coaches always tell you, make that second effort.

In this instance, that advice bore fruit immediately. I pushed through the front door, announced by the tingling of a suspended cat's bell, and Betty looked up from behind the counter at the end of the main aisle. She had a smile ready; when she saw me it went away. We'd never been formally introduced, but she obviously knew who I was and just as obviously wasn't too crazy to see me.

I walked to the counter. Fishing rods hung horizontally and vertically on the walls, more suspended from the ceiling. Every inch of shelf and display space was crowded with reels, hooks, bobbers, plastic-wrapped colorful flies, tackle boxes, almost everything related to fishing you could possibly think of. It was like walking through a tunnel of fishing gear.

I dug out a smile of my own to replace the one Betty had clamped a lid on. "Morning," I said.

She returned the greeting, somewhat grudgingly, then asked, "What can I do for you?" As she spoke the question, her eyes flicked anxiously to a doorway off behind where she stood, as if she feared someone might come through there.

I slid one of my business cards across the countertop.

Without looking at it, she said, "I know who you are, Mr. Hannibal." Another nervous glance over her shoulder. "This is about the tapes, isn't it?"

So. No awkward, building-up-to-it stage to have to work through here.

I nodded. "Yes, Betty, it is."

"I knew it. I knew when that bastard got killed those tapes were going to turn up sooner or later. And when you came on the scene I had a bad hunch it was going to be sooner. Damn my rotten luck anyway!"

"How long have you known about them?" I said.

"Too long."

"How did you find out about them?"

"How do you think? Mr. Charm was kind enough to show me the one he took of me and him. Do you know *when* the snake dropped that little surprise? The day before I was getting married, that's when. He'd barely spoken to me in months. He got what he wanted, then he was through with me, just like he'd been through with dozens of others, just like I'd been warned. But I couldn't see it when he was putting his oh-so-practiced moves on me, couldn't see it because I was too stupidly flattered that the dashing, handsome Alex de Ruth was paying even the tiniest morsel of attention to little butterball *me.* Anyway, after all that was long over and done with and I was lucky enough to find a new man, a real man who really loved me, that's when Alex stopped by my apartment with his lovely surprise. His 'wedding gift,' he called it. 'A little something to put some pizzazz back in those dull nights that are going to set in after the bloom is off the honeymoon.' What he was talking about was the cassette he had with him. He played it for me, enough so I could see what it was: me and him."

"And that was the first you had any inkling it existed?"

"Uh-huh. And I could have done real fine without *ever* knowing."

"But you said this was months after you and he were through, after he would have recorded it, in other words. He never hinted about it, never tried to bring it up in any way, say, to get something from you, favors maybe? Money?"

"Yeah, like I had money worth going after. I told you, he got the only thing he wanted from me when he shot his sick tape."

"So what was the object in bringing it up when he finally did?"

"Just to be a prick, as far as I could see. To make me squirm. When I yanked his cassette out of the machine and threatened to smash it in the garbage, he laughed. That was exactly the reaction he wanted. Then he laughed some more and said I should be happy to know I was in such good company, that he had tapes of lots of others who couldn't wait to wallow in the smut but then couldn't stand to have their dirty laundry held up for them to see."

"Did he say who any of these others were?"

"No. And I didn't ask. All I wanted was to be done with him and his dirty business." She snapped her head around and gave the back door her hardest, most anxious look yet. When her eyes swung back to me, she said, "Look, Hannibal, I've told you everything I know. Honest to God I have. Can't you just leave me alone now? My husband will be back any minute and I don't want him to find us talking like this. He doesn't know anything about me and Alex. He's a decent, understanding man. And everything probably would have been okay if I'd leveled with him up front. But I didn't. I don't want to hurt him with this and I don't want to risk his reaction in case . . . well, in case he can't handle it."

"I can appreciate that. Only neither of us can ignore the fact that a man has been killed and another accused of being his murderer—accused unjustly, many feel. These tapes, yours and the others, and their potential as alternative motives for de Ruth's death, have to be investigated. People like you could be the key, could know something helpful you don't even realize you know until it's brought out by the right kind of questions. I'm working as discreetly as I can, but I have to keep on."

She looked pained. "But I *don't* know anything that can help you. I certainly don't know anything about *murder*."

"Do you believe Tommy McGurk killed de Ruth?"

"I—I don't know. I wouldn't have thought so. Tommy was always so nice. But then the police arrested him, charged him . . . and a lot of people were convinced him and Paula had something going on. I guess it's the kind of situation where . . . well, anything could happen."

"All right, let's take that basic situation and play with it a little. Twist it around some. That's the kind of thing I do. What if, I have to wonder, your husband found out about your fling with de Ruth? Wouldn't that set up pretty much the same premise?"

"No!"

"What if de Ruth showed him the tape, either just being his prickish self or trying to get some kind of payoff in exchange for it?"

She shook her head. "No way. My Hank is no killer."

"Not even to protect you? Maybe it was an accident, maybe he lost his head."

"No, I tell you."

She was still shaking her head and the ring of her denial was still hanging in the air when the front door opened behind me and someone else came into the shop. Betty's eyes darted at the sound of the little bell but the fact that they remained reasonably calm told me without looking around that the new arrival wasn't her anxiously expected husband.

Turning, I saw Ava Coltrane striding toward us, her mane of jet hair billowing loose about her face and down over her shoulders. "Hiya, Bets," she said. Then to me: "Hey there, private-eye guy. Didn't know they sold supplies here for the kind of fishing you do."

"We don't," Betty said sharply.

Ava eyed the two of us.

Sensing that her tone had perhaps revealed more than she meant for it to, Betty tried to cover with a lighter touch. "So what brings you around this morning, kiddo?" she said conversationally. "I thought after last night you'd be going to the gym for a rubdown and a turn in the whirlpool before you did much else."

Ava made a face. "That's exactly where I was headed. But that stupid car of mine won't start again. I was hoping I could whine and look pitiful and Hank would help me with it one more time. I *promise* to get a new battery this week."

"Only trouble is, Hank's not here," Betty said. "He should be back any minute, though. Went over to Credit Island to pick up an order of leeches."

I couldn't let that one go by. "Leeches?" I said.

Betty gave me a "why don't you leave?" look, not ready to tolerate even a bit of simple curiosity on my part.

But Ava, who seemed seldom at a loss for words, was willing to fill me in. "Sure," she said. "Leeches make some of the best live bait you can use. Not very popular, though, because most folks—even some of your biggest he-man fisherman—don't like to handle 'em."

"Gee, I wonder why," I muttered.

The muffled sound of a door opening and closing and then the clomp of footsteps sounded from the back room at that point. Betty had time to shoot me a single plaintive look before the door she had been fretting over swung open and a man entered into the back counter area beside her.

It took me a few seconds to place the smallish, wiry little guy with the thinning hair and sharp nose. My first reaction was one almost of disappointment. After all the anticipation, all the anxious over-the-shoulder glances, I guess I'd sort of been expecting some big, boisterous bear. The contrast of what showed up instead was almost laughable. And then I remembered where I'd seen the leathery-faced guy before: the first time he'd been wearing a striped referee's shirt and struggling to maintain control over that match I'd watched between Betty and Paula, then later I'd spotted him, again in the company of Betty, at Alex de Ruth's funeral. So he was her husband, Hank Ryerson.

He gave a friendly nod in my direction, greeted Ava by name. Then walked up and patted Betty on the fanny. "Always good to see you piling up the customers, hon. Can I help with anything?"

Betty smiled nervously. "I think I've got everything taken care of, Hank."

Ava frowned. "You do? You going to be the one to come out and jump my stupid battery?"

"You having trouble with that again?" Hank said. "I thought you were going to get a new one?"

"I am, I am," Ava said defensively. "I just haven't gotten around to it yet."

Hank shook his head. "Girl, you'd forget your arms and legs if they wasn't attached to you."

Ava pouted. "I've heard the lectures, Hank. You going to help me with it or not? Have a little pity, I'm all banged up from the match last night and I need to get over and get some steam and a whirlpool and a rubdown or I'll get all cramped and hunched over like somebody's grandma or something."

"Oh, you know Hank will get you going," Betty said.

Hank wrinkled his brow. "I will, but she's going to have to wait a little while. Dennis Axelrod over at Credit had one of his tanks go out on him in the middle of the night and he's on the verge of losing a whole mess of his live bait. He's on his way over behind me, be here in just a minute. We got that old Burmessur down in the cellar I told him he could use until he got his fixed or got another. I need to help him load it up and get his stock transferred before I do anything else."

"Well, I guess that tells me where I stand," Ava said in mock seriousness. "Everybody thinks a bunch of smelly old bait fish are more important than my poor battered bod."

"The bait fish," Hank told her with a twinkle in his eye, "aren't in the fix they're in because of their own foolishness."

"Oh, yeah?" Ava came back. "They were foolish enough to get caught in the first place, weren't they?

Speaking of which, Hank, why don't you find the biggest, nastiest hook you got for sale in this place and go sit on it?"

Everybody had a pretty good chuckle over that.

"Tell you what," I said to Ava. "I don't profess to be much of a car mechanic, but if it's just a matter of jumping your battery, how about I lend a hand?" I paused to give Betty a meaningful glance. "I'm through here. And I've got a set of jumper cables."

Ava smiled. "Well, hey, Hannibal, that'd be swell. I'd really appreciate that."

Hank regarded me. "Hannibal? I thought you looked familiar. Damn, I'm poor on remembering faces. You're that detective fella looking into the de Ruth killing, trying to help Tommy McGurk, ain't you?"

"That's right," I answered.

He thrust out his right hand. "Hank Ryerson."

"Joe Hannibal." His grip had surprising bite to it and I knew for sure then what I had only suspected from looking at him, that he was one of those deceptively small men, almost spindly in appearance but all sinew and gristle at the core.

As we pumped each other's arm, Hank said, "Well, you can put me on record as wishing you all the luck in the world, mister. Tommy McGurk's a fine young fella and I think he's getting a bum rap. What's more, whoever *did* knock off Alex de Ruth probably did a service to the world."

"Hank!" Betty admonished.

"Well, it's the truth. Man was a piece of river scum."

"That's pretty much what I've been hearing," I said.

Hank furled a brow thoughtfully. "Something about your case bring you around here?"

Beside his shoulder, Betty's face flushed pinkish red then went pale.

"Just touching bases," I explained easily. "I knew you and your wife were associated with Big River Wrestling, figured you both must have known both de Ruth and McGurk. Wanted to get a sort of general reading from the two of you is all."

Hank nodded, satisfied. "Well, I reckon you got it then.

Don't suppose my redhead here gave a different picture, did you, hon?"

"Of course not," Betty replied. "Although I may not be quite as joyous over the man's death as you seem to be."

"You should be," Hank maintained stubbornly. "More than anything else, de Ruth had a filthy, lowdown attitude toward women." He swung his eyes to me. "If you ain't figured it out yet, Hannibal, you might be standing in the presence of about the only two women around who didn't fall victim to de Ruth's sugar talk and flesh-using ways. Truth to tell, my big redhead was even tempted at one point, but showed better sense before it was too late." He paused, his eyes taking on that teasing twinkle again. "As for Ava there, I expect she might have fallen prey to him, too, except with her faulty memory she probably kept forgetting whenever he tried to set up a date with her."

"Oh, very funny, Hank," Ava said. "Ha. I'll have you know if I ever *had* given that sharpie a tumble"—she placed her hands on her trim hips and rotated them suggestively—"his days of chasing after everything else would have been over. You know what they say about 'once you try black, you'll never go back.' "

"The way you two carry on," Betty said. "You're probably embarrassing Mr. Hannibal half to death."

Before anybody could say anything else, the cat's bell over the front door sounded once again and a guy wearing a ball cap and a checkered shirt poked his head and shoulders in.

"Yo, Hank," he said. "I got my truck out here, where you want me to pull up?"

Hank made swirling motions with one hand. "Come around to the alley, Dennis. You'll have to back in. I'll meet you out there. We have to bring it up out of the cellar."

"Okeydoke." The guy in the cap ducked back out of the doorway.

"As you can see, Hannibal, I got to scoot," Hank said to me. "You come back around any time, though. Me and Betty be glad to answer your questions, do anything we can to help."

22

In my Honda, after Ava had given me directions to her place and we were rolling that way, she said, "Got a little tense back there, eh?"

"How's that?" I said.

The question earned me a sidelong glance. "Come on. I thought we already established that dumb act won't wash with me. When I walked in on you and Betty I could feel some definite stress in the air. And when Hank showed up there was plenty more of the same on Betty's face. I suppose you wouldn't know anything about that?"

"Uhmm. Maybe a little."

"Uh-huh. I think I got it figured out. You heard about the fling Betty had with Alex and you came to question her about it, didn't you? Or was it the tape—Jeez, did you stumble on his collection of videotapes?"

This one certainly had some moves. "You know about the tapes?" I said.

She shrugged. "I've heard about them. I wouldn't say I *know* about them—turn here. It's the second driveway on the left, the pink duplex. That orange Chevette parked there, that's mine."

I turned where she indicated, pulling up alongside the Chevette, swinging onto an edge of the hard-packed lawn in order to do so. I left the Honda idling. We got out. A dog yapped at us from somewhere. Looking around, I saw the spikey-haired snout of some sort of small mongrel terrier bouncing against a screened window of the house.

Ava laughed. "That's Midge. My protector. Don't worry, he can't get out. And if he does, I think I could get him pulled off before he bit too many huge, bloody chunks out of you."

"Sure," I said. "Midge for midget, huh? Be about like getting mauled by an attack mosquito."

"Ha. You can afford to be brave and disdainful from a safe distance."

I popped the hood on the Honda, propped it open. Did the same with the Chevette. The Chevette's battery looked ancient, its markings faded and dirt-streaked. The terminals had been cleaned recently but the cables running to them were frayed and twisted.

"You sure this thing is going to get you anywhere even if I get it started?" I asked.

"Always has before."

"Where are you going for your new battery?"

"There's a Monkey Wards out at the South Park Mall. I thought I'd swing out there to their auto department after I get through at the gym."

I'd moved around to the rear of my car, had lifted the hatch and was pulling loose my jumper cables from beside the long, flat, special toolbox I have bolted across the back edge of the spare tire well. "You probably should get the battery taken care of first. Thing most likely won't start again once you shut it off."

She checked her wristwatch. "Yeah, but if I don't get to the gym pretty soon, the afternoon bunch will be in and I won't be able to get near the whirlpool. I'll just get jump-started again there if I have to."

"Why the dire need of the whirlpool?"

"If you had come to the matches last night, you'd know. I am one walking ache. Your friend Paula the Platinum Powerhouse gave me quite a pounding last night."

"You wrestled Paula? I thought your opponent was going to be the girl I saw you practicing with yesterday?"

"I thought so, too. Just like I thought I was going to get to win. But then Mel decided to insert Paula on the card and I was lucky enough to get picked to go against her instead. I have to admit it made a better show. The girl I was supposed to wrestle—Wynona, she goes as the Texas Tornado in the ring—had a pretty racked-up hip and we would've had to go awful light with it—"

"Go 'light'?"

"An insider's term, means take it easy with somebody's injury but still sell it as real combat to the customers. Something dear Paula knows nothing about. She's more into *causing* the injuries others have to go light with."

"Doesn't she read the script?"

"Oh, she follows the script. She just plays it a little more realistically than most of the rest of us care for. Don't get me wrong, she's a hell of an athlete and I'm not saying she sets out to purposely hurt anybody. But in practically every match, it's like she gives an extra shot or two, maybe goes heavy for a few seconds on one of her holds just to remind you who's boss in there. She gets away with it because she's a top draw and, well, frankly, because she's tough enough to. If everything was on the up and up, even if promoters like Mel and the others didn't decide who was going to win and so on, Paula would still be a champion: she's that good. Quite a different story from Brick Towers, the men's champ, who, in spite of all his lovely muscles can only seem to remember about three basic wrestling holds and probably couldn't win a real match if his life depended on it."

I had the jumper cables hooked. I motioned Ava behind the wheel of her car. "Okay, try it."

She got in, gave the key a twist. The engine rolled over with a slow groan. "Hold it," I said. "Let it just set and take a charge from mine for a couple minutes. It's deader than hell. You really ran it down."

"Didn't take much."

While we were waiting for my car to feed power to hers, I tapped out a cigarette and lit it. Setting one hip against the Chevette's fender, I said, "So how'd my buddy Bomber go over last night?"

"Are you kidding? He was terrific. He hasn't lost a step, at least not when it comes to working a crowd. He had them hating him in a matter of seconds. And by match's end—after he'd slipped his briefcase to Paula under the ropes then distracted the referee so she could bonk me over the head with it and knock me out for the pin—he had them on their feet in a frenzy. I guess that's going to be his gimmick: the briefcase and maybe some assorted nasties he'll carry in it. Tommy had his cane, for Bomber it will be the briefcase."

I shook my head, marvelling at the melodrama and shenanigans they find ways to work into the game.

"Bomber looked me up after the match," Ava went on, "to let me know he hoped him and Paula hadn't given me too rough a time. That was sweet of him."

"He seem to handle the booing okay? That was a first for him, you know."

"Uh-huh, that's what he said. But he acted like he got a kick out of it. Said it was exciting in a different kind of way than being cheered. I've heard other wrestlers say that, too, ones who've switched from being a good guy to a bad guy—or, as we say in the biz, from a babyface to a heel."

"Are you always the babyface?"

"Usually. I'm small, see, so it makes the heels look even rottener when they have to break the rules and resort to dirty tricks in order to beat me. Like Paula and that briefcase last night—made the crowd crazy. I mean, chick's a foot taller than me and outweighs me by forty pounds yet has to pull a stunt like that. How despicable can you get, right? Your hard-core wrestling fan goes nuts over shit like that, loving it and hating it all at the same time. That's what keeps bringing them back, and that's the name of the game."

I dropped what was left of my cigarette on the ground, mashed it underfoot. "Well the name of the game we're playing here," I said, "is seeing if we can get this beast started. Give it a try again, see what happens."

The engine turned over stronger this time and almost caught. But Ava got too eager with the foot feed and drowned it after one promising cough. The motor wound off in a series of weakened grunts.

"Forget it," I said, the sweetish stink of the unused gas in the carburetor reaching my nose.

Ava walloped the steering wheel with the heel of her hand. "Shit, now I flooded it. Shit, shit, shit!"

"Look," I said, feeling the pinch of impatience, "this could take a while and then you're going to turn right around and have trouble with it all over again. How long you figure you'll need to spend at the gym?"

"I dunno. Couple hours. Not any more than that."

"Tell you what. I was going to swing by there anyway, try to catch Bomber, maybe see a couple more people. Why don't you ride over with me. We'll each take care of our business, then I'll bring you back, pick up your new battery on the way, I'll slap it in for you and you'll be set. How's that sound?"

"Jeez, I couldn't ask you to do all that. You're in the middle of your investigation, you must have a million things to do . . ."

"If I didn't have the time or the inclination, I wouldn't have offered." I began unhooking the jumper cables. "Come on, get out of there. Let's do this right."

She piled out of the Chevette, her teeth flashing in a sudden grin. "All I got to say is if this is some kind of pickup line, it's an original one. I've heard about you smooth-talking white boys, though."

I held up one hand, palm out. "You caught me. That little bump and grind back at the bait shop and that talk about trying black and never going back—something snapped, drove me mad with desire. My plan is to haul you down the road a piece, tie you up with these here jumper cables, and ravish hell out of you. Better make a run for it while you still got the chance."

Ava laughed. "I don't know how good a detective you are, Hannibal, but you sure are a nut. I guess I shouldn't have to worry, I forgot for a minute you've been keeping company with Paula. After a six-foot blond amazon, hell, what would you see in a little black runt like me with boobs smaller than her lips, right?"

"Now who's trying to put on a dumb act?" I said, making a face. "You know damn good and well that in your own way you're every bit as attractive as Paula. If you were fishing for me to say so, there, I said it. If you're fishing for me to say anything more than business went on between Paula and me, you're SOL, kid."

"Methinks thou dost protest too much," Ava said, trailing me as I carried the recoiled cables to the rear of the Honda and stuffed them back down beside the toolbox. "And if you think I'm such a raging beauty, then don't call me 'kid.'"

"You got any tools around?" I asked.

"You mean like for fixing stuff or putting things together?"

"In this case, for taking things apart."

"I got an old flat-headed butter knife in the house I use for a screwdriver once in awhile, and I think I got a hammer around somewhere."

"About what I figured," I muttered, starting to spin the combination lock on my toolbox.

"What are you doing?"

"We'll take your old battery with us, get a few bucks knocked off the new one in trade," I explained.

"Good thinking."

The lock dropped open and I lifted the lid. Ava's eyebrows went up along with it.

"Holy shit," she exclaimed. "Are you going to shoot and kill my old battery before you yank it out, or what?"

Like I indicated, the toolbox is a little out of the ordinary, at least its contents are; covering a range considerably broader than your standard array of wrenches and so forth. The tools of my trade tend often to be more lethal. Without comment, I pulled out the heavy tray of guns and ammo, sat it crossways on the open box, rummaged underneath for what the job at hand required.

"Jesus," Ava went on, "looks like the kind of crate the Varsey clan might customize for somebody."

I straightened up, turning with a crescent wrench and a screwdriver in my grip. "Varsey? Where do I know that name from?"

A shrug. "They're all over these parts. You could have

heard it most anywhere. Say, aren't sawed-off shotguns illegal?"

I flipped shut the lid on the toolbox and batted my eyes innocently. "What sawed-off shotgun?"

"Yeah. Right."

"Getting back to Varsey . . ."

"Eugene Varsey is the guy who maintains BRW's rings. Hauls them around, sets them up for the matches and takes them down after, all like that. Does various other odd jobs for Mel, too, him and that brood of his. Likely that's how you heard the name. Bunch of shifty-eyed inbred white trash if you ask me. Maybe you know the type. Brothers and cousins and nephews all drifting around, never staying in one spot but never roaming too far from the general area either. Redneck macho jerks, for the most part. Into junking cars, hunting and trapping, a little fishing, doing patch-and-nail fix-it work here and there for quick cash. Lots of brushes with the law— that's why I said that portable arsenal of yours looked like something they might know about."

I had the name pegged now. "This Eugene, he have a wife named Glynnis?" I asked.

Ava shook her head. "No. Glynnis is his daughter. Eugene's wife drowned a few years back. Glynnis and I went to high school together for a while when they lived down New Boston way at one point. She remembered me when I showed up here and started working for Big River. She's like a diamond in the rough, being part of that clan. She has beauty and brains both, but she's too intimidated to use them. We palled around some when I first came here, but, like I said, her daddy's a redneck—to the bone. No way he'd stand for any daughter of his getting very chummy with a colored person. We went through that with him before when we tried to be friends in high school."

I wondered how daddy Eugene would feel about his daughter getting intimately chummy with a certified heel. Because that's where I knew the name from: Paula de Ruth had supplied it as the identity of yet another one of her husband's video sex partners. A coltish, dark-haired girl, if memory served, possessed not of spectacular beauty but displaying a youthful vibrancy and eagerness that had a special appeal.

Something must have shown on my face.

"What about Glynnis?" Ava wanted to know. She waited a beat, then: "You know about her romance with Alex, don't you? . . . Oh, shit, he didn't get her on tape, too, did he?"

I had her battery unhooked. I pulled it from the Chevette, lugged it to the rear of my Honda where I thumped it down to rest on the freshly coiled jumper cables.

Wiping my hands on an orange shop rag I took from the bundle at the opposite end of the toolbox, I said, "Before we go much farther, you and I are going to have to take time out to discuss exactly how the hell much you know about what's going on around here."

"I only know what I see and hear."

"You see and hear a *lot.*"

"You say that like it surprises you, makes you suspicious. Why? This is where I live and work. Why wouldn't I know some of the things you've managed to find out in only a few days?"

"It's my job to find out stuff. And when the bottom line is murder, I'm suspicious of everything and everybody. So how is it you know about Alex de Ruth's videotapes?"

She shrugged. "Simple. Betty told me. We're best friends. I'm the one she came crying to when Alex one-night-standed her, I'm also the one she came crying to when he popped his little pre-wedding day video surprise on her. And in between I was the one who introduced her to Hank. You saw how great they are together, how hard they're working to make a go of the bait shop, supplementing it with the extra money they make doing gigs for BRW. And you heard how Hank felt about Alex. Hank's a swell guy, but that's one part of her life Betty can never reveal to him. He wouldn't be able to handle it."

"And Glynnis? She another 'best friend' who bared her soul to you about how nasty, lowdown Alex humped and dumped her?"

"You can be a cynical fart, can't you? I already explained that Glynnis and I couldn't be close because her daddy didn't approve of the color of my skin. As far as anything going on between her and Alex, I have to admit that's pretty much conjecture on my part. I saw some things, I considered Alex's well-deserved reputation, I put two and two together. The only part that didn't fit was that it never seemed to reach the 'dump' stage like it should have. Although in a manner of speaking it did, I guess. When Alex went and got himself killed, you could say he effectively dumped everything."

I showed her a shark's smile. "Except he left behind enough questions to cause me to be hired. And I don't intend to get dumped until I find out the truth."

23

I paused in the narrow hallway just outside the Emergency waiting room long enough to draw a ragged breath of the thin, mediciney air, then went on in.

Melanie Dukenos's face looked the same grayish color as the fake leather upholstry of the chair in which she sat.

A half dozen feet beyond her, Bomber was on his feet, pacing around a low coffee table cluttered with magazines and newspapers.

On the other side of the table, Sam War Cloud, the Indian wrestler, was seated also, his bulk squeezed into another of the chrome and fake leather chairs that lined the walls. His head hung down and his fists were knotted together in front of him, as if he might be praying. His duskily beautiful wife sat motionless beside him, her left hand resting on his right shoulder.

All eyes swung to me when I entered the room.

I licked my lips and said, "How is he?"

Bomber's jaw muscles clenched and unclenched visibly. "Last report," he said, "they were calling his condition stable. Expected to be admitting him to a room before long. We may be able to see him then."

The subject under discussion was Abe Lugretti. The booze-frazzled, guilt-ridden old fool had tried to kill himself.

When Ava and I arrived at the BRW building, a pair of grim-faced Kolchonsky brothers had greeted us with the news. Their words hit as hard as punches from their fists. Seeing my reaction, Ava had been quick to urge me on to the hospital, assuring me she would be able to get a ride back home okay.

I'd stuck around only long enough to hear what sketchy details the Kolchonskys knew. It had been Sam War Cloud who'd discovered the suicide attempt, having dropped by Lugretti's house trailer earlier that morning to be met by the threatening reek of raw propane gas pouring out of every orifice of the kitchen stove, Abe snoring it in from a sprawl on the living room couch he'd pulled over next to the slatted room divider.

Reacting with exactly the kind of decisive heroics that had marked his ring style for going on three decades, the Indian star had charged in, killed the gas source and slammed open a handful of windows, then carried his unconscious friend outside where his shouts spurred neighbors to phone for help. Once Lugretti was in the hands of paramedics and the explosive danger of the gas had been quelled by a squad from the fire department, War Cloud had phoned Mel Dukenos at BRW, where Bomber had been present in her office when she took the call.

The head of Big River Wrestling stood up and faced me now. "I hold you directly responsible for this, Hannibal," she said without preamble.

I felt shitty enough as it was. I didn't need to listen to that. "If you're going to start laying blame, lady," I said, "I suggest you spread some a little closer to home. I wasn't one of the ones who stood by and watched Abe slide deeper into his booze dependency, waited until the bottles he kept tipping up started to suck out of him instead of the other way around."

Her eyes flashed. "No, you're just the one who dug up a shovelful of his most private dirt and had one of his oldest friends fling it in his face."

"Knock it off, the both of you," Bomber growled. "Biting at each other's throats isn't going to get us anywhere, and it sure as hell isn't going to help Abe."

Sam War Cloud stood up as well. "Bomber's right. There's enough blame to go around for everybody to shoulder a chunk. And that doesn't leave out Abe himself, not by any means. He was a man grown, he damn sure helped pack the burden he was carrying."

Mel tossed her hands in an irritated gesture. "Great. My whole organization is crumbling out from under me one key person at a time, and those I've got left want to stand around waxing philosophic."

War Cloud regarded her with a flat stare. "So where's your biggest concern, Mel? For Abe, or for the business?"

She blanched at the question, but quickly regained the fire in her eye. "That's a rotten thing to say to me, Sam War Cloud, damn you, and you know it!"

Leticia Cloud flowed out of her seat and moved to her husband's side in a single long stride. "That's enough, Sam," she said. "You're not being fair. BRW is bread and butter to all of us. Everyone knows how much Mel has riding on the upcoming pay-per-view card, she has every right to be concerned. That doesn't take anything away from how she feels about Abe."

"Look," Bomber said, "we're all pretty stressed out. Let's just cool it before somebody says something they're going to regret." His eyes went from face to face, challenging anyone to argue his wisdom. When no one did, his gaze came back and settled on me. "I'm getting cramped from sitting around here, need to walk out some kinks. How about hiking down to the cafeteria with me, getting a cup of coffee? I'll pop." Translation: You're the one who triggered this round of irritation, let's slide you the hell out for a few minutes and let things settle back down.

I nodded. "Okay by me."

"Mind holding down the fort for a little bit, in case the doc comes around?" Bomber asked Mel. "You can take a turn when I get back."

She shook her head. "Just bring me back a Coke or something, okay? I'm fine here."

Sam War Cloud followed Bomber and me out into the hall. "Okay if I tag along? I feel sort of outnumbered back there, especially since I managed to get the both of them already pissed at me."

The hospital's cafeteria was a broad, low-ceilinged room furnished with an arrangement of formica-topped tables and brightly colored plastic chairs. The lunch hour was winding down so we had little trouble finding a table to ourselves. Judging by the furtive glances cast after the three of us—in particular my two hulking companions with their grim expressions and cauliflowered ears and the latticeworks of ancient scars running around their eyes and foreheads—we wouldn't have had too big a problem clearing a spot regardless.

We sat down over styrofoam cups of steaming coffee.

"For what it's worth," I said to the Bomber, "I'm sorry as hell about this. I suppose I'm wasting my breath, but I hope you aren't going around blaming yourself in any way."

"Well I'm sure as hell not going around patting myself on the back for my part in it," he replied sourly.

I shook my head. "What could we have done different? We're not the ones who put him on that tape. But once we came across it, the questions had to be asked."

"Uh-huh. And those questions are what put him here."

I sighed. No sense gnawing that bone any more. If Bomber was bound and determined to take a turn at self flagellation, I wasn't going to be able to talk him out of it.

I turned to Sam War Cloud. "What's your reading on what happened this morning? Was it genuinely meant to succeed, or was it more a cry for help, the kind of suicide attempt that's undertaken with a pretty good chance of getting interrupted?"

The big Indian shrugged uneasily. "Hell, I'm not exactly an expert on the subject. But it looked pretty serious to me. Not only was Abe releasing enough gas to asphyxiate himself about ten times over, but the danger of the concentration he'd built up being set off by some kind of spark was way up there, too. From what I heard a couple of the firemen say, he could have blown off that whole end of town. No, I'd say he was out to get the job done all right."

"Good thing you showed up when you did. Mind if I ask what took you out there this morning?"

War Cloud grinned. "Bomber warned me you could be a nosy bugger. Said that's what makes you so good at what you do."

I grinned back, made a little "what can I say?" motion. But the question still stood.

"Okay," War Cloud said at length. "Matter of fact I went out there for that very reason: to check up on Abe. After the matches in New Boston last night, see, he stopped in The J.I. for awhile. The J.I.—the in joke is that the initials stand for Jock Itch—is a sports bar here in Davenport where a lot of BRW people hang out. Anyway, Abe stopped in there, something he doesn't do much of these days. Mostly does his drinking by himself at home, as you've apparently heard. So he stops, hits the juice pretty hard, and before long he's rambling and babbling about how miserable he is, how fucked up life is, how that no-good bastard Alex de Ruth held a loaded gun to his head for years and how now that he was gone the gun had fallen into the hands of people he thought were his friends but it turned out they were aiming the same gun at him.

"Eventually he got too drunk to be vague about it any longer, and it came out about the underage girl and the tape and all. Then he went on a crying jag and told everybody how sorry and ashamed he was, how he'd let us all down and that he wished he was dead so he could be with his Maisie so she could take care of him again. It went from being funny to being sort of sad to being downright scary, you know what I mean? Me and Letty finally got him out of there, got him home—I took him in my car, she followed in his—and made sure he got settled in okay. But after I woke up this morning I still had this uneasy feeling that there might be more to the things he'd said than just the booze running crazy in him. I finally decided to pay a visit and see. Like you said, I guess it's a good thing I did. You know the rest."

"Damn anyway," Bomber muttered. "I wish I'd have

been there, been paying closer attention. I'd have stayed right with the foolish old sonofabitch. I thought he was handling it okay."

War Cloud nodded with a kind of faraway look in his eyes, eyes that could be so piercing under their distinctive ridge of dark brows and the pattern of long, thin scars that crisscrossed his broad forehead. Bomber had almost identical scars and he'd explained to me once that they were self-inflicted, by razor blades secreted in the waistband or shoes of a wrestler to be used on those occasions when a promoter called for "juice"—blood, to me and you—to be spilled in a match. Contrary to popular belief, the blood you see shed in wrestling matches does not come from blood capsules or breakaway bladders of chicken blood, it is the real thing. In these AIDS-conscious days, the barbaric practice has been somewhat curtailed but is still a time-honored tradition called upon once in a while.

"Yeah," the Indian said, "us old timers got to look out for one another. Ain't many of us left. You, me, Abe . . . Mel and Tommy, I guess they'd have to be included as part of the old bunch. After that, what have you got? Lot of steroided-out muscle heads and acrobats with pretty smiles, in it for all the wrong reasons. Money and hype. Looking only to move on to the bigger federations, get their mugs on T-shirts and posters and plastic toys and video games, do movie and TV roles. God forbid they have to actually wrestle and sweat somewhere along the way, maybe bleed, get some bones broke, go to the mat four or five times a week in front of crowds of maybe only a couple hundred in towns nobody ever heard of, do some of their hardest fighting getting back to the locker room and out of town alive. That's the steel Abe is tempered with. With a little help from us, he'll be able to fight his way out of this, too."

It was a curiously stirring speech. Stirring in spite of the rah-rah rhetoric and echoes of the kind of melodrama that has been the foundation of pro wrestling for going on a full century. What made the difference was War Cloud's sincerity; he was talking from the heart. Or at least he managed to convince me of that.

I said, "Did Abe leave a note?"

"Yeah, he did. Short and to the point. I held it in my hands, I can remember every word. 'I'm sorry I let everybody down. I'm going to be with Maisie.' That was it. The police have the note now."

"Did the police question you?"

"Uh-huh. First some uniformed officers who were called to the trailer court. Then some plainclothes detectives who came here to the hospital."

"Did you tell them about the tape?"

"Didn't see any way around it. They wanted to know what the note meant, what had been bothering Abe. A lot of people heard him carrying on at the J.I. last night. If the cops looked into it at all, they were bound to find out."

"Did you tell them who has the tape?"

"I don't know who has it. All I knew was that Bomber here was the one who talked to Abe about it. I didn't give them Bomber's or your name, if that's what you're worried about. But they're probably going to get them from Abe when he comes around. They'll be back, and he'll have a lot of explaining to do."

"In the meantime," Bomber said, "I told Sam, and Mel and Leticia, too, the whole story on the tapes, about the collection of them that turned up and how you've been hoping they might hold the key to who really killed de Ruth."

I grunted. "Those tapes are fast becoming the worst kept secret since Howard Cosell's hairpiece."

"That's why I figured there was no longer any sense in not talking about them."

"That de Ruth," War Cloud said, "was an even sicker asshole than I thought."

I watched his face carefully as he said this, trying to see where the words were coming from. If he knew about his wife being on one of the tapes (something I hadn't mentioned to Bomber simply because I hadn't gotten into naming any names beyond Abe's, which was all he could deal with at the time), I caught no hint of it.

I drank some of my coffee. "Now look, don't the two of you haul off and take swings at me," I said, "but I want you to consider something. Is there any way Abe's suicide

attempt and his note could be construed as an admission
of guilt—an indication he might have been the one who
killed de Ruth?"

Bomber gave me a disgusted look. "Aw, for the love of
Christ, Joe."

"It's a fair question, dammit," I said defensively. "Abe
had as much reason as anybody to hate de Ruth, more
than most. The one staple in his life, the main thing he
still had going for him, you said yourself, was his loyalty to
BRW and his love of pro wrestling. De Ruth was the guy
who came along and yanked a chunk of that away from
him. Maybe he was threatening to do more, edge Abe out
the rest of the way or something. On the night of the
murder they rode together to the matches and back, at
least as far as Clinton, where the altercation with Tommy
in the parking lot took place. Maybe something was said,
or hinted at. Or maybe Abe figured it was just a matter of
time before de Ruth *did* get around to something like
that. Hell, he admitted he was the one who tried to break
into Paula's place to get at the tapes. That shows he was
desperate. And now this."

Bomber continued to glower. "Next you'll be suggesting he saw the fight between Tommy and de Ruth as
the chance he needed, the opportunity to off de Ruth and
get it blamed on somebody else."

"It scans as at least a possibility, or you wouldn't have
thought it."

"Fuck that. I hate this part of you, this part of what you
do—the constant, impersonal analyzing, rolling everybody's lives over and over, questioning every smudge and
speck of dirt."

"Like you said, it's what I do. What I came down here
for. To clear Tommy, remember?"

"But not to trade Abe for him, goddammit."

"You think that's the way I *want* it to be? It's not something we get to choose," I said, echoing Nicholas
Hatfield's words, feeling the sting of them once again
even as they came out of me.

"Hey, chill out a little, you two," Sam War Cloud cut in.
"Balls. I'd hate to see the way you'd go at each other if you
weren't friends."

Bomber and I suddenly got busy not looking at one another.

"Hannibal's right when he says those are fair questions to ask," War Cloud said at length. "It's the kind of thing he's supposed to do. And even the note Abe left was vague enough to fit in with that line of reasoning. But there's one thing wrong with it."

I waited for him to say what. I could feel Bomber doing the same.

"Last night in the J.I.," War Cloud went on, "when Abe lost it, broke down and started bawling and pouring everything out. If he'd killed de Ruth, and especially if he'd left Tommy holding the bag for it, it would have come out then. That was no act. I was there, man. He wasn't keeping anything back. I think it was the shame of what he bared to everybody—on top of his long-standing grief over Maisie and all his other frustrations—that pushed him too close to the edge when he woke up and thought about it this morning, made him decide to go on *over* the edge."

I drained the last of my coffee, wadded the styrofoam cup into a tight ball. Big accomplishment. "I guess you're right," I said to War Cloud. Then I added, somewhat lamely, "That other was just thinking out loud on my part. Spitballing. Should've kept it to myself."

"Oh, bullshit," Bomber groused. "Wouldn't be you, you started doing anything tactful like that."

I grinned. "And if I wasn't me, who would be, right?"

"Who'd want to be?"

I reached over and chucked him teasingly under the chin. "Tell me you wouldn't miss me, ya big lug."

He swatted at my fist like it was an annoying mosquito.

Sam War Cloud shook his head. "I think you two are nuts."

I let my grin fade. "I'll tell you what I think . . . make that what I know. And that is that those tapes are going to become a *very* hot property. The cops are going to want to get their hands on them, not to mention the state's attorney prosecutors assigned to the de Ruth murder once they latch onto the angle I've been working. The good side of it is that it should lessen the pressure on

Tommy McGurk. The bad side is that it will get real messy for a whole bunch of people who don't deserve to be dragged into it." I stood up. "I need to get in touch with Nicholas Hatfield, see what kind of advice he has on how to proceed. I don't want to get cornered here by the cops until I've had a chance to talk to him."

Bomber and War Cloud stood up, too. "You coming back down to the waiting room?" Bomber asked.

"Not if I can help it. I don't want to get cornered by Mel Dukenos again either."

"Yeah, she wasn't real happy she hadn't been told about the tapes sooner."

I thought of something. "Anyone notified Lori and Tommy about what happened concerning Abe?"

"No," Bomber admitted. "Shit, I never thought of it."

"You ought to. They're too close to him to have to hear it over the radio or on TV. While you're at it, prepare them for the repercussions that might be coming. And what about Paula?"

"The BRW building was buzzing with the news when Mel and I left. I figured word would spread to everybody quick enough. It never occurred to me to notify anybody specifically."

"I'll cover that base in case she hasn't heard yet. She still has possession of the tapes, I need to warn her, too, that the shit is about to hit the fan over them."

We walked out of the cafeteria together, then split up. The two scarred ring veterans headed back to their waiting women, Bomber dutifully carrying a can of Coke.

I went in search of the nearest pay phone.

24

Fifteen minutes of punching phone numbers and feeding hungry coin slots accomplished little except emptying my pockets of their accumulated loose change. Nicholas Hatfield wasn't in his office this time, nor was I able to catch up with him at any of the various numbers suggested to me as alternatives. And a half dozen attempts to get through to Paula de Ruth met only with the repeated electronic burps of a busy signal.

Growing impatient, cramped by the pay phone cubicle, I decided to drive over to Paula's (the busy signal indicating she was at home), then resume trying to reach Hatfield after I'd talked to her.

I exited the hospital and threaded my way through rows of cars in the parking lot to where I'd left my Honda. There was a hazy edge to the afternoon sunshine and the air had taken on a sultry heaviness.

When I reached the Honda, I discovered even more sultriness in the offing. Leticia Cloud was leaning against the front fender, waiting for me.

"It's about time," she said by way of greeting.

"If you say so."

"I told the others I forgot something in the car. I need to talk to you. I expect you have a pretty good idea why."

"Maybe. But I don't like guessing games. You call it."

"Very well. Those damn tapes everyone is buzzing about. You've seen them. Right?"

"Uh-huh."

"Am I on one of them?"

"Don't you already know the answer to that?"

"No guessing games, remember? Works both ways."

"All right. Yes, you're on one of the tapes."

Her eyes jumped away and she made a kind of groaning sound from deep within herself. After a while, her gaze found me again and she said, "Why haven't you been around to question me, like you did Abe and the others?"

"Simply hadn't gotten to you yet."

"Lucky me." She made an anguished, imploring gesture with her hands. "Shit! How could I be so dumb to get caught like that? How could I be dumb enough to get tangled up with Alex Goddamned de Ruth at all?"

"You tell me."

She considered the question. Looked for a moment like she was going to make a thoughtful reply, then dismissed the notion with a shake of her head. "It doesn't matter. Let's just say I was going through a screwed-up period . . . no pun intended. The thing that matters, Hannibal, is that I love my husband. Obviously there is a considerable difference in our ages. That's been the brunt of a lot of jokes and I'd be a liar if I said it hasn't been the cause of some genuine problems between us. But thanks to Sam's patience and understanding we've managed to work through all the crap. We're more in love right at this moment than we ever have been. It's not fair, dammit, for this to come up now."

"You could fill an encyclopedia volume with things that aren't fair in this life. I take it Sam doesn't know about your episode with de Ruth?"

She shook her head. "He knows I did some . . . bad stuff, some running around, retaliating when things were going lousy for us. But he doesn't know I stooped as low as Alex. And he damn sure doesn't know about the tape.

He's been a rock, so patient and understanding, as I said. And forgiving. But I don't know how he'd react to this."

"Maybe he already has."

"What do you mean?"

"Maybe he found out about the tape. Maybe de Ruth let something slip, either inadvertently or on purpose."

It took her a couple of blinks to see where that eventuality could lead. "And Sam's reaction was to kill him? Is that what you're hinting at?"

"The situation holds a lot of possibilities."

"That's preposterous! Sam's no killer."

"That's the tune I keep hearing. Nobody seems to think anybody could have been the killer. But there's a wrong note somewhere, because a man *has* been murdered. Somebody did it."

"This is insane talk. Next you'll be accusing me of pulling the trigger. I didn't come out here for this kind of craziness."

"What did you come out here for, Mrs. Cloud?"

Her nostrils flared. "I thought that much was obvious. You have access to the tapes, don't you? I want to deal. What would it take to get the one with me on it lost or destroyed?"

I smiled. "If you're trying to calm my suspicions, you're not doing a very good job."

"All I'm trying to do is cover my ass and keep Sam from getting hurt."

"Getting hurt by what's on the tape, or by what he might have done because of it?"

"Speaking of tunes, that one of yours is getting awfully monotonous. On the night Alex was killed, Sam and I were away together on a horse-buying trip for the business we're developing for when Sam retires from the ring. We weren't even in town and I can provide if necessary an auction barn full of people able to testify to that; we tend to make a rather memorable couple. Now can we drop that subject?"

"Fine. And we can also drop the subject of doing a deal for your video. I don't operate that way. Even if I did, I got a feeling any control I had over those tapes is about to be yanked out of my hands. Now that Abe's suicide attempt has broadcast the news of their existence, the authorities are going to be all over me for sitting on them in the first place. Doesn't seem like a real smart move to compound that problem by culling out a few choice selections on top of it."

"I'm willing to make it worth your while."

"Destroying evidence in a felony investigation is a felony in itself. I wouldn't be able to spend your money behind bars."

She pushed abruptly from the fender and pressed herself against me. Hard. "I can sweeten the pot with things other than money," she murmured.

"It's admirable," I said, managing to do a fair job of keeping my voice level even as she ground against me, "the lengths you're willing to go to protect your husband's sensibilities." I gave it a few beats, letting her grind away some more, before adding, "Trouble is, that's pretty much the same distance you traveled to put things in jeopardy to begin with. And you're still offering something I can't spend behind bars."

She took a step back. "You're a bastard."

"I can live with that," I said agreeably. "Can you live with what you are?"

On the drive over to Paula's, a massive, hollow roll of my stomach reminded me I hadn't had anything to eat yet today. I've often wondered whether it is a sign of character strength or weakness that I am able to maintain an appetite at all considering my line of work. At any rate, I took care of the immediate problem by coasting through the drive-up lane of a handy McDonald's and rolling away with a double cheeseburger, fries, and a Coke.

I was rattling ice in the bottom of the empty Coke cup and licking the last granules of French fry salt from my fingertips when I slid to the curb in front of the de Ruth house.

Both the IROC Z and Paula's Pontiac were parked in the drive, indicating she was still at home. A gleaming, high-slung Jeep Cherokee was pulled up behind them, indicating she had company.

I walked across the grass and thumbed the bell button.

I heard noises from within. But they sounded wrong somehow, not the sounds of someone coming to answer the door. Then it went quiet.

I hit the button again.

More quiet. The kind that makes the short hairs on the back of your neck crackle with a static charge.

I glanced back at the vehicles in the driveway as if their grinning grills might speak and give me a clue as to what was going on.

I punched the button a third time.

This time it got results. Results I was stupidly unprepared for. The door shot wide open and I had a brief sensation of everything within blocked from view by a massive chest and set of shoulders with wheat-colored hair spilling over them. Then a forearm as thick as my thigh swept out and thudded across my chest, knocking me backward off the front stoop as easily as you or I might tip over a chess piece with a finger flick. I landed flat on my back in a flower bed that felt a hell of a lot less pretty than it looked. What little wind the first blow hadn't knocked out of me, the crash landing took care of. I wheezed and clawed at the sky as ineffectively as a turtle on its back. Stars and pinwheels danced before my eyes, but across the bottom of that part of my vision still taking in reality I saw the giant who'd dumped me on my ass hurriedly leaving the house. In one hand he swung what looked like a black satin mailbag. I lay back and closed my eyes when he was out of sight, deciding I was hallucinating anyway.

I never really went all the way under, but things got awful spongy for a few minutes. I heard the usual bells ringing, strangely echoing distorted voices. The grunts and groans I made trying to suck home some air were magnified in my own ears to the level of test engines roaring in a wind tunnel.

When the world felt like it had turned back into a place of solid shapes and sounds, I opened my eyes to find Paula de Ruth's face hovering close over mine.

"Jesus Christ, Hannibal," she said. "Are you all right?"

There it was. The same dumb question that gets asked

ninety-nine percent of the time in situations like that, and
Christ knows I've been guilty of it myself. But for some
reason it seldom sounded dumber than it did right then.

"Just peachy," I said through my teeth. "It was such a
beautiful day I had this uncontrollable urge to flop down
here in the sunshine and do some upside-down pushups is
all."

Paula arched an eyebrow. "Your mouth seems to be
working fine."

I lifted myself on my elbows. My upper body felt like it
had been backed over a couple times by the Cherokee
instead of just manhandled by its driver. "So tell me," I
said, "what did I do to piss off your pet elephant?"

"Hardly *my* pet elephant." As she said this, Paula absently touched a hand to her cheek and for the first time I
noticed the fresh red welt there. She had on those baggy
shorts I'd seen before, above them a sleeveless pullover.
On her bare arms and legs I spotted more marks that
looked too recent to have come from the match with Ava
last night.

"It was Brick Towers, wasn't it?" I said. I'd only seen
the BRW men's champ twice before; once at Alex de
Ruth's funeral, again on the video segment that showed
Alex honking his skin trombone—the segment I'd kept as
a secret bargaining chip. And now it looked like the main
person I'd kept it a secret from had just paid the price for
my deviousness. All of a sudden the knock on my ass
didn't feel so ill-deserved.

I made it to my feet. "Let's go inside where we aren't
putting on a show for the neighbors," I said. "Then you
can tell me about it."

It didn't take long to start the replay. After dumping
ice cubes into a couple glasses and splashing some bourbon over them, she walked me through it as she talked.

"Brick showed up out of the blue about a half hour ago.
He's usually such a gentle, soft-spoken person, timid almost, outside the ring. It completely unnerved me to see
the rage he seemed to be in. He demanded to know
where the tapes were. At first I couldn't figure out how he
even knew about them."

"Everybody in the northern hemisphere knows about

those tapes," I muttered. "I'll explain about that later. Go ahead."

"When I wouldn't tell him anything, he hit me. The unexpectedness of it and the shock of who it was coming from struck me harder than the actual blow. Then he grabbed me and pulled me up and demanded to know where 'his' tape was, said if I thought he was kidding around I had another think coming. I lost my own temper, tried to fight back. He knocked me around some more, then dragged me into the bedroom and threw me across the bed. He said it didn't take a genius to figure out where the tapes had been shot from, said I was leaving him no choice but to do it the hard way. Then he started ripping the closet apart, smashing into Alex's little tunnel behind. He found the rows of tapes there naturally. He seemed to be after only one—'his' he kept calling it—but because of the way Alex coded the cassette cases he couldn't figure out which one that was. So he yanked a pillow case off the bed and began gathering them all. He'd banged me around pretty good by then, all I did was lie on the bed like a scared ass and watch. Hell, I *was* scared. I didn't know what else he might be capable of. That's when you started ringing the doorbell."

We were standing in her bedroom by then. The closet doors were ajar and shoes and clothing from within were strewn with windstorm abandon on the thick carpeting. Ragged chunks of paneling torn from the back wall of the closet lay among them. Uneven sections of the hidey-hole were exposed, its bare wooden studs looking like the bones of a skeleton showing through huge, dried wounds.

I grunted. "Some rescuing knight I made, eh?"

"You got the job done as far as preventing him from doing any more harm to me. This damsel in distress is grateful."

"You'd better hang on to that until you hear the rest."

"What do you mean?"

"You said Towers kept asking about 'his' tape. Remember? But do you recall seeing him on any of them?"

"Well. No. But—"

"You didn't see the one with him because I held it back on you. Matter of fact, because I'm such a cynical, untrust-

ing jerk, I held *two* tapes back on you. Oh I don't mean I
physically held them back; hell, I left them right in the
bunch with the others. He got what he was after. I just
didn't bother giving you a look or mentioning who and
what I saw on them during my solo screening."

I paused to toss down the rest of my bourbon. Then
took a deep breath and gave her the rest of it. Told her
first about the tape with Abe Lugretti; what was on it,
how I hadn't said anything out of a sense of loyalty to the
Bomber, then the outcome of Bomber's painful confrontation of his old friend. I moved next to Brick Towers,
reporting in a neutral monotone what—and who—I had
seen when I punched the PLAY on his cassette. Wrapped
it with a somewhat feeble attempt to explain my reasons
for tucking it as an ace in the hole.

When I was finished, Paula walked from the bedroom
to the kitchen. I followed her, watched her refill her glass.
She didn't offer me any. I went ahead and helped myself.

After we'd each taken a drink, she said, "Your objective
in not telling me about Brick and Alex had nothing to do
with protecting me from the ugliness of it?"

I thought I'd made that much clear. "No," I said. "I'm
afraid it didn't."

She studied her drink for a stretch. A pool of amber-
orange liquid fading in melting ice. When she spoke, she
said, "I'm not sure what I'm feeling right now, Hannibal.
Alex's bisexuality? That doesn't come as a complete shock
to me. When we were heavily into swinging I knew he
did some experimenting along those lines, although I
wasn't aware he pursued it any farther. I guess what it
amounts to is that by now I'm sort of numbed to any
revelation anyone could spring on me concerning Alex.
Brick Towers as one of his squeezes? Now I have to admit
there's a mind-blower. Mel would have a cow—a whole
herd of cows. Her carefully groomed, quintessential,
clean-cut all-American hero, her answer to Hulk Hogan
and the other champs from the bigger federations . . . a
fairy. God, it's almost funny in a pathetic kind of way. But
it all makes me angry. Angry at Brick for busting in here,
trashing my place, knocking me around. Angry at Alex, in
spite of what I said a minute ago, for being such a . . . a

pig. Angry at you for being—what did you call yourself, a cynical, untrusting jerk?"

"I was being kind. You have every right to your anger. If I'd leveled with you, you would have had something to deal with. Could have given him what he wanted, saved yourself getting roughed up."

"I wouldn't have willingly given that sonofabitch the dirt off my feet, no matter what."

"At least you'd've had the option."

"You know what I'm feeling most of all, Hannibal? I feel hurt. I suppose that sounds strange coming from the big, competent blond amazon, doesn't it?"

"Not necessarily."

"Damn you, I've been nothing but straight with you since you showed up. Through all the shit that's come down, I've cooperated every step of the way: with the police, with you. Mel. Bomber. Everybody. It hasn't exactly been easy you know. But I don't want to see Tommy railroaded for this mess either, and I don't want to see the Big River organization dragged through the mud any worse than it has been. Yet not a stinking one of you really trusts me, do you? I'm tainted by my association with Alex and because I had the audacity to be naughty with everybody's hard-luck kid brother, Tommy. That pisses me off, dammit. What do I have to do to prove to you assholes I'm on your side?"

"I guess," I said quietly, reaching out to wipe away the single stubborn tear that leaked from a corner of her eye, "you have to get the crap smacked out of you."

25

A hundred thoughts whirled and tumbled inside my head during the drive to Brick Towers's place. No clear answers took shape out of the jumble, certainly not the biggie: who had killed Alex de Ruth. But I nevertheless sensed a momentum building. The kind of momentum that past experience had taught me could bust a case wide open. That's the way it goes sometimes. You rattle around bumping against one apparent dead end or slammed door after another and then, out of the blue, when your resolve is starting to dim, something that looked like nothing, no lead at all, will topple away like the phony front of a stage set and suddenly you've got an opening you never counted on.

Brick Towers's actions had been those of a very desperate individual.

What had made him that way?

I brought up the possibility of alerting the cops to his smash and grab, but Paula wasn't having any of that. She was thinking primarily of Mel Dukenos. How would it look, she pointed out, for BRW's reigning women's champ to bring charges against the organization's reigning men's champ? Especially only a handful of days before the big pay-per-view card that was already operating under enough of a jinx. I didn't push her on the matter, for my own reasons.

Towers had obviously heard the latest buzz about the tapes, resulting either from Abe Lugretti's drunken babbling the night before or from his flubbed suicide attempt this morning. Or both. And he'd just as obviously had some prior knowledge about *his* tape because he knew right where to go for it.

But why, if he knew about the tapes before, hadn't he made an earlier attempt to retrieve his? Why hadn't he pulled his strong-arm act on Alex? Or had he? Did his wild display today indicate he might have played some part in Alex's murder and had missed getting the tape at the time of the hit? Was there something more on the video than I'd taken time to watch?

I didn't know the answers to those questions. But it was obvious who did. And I was grimly determined to make him share them with me.

Before leaving Paula, I'd had to lay one final bit of bad news on her. Told her the rest of it about Abe Lugretti, where he was hospitalized and why. Regardless of her concern for the old grappler, at first she still insisted she was going with me to brace Towers. I tossed that notion out of the ring in a hurry. She'd already gotten a taste of his rough side, I convinced her that might have amounted to little more than a prelim match compared to what could go down when I made the kind of horns-out run at him I had in mind. I didn't want her there to worry about on top of everything else.

In the end, she'd somewhat grudgingly aimed herself toward the hospital to check on Abe and that situation while I headed after Towers.

The address I had for the champion turned out to be a renovated farmhouse planted at the end of a long, tree-lined country lane. There was a freshly whitewashed wooden gate closed over the entrance to the lane but it was mostly for show, definitely lacking as an actual deterrent. Its padlocked chain popped like a paper streamer under one tap of the Honda's front bumper.

I rolled up by the house and braked to a halt behind the shiny Cherokee that had been parked in Paula's drive not so long ago.

The place was fairly isolated and under different circumstances was probably a soothing, peaceful spot to visit. But I was keenly aware of my intruder status. As I got out of my car, the slats framing the glass panes of the tall old house's many windows tracked me like rifle scope crosshairs.

I moved with careful deliberateness to the rear of the Honda. Lifted the hatch, spun the combination on the toolbox lock. I slid my trusty old .45 out of the shoulder rig it was wrapped in, tucked it into the waistband of my pants under my shirt. Relocked the box, closed the hatch.

I didn't really believe Towers was my killer. That would be too pat, too much to hope for. And for days I'd been hearing what an untalented wrestler he was, the perfect example of what old-timers like Bomber and Sam War Cloud and idealistic veteran Tommy McGurk sneered at, the kind of ring star who made it with good looks and pretty muscles and showmanship and little or no basic ability. But the fact remained his timing and balance and strength would still be honed to a much finer edge than mine. I'm a pretty good street scuffler and barroom puncher, a guy making it okay in a knock-around racket. But, as I sensed that time in the gym with Bomber and the Kolchonsky brothers, I was also smart enough to know when I was poking around outside my league. It would be dumb to think I could best Towers in a straight-up fight. The heavy piece was a precaution against getting my block knocked off or—in case I was wrong about his culpability for de Ruth's murder—maybe getting killed.

Walking toward the front door of the house with the .45 pressing against my bare belly, I felt a lot less vulnerable in those crosshairs.

Just before climbing the three steps of the wooden porch, I noted smoke pouring from the chimney high above. Somebody besides me apparently felt a chill in the air despite the afternoon's 85-degree temperature.

I wasn't in the mood for knocking. The door was obligingly unlocked, avoiding the fate of the lane gate.

The place was handsomely furnished, done in an interesting blend of modern and traditional. Intricate wallpapering and carpeting alternated with highly polished hardwood paneling and flooring. Overstuffed old davenports were somehow tastefully mixed with functional twists of chrome and Naugahyde. Ornately framed paintings balanced with sleek photo art.

I noticed these things only peripherally as I stalked among them.

I found Towers in a sunken denlike room through a door under the open stairway of the entrance foyer. He stood with his hands in his pockets before a crackling fireplace, intently watching orange flames give way to curls of black smoke.

"Knock fucking knock," I announced from the doorway.

He rotated his head almost lazily to look at me.

"You," he said. "Had a feeling you'd be showing up."

There was no denying what a fine physical specimen he was. Even in a shirt and baggy pants, you couldn't miss the perfect wedge of his body. An exclamation point with arms, as solid-looking as a slab of concrete.

I put my mouth to work before I started considering fan letters. "I'm the county gate inspector," I told him. "I stopped by to inform you that yours is defective."

He grunted. "A lot of things in my life are defective."

I inclined my head, indicating the fireplace. "That seems to be working fine. A shame, though, all the trouble you have to go to to find the right kindling."

"Some things are better suited for burning than others."

The flaming pile was giving off the distinctly acrid odor of melting plastic. Two or three tendrils of scorched black satin fell away at its base.

"What made you think you could get away with it, Towers?" I wanted to know.

He sneered at me. "What do you mean *think* I could? You blind?" He jabbed a finger at the heap of burning cassettes. "That shit is history. I *did* get away with it."

"Not necessarily. I'm here."

His sneer didn't falter. "That supposed to scare me?"

I sighed. "Probably not. You're probably not smart enough to be scared."

"Sure as fuck not of you."

"How about the police?"

"I don't see any badges. And don't bother showing me that one of yours you got out of a cereal box. Everybody knows how far removed from the real cops you private jobs are."

"Maybe the real cops are only a few minutes behind me. Maybe Paula de Ruth was on the phone with them, siccing them on you, when I left to come here."

"I doubt that very much. She wouldn't bring that kind of negative publicity down on BRW over some busted plasterboard and a handful of swiped videos. Even if she did, Mel would talk her out of pressing charges."

"So that's what you were counting on."

"Bet your ass."

"So why wait so long to make your raid then? Why not before? Why not when Alex was still alive?"

He shook his head in wonderment. "Because I was positive the slick bastard was too sharp to keep his tapes right there in his house. I figured he'd have them stashed in a safety deposit box somewhere, maybe duplicates made. Can you believe that? All the time that thing was hanging over my head like the sword of goddamned Damocles and I believed there was nothing I could do about it. Then a suicidal old drunk up and blubbers who's got it and how easy it is for me to get to."

"How can you be so sure there *aren't* duplicates somewhere?"

"If there are, nobody knows where."

"Exactly how much of a threat was the tape to you?"

"You're the private peeper who rutted through the whole collection. You must have seen it. You tell me."

I shrugged. "So you like to wag your weenie at persons who can wag one back. These are the 1990s, that kind of thing will rate a hot headline in the *National Shitslinger* for about one week and after that nobody will care."

"Uh-uh. There's where you're wrong. Pro wrestling

fans *will* care. They haven't evolved past the 1950s. Especially with my carefully manufactured image: the clean-cut, clean-living kids' hero—I'd be through just like that"
—he snapped his fingers with a sharp pop. "And because Mel and BRW have put so much into hyping me, have got so much riding on me, there'd be the risk I'd drag them down right along with me."

"How was de Ruth using this against you? Money? Favors?"

He shook his head. "None of those things. He was into just watching me sweat, knowing what he had on me. But what he wasn't putting into words was clear enough. If and when I got ready to make the move to a bigger federation, that's when he would have wanted his cut. Either to go along for the ride, or some kind of payoff not to squelch the deal."

"So why didn't you go to Mel in the first place? Have her put the squeeze on de Ruth, make him cough up the threat to her big investment."

"And then what? You think she'd keep me around after that, keep pumping a major buildup into a risk like me? I'd be lucky if she let me wrestle prelims in a mask and body suit. My career would be shit."

"Do you really believe you fixed everything with your caper at Paula's?"

"It can work. There've been rumors before about me being gay, but nobody had any proof. Now they don't again."

"In the process of destroying that bit of proof you also destroyed what might have been important evidence in Alex de Ruth's murder case. Do you care about that?"

"Not a lot, no. If he wouldn't have had the boxes marked with that stupid code, I'd have taken care of just mine. I didn't have time to play and sort. Besides, I probably got a lot of other innocent fools off the hook, too—innocent except for a moment of weakness for Alex and his oily charm."

"Gee, you're a regular Scarlet Pimpernel. How about the way you smacked Paula around and trashed her house, some noble purpose served there as well?"

"Perhaps. I don't imagine that cunt has been knocked

on her ass every time she's had it coming. So I've allowed you to barge into my house uninvited, thump your chest, ask your questions, break my gate. I don't want to have to hurt you. We'll call it even."

I shook my head. "Not hardly, asshole."

I hauled the .45 from my waistband, took casual aim, and blew apart the intricate glass-blown replica of a sailing ship that was the centerpiece on the mantle. Glass dust sprayed the room and a thousand glittery slivers tinkled down all around.

"Holy shit!" Towers bleated, throwing his formidable arms around his face and eyes.

Next I shot out the screen of a broad console TV, turning its docile blankness into a jagged black maw belching smoke and sparks. Then a pair of nearby stereo speakers swallowed slugs and went clattering off their perches.

"You're a crazy man!" Towers was hollering, still with his head ducked and arms up, protecting his classically chiseled profile. Glass shards sparkled on his mane of wheat hair. "What are you doing? Stop it, you lunatic!"

I walked toward him, firing off another round mainly to make him keep his head down. A big outdoorsy painting hopped off the wall and pulled a couple smaller ones down with it.

Three steps from the phony hero, I border-shifted the .45 to my left hand, reached out with my right and seized the fireplace poker. Hitched around and swung a hard backhand, laying the length of the rod along his beltline at the stomach. Air whooped out of him and he went backward in a jerky moonwalk before upending over a leather hassock and toppling heavily down. His shoulders hit the carpet with a satisfying thump and his eyes rolled as the rest of his air spouted whalelike out of him.

I stood over him, listening to him struggle to suck some breath back in.

"Now we can call it even," I said.

26

The cops were laying for me when I got back to Davenport. Twenty feet across the city line a black-and-white pulled me over and twenty minutes after that I was plunked in a hardwood chair down at headquarters with Detectives Janky and Brell circling me like a pair of hyenas waiting to tear off a chunk of my hide.

"I tried to be square with you," Janky was saying. "I stood back, held Brellsly here back, too; gave you breathing room, gave you a chance to do your job. All I asked was that you be square in return. Not stir up the citizens unduly, not hold out anything that might amount to anything. And the whole time you were smiling and nodding and agreeing to do just that, you were shitting all over my shoes."

"I told you," Brell said smugly. "I told you we shouldn't trust that smartmouth. These private jingles are all alike in my book, every bit as slimey and dirty as the rocks they hide under to do their peeping from."

Janky stopped circling and stuck his face down close to mine. "That's the thing that pisses me off the most, Hannibal. You made me look dumber than Brellsy because I cut you some slack instead of listening to him."

I passed a cigarette between our noses, hung it from a corner of my mouth. When I snapped my lighter to a high flame, Janky pushed back and straightened up.

Exhaling a cloud of smoke, I said, "Must be a pretty slow day, huh? You guys are sure getting corked up over a few dirty videotapes."

"You know fucking-A well why we're getting corked up over those tapes," Brell snarled. "They're evidence in a murder investigation."

"Oh?" I said innocently. "Funny, I thought that kind of evidence usually got tagged and stored for exclusive access, not left out in the private sector for guys like me to get our dirty, slimy hands on."

Brell looked at me like I was a bug on a drainboard. "Oh, you're cute," he said.

"So we blew it," Janky said. "We missed the fucking tapes when we shook de Ruth's house. The point here is that when *you* found them you should have immediately come forward with them."

"Why would I do that?" I said. "First I had to determine for sure what they were. For all I knew you guys left them behind because they didn't amount to anything."

Janky groaned. "That's an insult to my intelligence."

Brell put it more succinctly. "What a crock of shit."

"That old drunk who decided to suck down a couple lungfuls of propane gas for breakfast this morning didn't have any trouble deciding those tapes amounted to something, did he?" Janky demanded. "They damn near amounted to the end of him, thanks to the way you handled it."

That stung. "Fuck you. Tell me how tactfully you and Mr. Personality here would have gone about it. Besides, that had nothing to do with the de Ruth murder. Matter of fact, I don't think anything on those tapes does. They've been nothing but a waste of time."

Janky spread his hands in a sarcastic gesture. "Well, then. What a relief. You hear that, Brellsy? Hannibal here hasn't been keeping anything from us after all. He was just *sparing* us from wasting our precious time."

"I'll be eternally grateful," Brell said.

The interrogation room door snicked open and a uniformed cop with a nose like a strawberry stuck in his head. "Hannibal's lawyer is here," he said. "He want in on this."

Brell stiffened. "Oh, fuck that."

Janky gave his partner a tired look. "You know a way to keep him out?"

Brell gave each of us, including the cop in the door, a hard glower. Then turned away and glowered at the wall instead without saying anything.

Janky signaled the strawberry-nosed cop. "By all means. Send in whatever dedicated servant of justice waits without."

The cop ducked out of the doorway and a moment later Hatfield stepped through it. He looked rumpled but poised. Ready to take control.

"Evening all."

"Welcome to the First Annual Davenport Film Festival," I said. "Siskel and Ebert couldn't make it so Henry and Tony here are running things. They're interested in screening the work of the late avant-garde filmmaker, Alex de Ruth."

"Is my client being charged with something?" Hatfield asked Janky.

Brell remained standing apart with his back to everyone, still pouting.

"Haven't made up my mind yet," Janky answered. "But we got a whole smorgasbord to choose from. Obstruction of justice . . . Felonious misconduct . . . Tampering with evidence . . . want me to go on?"

"What I want is for you to be specific." Hatfield's gaze swung to me. "Have they read you your rights?"

"From what I could tell I had the right to get sneered at a lot."

Brell couldn't hold back any more. "That's bullshit," he said, wheeling around. "This is routine questioning as part of an ongoing investigation. We don't need to read him his rights for that."

"You do if you intend to detain him any longer," Hatfield replied.

The two men were a study in contrasts standing there
in that shadow-edged little room. Brell, big and beefy and
so obviously seething with an indignant rage. Hatfield, as
tall and slim and cool looking as a stiletto blade.

But I was watching Janky. He'd slipped on his bored-
looking facade again. I had a feeling that was when he
could be the most dangerous.

"Well?" Hatfield said after a full two minutes of stony
silence. "Do you charge him or do we walk?"

Brell lifted and lowered himself on his toes a couple of
times, like a fighter before the bell rings. "Oh, he can
walk alright. He can walk in front of a fucking semi for all
I care."

"Is that a threat, Officer?" Hatfield wanted to know, the
cutting edge of the stiletto in his voice.

"The tapes," Janky interjected almost softly. "All we
want is a look at the tapes."

Hatfield made a condescending gesture. "So do a lot of
people all of a sudden. I just came from a session with the
state's attorney about that very issue. That's where I
heard about Hannibal being hauled in over here. The
tape matter is going to be brought before Judge Flynn
first thing in the morning. I think we'll wait and hear
what the judge has to say before we start passing those
cassettes around."

Brell muttered something unintelligible and turned
away again. His hands were balled into white-knuckled
fists.

Janky raised his right hand and squeezed the bridge of
his nose, high up between his eyes. "All right, counselor,"
he said. "Take your man and go."

"The tapes are *what!?*" Hatfield sputtered into his
raised cup of coffee.

"Gone," I repeated. "Destroyed. Every last one of
them."

"By you?"

I shook my head. "That stupid I'm not."

I gave him a quick rundown of what had transpired
over the past few hours. My concern over the tape issue as
soon as I learned of their existence had become public

knowledge; my failures to reach him in order to discuss that development with him; my visit to Paula's house at the tail end of Towers's raid; my subsequent confrontation of Towers too late to prevent his incineration of the cassettes; the reasons he'd given for his actions when I questioned him.

With dusk settling outside, we had the tiny diner we'd driven to pretty much to ourselves. Just us and the waitress, an orange-haired black woman who stayed at the far end of the counter smoking cigarettes and watching the clock. From in back came occasional pot-clanging noises from the invisible cook.

"So as you can see," I summed up, "I've been running about a half step behind all day."

"Uhmm. I know that feeling. The hurrieder I go, the behinder I get, right?"

Hatfield drained his coffee, signaled the waitress for a refill. When she'd come and gone with her steaming glass pot, he said to me, "You realize everybody is going to have a shit hemorrhage over those tapes being a pile of ashes, don't you?"

"Yeah, I realize that all too well. That's why you didn't hear me bringing it up back there in front of Janky and Brell."

"I take it you're not ready to turn Towers in?"

"He's no more the killer than Tommy McGurk is."

"But think how much more popular he'd be in the shower room at the state pen."

"You think about it if you want. I'll pass. Besides, it isn't his lily white ass I give a hang about. I'm thinking of Mel and Paula and Tommy and War Cloud and all the rest at BRW. Throwing Towers to the cops now could screw things up royally for the lot of them. If I believed he was the one we're after, that'd have to be tough toenails. But the way things stand right now, I'm not anxious to feed everything else into the grinder."

Hatfield drank some of his coffee. "Look, I don't think I officially want to be hearing *any* of this, understand? Having said that, tell me, if Judge Flynn rules tomorrow that we have to hand over the tapes as court evidence—which is a good possibility, I think—how are you going to explain their disappearance and be able to leave the Brick out of it?"

"We'll tell them the truth. But only up to a point. I'm pretty sure I can get Paula—again, for the sake of BRW—to report the break-in and theft without naming Towers. There's nothing else to cover up. The ransacked bedroom, the empty hidey-hole, it's all there to be checked out. All she has to do is say it happened when she was out instead of at home."

"And then we can stand back and watch Janky and Brell and Keefington, the state prosecutor, blow their collective gaskets."

"Shit happens."

"And then what? As far as your investigation?"

I reached for a cigarette. Began somersaulting it between my fingertips without lighting it. I sighed. "I'm not really sure. I've got to stand back and spread everything on a table in front of me, look for a new angle to examine it from. In spite of all the promise it seemed to hold going in, this whole videotape/blackmail scam possibility feels like a washout. De Ruth wasn't playing it like a blackmailer, not in the regular way. He wasn't really squeezing anybody. The whole thing for him apparently was some kind of power rush—just *knowing* he had the goods on a bunch of different people. I can see where that made them uncomfortable as hell, but I can't see the pressure buildup that might lead to murder as a breaking point."

I finally stuffed one end of the butt in my face and set fire to the opposite. I held out my right hand, palm up, fingers curved slightly like I was cupping something. "And yet there's something right . . . *there.*" I squeezed the hand into a fist. "I can smell it, the nearness of it. Wading through all that videotape crap has somehow brought me close. All I have to do is figure out which way I need to turn in order to reach out and grab what I've narrowed the gap on."

Hatfield was staring at the fist I still held up. His nostrils flared with the scent of the hunt. "Do it, man," he urged. "Do it soon. Let's shut the lid on this bitch."

27

Hatfield and I quit the diner, went our separate ways in the lengthening shadows of early night.

I returned to the hospital.

Sam War Cloud and his wife had gone, but Bomber and Mel Dukenos were still standing vigil. Paula de Ruth was there, too. And Tommy and Lori McGurk.

I found them together in the second floor waiting room off one end of the psychiatric ward, where Abe Lugretti had been transferred and would be kept for the minimum three days of observation and counseling that is SOP for attempted suicides.

Surprisingly, the tension I would have expected to be crackling in the air with Paula and the McGurks present in the same room was undetectable. On the other hand, neither was there a palpable warmth emanating back and forth. The shared feeling for Lugretti, clearly, was the balancing factor.

Bomber brought me up-to-date. Abe was coming along okay. They'd been able to spend a few minutes with him. He was apologetic for the bother he was putting everybody to, yet obviously touched by the outpouring of concern; he'd shown some hints of relief at coming up short on the bid to take his own life. He was resting now.

First chance I got, I head-motioned Paula to one side and filled her in on how things had gone since I'd seen her last. "I'm *glad* the damned things are burned!" she'd said upon hearing the fate of the tapes. After I made sure she understood the potential for legal hassle, she was still willing (for the sake of BRW, exactly as I predicted) to file a truncated burglary report, leaving Towers's name out of it. Shortly following our talk, she said her good-byes all around and left to go home and "discover" the break-in.

I hung around, sensing that everyone there was weary, probably wanting to go home, too, but reluctant to make the next move. I tried to lighten things up a little by teasingly chiding Lori for calling me a horse's ass when I'd gotten her husband home that morning in the wee hours. I got a kick when Tommy joined in with me this time. He seemed in better spirits than he had in days. Sometimes it takes the misfortune of others to jar us out of our own self pity.

Mel Dukenos's attitude toward me had thawed a few degrees, but still gave off warning signals not to try and push the chuminess too far with her.

There can't be many places where time crawls slower than in a hospital waiting room.

I finally voiced my intent to call it a day and convinced Bomber to join me for a late supper. Mel declined an invitation to accompany us, allowing as to how she'd stick it out until visiting hours were over, maybe get a chance to spend a few more minutes with Abe if he woke. Lori and Tommy also made noises about leaving, but said they'd stay with Mel a while longer.

Bomber and I found our way to a franchised steak house where we proceeded to lay waste their all-u-can-eat salad bar until a panicky-looking assistant manager scurried out to shove our entrees in front of us with hope gleaming in his eye that this would be enough to stem the devastation.

Near the end of the meal, Bomber turned serious on me and offered his version of the sentiment recently expressed by Nicholas Hatfield. "This business with the murder and the tapes and all the other dirty little secrets is getting uglier and uglier, Joe," he said. "Don't you think it's about time you did your stuff and wrapped the damn mess up so we can get out of here and go home?"

I dropped him off at the BRW building after that, where he picked up his own car. Then we each settled for the places that had to pass for home until the matter *was* wrapped, somehow concluded.

I lay in the dark in my motel room for a long time, smoking, thinking, mentally shuffling and dealing the deck of cards that were the various pieces to the case. Reshuffling and redealing over and over, looking for the winning combination to fall.

Sleep fell instead.

28

Around three o'clock in the morning, the deck of cards got an unexpected bump off the edge of the table and landed aces up.

It started with a phone call.

"Hannibal? Hannibal, are you there?" The voice coming over the line was female and familiar, but not immediately placeable in my sleep-fuzzed brain.

"I must be here," I grumbled. "If I was there I would have stopped you from making this call and waking me up."

"Hannibal, this is Ava. Ava Coltrane."

"Right," I said. "Your car got you stranded somewhere again?"

I sensed her shaking her head. "It's not that. Nothing like that. This is bigger, more important. Life and death important. I think I've got a lot of the answers you've been looking for. It's too complicated to try and cover on the phone. Can you come over to my place? Right away?"

* * *

I scooped handfuls of cold water to my face from the bathroom sink. Ran a comb through my hair. Pulled on slacks and a T-shirt.

The derringer went into the boot clip as automatically as always.

Outside at the car I shrugged into the shoulder rig from the toolbox, socked the .45 home under my left arm. Pulled a loose shirt on over it, buttoned only a couple of buttons.

Phone calls in the middle of the night make me edgy. Especially ones requesting a rendezvous. Most especially ones promising hot information as a lure. I liked everything about Ava Coltrane, had no reason to suspect her of foul play. But there was danger in the air. And the more awake I became, the more warning flashers went off around the periphery of my instincts, alerting me to play it cool, approach this with caution.

I drove to Milan and parked in the alley behind Ryerson's bait shop. Walked the half dozen blocks to Ava's place, sticking to the deepest shadows. Watching hard for cruising cars, figures other than my own lurking on the black edges. A lone wolf hunting in new territory, on the lookout for signs of a pack already claiming the turf.

The night was comfortably cool. Still. Quiet. There were very few windows showing light. Nothing but square black eyes set in faces of night-blurred pastels.

Ava's duplex had lights on in her half. Lots of them. Even a dully throbbing yard light out front.

I went around back and tapped on kitchen glass with the barrel of the .45. Inside, the terrier, Midge, went nuts. Ava appeared before long, carrying him, trying to shut him up.

She frowned out at me. "Jesus Christ, Hannibal, are you trying to scare me to death and wake up the whole neighborhood in the process?"

"I was trying," I explained, putting the .45 back where she couldn't see it, "to be careful. I forgot about Big Mouth there. You want to turn off about thirty or forty of those lights and invite me in?"

Once she had me inside and had the lighting cut, Ava put the dog down. He'd been squirming in her arms, whimpering and emitting frequent yips the whole time. Now he ran at me and began leaping eagerly in the air, bumping against my leg. When I bent over and picked him up, he proceeded to try and lick me to death. "Some killer watch dog," I muttered.

Ava motioned me into the living room and it was there that I saw she had company other than me.

The brunette seated on the frail-looking couch was twenty-fiveish, with a generous mouth turned solemnly down at the corners and big, dark eyes that were sad or troubled or both. She had the kind of quiet, simple prettiness that withstood. Her faded jeans and black Batman T-shirt were neither stylish nor shabby, they were what she wore and to hell with you. Yet at the same time there was a hint of timidness, uncertainty, in her posture, the way she crowded the far end of the short couch.

I recognized her just as Ava was saying, "Hannibal, this is Glynnis Varsey. Glynn, this is Joe Hannibal, the guy I've been telling you about."

The Varsey girl regarded me. "You're the detective— the private eye they hired to look into Alex de Ruth's killing. Ava says you've known about Alex's private videos for two, three days. That you've seen them. I guess that means you know . . . well, that I'm in one somewhere."

I nodded. "Right on all counts."

"From the talk going around, sounds like everybody and his brother knows about those videos by now."

"That wasn't my doing."

"I know. But still." She paused, slid a quick glance over to Ava as if for support. "The thing is, Mr. Hannibal, I figure if it gets around about me being part of them . . . well, I figure that could get me killed, too. Just as dead as Alex."

I felt that prickle of excitement you feel at such times. "By the same person or persons who murdered de Ruth, you mean?" I asked.

"Uh-huh."

"Then Alex was killed because of the videotapes?"

"What? Oh. No, that wasn't why they killed him."

"They?"

"The ones who done it."

"You know who they are?"

"I didn't stand there and watch them with my own two eyes, if that's what you mean. But I heard enough talk afterwards. I know who it was alright."

"And now you're afraid they might come after you."

"Because of the video stuff, yeah."

"But that's not why they killed Alex?"

"No."

I unloaded Midge. He went trotting back to the kitchen where his water bowl was. It's hard to maintain the proper steely-eyed detective image with a miniature mutt in your arms, harder still while wiping dog lick off the back of your hands. But I did my best.

"Exactly who is it we're talking about, Glynnis?" I said.

This time when she looked at Ava she wouldn't look away, wouldn't look back at me.

Ava cleared her throat. "She's worried about protection, Hannibal. If she hands over the names of these people, what's to prevent their friends or family from coming after her, killing her anyway? That's the kind of people we're talking about here, the kind of thing they'd do. That's one of the reasons I suggested she talk to you. Would the police be able to guarantee her safety?"

"Frankly that depends on the police force, and I have to say I'm not that familiar with what you've got around here. I've met a couple of Davenport cops who seem pretty standard issue, but okay enough, I guess. For a solid witness, yeah, they should be willing and able to provide protection until a trial date is reached."

"And after that? What about this Witness Relocation business we see so much of in the movies and on TV? How does that work?"

"That only works for certain categories of crime. I don't know that a simple shooting and whatever else is involved here qualifies."

Ava's mouth pulled tight. "This is more than just a simple shooting. A lot more."

I let my eyes travel back and forth between the two young women. "I can't offer advice or help or anything else if you keep me blindfolded. You called me, asked me to come here because you evidently felt you could trust me. So you're going to have to go ahead and trust me the rest of the way, tell me all of it before you can expect me to do you any good."

Ava turned to Glynnis Varsey. "He's right, Glynn. You came this far. You can't go back. Tell him what he needs to know, exactly the way you told me. The only thing you owe those bastards is to do everything you can to see them put away like they deserve."

29

By daybreak, the assemblage in Ava Coltrane's duplex apartment had grown considerably. In addition to Ava, Glynnis Varsey, and myself, Nicholas Hatfield was there, along with a therapist from the county Family Crisis Center, and detectives Janky and Brell of the Davenport PD.

They had arrived in that order.

I'd called Hatfield first, wanting to make sure we proceeded in the smartest way possible from a legal standpoint while at the same time watching out for Glynnis's best interests. It had been Hatfield who suggested the crisis center representative—a woman he'd worked with in the past—to cover the emotional bases. Janky and Brell were contacted out of a sense of fair play, I guess, tempered by a dose of the old "better the devil you know" axiom.

In all, I sat through Glynnis's story three times.

It never got any prettier.

Hers was a tale of twisted love, greed, lust, intimidation, perversion, and murder that spanned more than a decade in time and reached practically the length of the

Mississippi, from the Louisiana bayous to the cold shores of Wisconsin and Minnesota. At its still blood-wet tip was the killing of Alex de Ruth. At its core, snarled together like the roots of an ancient, diseased tree, lay a great deal more.

Pathetically, in Glynnis's troubled young mind her episode with de Ruth remained a memory of splendid romance and the promise of love. She'd been so deprived of affection—except for the basest kind, received under the vilest of conditions—that Alex's well-rehearsed murmurings and expertly tender caresses had been like an encounter with a fairy tale Prince Charming. Unlike he had done with so many others, de Ruth hadn't seduced and then promptly dumped the young woman. Something had made him continue talking his smooth talk and arranging clandestine meetings for the two of them. But that something hadn't been love, not the kind Glynnis clung to in her imagination. That something had been what got him killed.

"Looking back on it now," Glynnis had said in her initial telling, "I can see where things started turning wrong for Alex and me was when he took so much interest in those special delivery packages I told him about."

"What packages would those be?" I'd asked.

"The ones Papa and Uncle Dub haul back and forth, up and down the river. Boxes of stuff. Their special delivery service, that's their own name for it; they call it that with a kind of snicker, like a dirty joke. Mostly they take the boxes to places where they're setting up for a wrestling show, and somebody comes around to pick them up. A lot of times they'll get other boxes of stuff in trade, like, to pass along at the next stop. Once in a while they'll make a separate trip to do an exchange like that. It's something Uncle Dub got them started in, after he got out of prison down in Louisiana that last time and after . . . well, after some other things."

"Do they get paid for making these special deliveries?"

"Uh-huh. Get paid real good."

"What's in the boxes?" I'd pressed. "Drugs?"

That's where it started getting rougher for her to talk about. "Not drugs," she'd answered in a small voice.

"God, I wish that's all it was." She had averted her eyes again at that point and I can't remember when she was able to lift them to meet mine again.

It took plenty of patient coaxing—from me and Ava both—to get the rest of it out of her. It came in ragged chunks, squeezed out between sobs and gnashing teeth and groans of shame. The telling was as disorganized as it was painful. When we finally had it all and were able to put it in order, it went something like this:

It had started back over ten years ago, back to within a few months of the death of Glynnis's mother. Her father, never exactly a teetotaler, had taken even harder to drink and Glynnis, twelve, the only child left at home, had responsibly taken to cooking and cleaning and caring for him, being "the woman of the house," innocently trying to fill the void left by her mother's passing, doing what she saw as her duty to help ease her father's aching grief.

And then, so unexpectedly to her young mind, he had come into her room in the middle of one night, calling her by her mother's name and reaching for her. Even in his drunkenness he was much stronger than she and, worst horror of all, in the end she had felt her body actually responding to his rough pawing and thrusting.

The next day had been filled with wails of lament and tears of shame and so-help-me-God promises, culminating in even more tearful self-abasement and cautious hugs and then loud prayers to the almighty for forgiveness and guidance in getting past such a wicked twist in the road.

But, slightly over a week later, it happened again.

And then again.

The almighty had clearly turned His back on the prayers. The cycle was locked in. The links of guilt and secrecy and fear and intimidation and misguided blame had been fastened tight, pulling father and daughter deeper and deeper into a nightmare netherworld in which each act, each unspoken cry for help, fed the nightmare hotter and numbed the soul colder.

It had gone on like that for months. Glynnis dropped out of school, avoided contact with others her own age (particularly guys—the few who were gutsy enough not

to wither under her father's baleful glare and actually
tried to talk to her). She traveled with Varsey and his
shifting band of kin to the wrestling shows, helping raise
and lower the ring, sometimes hawking programs, doing
various odd jobs as required. But always she kept to herself as much as possible. She feared that if she spent too
much time in the company of anyone, they would somehow sense her awful secret. At home she cooked and
cleaned and lay rigid in her bed every night, waiting,
listening, scarcely breathing, hoping her father would
pass out from his booze before he got ideas to try something else. She didn't pray anymore. Her faith in Papa's
liquor as her savior was stronger.

And when Uncle Dub got out of prison and came to live
with them, it only got worse. It hadn't taken him long to
figure out what was going on and to deal himself in on the
action. He'd played expertly on the young woman's guilt
and uncertainty—her feeling that she might have somehow *caused* the situation with her father, perhaps se-
cretly had wanted it; after all, she *had* responded that
very first time. Dub was a pig and that was how he made
her feel. Dirtier and lower than ever before. Nights when
Papa drank himself into a stupor were no longer times to
look forward to. On the contrary, they were doorways to
new and more debasing depths. And she didn't dare tell
because Uncle Dub would retaliate by telling about her
and Papa.

Many times Glynnis considered suicide.

Other times she considered murder.

But still it went on. And got worse. Uncle Dub, knowing there was a high-paying market for such things, hit
upon the idea of filming Glynnis having sex with her
father. He forced her to cooperate through continued
threats of exposure and, for the first time but hardly the
last, threats of physical violence. He rigged a blind outside her bedroom window, set up borrowed equipment,
and waited for the inevitable visit by Eugene on a night
when he wasn't too drunk to function. It was Glynnis's job
to keep the activity positioned in such a way that the
camera could catch it.

Glynnis never saw the filmed results, but was forced to

listen to plenty of bragging by Dub about the big bucks he received for it. Through contacts he'd learned of in prison, Dub was able to tap into a regional pedophile ring and market his film through their network. The authenticity of the perversions it detailed made it a hot item. The payoff and the potential for more was great enough for Dub to confront his brother with what he was up to and offer him a more willing partnership. Any moral or paternal reservations Eugene had, and whatever anger he might have felt at being exploited so unwittingly the first time around, were quickly outmatched by his basic greed. There followed a series of films featuring Glynnis performing sexually with her father and uncle, sometimes both at once, as well as with other men and occasionally older women, and even a few times with nameless teenage boys who were brought in like breeding stock, as mechanical and distant and dead in the eyes as Glynnis had become.

This particular chapter of the nightmare came to a close only after Glynnis grew too old and her body filled out with too many womanly curves to be of interest to the sick, select crowd it was being abused to entertain. By then her father and uncle had set up their special delivery service—the transporting of the kiddie porn magazines, photos, and tapes that were the lifeblood of the pedophile network—and were being compensated well enough for these duties to offset the forced retirement of their star.

And so it had continued. Glynnis withdrew deeper into herself, into a kind of protective shell that allowed her to function and go through her daily motions and cope adequately on the outside yet to still cling to a tiny sliver of her own true self on the inside. But that sliver could never gather enough strength to overcome the sensation of being hopelessly trapped. The middle-of-the-night visits by Papa and Uncle Dub came sporadically, just often enough to never let her forget all that had gone before, all that weighed her down and made her feel so enslaved and so unfit for any kind of purer love.

It was little wonder that when Alex de Ruth finally got around to casting his calculating eye upon her as yet another potential conquest, he found her so breathlessly primed for his brand of silken line. Never before had a male danced such an expert version of the mating dance around her. Never before had she been flattered, given gifts, made to feel special. Even though it was all done on the sly (another area of expertise for de Ruth) it still made Glynnis feel wonderful. The kind of wonderful she had dared only dream about in brief snatches scraped from the hard edges of what had been her reality for too long.

To give the devil his due—and regardless of the fact it was totally inadvertent—you had to hand it to de Ruth for at least providing her those moments. Even the videotape he made of their lovemaking became, in Glynnis's eyes, not a further invasion but rather a treasured record of a special event. It was the secrets locked up in her heart and soul that she spilled in return, however, that brought out the true nature of her seducer, even if she was too blinded to see it.

Her first reaction upon learning de Ruth had taped them together was a flashback to the old revulsions. She'd lashed out at him, accusing him of being one of *them,* and he'd instinctively known to pry into that unguarded moment and convince her to tell him the whole story while at the same time soothing her fears, assuring her his only motive for the video was to capture forever her beauty and the beauty they made together.

There was strong irony in the thought of de Ruth, after all his relentless manipulating and conniving to achieve a sense of power and control over people by getting the sexual goods on them, suddenly having this snake's nest of perversions dumped in his lap as a result of what he most likely saw in the beginning as simply another piece of ass on the side. The potential of learning the identities behind the multistate network of pedophiles linked by the Varseys' delivery route must have literally made him drool. It was his pursuit of this that put a bullet in his brain.

As best we could piece together from things Glynnis had overheard, de Ruth must have somehow approached Eugene and/or Dub Varsey with a "cut-me-in-or-else" proposition (although in Glynnis's version his motive was not personal profit, but rather to free her from their evil clutches). Whatever steps de Ruth meant to take to cover his ass clearly had backfired. From the darkness of her bedroom, Glynnis had heard her father and uncle return home the night of the shooting, drinking as usual, laughing and bragging to each other about how they'd taken the "pretty boy" out, how he'd gone down "skidding in his own blood." The shame and fear and low sense of self-worth that had kept her quiet all those years kept her quiet yet again, drove her deeper into her suffering hell.

It was only when Abe Lugretti's suicide attempt brought on the talk of Alex's secret videos that a spark of self-preservation finally flashed inside Glynnis. She knew if it came out that she was on one of the tapes with de Ruth, her father and uncle would have no trouble deducing where the secret of their contraband deliveries had leaked from. They'd think no more of killing her—probably less—than running down a rodent on the highway. And despite her earlier contemplations of suicide, Glynnis decided she didn't want to die. More important, that she didn't *deserve* to die. The spark of preservation flared into a flame of resolve, of retribution, and she at last felt the strength to take action against her tormentors no matter what other consequences she had to face.

As a final sad commentary on the bitter isolation of the life she had been leading, the only person she could think of to turn to for help and guidance was a friend of painfully brief duration from so many years ago, Ava Coltrane.

After Janky and Brell took Glynnis away, the apartment seemed suddenly huge and empty. Hatfield went along, of course, and so did the crisis center therapist who had demonstrated her skill by gently, expertly, gaining the girl's confidence and then aiding substantially in the questioning that helped smooth out the rough initial picture I'd been able to put together. Their immediate destination was the station house, where a statement would be prepared for Glynnis to sign, and then on to a safe house, where she would be secure as the various actions she'd set in motion began to unroll.

As I watched the young woman being escorted from

the duplex, I felt a curious surge of guilt, as if I somehow shared in the blame for what had happened to her. Maybe it was a breath of the common guilt all men must share for the way we've treated our women over the centuries. Or maybe it was remembering a specific case I'd been involved in not so long back that had dropped me in the middle of a troupe of performers and others turning out X-rated videos. My actions then had not only protected the existence of the troupe, but in my mind I'd come to advocate pretty strongly their right to do what they were doing. Now this. Did advocacy of one perpetuate the other? No, dammit, it didn't. I shook myself out of it. Pornography involving consenting adults was one thing, a nebulous thing perhaps that could be argued about forever. But what had been done to Glynnis—incest, child molestation, messing with the mind and body of an innocent—there was nothing nebulous there. These things were aberrations. Participated in at any level, they were crimes against nature as well as society. No amount of argument could make them right, could ever alter the wrongness and damage of their practice.

I took a deep breath.

Outside, the sun was pouring over everything and the day looked as bright and clean as a day could look to anyone who'd heard the things we'd listened to in the more appropriate grayness of dawn.

Ava felt it too.

She stood in the doorway, hugging herself, watching the cars drive off. "That poor thing," she said. "All those years . . . the weight of carrying around such awful secrets."

"But it's over now," I told her. "She's in good hands. She was tough enough to get this far, from here on out should be downhill."

Ava turned to me. "Do you really believe that?"

"I have to. If I couldn't dredge up a chunk of optimism every now and then, the kind of shit I wade through—stuff like this—would drag me down and swallow me."

"Then why keep doing it?"

I shrugged. "The cards I got dealt. It's what I know how to do best."

She regarded me for a long moment. "I think there's more to it than that, a more conscious decision. I think you're a better man than you want to admit."

"Yeah, I'm a pip."

"Look at what you've accomplished with this case," she went on stubbornly. "You've cleared an innocent man, Tommy McGurk, of the charges against him *and* aimed the cops in the direction of the real killers. You've helped free Glynnis from a horrible situation that might have gone on for God knows how much longer. In a more roundabout way, you brought attention to Abe Lugretti's problems so he'll be getting the kind of professional help he's needed for a long time—"

"Roundabout," I cut in, "is the key phrase there. Everything you just said was pretty goddamn roundabout, if you ask me. Hell, I was off chasing the trail of de Ruth's videotapes, trying to run down a blackmail angle. It was *you* Glynnis came to with the information that cracked the case."

"All the same, it was your chasing and keeping things stirred up that caused the rest of it to happen, to fall in place. You have a right to feel good about that."

"I feel thankful it's over—or soon will be. I feel glad it worked out. Mostly right now I'm feeling tired."

"You could rest here." The words brought a subtle shift to her voice, and I became aware that we had somehow edged very close together. She lifted her face and gazed up at me with eyes deep enough to get lost in for a long time. Her suggestion shimmered in the space between us like heat rising off summer pavement.

"Is it wicked to be feeling this way?" she asked in a sultry whisper. "Listening to Glynnis . . . the ugliness of what she went through, how alone she felt all the time. The thought of *all* the ugliness that's out there in the world. I need something . . . nice, to balance those things in my head. What I'm saying, Hannibal, in case you're not getting the message, is that I could stand to be held and talked softly to. And I damn sure don't want to be alone just now."

I got the message all right.

I took her in my arms, held her, talked the soft-talk she
needed to hear.

It turned into more.

And as she clung responsively, I discovered my need to
share in such a moment was as desperate as hers.

30

Later that afternoon Tommy McGurk received notice that all charges against him had been formally dropped.

Within the hour Eugene Varsey was taken into custody at his house on the southern outskirts of Davenport by a heavily armed force of county sheriff's deputies and Davenport blues operating jointly under the direction of Detective Sergeant Henry Janky. Apprehended along with Varsey, as material witnesses, were two second cousins, Al and Dennis Bordeen of Mississippi. Also seized in the raid were three unregistered handguns, five rifles (including two 7mm Savages, potential matchups to the weapon that had killed Alex de Ruth), and two 24″ × 24″ cardboard cartons of magazines and photographs depicting underage boys and girls in various stages of undress and sexual activity. Alvernon "Dub" Varsey, the subject of a second primary arrest warrant, was not found at home and thus evaded capture. A 500-mile radius APB was immediately issued on him.

While all of this was going down, Glynnis Varsey, having delivered her statement, was being tucked away under heavy guard in a safe house, the location of which was known only to a select handful.

After leaving Ava's, I did some scrambling to touch bases, contacting Bomber, Lori and Tommy McGurk, Mel Dukenos, and Paula de Ruth, giving them the facts as best I knew them before the news reports started blabbing their versions. Lori thanked me and hugged me, then hugged Tommy and cried, then thanked me some more and cried some more. Tommy shook my hand, damn near pumping my arm off. It was good seeing them like that, together, happy, their future more promising than it had been for some time. It occurred to me that in all that had happened over the last few days I had somehow never gotten around to delivering on what Lori had originally hired me for, the question of her husband's fidelity. I hoped Tommy had answered that, told her things exactly the way he'd told them to me the night we drove to the graveyard. If she ever got around to asking me point blank, I couldn't duck it. But I was more than willing to leave the matter unaddressed in the meantime, let them work it out themselves.

That evening, a sort of instinctive gathering at the BRW building turned into an impromptu celebration party. Much as Arsenal Island was the hub of the Quad Cities area, BRW had been the hub of this murder investigation. I guess it was natural enough for things to gravitate back there once again at the wrap.

Mel Dukenos was present, of course, drifting mother hennishly among her flock, looking less stressed than at any point since I'd met her. She even had a smile for me. The only problem she seemed to have left was putting together a new ring crew.

Bomber was in fine form, working the room gregariously, his bulk blotting out great chunks of landscape, his booming voice and laughter often rolling over that of everyone else. At one point he and Tommy slipped muggingly into their manager roles, Tommy warning that he'd be coming back to reclaim his champion wrestler now that he was exonerated and Bomber reacting with outrageous indignation. They verbally sliced each other up pretty bad. What made it funny was the insight on what good friends they actually were and the fact that much of what they were saying would probably be played out verbatim for the fans in weeks to come. Even Lori and Paula, who kept warily edging around one another, were able to share in the enjoyment of the hammy performance.

Almost everyone showed up sooner or later. Sam War Cloud and his wife, Leticia; the Kolchonsky brothers; Bouncing Betty and Hank Ryerson; a somewhat sullen-looking Brick Towers; plus a dozen or so others I'd bumped into during my comings and goings from the building. At one point somebody even got Abe Lugretti on the phone from his hospital room and the handset was passed around so different ones could say hi and allow him in on the party as well as circumstances would allow. The party mood further extended to the point where I was surprised to see Paula and Brick off to one side carrying on a conversation not nearly as heated as I would have expected. She later told me he had apologized for his actions in her home the day before and offered to pay for all damages he had done.

More than once I caught nervous glances being slid in my direction from Leticia Cloud or Betty or the Brick. As if they feared I would suddenly halt the proceedings with a shout and a wave of my arms and then trot out some new evidence of their videotaped former indiscretions. I have to admit to a nasty little part of me tingling with the sense of power over them that this provided, a whiff of the kind of trip that had apparently been such a turn-on for Alex de Ruth.

Ava Coltrane caused different kinds of glances to be cast my way. With her body language, her attention to me, little woman tricks with her own eyes, she let it be known as clearly as if she'd been wearing a billboard that something was going on between us. I can't say that I minded. It made me feel a little uneasy at first, but I got over it quick enough. There is, after all, enough male peacock in me to strut and unfurl my feathers a bit upon gaining the attention of a pretty female. Speaking of which, the only troubling thing about this development was having to face Paula. Maybe it was just my imagination or ego that let me think it bothered her at all, but a couple of times I thought I saw her watching Ava and me with a hint of jealousy, maybe sadness playing across her face.

Things broke up before it got too late. Some of the more dedicatedly party-minded made noises about regrouping over at the Jock Itch, but I passed on that.

I returned with Ava to her place.

Where our lovemaking that morning had been slow and gentle and reassuring, that night it became more impassioned, less inhibited. Not quite the near-competitive sexual workout I had experienced with Paula (I guiltily found myself recalling), but nevertheless a driving, aggressive exchange of physical pleasure. Her sweat- and saliva-shiny black nipples danced in the moonlight like animated licorice drops. Her arms and legs and lips reached for me, tugged at me, entwined and engulfed me . . . drained me.

Our soft cries and moans hung in the night long after we lay spent, motionless, still pressed close as if fused by the heat of our exertion.

Everything seemed right with the world.

Later, after dozing and then waking, still in each other's arms, we got to talking the way new lovers sometimes will. Exploring beyond the physical.

At one point we found ourselves going down the "how did you get to be . . ." road.

I gave her my standard summary. Ex Chicago cop, quit the force and quit the whole area when my marriage went down the drain, bummed around the country, returned to the Midwest and settled in Rockford, drifted into the P.I. dodge as a means of putting my instincts and previous training to use.

For her part, Ava told me how she had been a track star in high school but had missed a scholarship that was her only hope of going on to college. So she'd stayed in the area, done some store clerking and dancing and modeling. It was on a modeling assignment, a promo for Big River Wrestling, that she had met Mel Dukenos and had been persuaded to don tights and step inside the ring. Mel convinced her her athletic training made her a natural and her size made her a perfect babyface foil for the bigger villainesses. She'd tried it and been hooked ever since.

"Funny, isn't it," Ava said wistfully, "how our childhood dreams and hopes turn out? You know what I always wanted to be more than anything else in the whole world?" It was a rhetorical question, one I just lay there and waited out. "A ballerina," she went on. "When I was only four or five I saw this picture in a book of a ballerina and, God, I was mesmerized. I started sneaking pieces of Mama's frilly curtains and tying them around my waist like a tutu, then I'd go spinning around the house on my toes with my arms drifting out at my sides. Every Christmas for years I begged and prayed for a pair of ballerina slippers, you know those silky little slip-on things with ribbon laces? But in a field hand's family you got what was practical, not necessarily what you wanted. I longed for dainty slippers but got sturdy work shoes that could be handed down to my younger sisters or brothers after I outgrew them.

"Years later, after I started wrestling, the whole thing became a big joke in my family. My older sister, Mabel, would always tease me about going from wanting to be a ballerina to being a bone-breaker. I had a good comeback, though. I told her I was performing choreographed moves on a lighted stage in front of a paying audience . . . it was just that I was dancing the brutal ballet of pro wrestling, instead of *Swan Lake*. She got the biggest bang out of that. Now, whenever she tells anybody about me, she tells them I'm a ballerina in the brutal ballet."

After the talking, we made love again. Less as strangers than before.

31

The finger still rested in the box it had arrived in—one of those waxed white cardboard rectangles in which a retailer might package an inexpensive bracelet or necklace. The digit was the ring finger from a man's right hand, hacked off none too neatly at its thick base, leaving a puckered orifice of ragged tissue, crusted over by dried blood. The lid of the box had been tipped off and lay beside it on the kitchen table, along with the red rubber band that had secured it.

"When Mel stepped out on the front porch this morning to bring in her newspaper and juice delivery," Bomber was saying, "she found that tucked through the handle on a bottle of citrus blend. This note was inside the box."

He handed me a sheet of lined notebook paper. It bore creases from having been folded to fit the confines of the box and was stained by rust-colored streaks of blood from having shared the space with the severed finger. But its message, crude all-cap block lettering done by a felt-tipped pen, came through just fine: BOSS LADY—YOU GOT MONEY AND YOU GOT INFLUENCE. UNLESS YOU WANT

THE REST OF YOUR CHAMPION HANDED BACK IN LITTLE
PIECES LIKE THIS, YOU BETTER USE THEM TO MAKE SURE
THAT SLUT BITCH GLYNNIS DROPS ALL HER CHARGES.
Naturally there was no signature.

I looked up after reading the demand carefully through
for the third time. The clock over the kitchen sink told
me it was about forty minutes short of noon. Less than an
hour since Bomber's booming knock had roused me out
of Ava Coltrane's bed so he could tersely inform me we
had big trouble, that I needed to go with him right away.
On little more explanation than that, he'd dragged me
from Ava's waiting arms and puzzled questions and
brought me here, to Mel Dukenos's hilltop house in one
of Davenport's highest-priced neighborhoods.

And now I knew why. Knew what had gone wrong,
what the big trouble was.

"Where's Mel?" I asked.

He made a motion with his head. "I took her over to
Sam War Cloud's. Sam and Letty are trying to calm her
down. Finding that box—what was in it—really knocked
her for a loop. She didn't want to be here in the house
with it and I didn't want to take it away—you know,
disturb it for evidence or anything—so I got her out instead. After that is when I swung around to pick you up."

"Yeah. Which reminds me, how were you so sure where
I'd be?"

He twisted his mouth. "Come on. I know you, and me
and everybody else saw the way you two were making ga-
ga eyes at each other at the doings last night. Didn't take
psychic powers to have a pretty good idea what was on
the agenda next."

So much for that. I backed up a square. "So Mel called
you over right away after she received this surprise package, is that the way it went?"

His expression turned a little funny. "She didn't have
to, uh, call me over . . . that is to say, I was, uh, already
here. She was making me breakfast." And then the big ox
actually blushed.

It still took me a handful of seconds and a couple dumb-
founded blinks to get what he was driving at. When I

finally did, I felt my mouth spread in a lopsided grin and I said, "Why, you old dog, you."

He puffed up a bit in spite of himself. "What? You think you're the only cowpoke can ride into a strange town and find a female willing to spare him a kind word or two?"

I kept grinning and said again, "You old dog."

"Knock it off already," he responded with a choppy wave of his hand. "We got more important stuff than that to be discussing. And don't you go blabbing it around, either, you hear?"

"Oh, sure. That's the business I'm in, right?"

"The business you're supposed to be in is detecting." A jerk of his head indicated the grisly fare spread on the table. "So what do you make of that?"

"Easy. Somebody got their finger lopped off."

"Brilliant."

I tapped out a cigarette and got it going. "The note says 'your champion' and the finger obviously is that of a male, indicating they're referring to Brick Towers. Anybody verified anything—tried checking on him, getting hold of him?"

"I drove out to his place after I left Mel off, before I came to get you. The front gate to his property had been busted and there was nobody around, no answer when I knocked and hollered."

"Don't put too much stock in the broken gate. I did that the other day."

"You?"

"I'll tell you about it another time. The important thing is that Towers *does* appear to be missing. How about the ring—Mel recognize it?"

I was making reference to the ornate band wrapped around the chunk of meat in the box, filling most of the space between its gory base and the first knuckle. It bore a big, glittery, jewel-encrusted "B." I thought I recalled seeing a similar ring on Towers's right hand when he was covering his head and ducking the fallout from my shots, but couldn't be positive this was the same one.

Bomber took away any doubt when he said, "Yeah, Mel recognized it right away. All the members of one of Towers's fan clubs chipped in and bought it for him for

Christmas a couple years ago. I guess the recognition factor was the reason whoever took him picked that finger to send."

"The fact they chose to whack off a finger at all—as opposed to sending just the ring, say, to establish their bona fides—shows we're dealing with some seriously dangerous characters," I pointed out.

"Who do you figure—Dub Varsey?"

"I haven't heard any news reports lately. He still on the loose?"

"Yep."

"That'd make him a logical suspect then. Not only trying to clear the way for Eugene, but himself as well. On the other hand, from what I've heard of this Varsey bunch they've got relations of one kind or another all over these parts and they hang pretty tight. Could be any one—or a dozen—of them."

"You'd have to bet they'd send more than one to take Towers alive."

"Uh-huh. Of course there's no guarantee he *is* alive. Way easier to chop parts off a dead man than a live one, to say nothing of trying to keep him captive in the meantime."

"Jesus, Joe. You're a real ray of sunshine."

I shook my head. "Not much sunshine to spread on this situation, old buddy. How does Mel feel about calling in the cops?"

"Said it was up to you."

I sighed. "Looks to me like it's about that time."

Janky and Brell kept it real low key. Just the two of them and a pair of lab boys showed up.

Bomber reviewed the events of the morning, answered a line of standard questions. After that, while the lab guys tinkered with the little box and its contents and examined the front step area where it had been left, we stood around chewing over things in general.

"I have to hand it to you, Hannibal," Janky was saying, "you sure have a knack for stepping right in the deepest part of the pile."

"Yeah," I had to agree, "I tend to give a whole new meaning to the term 'gumshoe.'"

We laughed a little harder at that than it deserved, the way people sometimes will when they feel a common tension drawing at them.

Into the hollow quiet that followed, Brell said, "This Dub Varsey—assuming this *is* his handiwork, which seems a pretty safe assumption—is a plenty bad actor. I've been reviewing his file. The Varsey clan has its share of hell-raisers and no-goods, but old Dub takes the prize. Goes way beyond hell-raising into plain mean and dangerous. Which makes the implied threat in that note all the more serious. Believe me when I say he'd think no more of chain-sawing Towers into a pile of soup meat than any of us would of squashing a waterbug."

Bomber grunted. "Kind of makes you wonder why they let him walk out of that Florida prison, don't it?"

"I can't afford to wonder about that," Brell said, his mouth pulling into a hard line. "All guys like me and Janky can do is keep putting the assholes in—or *back* in, as is too often the case."

"No kind of lead on where Dub might be?" I asked.

"Not a hint," Janky answered. "Even before this came up we had the feeling he didn't make a run for it, that he was laying low right here in the area. All the kinfolk he's got around and the way they tend to feel about the law, there's hundreds of places he could go to ground, practically a network right under our noses."

I said, "The incest, the kiddie porn angle—not even that makes a difference? Even hardass prison inmates have the instinct to draw the line in those areas."

Janky spread his hands. "I don't see anybody lining up to hand him over."

"You got to remember," Brell said, "in the Varsey family and its offshoots there's probably already been a good deal of inbreeding over the years. You don't have to go too far south of here, on either side of the river, to run into some pretty boondock attitudes. Attitudes that look on women as being mainly useful for cooking or fucking. For the sake of convenience, little matters like age and bloodlines can get shoved aside pretty easy. As far as the kiddie porn thing, hell, wouldn't have been hard for Eugene and Dub to rationalize that away either. You know, that they were just deliverymen, not like the sickos who actually enjoyed the stuff. The old 'Somebody's going to do it anyway, might as well make a buck off it' attitude."

"All this talk about Varsey kinfolk and how close they are and all," Bomber said, "is that girl completely safe where you've got her?"

"Safer than the Pope taking a poop in the Vatican's bombproof toilet," Janky answered flatly.

"Affirmative," Brell clamped on.

I nodded. "That makes this run at the thing through Mel and BRW a kind of desperation move. Can they really believe she swings that much clout, could somehow force the kind of trade they're suggesting even if she wanted to?"

"Like you said," Brell pointed out, "they're desperate."

"Besides," Janky added, "look at it from their viewpoint. All through the years Varseys have been going to jail for everything from boosting cars to spitting on the sidewalk. But pick up a newspaper any day of the week, turn on the TV news, how many rich movie stars or politicians or sports celebrities are walking away from their crimes with a slap on the wrist and a few hours of public service? Money talks real loud in this judicial system. Money and influence, like the note says. They figure they hit on a way to make Mel Dukenos put her money and influence to work for them."

"When is Eugene Varsey's arraignment scheduled?" I asked.

"Tentatively for tomorrow," Janky answered. "There's a team due in this afternoon from the FBI's Pedophile Task Force. We need to review everything with them before we decide on all the charges to be brought. In the meantime, Eugene ain't saying shit. The two cousins from Mississippi, on the other hand, are willing to sing like tweetie birds. Only trouble is, they don't know much, haven't been on the scene long enough."

"Since the note doesn't stipulate any other time frame," I said, "sounds like we've got until tomorrow then before the Varseys make another move. They'll know by the arraignment outcome if this bit today accomplished anything."

"And since it won't have," Bomber said pointedly, "we can only expect things to get messier."

Brell's jaw muscles worked. "Yeah, you can figure they won't give up. They're not the type to stop at this."

I bared my teeth in a cold smile. "That's fine. Because whether they know it or not, they just tangled assholes with the type who won't *let* it stop at this."

The afternoon crackled with activity.

It didn't take long for word to work its way through the BRW ranks about this latest piece of bad luck to befall the organization. Because she was still too upset to return home or to go to her office, Mel Dukenos remained at War Cloud's place, a horse ranch setup on the outskirts of Moline, not far from Quad City Downs, where the Indian and his wife raised and trained trotters as an alternative to their days in the wrestling ring. The ranch became the center of a more or less constant flow of BRW personnel phoning or stopping by to check on Mel and the status of things in general.

The FBI team arrived in Davenport and immediately closeted themselves with Janky and Brell. As is usually the case when the Feds get involved, everybody's asshole tightened up like a vise and things got so hush-hush you could've heard a mouse peeing on cotton anywhere around police headquarters.

I did learn that the same two lab men who came to Mel's house were accompanied to Brick Towers's place by a sheriff's deputy so they could scour the scene for any signs that might be helpful. I'd warned Janky and Brell of the damage I'd done there. It was still undetermined exactly where or how Towers had been abducted. I also heard that prints from the severed finger had been matched to Towers's National Guard records (back when he had been plain Paul Stervol from Akron, Ohio), thus pretty much eliminating the possibility of a hoax.

TV and radio news broadcasts were airing that the wrestling star had been reported missing. They failed to tie it in with the de Ruth murder and subsequent Varsey arrests, however. More than one smug anchorperson presented the item with thinly veiled implications that they believed it to be some sort of publicity stunt.

I got back to Ava and we met for a late lunch at a seafood joint she suggested. She looked stunning in that way that a woman looks when you see her for the first time after making hard, sweet, passionate love to her. I brought her up to date over shrimp and rice. My words turned her pensive, angry. "Those dirty bastards," she kept muttering.

After the meal I headed back to War Cloud's. I thought Ava might accompany me but she begged off, claiming a number of backlogged personal things to take care of. We agreed to hook up again later that evening.

It was past six P.M., dusk was starting to lengthen the shadows on the trees and outbuildings, when I recognized the orange Chevette rolling in a cloud of dust down the long graveled lane to Sam War Cloud's ranch.

I was hanging out. Wasn't much else you could call it. Too far off my own turf, with no leads and no snitches to send digging, I couldn't see any angle to pursue except to wait for something to break and be ready to pounce all over it when it did. It wasn't a role I was good at, and sure as hell not one I liked having thrust upon me.

I had some help playing this waiting game, and the frustration level was climbing all around. A handful of us —Bomber, Sam, the Kolchonsky brothers, myself—were leaning on one of the corral fences, sipping cold beer out of cans from a refrigerator in the barn, absently watching War Cloud's grazing horseflesh while we went round-robin on the theme of "if I could get my hands on . . ." Leticia Cloud and Mel Dukenos were in the house. Nicholas Hatfield had showed up about a quarter hour earlier, having no news to speak of and looking somewhat incongruous in a blazer and tie, but proving especially adept at flights of fantasy justice.

It was this scene that Ava rolled up on.

I pushed away from the fence, walked over toward the car as she braked and cut the engine. There were some catcalls from behind me, the way a bunch of guys will do to one of their own whose hormones might be causing him to stray. "I think she's checking up on you, Hannibal," one of the Kolchonskys said. And then the other one suggested, "Maybe she's been out shopping for bull rings. Came to have old Sam here help clamp one on you."

Ava was grinning when I leaned in at the driver's side window. "They giving you a hard time?" she said.

"They're just jealous."

She winked. "Don't you forget it, big guy."

There were two teenaged boys of about sixteen also in the car, one in front, one in back. It looked like the one in the seat next to her bore something of a family resemblance.

Ava saw me speculating. Gesturing toward the kid on her right, she said, "Hannibal, this is my brother, Rudy. In back there is his friend Raymond. Guys, this is Joe Hannibal, the man I've been telling you about."

"Rudy. Raymond," I acknowledged.

They returned nods of greeting, two dark, smooth faces bobbing in unison. Nowhere was their youth more evident than in their eyes. Devouring gazes, uncertain but damn sure unimpressed.

"It so happens," Ava picked up, "the boys did a little fishing this afternoon. Out on the river south of here a ways. Didn't spend much time at it, didn't catch much either. Nothing so unusual there. But what I thought you might find interesting was what they *saw* while they were out."

She was obviously setting something up. I went along. "And what was that?"

"Men with guns," Rudy answered. "Lots of men. Lots of guns."

"That's right," Raymond added. "That ol' island was crawlin' with 'em."

"What island?"

Both of them blinked at me as if my question was astonishingly dumb. After a couple beats, Rudy said, "Why, Wild Pig Island, man."

"That's right," Rudy tagged on. "Right where Ava told us to check."

I was tempted to ask them something else, just to see if

they always answered in tandem that way. But I passed, went back to Ava instead, saying, "You into booking fishing excursions on the side?"

"The boys go fishing about every day anyway," she said offhandedly. "I just sort of borrowed them a boat and suggested a particular spot for them to try."

"At this Wild Pig Island."

"Uh-huh."

"Where there are a large number of men with guns."

"That part I didn't exactly figure on. But it sure makes you wonder what they got there so important they have to guard it with all that firepower, don't it?"

"I get the feeling you already have a pretty good idea what the answer to that might be."

"Matter of fact I do. But first let me tell you about Wild Pig Island. It's a ways south of here, like I said. Down near New Boston—where I used to live and where I went to school for awhile with Glynnis Varsey, remember I told you? My folks still live down that way, as far as that goes. And Rudy here. And Raymond, too. Anyway, it was while I was chumming around with Glynnis—before her old man put his foot down about her hanging out with me—that I first heard of Wild Pig Island. Me and her took a skiff out there for a picnic and swimming one time. We were at that pimply, awkward stage where boys weren't in the picture very much—not that they ever were for Glynnis, only now we know the reasons why. But getting back to the island, it was this narrow, spiney twist of land, not very many places along the shoreline where you could even put a boat in, all humpy rocks and hills inland, grown over with trees and scraggly bushes and peppered with shallow caves and a few that weren't so shallow."

"Way it still is today," Rudy said, nodding. "Ain't changed a lick hardly in years."

"That's right," Raymond agreed on cue.

"Not likely to ever change," Ava said, "because there's nothing there worth the effort it would take to fix the place up. Not all that big to begin with, plus no decent shoreline, like I said, or no decent spot to build a house or anything on. Maybe a fishing shack or two, that'd be about it. That was Glynnis's whole point, see, the day we went out there. The one piece of property her family ever managed to accumulate over the years, she said, and it turns out to be this rocky chunk of nothing."

"The Varseys own the island?" I said.

"That's what Eugene Varsey was claiming back then. I never heard of anybody disputing him. But, then, who would bother? His big plan was to build a tavern and a boat service dock out there, cash in on the pleasure boat trade in the spring and summer. Donald Trump couldn't afford the dredging and blasting and ferrying it would take to do something like that, even the most simple version. I think old Eugene got as far as posting some hand-painted No Trespassing signs and that's where he ran out of money. I don't know what all his excuses were because by then Glynnis and I weren't allowed to be friends any more. Within a few months they moved away."

"The signs are still there," Rudy said. "Nobody pays any attention to them, though, on account of there's never anybody around to enforce them. Except once in a great while. The island is a popular place with kids, see, because it has cliffs for diving off of and the caves are spooky and fun and after the water has been high they're a good place to trap turtles."

"That's right," Raymond said. "It's a good place for beer parties, too." When his buddy shot a hard, over-the-shoulder warning with his eyes, Raymond added with comically sputtering urgency, "I mean, not that *we'd* know anything about that firsthand, of course."

Ava couldn't help grinning in spite of herself. She also couldn't help laying on a dollop of big-sister lecturing. "You little shits better not know anything about it firsthand. And if you do, you'd better double-damn sure not let your fathers ever find out about it."

"When you say 'once in a great while' somebody enforces the No Trespassing postings," I said to Rudy, "you mean there have been other incidents like today?"

Rudy shook his head. "Never like today, no. Always before it'd be a case of a couple, three guys—white trash, some kind of Varsey kin we always figured—who'd turn up there unexpected, be there camping out, like, when somebody went to do some swimming or turtling. The swimmers'd get hollered at and run off, you know, 'Can't you trespassin' brats read? Get outta here!'—like that. Wait a few days until somebody was brave enough to row back out for a peek and usually the island would be empty again and things would go back like before."

"Never any guns before?"

"Probably were times when those Varsey trash had hunting rifles in their camp. But I never heard of anybody getting them waved right in their faces like today."

"Were the guns you saw today rifles?"

"Yeah."

"That's right," Raymond said. "And the guy up on the hill had a pistol, too. Stuck in his belt."

"You said there were a 'lot' of men and a 'lot' of guns. Think a minute now. By count, how many of each did you actually see?"

The boys exchanged glances.

After a bit of a hesitation, Rudy began marking off the answers to my question. He said, "Okay. First there was the guy who came to the shore right where we were getting ready to put in. He's the only one who said anything, told us if we knew what was good for us we'd keep on moving, that the island was private property. He was carrying a rifle. Up the slope, up near the top, like a lookout, then we could see another guy with a rifle. Big sucker, with one of those big curved clips. That'd be the one Raymond said also had a pistol. Then, as we were getting away from there, two more guys, both with rifles, came into view at different spots on the shoreline, watching us."

"That's right," Raymond said. "Watching like they were trying to look holes right through us."

"Better than trying to *shoot* holes through us," Rudy said.

"All right," I summed up. "So you saw four men, four rifles, one handgun."

Something in my summation must have sounded accusatory because Rudy got defensive. "Hey. It *felt* like a lot more."

"That's right," Raymond said. "Felt like there was a

whole doggone army there. In the bushes, watching with their eyes and with their gun barrels."

"I know the feeling," I said appeasingly. "One set of eyes over one gun barrel is enough to make you feel that way."

I let my gaze drift down to Ava. She was regarding me under a sharply arched brow. "Well? Are you thinking what I'm thinking?" she asked.

I was, but I wanted to go careful with it. "It's a ways to reach," I said. "But it's certainly a possibility."

"A damn good possibility, if you ask me. I've been thinking about that island ever since we lunched today. About the Varsey claim to it, how they've used it before, how Dub Varsey is in hiding somewhere and now he's got Brick Towers his hostage . . ."

"We can't be positive it's Dub who has Towers."

"Oh who the hell else would it be? And what better place to hold him—*and* lay low at the same time—than Wild Pig Island? Why else would they have all that artillery out there? I guess it was pretty foolhardy of me to send the boys the way I did, but it worked out okay. We verified there's something heavy-duty going on, and it isn't likely Rudy and Raymond aroused any suspicions in the process. *Whoever* is on that island, they'll still be there, like sitting ducks."

"Only sitting ducks aren't usually armed to the teeth," I pointed out. "And if everything is the way you have it figured, then the next move we make had better be exactly the right one or Brick Towers will end up a cooked goose in the crossfire."

32

Anthony Brell's expression was that of someone who'd just bitten into a dirty sweatsock. "Man oh man," he groaned, "talk about your jurisdictional can of worms. We've already got strings shooting off this case in every direction you can think of, enough to bring the Federal-fucking-Bureau of Investigaion here to stick their pointy little noses up our ass. Now you're suggesting yet another state, another county, maybe even the Coast Guard."

"What we're suggesting," Nicholas Hatfield pointed out forcefully, "is action that could possibly save a man's life."

Brell aimed a finger. "There's the key word—'possibly.'"

"You have to admit there appears to be *something* mighty suspicious going on on that island," I said. "Even if it turns out totally unconnected to this Varsey-Towers bit, doesn't it deserve looking into on the basis of a reported concentration of heavily armed men?"

Brell nodded. "Looking into, sure. I could probably convince the Coast Guard or a couple sheriff's deputies from Mercer County over on the Illinois side to take a boat ride out there for a look-see. That's the way it is with islands on the river, understand; whichever side they're closer to is the state and county that has jurisdiction. From the map, this Wild Pig Island clearly belongs to Illinois. I'm never sure when it is the Coast Guard gets involved. But anyway, if you're right, if Varsey and/or Towers are there, seems to me that kind of minor check would be the *last* thing you'd want. Be too easy to hide them through something like that. All it would accomplish would be to put the bad guys on alert so they could move things somewhere else. What you really need is a strike force to hit the island under the auspices of a warrant, a sweep and seize like we did at Eugene Varsey's place yesterday. Trouble is, I don't think you've got enough this time to convince a judge to issue that kind of warrant. Especially not with the Feds on the scene, sifting every little detail through their tight starched asses and bogging down everything and everybody around them."

The three of us were seated at the broad, cluttered desk Brell shared with Janky in a dim corner of the Davenport PD squad room. Hatfield and I had come here seeking help and/or advice on how to proceed with the information Ava and the two boys had provided. As senior partner of the team, Janky was still cloistered somewhere in the building with the FBI agents. Hatfield had used his influence to pass a message through the lines and Brell had availed himself in response. Judging from the attitude he was displaying toward his federal cousins of the badge, parting their company for a while was no real hardship on him.

"Come on," Hatfield said now. "You cops nurture judges all the time. Don't you have one who owes you some kind of favor, one who might be willing to consider a warrant under less-than-ideal circumstances?"

Brell blinked with exaggerated innocence. "Why, counselor, I'm surprised at you. To hint not only that such practices take place but to actually be encouraging something of that sort."

Hatfield twisted his mouth wryly. "Bite my habeus corpus, Brell."

"Besides," the cop said, "even if—*if*, counselor—I had

that kind of arrangement somewhere here in my back yard, what good would it do in Mercer County across the river?"

"Maybe your judge friend has a judge friend over there?" I tried.

Brell shook his head.

"How about using the APB on Dub Varsey as an angle? Claim he was spotted on the island?"

"Hell, there've already been dozens of reported sightings on Dub everywhere from St. Louis to Minnesota. Nobody's going to get too excited about another one."

Brell spread his hands. "Look, you both know my reputation. I'm a hothead. Your island story smells good to me, which is to say it stinks of something rotten as hell going on there. Nothing I'd like better than to go there with you and bust a bunch of Varsey heads, maybe shoot a couple of the fuckers. Wouldn't be a lick amiss, I promise you, no matter what. And there's one or two more places right here in town I'd like to hit in the same way. But there's bigger stuff to consider, fellas. The murder rap looks like a lock. Preliminary ballistics on one of the 7mms seized at Eugene's matches as the weapon that killed Alex de Ruth. And then there's the kiddie porn angle—the main thrust of the FBI's involvement so far. Plus the way that poor girl Glynnis was treated all those years. It all makes you sick enough to vomit. That's why I don't want to see anybody—me, you, whoever—go off half-cocked and do something to queer some bigger aspect of the case. You understand what I'm saying?"

Hatfield sighed frustratedly.

I said, "I also understand that when Eugene gets arraigned tomorrow, Brick Towers—wherever he is—is almost certainly going to get more pieces of his person hacked off. Maybe get hacked to death."

"You realize there's a good chance he may already be dead," Brell said.

"I've thought of that. Doesn't sit very damn well one way or the other—especially not when I figure I got a good idea where to lay hands on the ones responsible but just don't know how to reach them."

Brell eyed me. "You're all right, Hannibal. I had you

wrong at the beginning and I'm a big enough man to admit it. You've played pretty square with us. Jesus, don't you think all the things you're telling me is putting a knot in my gut, too? Janky's the one who's got a sharp, level-headed way of looking at these kinds of things. He's been keeping me in line for years. As soon as I can get him away from those Federal fucks, I promise to run this by him. Maybe he can see something. Maybe he's got a good Mercer contact he can put you in touch with, have the island put under surveillance. Maybe we can get a helicopter to fly over, get some photographs or something more solid to take to a judge."

"We don't have time for anything as elaborate and drawn out as that. Not with the arraignment scheduled for tomorrow."

"That's up to the Feds. In the meantime, my advice is to grit your teeth and sit tight. Give me a chance to get back to you."

There didn't seem to be anything more to say. Hatfield and I stood to leave.

When we'd gone about a half dozen steps, Brell said, "Hannibal."

I looked back over my shoulder. He was messing with some papers on the desk, not meeting my eyes. Offhandedly, he said, "I just remembered that I have a couple buddies on the Mercer County sheriff's force. I might get a chance to call them after a while and mention to them to sort of keep an eye on Wild Pig Island tonight. Just in case there might be . . . oh, I don't know, some kind of disturbance or something out there later on. They'd be sure to be in a position where they could scoot right out and help get things under control. And naturally they'd have to thoroughly investigate the cause of the trouble."

I stood looking back at him for the better part of a minute. He kept busy with the papers.

"Okay," I said measuredly. "You never know. That might be a real good idea."

In Hatfield's car, as we rolled away from the cop shop, he said, "What Brell was hinting at there at the last, you wouldn't actually consider something so crazy, would you?"

The night air sliding in through the open windows was growing warmer instead of cooler, getting heavy and stickily humid.

"Is it so crazy?" I said.

"Come on, for crying out loud. You know damn well it is."

"Crazier than just backing away from it—leaving a man to be carved to hamburger, or worse—because of a few legal technicalities?"

"Maybe Janky will come up with something."

"Shit. When? Tomorrow? Next week? We're running out of fucking time. Do *you* know a persuadable judge who'd back a police strike on the island tonight?"

"If I did, don't you think I'd have said so by now?"

"There you go."

"Dammit, doing something as cockamamy as you're thinking could have disastrous repercussions on the rest of the case. Even Brell could see that."

"I don't care much for the repercussions of *not* doing something as cockamamy as I'm thinking, either. Besides, how could anything I do tonight screw up what's already gone down? That was all legal and by the book."

"You can never be sure. Things can get twisted around, doubts can be cast. Accusations made that can sway a jury in ways you can't measure, even on something officially stricken from the record. Sometimes that's all it takes. I should know, that's what guys like me do for a living, remember?"

"Uh-huh. And you should remember that guys like me aren't much for sitting on our thumbs on the sideline. I've had my fill of that for today, thanks."

Hatfield grunted. "Jesus, next you'll be telling me that a man's got to do what a man's got to do."

I looked at him in the shifting pattern of streetlights and neon that was about to give way to hazy starglow as we passed out of town. "As corny and clichéd as it sounds," I told him, "that's exactly what it comes down to sometimes."

* * *

We arrived back at War Cloud's and it didn't take long to discover that Brell and I weren't the only ones with cockamamy notions dancing in our heads. The congregation had grown while we were away and had all gathered in the den of the ranch house, a comfortable, sunken room furnished with a nod toward Sam's and Leticia's Indian heritage. Exceptions to the theme were a wide-screen TV not in use at the moment and a wet bar toward the back that was getting a good deal of use. The walls were adorned with wrestling memorabilia and a smattering of ribbons and trophies from the more recently undertaken horse racing pursuits.

Ava was there, having returned after taking her brother and his friend home, and it was clear that all present had been filled in on her suspicions. In addition to everyone else who'd been on hand when Hatfield and I left to have our discussion with the police, Lori and Tommy McGurk had shown up. As well as Betty and Hank Ryerson. And Paula de Ruth, looking pale and lovely and lonely, a part of the scene yet somehow removed from the others.

It occurred to me that this same group only a day or so earlier would have constituted a gathering of practically all the suspects I'd had in the case, the way they used to bring them together in the old Charlie Chan movies for the big unmasking of the killer. I'd never been much of a Chan fan, and I guess you can see why. If I'd tried something like that, look what a fool I'd have made of myself.

There was no longer a killer to unmask. That part had already been taken care of. But what was left was no less grim a task.

"Well?" Bomber asked of Hatfield and me. "How'd you make out? What are the cops going to do?"

The lawyer and I exchanged glances. I took a breath and told Bomber and the rest how we'd come up empty and tried to give the reasons why. Their mood wasn't exactly what you'd call receptive.

"What a crock of bullshit!" Sam War Cloud boomed.

"I can't believe it," Mel Dukenos said. "They're going to just *leave* Brick there at the mercy of those . . . those animals?"

"We can't offer enough proof that Towers is actually on that island," Hatfield attempted to explain. "A hurried, ill-advised move by the police or anyone else at this juncture could do more harm in the long run than good. We need to wait until—"

"Until what?" Mike Kolchonsky cut him off. "Until they mail more pieces of the champ? Maybe they'll provide a fucking return address next time—will that be enough for the cops to go on?"

"They can put the island under surveillance. If Towers is there and his captors try to move him—"

This time it was Bob Kolchonsky who wouldn't let him finish. "What if he's *dead* by the time they go to move him? Chopped to bits, like the note said? You expect us to wait around for that?"

I edged closer to the Bomber. "You got any control over this?" I asked him.

"Control over what?" he asked back.

I jerked my thumb. "This. This vigilante groundswell I feel building here."

He regarded me with a hard, flat stare. "I'm not sure it needs to be controlled. I'm not sure I disagree with it, Joe. I kind of thought you might see it the same way."

"What I see is a bunch of well-intentioned amateurs working up a head of steam to go out and run head-on against armed hardasses who've demonstrated beyond any doubt how cheap they value human life."

"We can get guns. We'd be armed, too."

"That'd just make it worse, not better."

"It's the kind of thing *you'd* do."

"That's the whole point. It *is* the kind of thing I do. I'm not a goddamned amateur."

"Oh. So you figure on making a run at it by yourself, is that what you're saying?"

"I don't know what the hell I'm saying. The idea is to *save* a life, not spend more. I know that much."

Our conversation had started out on the QT, while the rest of the room was buzzing around us. I'd become aware, however, of the others going quiet, leaving this exchange between Bomber and me the center of attention.

I felt uncomfortable under all that scrutiny. I dug out a cigarette, snapped fire to it, blew a wall of smoke. Tried to think.

Tommy McGurk stepped forward. "Brick Towers is one of us, Joe," he said. "We take care of our own. That's the way it's always been."

"You'd be out of your league," I said. "Can't you get that through your head? These bad guys are *bad* fucking guys. They don't have a script to follow, they don't know about choreographed moves. Anybody gets carted off after this matchup it won't be for show, they won't be hopping off the stretcher good as new back in the dressing room."

Mike Kolchonsky said, "My brother and I grew up on some of the meanest streets in Chicago. We tasted blood, heard bones break—heard gunshots, too—before we were out of grade school. We know about living and dying and surviving, Hannibal. We're more than just the pretend fighters you seem to think."

"Back in the early fifties," Sam War Cloud said, "I fought on a bare-knuckle circuit in Oklahoma. I split skulls and caved in teeth for twenty bucks a bout. There was no money and no mercy for the loser. When I lost, I lay under a porch like a dog in my own sweat and blood and healed my own wounds. I learned real good about the importance of *not* losing, not when it counts."

"There's no denying you're better suited to this kind of thing than any of the rest of us, Joe," Bomber said. "That's why we need you. Show us a plan. Take us in. Give us a chance to get Brick out of there, we'll come through for both of you."

"What if I just walk away from it?"

"Nobody'll try to stop you, if that's what you mean. We'll go ahead on our own."

Paula de Ruth strode over. Given her recent trouble with Towers, I thought she might be another voice of reason. I was wrong. "These people have already killed one of ours," she said. "No matter what else he might have been, Alex *was* one of us. And now Brick. Like

Tommy said, we have to take care of our own. There's an old saying, Hannibal: Either lead, follow, or get the hell out of the way. Time to decide which one it's going to be for you."

33

Seven of us went in.

Myself, Bomber, Sam War Cloud, Mike and Bob Kolchonsky, Ava Coltrane, and Paula de Ruth.

Bomber because he was the one I knew I could count on completely; War Cloud because of his sheer toughness; the Kolchonsky brothers because of their youth and strength; Ava because she knew the river and the island; Texas born and bred Paula because she'd been handling and shooting guns since before she could walk (a claim which she'd backed up with an impressive demonstration out behind War Cloud's barn); and me because I was a goddamned idiot.

Tommy McGurk had wanted to go in the worst way. I'd tried to fend him off with a feeble excuse about him having gotten cleared of murder charges too recently to consider such a gamble, but he saw through that quick enough to what I was really thinking.

"It's my bum leg, isn't it?" he'd demanded. "You don't want to have to worry about a gimp stumbling around out there in your way, is that right?"

I hadn't been able to meet his eyes and that was all the answer he needed.

Hatfield, while unable to bring himself to sanction the undertaking, nevertheless made it clear he'd be in our corner as a legal representative whatever the outcome.

Most of the rest of them expressed a willingness to participate to the fullest, but I kept the raiding party to seven. I figured six to ten men on the other side, so if the element of surprise worked for us at all, seven should be plenty. The more I took in, the greater the chance—especially with such hurried preparation and such a green team—of some part of our plan getting screwed up.

Our armaments consisted of a pretty basic supply of man-stoppers culled from my special toolbox and the personal collections of War Cloud and Paula. I stayed with my trusty old .45 auto; Bomber chose the 12-gauge sawed-off from my toolbox (about the only piece he was likely to hit anything with considering what a lousy shot he was and, loaded with 3 1/2" Magnum shells, a weapon that required someone of his bulk to operate); War Cloud shouldered a .30-06 Remington autoloader with a short-barreled .38 stuck in his belt for good measure; the Kolchonskys selected a pair of pump action 12-gauge Ithacas, packed with long-range 3" loads; although I didn't anticipate her being in the thick of any shooting, I equipped Ava with a snub-nosed .38; and Paula, laying the Annie Oakley bit on perhaps a little thick, carried a lever action .307 Winchester and a Colt .45 in a Western style holster.

Thus equipped, after a too brief and too poorly lighted round of practice shooting behind the barn, we struck out for the river. Our plan was to tube in. "Tubing," for those not familiar with the expression, is the term used to describe a popular means of leisurely traversing streams and rivers throughout the Midwest. You simply take a big old-fashioned rubber inner tube, inflate it, lay across the top with your butt hanging down, and let the current take you at its own pace. Smaller floatation devices can be tied to the sides to provide access to beer, pop, sandwiches, a radio to listen to, etc. For our purposes that night, we used such tie-ons to support our guns, wrapped in plastic freezer bags. We also tied some tree and bush branches onto the main tubes, the idea being to better blend in with the various other bits of flotsam being carried by the river, still high from the early spring rains.

Hank Ryerson (who'd also secured the tubes and other floatation gear) arranged to borrow a broad pontoon boat on which he took us out to the middle of the river and down to within a mile and a half, two miles of Wild Pig Island. We put in from there.

It was around four A.M. The water had a piercingly cold bite to it, in sharp contrast to the heavy, humid air that had continued to warm through the night. Overhead the moon was only a sliver of pale white, although the stars were out in full force. The thick air of the unexpected warm front seeping in, however, subdued their glow to a soft fuzziness. And here and there wisps of low-lying fog crawled across the water.

The Mississippi was too sprawling and unpredictable for tubing as the idyllic pastime it was intended to be. For that reason, Ryerson had furnished short canoe paddles to enable us to stay on course. Ava, me, Bomber, Paula, War Cloud, Bob, Mike—that's the order we drifted downstream in. Luckily, no barges or other large boats were active on that part of the river at that hour.

Dawn was a whitish gray smudge above the eastern horizon as we reached the northern tip of the island. We deflated the tubes (holding the stems underwater to mute the hiss of escaping air), unbagged our weapons, and waded ashore. In addition to being easily disposed of, the tubes provided the advantage of our not having to pick a spot on the island's perimeter accessible to boats (of which there were only a handful, according to Ava, making it potentially convenient for whoever held the island to keep those points under watch). We stuffed the paddles and folds of flattened rubber into brush-covered crevices and fanned out, briskly rubbing our feet and hands to counteract the numbing cold of the river.

So far so good.

The thing to do now was wait for it to get a little lighter, then make our next move. The beginning of our most crucial series of moves.

As I lay in the rugged underbrush flanked by Ava and Bomber, my thoughts strayed back to the story Hank Ryerson had told us on the boat about how Wild Pig Island got its name. In the 1800s, a keelboat wreck had dumped a cargo of hogs and other livestock onto the then unnamed clump of land. Through a bitter winter, the porkers managed to survive there but in the process took to eating many of their own weaker members as well as most of the rest of the chickens and goats that had been unfortunate enough to be stranded with them. The following spring, unsuspecting river travelers who happened ashore for various reasons began being savagely attacked by the flesh-eating pack that remained. After enough such incidents had been related up and down the river (to the tune of a certain amount of derision, one would guess) a couple of boatloads of hunters had gone out to the island and blasted the hungry hogs into extinction. The spot came to be called Wild Pig Island after that, and more than one spooky legend sprang up about a single, super-savage, maimed and wounded killer pig who'd survived the slaughter and lurked with crazed patience to exact retribution on any human who ventured near.

I appreciated the grim humor of the tale, and the dark psychology behind Ryerson's telling followed the same logic as jump squadron leaders who pipe a perverse ditty called "Glory, Glory What a Hell of a Way to Die" (to the tune of "The Battle Hymn of the Republic") over the airplane speakers when they take a training team up for its first airborne tactic. Learn to relax a little by laughing at Death and you're more apt to make it through and not actually have to face the bony bastard and his reaping scythe until another time.

When the morning twilight had brightened the sky to a pale gray, I repositioned myself and motioned the others in close. All around us, the river glided on with an almost surreal sensation of perpetual motion and breathy, tireless rustle of sound. Even in the dark I'd been able to hear it and smell it and feel it. Like a living thing. A pulse feeding the heart of the land. It had been going like that for thousands of years and would be for thousands more after we were done here this morning, done with our puny human trials and tribulations. Just like it washed away hopes and dreams and troubles in its different moods, it would wash away the blood we spilled today and, in time, any memory of why we'd had to do it.

"It's showtime, boys and girls," I said in a tight whisper. "This is it. No prelim matches, no best two-out-of-three, no getting saved by the bell. One fall for all the marbles and coming out alive amounts to getting your hand raised in victory."

Six pairs of eyes watched me intently. Hard muscles, trained reflexes, strong hearts. They were as ready as they were going to get.

"War Cloud," I said to the big Indian, "for about a hundred years Hollywood has been teaching us that your people have some kind of inbred something that enables them to sneak around under almost any conditions like a puff of smoke. You're not going to disappoint me now by telling me that's all a bunch of crap, are you?"

He grinned with half his mouth. "I'm about thirty years and half again that many pounds past my prime sneaking days. But I can damn betcha still slip up on any white-eyed vermin infesting this piece of rock, if that's what you're getting at."

I nodded. "That's what I wanted to hear. Now, according to Ava, this ridge above us runs like a spine down the center of the island. Somewhere along there the nasties ought to have a lookout. If he hasn't been on post all night, he ought to be coming on soon. I want you to find him and take him out without alerting the others. Can do?"

"Done."

I swung my eyes. "Paula, you trail along a ways behind Sam. After he chills the lookout, you take up that post. You're our best shot. From there you'll be looking out for *our* asses. Got it?"

A quick bob of her head. Then, calmly: "Where will your asses be?"

"Bomber, Ava, and I will be working our way along the east side of the island. Mike and Bob to the west." I hand-gestured in each direction. "Five or six hundred yards down, that central ridge makes a dip, like a cut, then continues on. In that cutout area is where the island's deeper caves are. I'm betting that's where they're holding Towers. I'm also figuring around the top of the cut is where they'll have their lookout post. That's approximately in line with where Ava's brother and his friend tried to go ashore and where they saw one of the armed men stationed on higher ground. If all of that is on the money or close, and neither of our groups run into any trouble in between, then we should be converging there right under your pretty nose."

"What about me and my pretty nose?" War Cloud wanted to know.

"After Paula is in place," I told him, "work your way down that cut, try for a better look at the cave area. See if you can determine where they're holed up, what their setup is. If you're able to, then shift to link with one of our converging groups so you can key us in."

All eyes stayed on me. The anticipation and the talk was about finished, about to give way to the reality of getting it done.

"Ava," I said, "you're the one who schooled me on the terrain. Have I got it right? Anything else? Any questions?"

She shook her head. She was clearly tense, more so than I would have liked.

"Mike and Bob," I said to the brothers, "don't forget we're going to be coming in face to face at about the time the action pops. Let's not get excited and start shooting each other, okay?"

"Fine by me," Mike allowed. "Just make sure our big pal there with the blunderbuss understands, too, huh?"

Bomber waggled his sawed-off. "When this baby speaks, everybody'd better listen."

"I just hope I got a head left to listen with," Bob Kolchonsky muttered.

I scanned their faces. Came back and settled on War Cloud's. "Let's get this show on the road, Sam," I said to him.

"Get it done, Indian," Bomber said.

"Rock and roll," one of the Kolchonskys offered.

We gave War Cloud five minutes.

Then Paula went after him.

Another five minutes and the rest of us split into our groups and began working down the length of the island on opposite shores.

We should have all been dog tired, having been awake and on edge throughout the night. But our edge now was adrenaline, carrying us beyond our normal limitations. Maybe beyond our better judgment.

In a short time, the first glimmer of sunshine would be breaking over the horizon. Long tendrils of fog seemed to be wrapping themselves tighter about the island, as if seeking something to cling to for protection from the burning, dissipating rays.

The sticky air had me sweating hard in a matter of minutes. I led our procession, followed by Ava, then Bomber. I walked with the .45 drawn, cocked, hanging at my side.

Eventually the riverbank began to smooth out and the tree line shifted over off the slope of the ridge. We came upon a twelve-foot motorboat chained fast to a tangle of thick roots.

"The cave area shouldn't be much farther," Ava whispered. Her hand touched my arm, lingered there. The soft heat of her fingertips was like sparks, triggering thoughts of the time we had spent together so recently yet so long ago. Too long ago. I kept moving.

The ridge fell away into the cut. We started to angle in from the bank. At the edge of a meadowlike clearing, I paused to scan the higher ground. Looking for some sign of Sam. Or Paula. Something. All I saw was nothing, nothing but rock and shrub and stunted trees.

The rising sun was hot on the back of my neck, making the beaded sweat there tingle.

On the far side of the meadow I paused again. Turning to Ava, I said, "I think it might be a good idea for you to stay here. We could use somebody covering our exit."

She considered about two seconds before giving a firm shake of her head. "Nice try, Hannibal. But when I dealt myself into this, I dealt myself in all the way. I won't let you make any special exceptions for me, so don't even think about it."

I glanced at Bomber appealingly. He shook his head, too. "It's her call to make, Joe."

So we moved on. Picking our way carefully through a stand of thick, gnarled timber. My shirt was plastered on me and Ava's and Bomber's faces shone with perspiration like they had been butter-basted by a chef.

At length, the ground grew rockier and the timber grew thinner. Then the twisted trees gave way to an opening where the notched ends of the ridge dropped both from the right and left to form a kind of jagged V. The inner tip of the V was choked with a jumble of boulders and thorny-looking underbrush. The slanting walls of the cut were pocked by fissures and caves. Whiskers of fog hung over the scene, trailing down.

We knelt just inside the tree line, wiping the salt sting from our eyes, catching our breath.

"Downtown Wild Pig Island," I muttered.

Again my eyes swept the higher reaches of the ridge. Again I spotted nothing of what I was looking for.

A faint odor of woodsmoke seemed to ride on the still air.

"There," Bomber said, pointing.

I followed the line of his finger to one of the caves on the right, a broad, shallow scoop out of the pale rock. Concentrating, I saw that what a cursory scan had taken to be clumps of debris scattered across the floor of the cave were instead supine figures lying on and partially wrapped in dusty sleeping bags. Men. Three or four of them. Not yet awake. Out near the lip of the cave, a pile of ashened logs, a dead campfire, emitted a minute curl of smoke.

"Looks like we're in luck," I said. Then I asked of Ava, "Is that one of the caves that has a deeper tunnel running back in it?"

"I don't think so. The deeper caves are to the left. See that smaller, darker hole over there, with the flat-topped boulder sort of leaning right underneath it? That's one. And then back and up a little higher, that other dark hole in the rock? That's another. Then there's one or two down lower, back around the angle of the cut where we can't see. Those are where the water backs up, where they go for turtles."

"You'd think they'd have Towers hidden better than in that big, shallow cavern there where they're sleeping," I mused.

"Not necessarily," Bomber said. "They'd want him where they could keep an eye on him, right? They must have him tied up. And it's not like they're expecting company."

"Looks like there's only three or four of them there. Should be more."

"Hard to tell from here, what with them lying down. Gets awful shadowy off in the back. And you reckoned a lookout or two to be posted, didn't you? That would account for more. Got to figure War Cloud took care of them okay or there would have been a disturbance."

Ava said, "Are we going to talk away our advantage or make our move while they're still asleep?"

I grinned at her feistiness. "Point well taken, Private. Come on. Spread out a little and keep a sharp watch, especially for Mike and Bob to be coming up across the way. Let's hope War Cloud and Paula are up there somewhere overlooking all of us."

We quit the trees and started across the rocky, open terrain in a triangle pattern with me on the point and Bomber and Ava behind me to the right and left, respectively. I held my focus centered on the cave and as many of its snoozing occupants as I could keep in sight, peripheral vision on alert for anything additional.

It only took a couple weeks to cross that open area.

As I topped the first of the bigger boulders in the rubble at the base of the V, motion on the opposite side of the cut caused me to freeze and swing the .45 into firing position. A heartbeat later, Mike Kolchonsky's grinning mug was in my sights. He snapped me a jaunty salute.

I let my breath out through my teeth and lowered the .45 a little shakily. Bob Kolchonsky stepped into view also.

Pantomiming *Do you see them?*, I jerked my head to

indicate the sleepers to my right, now only a few dozen yards away.

Both brothers held up encircled thumbs and forefingers in the universal OK sign.

I motioned again, signing them to converge on the cavern with us.

I turned and climbed another boulder closer. I remember thinking: What a cake walk this is going to be.

Approximately one second after that random jinx of a thought, everything turned to shit.

It started simply enough with a guy strolling out of the thorny underbrush swinging a partially used roll of toilet paper in one hand and a military surplus carbine in the other. He'd been traversing a narrow gravel path that ran, I saw now, tight along the side of the ridge, keeping him out of sight of any of us (including War Cloud and Paula, wherever the hell they were) and vice versa. A still puffy-eyed early riser who'd wandered off to tend in private to that traditional morning duty, taking a dump, and was returning from same enlightened and refreshed.

Fresh enough to react every bit as quick as I was able to.

He stepped out not ten feet from where I poised on my newly gained purchase. Our eyes locked. Simultaneous intakes of breath. I was crouched slightly off balance, bracing myself with my left palm and the heel of my right hand, the hand that gripped the .45. I saw the toilet paper drop and the carbine swinging up. Nothing I could do but pitch myself back and away, snapping a blind shot as I rolled down the gritty curve of the boulder.

The carbine spoke at the same time. Dust spurted and rock shards rattled.

The dumper began hollering at the top of his voice. "Dub! Dub! Granger! Everybody wake up! Somebody's on the island! Somebody's on the island!"

His shouts—not to mention the gunshots—reverberated off the sharply angled rock surfaces of the cut. From where I tumbled, I could hear him plainly but could no longer see him. No matter, he signed his own death warrant with his big mouth. Bomber's sawed-off cut loose, a cannon's roar smashing the air. And from a rugged ledge directly above the cavern, Sam War Cloud popped into view, sighting down the long barrel of his .30-06 and squeezing off three rapid rounds. Nothing more was heard from the dumper.

But it was a different story for the men in the shallow cave. Slumber and stillness turned into a flurry of desperate activity. Curses were spat loudly, bodies rolled and scrambled, more guns were swung into play.

I did some scrambling of my own, retreating to better cover. It occurred to me that if Towers was somewhere up there in that cave, we needed to be careful where we sent bullets flying. But after a fusillade of shots sang out from the cavern's mouth, there was no stopping a return volley. The Kolchonskys opened up from their side of the cut and Bomber's sawed-off boomed again. I didn't hold back either. I saw at least two of the cavern's shooters jerk and go down.

From his position above the cave, War Cloud was of no use in this exchange. But a moment later, his position proved to be crucial.

Shots crackled from behind me and slugs gouged into rock only a handful of inches above my head. I threw myself to one side and twisted around. More figures had emerged from one of the caves on the other wall of the cut, the dark hole just above the flat-topped boulder that Ava had pointed out as being one of the deeper tunnels. A man and a woman crouched there now atop the flattened massive rock. The man was big and bulky with long, dirty blond hair, the woman a scrawny redhead. The man I had no trouble recognizing, from descriptions I'd heard, as Dub Varsey. I had no idea who the woman was. Varsey wore faded blue jeans, no shirt or shoes; the woman had on a pullover sleeveless top, was bare below that. It was obvious why they had taken separate nighttime lodgings from the others, just as it was obvious the woman was a real redhead. I don't know why I bothered noticing a crazy thing like that under the circumstances, but I did. Both of them wielded big, glittery revolvers that looked like Magnums and our relative positions had me at an unhealthy disadvantage.

That's when War Cloud being where he was came in lifesavingly handy. Before the new pair could zero more rounds on me, his .30-06 barked across the width of the cut and chased them back into their hole. And from a point higher on the Indian's ridge, the sharp crack of a Winchester—Paula's—joined in to help. Grateful that at least part of my plan had paid off, I squirmed once again for better cover.

We traded fire sporadically over the next several minutes. As best I could tell, there were two left in the shallow cave and two in the deeper one. Figure War Cloud and Paula had taken out at least one lookout, plus the dumper, plus the two I'd seen go down in the cavern; that meant there had been eight altogether. I could buy that. The thing that bugged me, though, was where was Brick Towers? Had we been only half right? Had we hit Dub Varsey's hideout while the wrestling champ was being held hostage somewhere else?

Once again, thinking about it seemed to jinx it into coming around in an undesirable way.

"Hold it!" somebody called from the shallow cave. "Hold your fire out there. We're nearly out of ammunition. We got one man dead in here, another dying. We've had enough."

Before me or any of my people could say anything, Dub Varsey hollered from his hole, "What kind of chickenshit talk is that, Stuckey, goddamn you? You think you're going to hand me over?"

"You do what you want, Dub. We can't be no help to you anyhow. We're about out of bullets, like I said. Marvin's dead, Granger's bleeding to death. What good is it going to do me and Bradford to hold out until we eat lead, too?"

"I always knew you was yellow, Stuckey. Ever since that time in Natchez."

"Fuck you, Dub. I'm getting tired of fighting your fights. I'll be damned if I'm going to die for you."

While this exchange was taking place, I caught the attention of the Kolchonsky boys and signaled them, *Whatever you do, keep an eye on Varsey's cave.* They nodded grimly that they understood. I did the same with War Cloud and, although I'd never spotted her exact position, I hoped Paula got the message also.

"How about it, down there?" Stuckey called out. "You willing to let us out alive?"

"Throw your weapons out," I told him. "Then come ahead. Keep your hands where we can see them at all times and move real slow."

"Fucking chickenshits!" Varsey screeched from his cave.

Rifles and handguns came slipping and clattering over the lip of the shallow cavern. After about a minute, two men eased into view. I had no way of knowing which was Stuckey and which was Bradford. Both were streaked with dirt and dust; one was scarcely more than a kid, his chin speckled by red and sore-looking pimples. They moved slowly, awkwardly, starting the descent without using their hands, keeping them held high.

They'd gone maybe ten careful steps when the Magnums from the deep cave across the cut spoke viciously and mowed them down. I'd anticipated Varsey using the surrender to try some kind of trick, maybe pick one of my group off while we were concentrating elsewhere, but I'd never in Christ's world expected him to do something like that! I wheeled and opened fire on the murderous hole along with everybody in my party. I even heard the snap of Ava's .38. A rain of slugs riddled the flat-topped boulder and the cave mouth. It was hard to believe anything could survive such a volley but somehow—even as I was squeezing off a full clip—I knew the evil bastard had.

The echo of the barrage hung over the cut for a long time.

"Jesus Christ," Bomber said, "did you see the way that sick fucker slaughtered his own men?"

"The man's a monster," Ava said, an edge of awe and fear in her voice.

"But not one who can't be taken down," I told her, perhaps trying to reassure myself at the same time.

Not long after that, the monster had something to say.

"Hey, you sneak-attacking motherfuckers out there," he called. "I got a present here for you. I got the prize you all came after. Better hold your damn fire unless you want to shoot this pretty package full of holes."

With a sinking feeling in my gut, I knew what was coming.

Varsey edged out of the cave and stepped onto the flat top of the boulder. He held Brick Towers close in front of him, like a shield, the barrel of his Magnum jammed into the wrestler's right ear. Towers was filthy, his hair matted, his face pale and pained. His hands were tied behind him with what looked like duct tape and Varsey had a tight hold of the wraps, keeping the prisoner's arms wrenched up high.

Varsey was smiling triumphantly. "Take a good look at your musclebound pretty boy," he said. "This what you're all so hot after, huh?"

The scrawny redhead slithered up beside him, Magnum flashing, eyes darting above a maniacal smile of her own.

This didn't help the overall situation a bit, but at least I could find some satisfaction in the fact Towers was still alive. Now to keep him—and the rest of us—that way.

"What's your deal, Varsey?" I called.

"You know my fucking deal. I want my brother out of jail and I want me and him allowed the hell away from here."

"That's impossible, and you know it."

"If we was some rich bastards instead of Varseys, though, it wouldn't be impossible, would it? Eugene wouldn't even *be* behind bars."

"That's for somebody else to debate. Me and you have to deal with the here and now."

"The here and now is that I want to see you sonsabitches clearing out of here—off my island—or I make this chunk of rock run red with pretty boy's blood."

"That's no good either. Release Towers, turn him over to us. *Then* we'll back off, give you your lead. That's the best I can do."

"Oh, sure. *Then* you'll back away. That sucks river mud. You think I'm crazy enough to buy that?"

I thought the fucker was crazy all right. I wasn't sure what I could make him buy, or even what else I could try to sell him on. We had him covered from a number of different angles, I guess I was hoping for him to lean far

enough away from Towers in his excitement to offer one
of us a target.

The answer came, shockingly, in the form of Tommy
McGurk. He appeared in the cave opening directly in
back of Varsey and the redhead, his face, then body re-
verse-melting out of the blackness like a movie image
coming into focus.

He carried a hunting rifle. As I watched—stunned, ex-
hilarated—he took a long step forward, carefully bracing
his bad leg, then raised the rifle's heavy butt and sliced it
in a savage chop across the back of Varsey's head.

Varsey's knees buckled and he went down like a ham-
mered steer, the Magnum dangling harmlessly from his
nerve-deadened fingers. He pitched forward and
dropped over the flattened top of the boulder to land
with crunching impact on the rubble below. Towers, released suddenly and then bumped by his falling captor,
nearly went over, too, but managed to fall to his knees
and maintain his balance.

The redhead, meantime, let out a screech at the sight of
her man going down and wheeled about with her big
handgun. Tommy was caught leaning from the blow he'd
delivered to Varsey. He might have had time to twist
back and swing the rifle in reverse. But it became a moot
point. Paula's Winchester cracked once and the .307 slug
it discharged took the redhead high on the rib cage, just
under the right armpit, and flung her like a rag doll back
against the rim of the cave.

As the echo of that final shot was still fading, I moved
toward the flat-topped boulder. I felt my feet picking up
momentum, breaking into a trot over the rough ground.
My heart was pounding in my chest like a speed bag
under a prize fighter's rhythmic punches. I sensed
Bomber and Ava hurrying up behind me, saw the
Kolchonskys coming in from their side.

I wanted to let loose a cheer.

Sonofabitch, we'd done it. We'd pulled it off!

I clambered up the boulder and grabbed Tommy, clapping the broad expanse of his shoulders between my
palms, shaking him. I could feel my mouth spreading in a
wide grin. "Where the hell did you come from?" I wanted

to know. He was grinning, too, like a big, proud kid. Before he could say anything, I said, "Never mind, never mind. I'm just glad you're here."

"Not bad for the gimp you left behind, eh?" he said.

"Go ahead and rub it in all you want," I told him. "I'm just happy as hell you didn't listen to me."

Ava and Bob Kolchonsky were helping Brick Towers to his feet. I could see that the hand the finger had been cut from was swollen to the size of a baseball mitt. The champ grimaced painfully as they began slicing away the duct tape that bound him.

Bomber came up and took a turn at thumping Tommy on the back. "How the fuck did you get in that cave?" he demanded. "I was never so surprised in my life as when I saw you sliding out behind those two."

"Most of these deep caves have more than one way in and out," Tommy explained. "If Hannibal here would have given me half a chance, I could have told him that. I also could have told him that I spent the better part of a day on this island once a couple years ago when an old Cajun hunting and fishing buddy of mine brought me here. When the fishing turned out not to be so hot, he showed me the caves and told me the legend of the island. That's how I knew about the other entrances. Because you were all so eager to take off without me, I decided fuck it. Then, after I got done pouting, I got pissed. Made up my mind to come here and help in spite of your bullheadedness. Seemed logical to expect they'd be holed up here in the cut. I outfitted in a life jacket and flippers and swam over from the Illinois side."

"You *swam* over?" Ava said incredulously.

Tommy shrugged. "We gimps tend to overcompensate sometimes."

We were easing Towers down off the boulder by then. Mike Kolchonsky had fashioned a sling from his shirt to support the mangled, infected hand.

"Anyway," Tommy continued, "I came in on the southern end of the island and found one of the places where the caves feed out. Started working my way through from there. Just dumb luck I happened to pick the very tunnel Varsey had Brick stashed in. I heard the gunfire start up.

In my haste to get out where I could do some good, I tripped over Brick in the dark. In another minute I'd have been able to drag him out of there, but that's when Varsey came to take him to use as a shield. I had to hold back, no way I could open fire there in the tunnel for fear of ricochets. I had to wait until they were all out on the ledge to make my move."

"And a damn fine move it was," Sam War Cloud said.

He and Paula had made their way down from the ridge and had joined us now. Our raiding party was reformed. Intact. Had even gained two in number. I might leave something to be desired when it came to screening personnel, but on my first outing as a general I'd nevertheless managed to bring my troops through all in one piece.

"Speaking of fine moves," Tommy said, his eyes finding Paula, "that shot of yours that saved my ass looked mighty fine from where I stood."

"It was what I was put in place to do," Paula replied somewhat coolly. "We'll see how fine the police think it was when they get here. They've got boats coming across the river now with lights and sirens going."

"Brell," I said under my breath, "the old shit kept his word."

And that's when Dub Varsey came back to life.

Or so it seemed.

He'd taken such a bad fall that in our excitement to congratulate Tommy and tend to the injured Towers no one had bothered to check him closely enough to make certain he was out of the game. Big-time mistake. He reared to a sitting position now—battered and scraped and bloody, the Magnum he'd somehow managed to keep hold of catching a dazzling glint of sunlight—and began squeezing off rounds into where we were bunched like birds in a box. Chunks of meat and bone were torn away by the impact of the heavy slugs. Gore splattered the rocks.

"Die, cocksuckers!" I heard the monster bellow as he rolled to his feet and began backing away.

I saw Ava go down, an arc of blood pumping from where one of her breasts used to be.

Tommy McGurk took a hit.

Then War Cloud.

Paula screamed and managed to draw her Colt but was unable to get off a shot before the big Indian fell against her and knocked her off balance.

I was screaming, too. I held the .45 in front of me in both hands and was firing at where I'd caught the glint of the Magnum. I ran after my bullets, leaping over fallen and scrambling bodies.

A quivering patch of underbrush and a handful of loosened rocks, still rolling, showed me the route Varsey had taken, fleeing his carnage. I plunged after him, giving no regard to the foolhardiness of the move, thinking only of getting him in my gunsights or between my hands, thinking only of making him dead for positive this time. There were shouts and cries from behind me, but I blocked them out, not wanting to imagine what they meant. I focused everything I had on what was ahead of me . . . the one responsible.

When I broke from the underbrush, a bullet shredded the thorny leaves beside my shoulder. The sound of the shot was followed immediately by the hollow snickety-click of a hammer falling on an empty chamber. I saw him then, crouched on bare, bleeding feet in the black mouth of another cave, down low on the wall of the cut, aiming his useless piece at me. I barked a crazy laugh, loud enough for him to hear, then ran straight at him. He leaped into the blackness and I followed.

The tunnel was tubular, almost a perfect cylinder. I had to stoop to negotiate it but was able to put my arms out in each direction and feel the sides for guidance. The walls became cold and wet in a matter of yards and the blackness was impenetrable after the same distance. I could hear Varsey ahead of me, breathing heavily, stumbling, cursing. The same threat of ricocheting that had held Tommy McGurk in check in the other cave, forced me to hold my fire here. After his clubbing and the fall he'd taken, I had to believe I was in better shape than Varsey was. If I could keep from bashing my brains out on a low-hanging section of the ceiling or a sudden turn, I ought to be able to close the distance between us. And once I got my hands on the fucker . . .

I don't know how long we proceeded like that. The blindness distorted time, distance, everything. You don't know what dark is until you've been in the bowels of the earth with no kind of light. All I had was the sounds of Varsey ahead of me. That's all I needed.

I sensed the tunnel was taking us downward. The walls seemed to be growing colder. Wetter.

And then, just ahead, I heard an echoey splash. Followed quickly by another. Then a much louder one. Varsey swore. He had slipped and fallen. Landed somehow in a pool or puddle. I remembered what Rudy Coltrane had said about some of the lower tunnels taking on water after the river had been high, about them being a good place to trap turtles.

But it wasn't turtles I was out to trap.

I lunged recklessly after the sounds of Varsey's struggle. I ended up falling, too. Over my quarry.

We locked there in four inches of cold, brackish water, pounding and kicking at each other blindly. My rage exploded completely then, made me impervious to the iciness of the water, to the slams from his knees and fists. While my eyes could see nothing but blackness, inside my head I saw many things with crystal clarity. I saw Glynnis Varsey pale and rigid on the couch in Ava's living room, quakily reliving the horrors of incest and other debasements at the hands of this man and his brother; I saw Stuckey and Bradford doing spinning dances of death, dying with expressions of horrified disbelief frozen forever on their faces; I saw Brick Towers's bloated, untreated hand; I saw Ava collapsing into the dirt with bloody fragments of her insides painting the rocks a dozen feet away.

Most clearly of all, I saw what I had to do.

They say a grown man can drown in less than an inch of water. I don't know about that. But I know it can happen in four.

EPILOGUE

They buried Ava Coltrane on a Wednesday. Everybody said it was a nice ceremony. I couldn't bring myself to attend.

Neither Tommy McGurk nor Sam War Cloud made it either. They were both still in the hospital. Tommy had taken a slug to his bad leg. ("Dumb bastard tried to kill what was already dead," he downplayed. "What's everybody getting so excited about?") War Cloud lost a fist-sized chunk of meat out of his right love handle and broke his left hip falling from the hit. He tried to downplay it, too, claiming he'd been hurt worse by overzealous female fans swinging purses, but the doctors remained concerned about blood loss and infection.

The cops raked us all over the coals pretty good. I never got the feeling their hearts were really in it, though. Not even the Feds.

We got away with it primarily because Dub Varsey had surrounded himself with so many sleazeballs. It turned out every one of them was wanted on at least one felony charge somewhere along the Mississippi. Two of them—Granger, the one who'd been wounded in the shallow cave, and the lookout War Cloud had coldcocked and left bound and gagged back up the ridge—survived to stand trial for their previous illegalities as well as face charges stemming from Brick Towers's kidnapping and the shootout on Wild Pig Island. Varsey's redheaded cave mate had been Granger's half sister, a bail skip on a dope dealing bust in Little Rock, Arkansas. Because they were all fugitives and because I was known to do bounty work from time to time, Hatfield managed to fly the notion me and my party had been acting as freelance officers of the court attempting to bring these scoundrels to justice and had resorted to gunplay only when given no alternative. It wasn't that far from the truth.

Eugene Varsey went down on Murder One for the killing of Alex de Ruth, plus charges related to incest, possession and distribution of kiddie porn, and possession of unregistered firearms. I'd like to say they put him behind bars for a long, long time, but with prison overcrowding and parole board mentalities and so forth to factor in, that remains to be seen.

Glynnis Varsey stood bravely and unwaveringly by her testimony, even through the cruelest cross-examination. When her ordeal was over, she went away under the Witness Protection Program and I can only hope that somewhere today she's living out a life touched by some genuine love.

The Feds staked out the Varseys' various drop points and busted a bunch more mules, but unfortunately were never able to penetrate very far into the actual underlying pedophile network.

Mel Dukenos's big pay-per-view wrestling card from St. Louis was a success, hyped tremendously by the news reports surrounding the shootout (not that she wouldn't have preferred to get her publicity a different way). A number of bigger-name grapplers working the independent circuits came forward to offer their services to help fill the gaps in BRW's roster. Abe Lugretti, released from his hospital stay and started on an alcohol rehab program, was able to handle the announcing chores just fine. Bomber was a big hit as his co-anchor and as Paula's new, nastier manager. Brick Towers demonstrated the kind of moxie the old-timers were always talking about by allowing his abused hand to be pumped full of novacaine and wrapped in a special glove and then going out to successfully defend his title in the climactic main event match. That might have made him a better man in the eyes of some, but to me he'd never come close to being worth the trade for Ava's life.

Bomber continued working for BRW for a couple months, until Paula jumped ship and joined up with one of the bigger east coast federations. He kept a long distance romance going with Mel for a while, but it eventually petered out. When Tommy was on his feet again, he returned to the wrestling wars, this time as a "good guy" manager to a pair of former pro footballers who'd formed a new tag team billed as Two-Minute Warning, their gimmick being to win their matches in under two minutes. War Cloud retired from the ring except for occasional stints as a special referee, and he and his wife settled into training and racing their trotters. Despite my misgivings about her, Leticia showed nothing but unselfish devotion to the big Indian throughout his recovery and beyond.

A long time later, on a bleak and blustery day near the onset of winter, I drove back down to the Quad Cities and found the graveyard where they'd laid Ava to rest. Found her marker on a bare hill overlooking the river. There was no one around. That was the way I wanted it. From the back of my Honda I took the long cardboard box. I remembered how the lady at the florist shop had looked at me when I'd placed my order; but I was willing to pay so she was willing to make the arrangement I'd asked for. I took the flowers from the box and laid them on the coarse brown grass over Ava's grave. In the distance you could see the waters of the Mississippi turn a rough gray as gusts of wind rolled across them. Then, after a minute or so, the same gusts, carrying the smell of the river, would sigh up over the cemetery hill. She'd like that, being where she could get the scent of the river. The flowers stirred in the wind. The pair of dainty, pearl-

colored ballerina slippers laced through their stems
stirred, too. If you used your imagination a little, you
could almost believe they were doing a little dance there
. . . a soft, gentle ballet.